"COME HERE," HE ORDERED, SMILING DANGEROUSLY

"I won't!" Liza declared. Then, despite herself, she walked slowly toward him. As he drew her into the warmth of his arms, an inner voice warned against the treacherous pleasure she felt. Still, she raised her lips for his kiss.

"I won't give you the illusion of being forced," he told her. "There'll be no excuses when you have to face your doubts about your fiancé—"

"But I have no doubts," she insisted.

"Nor devotion," he finished cruelly.

"Christian...don't spoil it, please."

"Spoil what? Your affair with him? Or, with me?" He kissed her with such savage sweetness that all the stars in the heavens seemed to fill her breast. The invader was welcome now—and she could only give what he'd come to claim.

AND NOW...

SUPERROMANCES

Worldwide Library is proud to present a
sensational new series of modern love stories—
SUPERROMANCES

Written by masters of the genre, these longer,
sensuous and dramatic novels are truly in keeping
with today's changing life-styles. Full of intriguing
conflicts, the heartaches and delights of true love,
SUPERROMANCES are absorbing stories—
satisfying and sophisticated reading that lovers
of romance fiction have long been waiting for.

SUPERROMANCES

Contemporary love stories for the woman of today!

SHANNON CLARE

SWEET TEMPTATION

A SUPERROMANCE FROM
WORLDWIDE

TORONTO · NEW YORK · LOS ANGELES · LONDON

Published December 1982

First printing October 1982

ISBN 0-373-70043-1

Printed in Canada

Prologue

Who could say whether a man like that would answer—or whether he would even remember the way it once was. So many years had gone by. Angus Cavanaugh, though, had kept up on all of it—the changes in government, inflation, recession, or whatever else descended to try the Western world. Even the inexplicable, annual wanderings of women's hemlines.

That was how Angus knew what business the man was in. Every now and then his name crept into a newspaper article—some reference to a deal in Amsterdam, Hong Kong, or Johannesburg. Of course, Angus reflected, you had to be able to read between the lines to figure out what part *he* had played in the transaction. But by now, he decided, he ought to be pretty good at ferreting out the facts. He made an odd noise, half laugh, half snort. The old man at the table next to his, with his stubs of teeth and smoking hookah, glared at him suspiciously.

Angus fingered the morning's stubble on his chin, still lost in thought. How many men could claim a profession like that, he wondered. How many could take the globe-hopping pace and the tension, the responsibility for so much wealth? A couple of dozen in the entire world? No, probably not even that. And out of those, he'd be the best. Angus wasn't sure whether or not to draw comfort from knowing that.

He grimaced suddenly and looked down at the pad and pencil in front of him on the table. He was taking pains with the cable to London. Several drafts already lay there, crumpled and discarded. Words were important and Angus was a careful craftsman. He was a bit vain about that. And he knew that in this situation he had to get the message just right.

He mopped his brow as he wrote. Doves in a cage above him were the serene observers of his labors. Lord, it was impossibly hot in this place! Even the gnarled olive tree that shaded the café courtyard didn't help today. Angus raised a finger and Gumaa the Arab boy, in his white robe and little skullcap of coarse cotton, refilled his cup with the syrupy, inky coffee he had come to love.

When he had finished his writing, he leaned back and watched the shadow of the olive tree play against the whitewashed brick of the low, plain café with its tiled roof. He was in a brooding mood, something this country of Jordan seemed to encourage in its motley population of expatriates. Anyway, it was almost a hobby of his, trying to unravel the tortured knots of human motivation.

Now what sort of man, Angus mused, chooses work like that? He would have to be part scholar, part sleuth. A man of finely honed sensibilities with the instincts...and skills...of a thief. Or worse. It was a rare mix. Very rare indeed. Beauty and corruption, serenity and violence. How could anyone live, balancing all that, always existing on the brink?

Angus crumbled the corner of a chunk of halvah—that luscious Middle Eastern concoction of nuts and honey—and sucked on a piece absentmindedly. An ordinary man, he thought, couldn't just wake up one morning and say, "Well, *that* looks like an interesting profession, I think I'll try it." No, part of it had to be in the blood, really. The eye, the instinct, the plain luck to survive had to be there or it was game over. And it couldn't hurt to have a leg up on it through inheritance either. It wasn't just the money that mattered; it was the intangibles—the taste, the confidence he would have absorbed unconsciously since birth.

Still, could you really educate your eye for beauty and your body for brute survival at the same time? Apparently some men could. But very, very few.

Angus glanced at the cable he'd drafted. Did it appeal to all those traits of his friend of so long ago? For that would be the key, of course. He saw that now. Would it arouse the man's taste for rare beauty and high stakes? Would it stimulate his natural—or unnatural—appetite for danger? Did it raise the possibility... well, Angus decided, it was far too soon to judge whether there was a criminal twist to all of this. Best to leave that for him to wonder about. In fact, it might well be his first thought.

Angus left the café and stepped out onto a narrow road baking under the harsh white sun. He smelled heat and cloves and oranges. Across the hard, mud road two young soldiers, handsome and cocky and dark-lidded, with automatic weapons cradled in their arms, ate almond cakes acquired from a wooden cart. A street vendor with a creased mahogany face and black teeth, wearing the trailing *arabaya* of the desert, squatted by a crate of scrawny white hens. There were no women about. None.

Usually Angus preferred to walk. He coped with the Jordanian sun—some Westerners couldn't. But this business of the cable mustn't wait another day and the telegraph office, whose hours were capricious at best, would close soon. Angus sighed. He would have to take a taxi, and God save him from the cabdrivers of Aqaba. Ancient Mercedeses, most of them drove—although why that should be was one of the trivial mysteries of the Middle East that he'd never solved. Inevitably the vehicles were held together with string and hope and shrouded with that ocher dust.

Angus raised a polished walking stick and waggled it at a knot of men lounging against one of the taxis. The drivers, with their baggy trousers and fierce mustaches, wore grimy *keiffiehs* draped over their heads and shoulders and bound around their foreheads by black cords. The men held a brief, ritual squabble for the fare, then fell back into disinterested silence when one of them prevailed.

Angus told the driver his destination, was quoted a price, and responded with his own. The matter of the dinars was decided as far as he was concerned. He was far too old a hand in the Middle East to be drawn into interminable haggling. Occasionally he was amused by it, but today his mind had other claims on it.

He settled back in the cab and gazed out the

window, down toward the Gulf of Aqaba where the Bedouin laborers would be loading rusting, ungainly ships with sacks of lentils and Syrian phosphates. The driver took off like a maniac for the Mudaw-warah Road.

CHAPTER ONE

FALL HAD BLOWN IN EARLY, sweeping down the canyons of Wall Street, chasing newspapers and candy wrappers before it, flipping up coat hems, and scattering office workers into the shelter of their glass towers. In Central Park, the trees ignited in a blaze of gold and scarlet. Window boxes on the brownstones wept cascades of bronze chrysanthemums, and bouquets of Indian corn sprouted beneath polished knockers.

From rambling Victorian summer houses on Long Island, salt boxes in Connecticut, and cabins in Maine, wives and children made the annual trek back to the plush apartments overlooking Fifth Avenue and Sutton Place. Husbands moved out of private clubs and rejoined the family circle. Dust covers were stripped off furniture and rooms aired. The children were shorn of sun-bleached curls in preparation for school and consoled themselves by lining up the summer's haul of seashells along the window ledges.

People lamented, of course, the end of the long, laughing days of sailing and tennis and clamming. Their complaints, though, were halfhearted at best. The warning edge of cold in the air had energized them, and they opened engagement calendars to snowy, unblemished pages and set their minds contentedly to the coming months.

In the superb plum and charcoal dusk of one of those late September days, with a huge copper moon sliding from behind a skyscraper, a young woman hurried down the steps of a town house. It was a tiny apartment she had just turned the key on, only half a floor at the rear of the house. But it had a charming view of the cobbled garden, and a white marble fireplace to be cherished. The brownstone itself was old and beautiful, and the street on which it stood was one of the prettiest in all Manhattan.

Skirting puddles of crimson leaves, the woman walked purposefully toward Park Avenue where, she had decided, she at least had a chance of finding a cab on a near-perfect Saturday night in New York. She clutched a small, black silk purse to her and, from time to time, glanced at the thin gold watch on her wrist. She began to worry now, as she bent her neat head against the wind, that she would be late.

Her name was Liza Downing, and she was on her way to an event that would launch "the season" of galas, benefits, and openings. It was certain to be celebrated in the morning papers of every major city in the States and Europe, Liza knew. The headlines would be in two places—the social pages and the financial section—for there was not the slightest doubt anymore that art was now a matter of both social status and big business. And, if events went as planned, her own picture would adorn the respectful yet rapturous text.

But Liza, annoyed with herself now for turning

down the offer of a limousine, wasn't thinking about the glamour ahead. Her feet hurt from a long day at work and were protesting vigorously against being thrust into the high, thin-strapped evening sandals. Nor was she thinking about the publicity she might receive. She had never been particularly in awe of this sort of social spectacle, even though she was a very recent entrant into the closed, exclusive world of New York society. Liza was fretting, rather, about Penn.

He was probably pacing already, she thought, frowning. He had been keyed up about this auction for weeks. Not that he would need her professional opinion tonight. He had long ago made up his mind firmly to acquire the jewellike little Renoir. But he loved, even thrived on, the tension and the competitiveness of these events. And he wanted her there beside him as he bid the extravagant amount that would no doubt be required to claim the painting.

At the corner of Park Avenue, a gust of wind caught her, carrying a sharp promise of colder nights to come. Liza hugged herself and shrank back into the black velvet coat with its wide taffeta ruffle that circled her neck and spilled to the flaring hem. Across the broad center divider she spotted the roof light of a lone, cruising cab. With the sure arm of a longtime New Yorker, she made the circling, pointing gesture that told the driver to turn and pick her up for a trip back downtown.

The driver twisted around as Liza hurried into the back seat. He opened the small slot in the plastic partition that separated him from his sometimes dangerous passengers, and raised a questioning eyebrow.

"The Fairchild Auction Gallery...Madison at Sixty-sixth, please," Liza instructed.

The driver took in her face, her clothes, pondered her destination and smiled. Then, anticipating a generous tip, he flipped down the flag on the meter, draped one wrist over the steering wheel, and sent them hurtling toward the lights of midtown Manhattan.

Liza Downing wasn't beautiful. She was more than that. It didn't matter in the slightest that her mouth was a whisper too broad for the delicate, heart-shaped face. Or that the fine, straight nose stopped just short of classic elegance. Her eyes were a marvel—large, bright, thickly lashed, with a slight tilt and taper at the corners that was unexpected yet just right. Their color was a light, liquid violet circled with a deeper amethyst. Her skin was pale as porcelain and just as flawless, set off by an abundance of long raven hair. Tonight, she had swept it back from her forehead into an elegant knot. Two tortoise combs secured the twisted strands drawn upward from her temples, emphasizing the exotic breadth of her high cheekbones.

She was unusually petite and fine-boned, a fact that sometimes caused her to eye wistfully the leggy models that stride the streets of New York. Yet she was sweetly and devastatingly put together, her waist slender above gently rounded hips, her breasts small and perfectly shaped. "Intriguing" was a word that could frequently be heard floating around her. A study in ivory, ebony, and the surprise of that violet. No, people conceded agreeably, she couldn't be called classically beautiful. But it hardly seemed to matter.

The taxi nudged into the line of cars outside the Fairchild Gallery, its canary yellow the only break in a solid black column of Rolls-Royces, Mercedeses, and BMWs. "You ought to be in one of those," said the driver, nodding sagely as his eyes met Liza's in the rearview mirror. "You won't make what I'd call a grand entrance from this hack of mine."

"I like taxis just fine," Liza said, and gave him the tip he'd hoped for, plus the bonus of a smile that he took home with him to Brooklyn that night.

Liza threaded her way down the center aisle, drawing stares that were either curious or envious, depending on the bent of the viewer. The large, principal salesroom of Fairchild's was filled, as were the side rooms where the slightly less favored would follow the bidding by closed circuit monitors. The gilded chairs, set in precise, curving rows, were spindly faux bamboo. The women seated on them looked suitably elegant and decorative, their dinner-jacketed male companions appearing vaguely uncomfortable on the diminutive wine velvet cushions. The usually sedate gallery was buzzing, reflecting the extraordinary excitement over the night's offerings.

Liza wasn't worried about finding Penn. Since he was one of their best customers, his favorite seat would have been held for him by one of the gallery's bright-faced junior trainees. And yes, halfway down, on the aisle, she saw the broad back and the thick, close-cropped hair.

"Liza!" Penn Livsay stood, relief and pleasure flooding his square, tanned face.

"I know, I know—don't scold, Penn!" she implored, her eyes dissolving the last traces of tension at the corners of his mouth.

He stepped aside, pleasantly aware of the ripple of interest that attended her entrance, and felt the familiar rush of possessive pride. "I wouldn't dream of it—I'm much too delighted to see you. It's your boss I'd like to have a word with."

Liza squeezed by him, picked up the thick, glossy catalog that lay on her chair, and sat down. "Now don't go blaming Julian," she cajoled gently. "It's always mad this time of year. We're swamped with requests for school tours, the evening lecture series starts next week, and I've got two major exhibitions to mount this season...not to mention *your* little event."

"Quite," he replied, charmingly chastened. He slipped the coat from her pale, bared shoulders, revealing the starkly simple, strapless wrap of black silk that clung with effect to her body. "But that's exactly my point—Julian should get you some proper help. You're assistant curator now, after all."

Liza smiled and didn't argue. It was a familiar complaint from Penn. He couldn't see how she functioned so cheerfully without her own private contingent of assistants. The reality of her situation went against everything in his own experience and expectations.

Liza remembered the gauntlet of secretaries she had to run to reach Penn's hushed office. And at his home, in the small, paneled penthouse overlooking Central Park, the capable Mrs. Green came every other day to tidy, although what she found to clean Liza couldn't imagine. Penn ate most of his meals out, but Mrs. Green saw to it that the immaculate refrigerator always held the makings of at least one perfect meal—lamb chops, usually, with some fresh asparagus in season. And strawberries, even in the dead of winter, from a greenhouse on the Island. Nor did she forget to keep a perfectly ripe grapefruit and buttery brioche on hand should her employer decide to eat breakfast in.

Then there was his man, of course. The first time Liza had met Peters, she had blinked with astonishment. "I didn't realize young men kept valets in this day and age," she'd whispered to Penn as they stood at the stone balustrade of the terrace, sipping sherry deftly poured by Peters. "Or is he a butler? The job descriptions of domestics is something I'm not quite up on."

Penn had shrugged and smiled. "I believe he might be offended if he was confused with a butler. They're very fierce about their territories, I'm told. I sort of inherited him from Uncle George. But it's true, there really isn't much call anymore for a gentleman's gentleman. So when George passed on, it was just understood, I suppose, that I would take him on."

"But what does he *do* all day? You're so neat—I've never seen you so much as leave a tie hanging over a doorknob!" Then, frowning, she had added, "I don't know that I could stand someone, even

someone as silent and polite as Peters, lurking about
in the background all the time. I'd feel. . . funny.''

Penn raised a perplexed eyebrow. ''I never really
thought about it. One just gets used to it, I guess.''

Gets used to it, Liza thought, looking out over the
city. But did one, when not born to such a pampered
existence? Could she?

She turned now and studied the strong profile of
the man seated beside her. His face was smooth,
utterly unmarked by the tension she knew to be there.
Penn Livsay was an attractive man, his dark good
looks polished by the privileges of birth. From the
clear, confident eyes to the manicured nails, he
reflected a lifetime of good food, good doctors, good
habits and education, all carefully supervised by a
procession of strict but adoring nannies, tutors, and
assorted servants. He was of moderate height, his
shoulders broad and well-muscled from regular
workouts at his racket club. His features were blunt
but pleasant, his jaw square, his nose slightly snub,
the brows that overhung the hazel eyes thick but
tamed.

At twenty-nine, he was the head of a family that
had been a power in New York for generations.
Although he was officially employed as a partner in
an investment banking firm, most of his time was
devoted to managing his family's extensive business
interests and portfolio of assets. And a large part of
the Livsay wealth lay in a private art collection that
was the envy of many a museum.

Investing in art had begun as a family amusement
of sorts, if the shifting of vast sums of money could

be thought of as a diversion. Penn's father had introduced him at an early age to the rituals of the auction
house. It had not taken long for an impressionable
boy, flattered to be included in the adult world by a
rather intimidating father, to become addicted to the
heady atmosphere in which fortunes are made—and
lost—by the almost imperceptible lift of a finger.

It was art, not mutual friends or family, that had
brought Penn into Liza's life. Liza had no family—
no close family, at least. Her mother had died when
she was young, and her father, a professor at the
state university, died more recently. Liza hadn't any
brothers or sisters, only a global scattering of
relatives to whom she wrote dutifully yet affec-
tionately at Christmas. But in all the ways that
counted, she had been alone in the world since she
was nineteen. Her background was academic, respectable, but decidedly out of the Livsays' social
orbit.

She had a graduate degree in fine art, a sheaf of
references in her hand, and three summers of work
experience behind her—two at archaeological digs in
Egypt, one cataloging a collection of old manuscripts—when she applied for a job at the Cavendish
Museum of Middle Eastern Art. The fact that she'd
been hired she saw as more than a dizzying stroke of
luck for a raw graduate in a dismal job market. She
claimed it as a good omen, and allowed herself to
hope that the darker days, the ones of loss and
lonesomeness, were over.

She loved the Cavendish and knew it well, even
before her application had been accepted. It was

there that she had spent countless hours as a student. And it was in the Cavendish's dim, stone basement where she'd worked that one summer, sifting through the dusty cartons of old books willed by a patron—counting, labeling, typing the file cards, searching for a nugget of gold in the piles of dross.

A small, private museum on upper Fifth Avenue, the Cavendish was once a mansion and was now a pleasant example of the solid, ornate architecture favored by turn-of-the-century grain and railroad barons. It had a grand central staircase, cool marble halls, and a tiny, arcaded inner courtyard with a formal garden of boxwood and roses as exquisite as a Persian carpet.

Liza's working relationship with the curator, Julian Sloane, had been wonderful from the beginning. Now, at the age of twenty-six, she was his assistant and widely acknowledged to be his likely successor. The Cavendish, whose reputation had always rested on the strength of Julian's scholarship, had become a bright and vital place with the infusion of energy and ideas Liza had brought with her. Her somewhat unorthodox approach initially hadn't been favored, though, at least not in one quarter.

The board of directors had knit its collective brow at the very thought of hordes of school children trampling through halls that usually heard only the sedate click of the heels of well-to-do matrons on an afternoon's outing. They'd howled about security when the evening lecture groups crowded the rooms that had been the private domain of a handful of scholars. And they had delivered a firm no to the idea of guest musicians playing the ancient instruments of the East in the courtyard on summer Sundays. But they began to look at Julian's choice of second-in-command with new interest—and respect—when the museum became the subject of frequent, admiring newspaper articles, when attendance soared and an increase in bequests and donations was announced by the treasurer.

One of those who turned an appraising eye on Miss Downing was Penn, who had assumed his father's seat on the board at the elder Livsay's death. His work for the board, which he had once viewed as both a family duty and a bore, assumed a new appeal. He volunteered for committees he normally avoided and sought out Liza's small, back office with increasing frequency. Gradually, he forgot to make excuses to see her. Business lunches became midnight dinners and for a year now, there had been no other man in Liza's life, no one of more than a few nights' interest in Penn's.

There was no formal engagement yet, no moment in time when Penn had asked and Liza assented. Neither was inclined to hasty marriage, she out of temperament and an enforced habit of self-reliance, and he out of tradition—few Livsay men married in their twenties. Still, there was an understanding, an unspoken acknowledgment on both their parts that they were well along a road that led to only one place, a road that seemed pleasantly free of obstacles.

Penn had even pressed a gift upon her, an amethyst ring Liza had once casually admired. He had been indulging a whim, she suspected, when he bought it, although he made much of the fact that it mirrored her eyes. But the ring was both small and new, and Penn was of the school of thought that believed jewelry should be tasteful yet "important," mellow with the patina of family history—plucked from grandmama's jewelry box, perhaps, where it had lain among the lavender sachets.

When the time did come for an announcement and portrait in the *Times*, Liza knew the amethyst would be put aside in its blue velvet Tiffany box and the real thing, the Livsay Diamond that had graced the hands of generations of their brides, would be brought out of the vault. Penn had shown it to her once when she was at his bank on museum business. She thought the priceless jewel dazzling, but too large for either pleasure or safety. No doubt there would be an escort—a large man with quick eyes and a slight bulge beneath the left side of his nondescript suit jacket—to the photographer for an official portrait. There would be more men drifting about the edges of the engagement party, similarly faceless and discreet, but with the same telltale bulge.

"It's the insurance people," Penn had grumbled. "Won't insure it unless you provide your own palace guard whenever it's out of the vault. Even at that, what they charge for a year's coverage would have bought the stone once." Liza tried to be sympathetic. She did think it a shame to consign such a shining object to the murk of the vault. But it belonged to another era, another life-style, and she was secretly relieved that the wearing of the Livsay Diamond had become a ceremony performed only a few times a year.

Liza's experienced eyes now swept the tall, wainscoted gallery and she considered for the hundredth time the very satisfactory way in which her world and Penn's met, the way the lines between them blurred at an event like this. It was not, she decided contentedly, an unreasonable basis for a relationship.

If there was an awkwardness between them, it lay in the difference of their social backgrounds. The concept of "breeding" was a stubborn survivor, even if those who had it no longer spoke of it openly. Penn discounted it entirely. In fact he'd refused to discuss it on the one occasion Liza, in her forthright way, had raised the issue. Yet Liza would have bet the Renoir that his mother and sister had not been so easily put off by his indifference. But here, at least, she felt her expertise and reputation seemed to bring the scales into better balance.

She glanced around and, toward the front of the elegant assembly, saw the familiar aquiline profile of Marcus Johns from the National Gallery in Washington. Her gaze traveled to the other side of the aisle, where Casey Ashton from the Metropolitan was seated. Then a hand caught her attention and she spotted Whit Manning, the art critic of the *Times*. She returned the wave and the smile. Whit had been a keen observer of Liza's blossoming career, and an unexpected ally, sending reporters to cover new events at the Cavendish, giving high marks when she deserved them and tough but helpful criticism—not the condescending, cruel sniping some of the other columnists indulged in. Liza respected and appreciated his professionalism; she was not the sort of person to be careless with the kindnesses shown her.

From where she sat, she could recognize almost every major art dealer from the United States and Europe. Some, she knew, would be buying on speculation for themselves, banking that the value of the art acquired tonight would continue its phenomenal escalation of the past few years. Others would be acting as agents for collectors, or even corporate conglomerates that preferred to remain anonymous.

One of these, the elite among dealers, was Victor Morneau, a dark, smoothly attractive Frenchman who was a great favorite of Penn's. For a moment, the man's watchful black eyes caught and held Liza's. He inclined his head a fraction and smiled. It was a slow smile, a private smile, as if they alone were in the room. It was an act of undeniable, European charm—the kind a sensible American woman might resolve to resist but happily succumbs to anyway.

No man, Liza thought, has the right to be so confident. She sensed her attitude sprang more from self-protection than criticism, but wasn't there a hint of complacency there that detracted ever so slightly from his appeal? Of course, Victor must be almost old enough to be her father, she judged, so his attentions came more under the heading of harmless flattery than risky flirtation. Really, you couldn't take Victor seriously! Which wasn't to say a woman couldn't enjoy him. Or at least be amused. Her own nod, her glance, were spirited, and she quickly hid the merest hint of a smile behind her catalog. Perhaps, she mused, it was a man like Victor, a man of such ego, who was the most fragile after all. She made a mental note to speak to him after the bidding.

So much wealth, from so many places and enterprises, she thought, her long, buffed nails tapping her crossed knees in unconscious nervousness. Penn would know all the names, but she herself had met many of these people. Over there was the head of a Japanese electronics firm, there a German arms dealer and the British owner of a large string of newspapers. Ahead of them was a long ripple of cream wool, the backs of Arabs in their robes. Probably looking for some way to spend their seemingly uncountable oil-earned dollars, Liza decided. She saw, too, that there was a liberal sprinkling of stardust: the boyish dress designer who was the city's current darling, an actress who made Liza feel ancient, a rock singer in tux and tennis shoes, charming an aging dowager in a dog collar of pearls.

New money, old money, all looking for the same thing—a safe haven in a world plagued by monetary crisis. Dollars could be printed, their value could plunge. But there would be no more Rembrandts, Rouaults, or Renoirs. Their value could only increase. People were rushing to buy whatever came on the market. New records were set daily at the great auction houses.

And art, the apparently foolproof investment, had a not unpleasant side effect that didn't come with buying gold bullion or blue-chip stocks. It conferred a certain aura, deserved or not, of culture. The buyer became an instant patron of the arts. If the painting was of world-class importance, its owner would take a place in history; his name would be noted by art historians and become an addition to the painting's provenance.

A gangly young man came sauntering down the aisle. He stopped, leaned behind Penn, then tapped her on the shoulder in a familiar gesture. "Here to pick up something for the guest room, Liza?"

She jumped, then laughed as she recognized the face of a former classmate now on the staff of a Washington gallery. "Forgot my checkbook, Eric," she replied, shaking her head in mock dismay. "Maybe next time."

The young man grinned. "Catch you later," he said, and went to take his place beside his boss, Marcus Johns.

Beside her, Liza saw Penn shift in his seat in what she thought might be disapproval of such casual banter. Dignity when in the public eye—she was going to have to remember that if she was to become Mrs. Penn Livsay. Sighing, she opened the catalog and scanned the list of paintings up for auction.

It was a respectable showing, she concluded, but the Renoir, last on the list, was definitely the best. It wasn't one of the artist's major works, but it was charming to be sure, and it would fill what Penn considered to be an important gap in his family's collection of Impressionist paintings.

The timing of the offering was convenient, too. Although Penn had not spoken of a direct connection, Liza knew that he'd recently sold a small manufacturing concern, which he'd never been particularly interested in, to some conglomerate. He'd been scouting for a while, now, for places to put the profits. It still made Liza's head spin. One day you owned a business—people, trucks, clanking machines—and the next, all of that was somehow converted into a small square of canvas.

Unobtrusively, she leaned toward Penn, kept her eyes on the catalog and said quietly, "Do you know who you'll be bidding against tonight?"

"Rumors, no more," he murmured, his eyes fixed straight ahead. "I do know that Johns wants it badly, but he doesn't worry me."

"Oh? Why not?" How could he *not* worry about Marcus, she wondered. Surely even Penn couldn't be so confident against such a well-backed opponent?

"He's been given a cutoff point by his board," Penn told her. "He's not authorized to go a cent higher."

"But what if his cutoff point is higher than yours?" she whispered. "Marcus has a very good budget, you know."

"It's *not* higher," he said flatly.

Liza pulled back and searched Penn's profile. "Are you sure?"

"I'm sure."

She regarded him for a second longer then turned away. She would not ask him how he knew—such things were supposed to be confidential. But Penn certainly knew people on the other museum's board. At business lunches no doubt things were sometimes said that shouldn't be.

A side door near the gallery's raised platform suddenly opened and a stream of brisk, well-groomed young men and women emerged, the men in tuxes, the women in pin-plain black silk dresses. They fanned out, taking positions along the side aisles. They stood, erect and impassive, hands clasped behind their backs, waiting. These were the "spotters" who would see that no bid, even the most subtly coded, would go unnoticed by the auctioneer.

Then the auctioneer, a thin, aristocratic-looking man in his forties, entered. He appeared completely at home in his dinner jacket as he climbed the few steps to the rosewood rostrum and took his place behind the shaded light of polished brass. At his side, a clerk sat with pen poised over the official ledger, looking alertly at him. A wave of expectant chatter rose and washed the length of the room, then subsided. The auctioneer's gavel fell into a now total silence, an unnecessary but ritual call to order.

"Good evening, ladies and gentlemen. Welcome to the Fairchild Gallery. Tonight we have the pleasure of offering for your consideration twenty lots of paintings, and we invite you to begin with lot Number One in your catalog, *Still Life with Pears*, dated 1890, one of many still lifes by Gauguin."

And so the rhythm of the auction began: the escalating bids, the increasing tension, the painful pause before the final fall of the hammer. Then, after a collective release of breath from the audience, an explosion of applause and the scene was replayed.

Prices were high, the bidding brisk and unhesitating. It was a good sign; the market remained strong.

Liza took a furtive glance at Penn. His face was a mask of indifference, but she knew him well enough to sense his pleasure. He would have enough competition for the Renoir to make a delicious game of wits. He would have found it a flat, tasteless victory to have walked away with the painting with none of the jousting, those twists and turns of bidding designed to make the competition unsure of the strength of his desire for the painting, the limits he was willing to go to get it and, indeed, the very worth of the painting.

Liza struggled with inelegant fidgetiness as the numbers were ticked off. Her heart fluttered. Finally, two hours after the first fall of the gavel, she heard what she'd been waiting for.

The auctioneer spoke, his voice still silvery and cultivated, the one dispassionate note in the fevered climate. "And now, ladies and gentlemen, our final offering of the evening, lot Number Twenty, *La Baigneuse*, one of several having this subject and dated 1896, by Pierre Auguste Renoir...."

A man in the dove-gray uniform of the Fairchild porters entered from the side, bearing the oil painting in his white-gloved hands. With reverent care he placed it on the easel beside the rostrum. The canvas itself was small, not more than twelve by twenty. The frame was massive, heavily carved and gilded. There was a moment of utter silence. Liza felt deeply moved and tears threatened to spring to her eyes. Art had always had that power over her—sometimes at the most inopportune moments. And *La Baigneuse* was so very beautiful!

It showed a young woman from the waist up, her bared back to the viewer, her ivory gown draped about her hips. Her head was turned to one side, the profile just visible above the soft curve of her shoulder. Masses of daffodil hair were swept up on her head. The background was a bright blur of flowers, a dozen blues of cornflowers, delphiniums, and heliotrope, all gilded by a wash of sunlight. It was a shining moment in time caught by true genius, and Liza involuntarily gripped her catalog to still the trembling of her fingers.

The auctioneer paused a moment, allowing *La Baigneuse* to have her full effect before his reserved voice cut through the excited hum. "I have $100,000 to start," he began.

Immediately, from all around the main room and from the side rooms, relayed by spotters, the bids came in. Some were signaled openly by raised hand, some furtively by codes known only to the auctioneer—the slight adjustment of a tie, the subtle touch of a finger to an earring.

Liza sat tensely, alert and waiting for Penn's first move. She knew he would not join in this opening flurry of low bids. Often they were made by those who knew there wasn't a chance of winning, but who left with what they'd come for anyway: experience, possibly, or just the perfect icebreaker for a clutch of cocktail parties. "When I was at Fairchild's last week, bidding on that little Renoir...."

Timing was vital. It didn't pay to give away too much, too soon. There were some serious bidders who would try the ruse of bidding early and dropping out, as if to suggest they could afford to go no further. Or that the painting was worth no more. Then, they would sit back while their agents in a now wary and confused audience finished the bidding for them. At the other extreme was the buyer who came in only at the end, forcing his opponents to decide very quickly whether his bid was an opening move or a final offer. Penn's technique fell somewhere in between. He seldom used agents, and preferred to enter the bidding toward the end, indicating he was there to win.

The bidding got higher and, one by one, the less serious buyers dropped out. "Do I have $400,000...? $400,000 on my right," called the auctioneer, noting for the first time a bid from Marcus Johns.

Something told Liza that Penn would enter now. It seemed...gentlemanly, she thought, for him to acknowledge Marcus's serious intent by exposing his own. She was not disappointed. With a quick, sure gesture, Penn touched one finger to the pearl stud on his dress shirt.

The auctioneer, who had been glancing at Penn from time to time in the past minute of bidding, caught it smoothly. "In the center, $450,000," he said, and Liza felt her heart thud. Then, without missing a beat, the man continued, "On my left, $500,000...."

That would have to be the Italian industrialist, Liza realized. What was his name...Sarti? She willed herself not to stare at the small, dark figure a few rows ahead of her.

"Do I have $550,000...?" A British dealer raised his catalog and the bid was acknowledged.

Immediately, Marcus Johns raised his hand. "We are at $600,000," the auctioneer called in response. His eyes went back to the British dealer. The man was visibly tense, chewing distractedly at the corner of his lip. With a defeated little shake of his head, the Englishman withdrew from the competition.

A three-way battle among Penn, Marcus and the Italian nudged the price up to $700,000. The audience viewed the seesaw struggle with fascination. Forgetting decorum, they shifted in their seats and craned their necks like spectators at a tennis match, now that the players and the rhythm were established for all to see.

Liza began to feel strangely uneasy. Something about the atmosphere was unsettling. The young bather, her nakedness so beautiful a short while before, now seemed exposed. A shadow had passed over her, stealing her warmth. This fight for her seemed somehow indecent. Liza thought about the artist and his vision. It seemed now so transformed that it might have been *any* commodity they were bidding for. She knew that this was the way it had to be done. But how sad, she thought, that an artist's creation could come to mean a hedge against inflation for the very rich.

She was sure she could see a slight slump to Marcus's shoulders and decided that the end of his bidding must be very near. Suddenly she felt a surge of sympathy for him. Their work was the same and she knew what he must be experiencing—the sense of loss and the frustration that this painting would not find a home in a public gallery where it could give pleasure to thousands. She felt a quick stab of guilt as her loyalty was torn between Penn and Marcus. Then, as the curator raised his hand, she knew with sad certainty that the fight for *La Baigneuse* was about to end.

"I have $750,000 in the front," the auctioneer announced. "Do I have $800,000?"

The silence was long, and for Liza, painful. Why doesn't Penn respond, she wondered. Was he forcing the Italian's hand? If he was, the next moment he received his satisfaction.

"I have $800,000 on my left," the auctioneer intoned, acknowledging Sarti. He looked back to Penn and waited.

The gesture was lightning fast, so totally unexpected that Liza could hardly credit her eyes. Her shock was apparently shared by the auctioneer. This time he didn't react with speed to translate the bid for the audience. Instead, his eyes went in appeal to the spotter nearest Penn and Liza.

There was a low murmur of confusion from the gathering. The spotter turned to Penn for confirmation. Again, Penn's gesture was too quick for any but the professional to catch. Or the woman beside him. Yet he definitely had brushed the pearl with the tips of four fingers. The spotter nodded almost imperceptibly to the auctioneer.

"I have $1,000,000 in the center," he noted casually, and the audience swooned with delight.

In the trade, it was sometimes known as "jump-bidding," a sudden major change in the standard of increment that had been established. In the beginning, the bidding had escalated in units of $25,000. When the serious buyers came in, it became $50,000. Now, Penn had changed the rules. He had made it $200,000. It was an offer that held an enormous challenge for any remaining bidder, a dare that was not only monetary, but also psychological. It was as if Penn had said, "We have been playing, gentlemen—now, let's get down to business!" But who could afford such daredevil business?

Even the auctioneer allowed Penn a fleeting look of admiration. His eyes fell on the Italian almost apologetically. But Sarti himself was enjoying the drama immensely, and gracefully accepted defeat. He made a courtly nod in Penn's direction and lifted his palm slightly, conceding the prize. Across the aisle, Morneau flashed a dazzling smile of congratulation.

For the first time that evening, Liza felt the tension flow out of Penn. He turned to her and actually smiled. Quickly she extended her hand to him and he took it, holding it between his palms for the inevitable but exhilarating conclusion.

"I have $1,000,000 once...twice...." The audience was poised to shower applause. The auctioneer ventured a rare smile and his hand moved toward the gavel.

He did not pick it up. Instead, his hand remained oddly suspended above it. A small frown appeared on his brow and he inclined himself toward another of his spotters. One eyebrow then lifted a fraction as he withdrew his hand from the gavel. "I have $1,200,000 at the back," he said crisply.

Penn's jump had been acknowledged and met.

There was a moment of audible silence and then a breathless "Ahhh...!" from the audience. This was much higher drama than anyone had expected and they were in raptures. They strained and twisted in their seats, frantic to see who had entered this late, stunning bid.

Liza felt her stomach turn. A man in front of them, an associate of Penn's from the bank, put his elbow over the back of his chair and spoke briefly to Penn under his breath. She saw Penn's jaw tense and felt his hand tighten around hers in unconscious response. Still, he neither turned nor spoke to her.

Well, perhaps *he* could retain that icy self-control, but at that moment Liza was feeling her human frailties just a little more acutely than Mr. Pennfield Livsay. She turned slightly in her chair. Then, even more. Finally she looked back over her shoulder. At last, she saw who had made that audacious, intimidating bid. Every eye in the room was fastened on him.

He was lounging casually against the pillared arch of the main entrance—a lean figure, decidedly unattractive, and devastatingly confident. Liza turned back and searched Penn's face. A question—who?— began to form on her lips but she silenced it, seeing the purple stain of rage rising above the stark white of his collar. She glanced toward the rostrum and saw that the auctioneer was also gazing at Penn in mute appeal.

Surely he would not embark upon another slow, agonizing round of bidding, Liza thought. Not at a

cost like that! He had made his gesture. There was no
card left to play. She saw him fold his arms in the
traditional gesture of withdrawal and was conscious
of relief. Unknowingly, she played her fingertips
soothingly across the back of his hand and in return,
he gave hers a bracing pat.

"I have $1,200,000 once...twice...to you, sir!"
The gavel fell three times, its crash lost in the explosion of applause. Liza turned again and this time
stared openly—bad form, she thought quickly, considering her position next to the man who was smart-
ing from the humiliation of being outmaneuvered.
But who was this show stealer? Mentally she ran down
the list: dealers, curators, collectors, investors. She
drew a blank. His was an utterly unknown face in a
group she thought she knew well.

It was then that she noticed he was returning her
scrutiny. A smile lifted one corner of the too-thin
mouth and she was forced to alter her initial impression—slightly. He was not precisely ugly. The face
was too intelligent, too mobile and expressive for that.
Suddenly conscious that their eyes had remained
locked too long—his amused, hers angry—she
blushed furiously and whipped around in her chair.

Penn, at least, had regained his composure. The
public lapse into anger had been brief. He rose and
shook hands with friends who clustered around him
offering words of consolation. He accepted their
sympathy with a shrug of his large shoulders and a
disarming grin. He even joined in some head shaking
and self-deprecating laughter with his fellow-
sufferer, Sarti.

In the foyer, they accepted champagne. "I'm sorry, darling," Liza murmured, her eyes somber over the rim of her glass. "I know the Renoir meant a lot to you."

"It's not losing it that bothers me," he said. "It's the *way* I lost it—the damned theatrics of a bid like that! If he'd declared himself earlier, participated—" He bit off the rest of the sentence. "But it's what you would expect from his sort, I suppose," he finished sullenly.

Suddenly she realized that he *did* care. The studied nonchalance was just a front, and beneath it he was stinging. "Why are we hanging around here, Penn?" she said crisply. "Let's go on to dinner—someplace bright and noisy. The little Spanish place in the village would be fun, I think."

"And slink out of here like a poor loser? No, Liza, we'll finish our champagne and mingle a bit first."

There'd be no moving him. Liza accepted his decision without argument. Although she wished just *once* he'd make things easy on himself, she knew he'd have to work through this in his own way. "Who was he, anyway, Penn?" she asked. "I don't think I've ever seen him before."

"His name is Chase. Christian Chase," he replied in a tone of voice she couldn't quite decipher.

A small gap developed in the tightly-packed, glittering crowd and Victor Morneau emerged, with suitable dramatic effect. A large, vigorous man, looking much younger than his fifty or so years, he embraced Penn forcefully, oblivious to the other man's slight stiffness. Victor's musical voice was richly accented and, Liza thought dryly, just a shade too loud, given the circumstances.

"Bad luck, Penn, bad luck—but a gallant effort all the same! Good evening, Liza. You're looking particularly delightful tonight. I trust you will cheer up our friend here?"

"Hello, Victor—yes, I hope so. I was just about to say to Penn that I thought *his* bid was perfect. But if he'd taken the bait of that man—Chase—he'd have ended up having to pay close to two million and that would have been simple foolishness."

"Precisely, Liza! Only the amateurs get sucked in like that." He drew back and looked down at her for a moment, frowning, as if appraising something. "What a joy a beautiful *and* intelligent woman is!"

Liza cocked her head. "You don't suppose he was a plant in the audience, do you? Someone who was just trying to force the price up? Maybe he was shocked that Penn didn't bid up and he was stuck with the painting—it would serve him right!"

Victor pursed his lips. "That happens, of course. But not in this case, I think. Chase meant to buy. Still, it's easy to be free with money when it's someone else's." He stared into his champagne almost wistfully.

"He's not a private collector, then?" she asked.

"Hardly," replied Victor with a sniff of disdain. "He's a step above messenger boy."

"Messenger boys aren't usually entrusted with small fortunes, are they?" Liza was eyeing the Frenchman skeptically.

"Oh, I have no doubt Chase sees large enough sums pass through his hands with some frequency," interjected Penn.

"He's not here, then, under false pretenses?" She said that lightly, but Penn's mood was stubbornly heavy.

"Chase's background is decent enough," he said, with an air of conceding a great deal. "His family's British aristocracy—titles, country estates, the whole business. But they went broke when the father died...a combination of death taxes and mismanagement, I understand. They used to own a very fine art collection, didn't they, Victor?"

Victor nodded solemnly. "A *beautiful* collection. Magnificent—I saw it once at their London house. The house was sold to pay off some of the debt, of course. And the paintings, too. Gainsboroughs, Turners—all gone, scattered around the world!" He made a properly dramatic sweep with his champagne flute. "My father used to sell to his father—that is how I came to see the London collection—and later he bought from him, to help out when the trouble began."

"So that's how Mr. Chase comes by his taste for Renoirs," Liza remarked.

"Probably the one thing he comes by honestly," added Penn through firmly clenched jaws.

"He hardly seems down-and-out, though," she noted. "Presumably there are still a few shillings in the pockets of his dinner jacket—which *doesn't* look rented by the way."

"Ah, a few shillings!" said Victor, pouncing.

"There you are closer to the truth than you may know, my dear. Christian Chase has a very unusual problem—he is both very wealthy and very poor, depending upon how one calculates wealth."

Liza shook her dark head. "You've lost me, Victor...."

"It's simple, really. The Chases are land-poor. They still own the original country estate. It's one of those monstrous places with more bedrooms than anyone ever bothered to count. It has its own farm, houses for the herdsmen and gardeners and what have you. But who can afford to keep it as a private home in these times?"

"I don't know," Liza smiled. "How does he do it?"

"Not *he*, darling," Victor corrected. "His brother. There are two Chase sons. It's Alister, the younger one, who keeps it going and in the family. He runs it as a national museum of sorts—gives house tours, takes in overnight tourists, that kind of thing. Quite a comedown, admittedly, but at least it's the honorable thing."

Across Penn's shoulder Liza saw the finely chiseled profile and dark blond, sun-streaked hair of Christian Chase. "And the other son?" she asked, sensing the unspoken accusation.

Victor Morneau bent over her, his voice conspiratorial. "Walked out and left the mess for his brother to sort out. Now he lives wherever he happens to find an accepting bed."

"But this business tonight..." Liza said, changing the topic. Much as she liked Victor, and much as she was curious about the odd history of Christian Chase, she didn't care for this sort of gossip.

Victor's nostrils flared slightly and his sigh seemed to indicate regret. "He does act as an agent in the buying and selling of works of art. But he works at the fringes of the profession, everything very speculative, very vague and off-the-record. He also deals in another facet of the business an agent like myself doesn't touch—security. Occasionally he is retained to trace and recover stolen art. At least, that's the side of it he *claims* to be available for." He took a sip of champagne and tossed a glance in Penn's direction, but it was Liza who intercepted it.

She turned her large eyes on Penn. "You don't think he's mixed up in anything illegal, do you?"

A shade of distaste flickered at the corner of Penn's mouth. "We'll probably never know—just as we'll never know where the Renoir goes after tonight."

"But we can guess, eh, Penn?" said Victor, raising a silvered eyebrow. "Right now I can think of several interesting possibilities," he added, and Penn smiled a little grimly.

"What are you two hinting at?" asked Liza cautiously.

"You have to understand what drives a man like Christian," Victor began. "He is embittered—he has a deep sense of being wronged by life."

"And," Penn cut in, "he's ambitious."

Victor nodded. "But perhaps not precisely in the way you mean, Penn. He has ambition to reclaim what he considers to be his by right, by whatever means are left to him. Christian has an impeccable family background, an intimate knowledge of art, and all the necessary social graces. But he lacks capital. So, he cultivates people who will be useful to him . . . particularly if they are old, rich and female.''

Liza smiled, but couldn't help shuddering, too. ''Oh, Victor—you make him sound horrid!'' she scolded, and the man laughed heartily, delighted to think he shocked such a pretty young woman.

She looked at the two men as sternly as the two glasses of Fairchild's excellent champagne that she'd had would allow. ''So, you two think he's bought the Renoir for some desperately lonely, aging divorcée. I'll bet you even have some silly fantasy about his delivering it to her silk and satin boudoir, hanging it over her bed and being generously rewarded for his efforts. Really, you're worse than schoolboys!''

For two brilliant men, their replies were slow and Liza knew she hadn't missed the mark by much. They changed the subject and as they droned on— something about foreign currency exchanges—Liza sipped her champagne and regarded the disreputable Mr. Chase across the rim of her glass.

Could he really be the sort to court and take advantage of lonely, older women, she wondered. Perhaps that was just another of Victor's theatrical exaggerations. Yet as she watched him, she could believe it was true. He was ringed by admirers pressing congratulations on him. The women were utterly lost to him, faces upturned and adoring.

She felt a flash of dislike, which, in her scrupulously fair way, she conceded to be unreasonable. He had, after all, done nothing wrong. His only crime was winning. Yet Liza felt Penn's disappointment keenly. Piqued, she continued to study the utterly self-assured winner through lowered lashes, as if his body would yield hints of inner weakness and past sins.

She remembered her first impression of him, that he was unattractive, and began to understand her reaction. Christian Chase had no pretensions to conventional good looks. He was too thin for his unusual height, she thought, although he compensated with a lithe, loose-limbed grace. It was the sort of body on which expensive hand-tailored evening clothes hung well, lending an unmistakable elegance to his natural grace. His hair, a sun-shot shade of blond, was fine and fell mutinously across one side of his high forehead. The planes of his face were sharply defined, the cheekbones dominating slightly gaunt cheeks. His nose was large and thin, yet aristocratically straight. The lines running from it to the edges of his mouth were deeply incised, indicating his life had not been easy.

That mouth was broad, perhaps too narrow, and his smiles tended to be crooked. But it was an expressive mouth, one that some might call sensual. Or cruel? Liza wondered, still searching for some key to him. His eyes were deep-set, with a disconcerting tendency to squint when he looked at you, emphasizing the network of lines at their corners. They were a clear, light blue, striking, she admitted, against his high, ruddy complexion.

It added up to something a little sinister, Liza concluded, recalling the way he had made her flush back in the salesroom. In fact, she thought, that memory still pricking her, he reeked of deviousness. But the man had charm, there was no denying that. Victor's claim that he was a professional dazzler of vulnerable women took on a new credibility.

"Liza?"

She started. "I'm sorry. . . what was that, Victor?"

"I was just saying to Penn, what does he need *La Baigneuse* for when he has his exquisite Liza?"

Liza smiled and said easily, "Don't you ever tire of flattering women outrageously, Victor?"

"Never. Although with you it's not flattery, my dear. But now I'm afraid I will have to ask you to excuse me. There is a woman over there who has shown an interest in acquiring a small piece of sculpture I have and I must speak to her." He shook hands with the couple, declining their invitation to join them for dinner. "I will be in touch with both of you soon anyway. Don't forget, Penn, tonight you missed one minor Impressionist painting among thousands. Next week you will have the art coup of the decade, the century even. And no one can take *that* away from you!"

The light came on in Penn's eyes again and the furrows of tension on his brow smoothed out. "Not from *any* of us. It will be a wonderful moment when we unveil the Constantine Cross. But we'll savor it together, you, me—and Liza."

Liza couldn't say how she knew that Christian Chase was watching them at that moment. But she knew. And with slow, deliberate pleasure she slipped her arm through Penn's, twined their fingers, and gifted him with a radiant smile. They were a couple—united, joyous, invulnerable. Then, with a defiant toss of her head, she looked back over her shoulder as they walked together toward the door and the waiting limousine.

From the thundercloud that had settled suddenly on Mr. Chase's brow she knew the dart had hit its intended target.

CHAPTER TWO

"You're sure you don't mind...?"

Liza, tucked into the curve of Penn's arm, turned her head contentedly on his shoulder and ran her finger slowly down his cheek. They were gliding through the now-still streets in the Mercedes, a window and fitted mahogany bar separating them from the liveried chauffeur.

"Of course I don't mind," she assured him. "I couldn't have eaten anyway."

"You make a terrible liar. I know you must be famished."

"I can scramble an egg when I get in...really, I'm rather glad you decided against going out. You may have put on a good front for everyone else tonight, but you can't fool me, my darling...I see you as you really are."

Penn smiled and tipped her chin up to him. "And what does Liza see?"

"She sees a man who drives himself hard. A man who has farther to fall when things go against him...as they did tonight."

He studied the palm of the small, tapering hand lying in his and brought it to his lips. "You're very good for me, Liza. I'm beginning to think I wouldn't know how to get along if I didn't have you."

She laughed gently. "You would get along very well indeed. You are one of the most driven, vigorous men I have ever known. As long as there's a challenge left in life, you'll move heaven and earth to meet it."

The car came to a smooth halt before Liza's building, although neither of them seemed to notice. The driver sat unmoving, waiting for the phone to ring with his instructions.

"Will I see you tomorrow?" Penn asked, his lips brushing her ear softly.

"If you don't mind, I think not, darling. I'd planned to spend Sunday in the glamorous manner most working women must—relaxing between cleaning and laundry. I should get some extra sleep, too, for next week. I've cleared my calendar of everything else so I can devote myself to the unveiling."

"How are the arrangements going?"

"I can't say it hasn't been hectic. . . but I think—I hope—you'll be pleased."

"I've never had any doubts about that. I've seen your talents in action before. That reminds me of something, though. Mother asked me to pass along her offer of assistance—caterers, the press, extra staff. All you have to do is ask."

Liza considered the "assistance" she would receive from Victoria Livsay. Let her have a part in the smallest detail and she would somehow have it all.

"Tell her I thank her sincerely, but she's a guest. A very honored guest," Liza added. "It's more than generous of her to be giving a party after the public ceremony.'' Mrs. Livsay, she knew, wasn't used to bits and pieces in life, but the unveiling was museum business that should be kept strictly separate from the event's social aspects. Liza didn't want anything to distract from the historical significance of the discovery of the Constantine Cross. It was only right, though, since it was Livsay money that had made it all possible, that Mrs. Livsay entertain afterward—Liza had never had any quarrel with that.

She felt a brief wash of desolation. Her relationship with Penn's mother was still uneasy and unformed, although it had always been carefully cordial. They were like two birds, nervous and fluttering, unsure of where to settle. If she and Penn were to become engaged, she'd have bridges to build there. . . .

It was at a time like this that Liza felt she missed her mother most—more, even, than when she'd been so young and the hurt so sharp. The loss of her parents had torn a hole in the fabric of Liza's life. It had been so beautifully stitched and appliquéd over the years—her achievements at school and at work, her grace and style in living—that no one, not even Penn, sensed the vulnerability, the possibility of a sudden giving way.

She knew so few women of Victoria Livsay's age. Without her mother, and the company of friends she would have had, Liza was aware of a gap in her understanding. What did Mrs. Livsay think, how did she feel, what did she value at this point in her life? Had she lived, Kathryn Downing might have given her daughter wise counsel and insight into another woman's mind—although they would surely have been very different from each other. But there was one thing Liza did not need to be told. Victoria Livsay was fiercely devoted to her only son.

Penn...but she cared for him so, too! Shouldn't that be a bond rather than a barrier? He was the new strength in her life, a vital, sustaining force. Through him she could rejoin the warmth and continuity of family that had reached such a tenuous conclusion in her own life.

In the watery gold light filtering in from the street she saw his dark eyes fall on her, warm and wonderfully tender. Understanding, she offered her lips to him, soft and full with the pleasure and comfort she wished to bring him.

He shifted and turned, pressing her back against the soft leather of the seat. She sighed, feeling the firm, welcome weight of his body. Her fingertips brushed his square jaw and felt a different tension there. He gave a low murmur of response and slipped his hand beneath the ruffle of her collar. His fingers played over her neck, lingering on all the sweet, remembered curves, then settled reluctantly on her shoulder.

Her own body answered with a slow, warm surge to his patient lovemaking. She knew and accepted that it wasn't a grand passion she felt for this man in the circle of her upraised arms. Nor a madness that confused itself with love. She could admit that freely and without guilt, for what she felt rising in her now was a reflection of the building affection and growing intimacy between them. And increasingly, she did feel the need for sexual fulfillment tug at her as she savored the still-gentle pleasure of his caresses.

It was the way she wanted it. She did not precisely fear what might lie beyond the crest of their passion. Surely they would never confront some bleak moment when the kiss they had just shared meant a little less than the one before.

But falling in love was easy. It was the loving, the commitment once physical passion had faded, that demanded strength. And her marriage to Penn, Liza knew, wouldn't fail. It couldn't. They were willing to wait and work for a deeper, richer intimacy to build.

His mouth found the soft hollow at the base of her throat and her head tipped back, her eyelids closing. What a deliciously baited trap, she thought, this freedom to reach out and take the physical part of love. The body could so easily claim what the heart barely knew. But she and Penn would build their marriage on a firmer, more faithful foundation. And the sexual love, such a tender pleasure now, would grow and blossom in its own time.

Penn knew that he was not the first man to kiss her, but he certainly meant to be the last. And Liza sensed deeply that to make the ultimate gift of her body would be to count her life totally committed to him. He would be a good husband—to her and for her. He would be kind, sensible, generous, possessive. Yet she couldn't help wondering whether it was cruel to deny him the fulfillment he longed for with such strained patience. Gently, she began to separate herself from him.

He drew a long, hoarse breath. "Oh, damn it, Liza—please!"

So, it was to be one of those nights when their parting would be particularly wrenching. Her hand groped across the seat, found her purse and then the door handle. "I love you," she murmured.

He brushed back his dark hair roughly. "Wait, I'll ring the driver," he began, sounding momentarily disoriented.

"Too late, I'm gone!" she said with a casual cheer that hurt her throat, it was so false.

She kissed him quickly, lightly, and *was* gone, gone before she could give him the answer that was on her lips.

As she ran up the broad stone steps she realized her relationship with Penn was about to change. And that night her bed did feel lonely and her dreams brought unsettling glimpses of a still-veiled ecstasy.

LIZA WAS AT WORK by seven on the morning of the presentation, blue-jeaned, her hair pulled back in a lopsided braid. She had a brief moment of blind panic.

"Blythe!" she howled at her pretty secretary. "Did I remember to mail the invitations?"

Blythe, usually as dreamy as her name suggested, but today the steadier of the two young women, assured her that she had. She stabbed her halo of copper curls with a pencil and counted off on her fingers, "Press, patrons, city officials, staff from the competition—plus a lavish assortment of Livsay friends and business associates. You got them all."

"They cost the world, you know," Liza sighed, remembering how grand and festive they had looked as she slipped each of the coveted, engraved invitations into its heavy cream envelope.

"But they were worth it. It's not every day we get a gift as fabulous as the one Mr. Livsay's giving us." Blythe dipped her head and looked at Liza thoughtfully through her fringe of short, dark lashes. "He's pretty special, isn't he?"

Liza considered, hugged her clipboard to her T-shirt and smiled. "Yes, yes, he is, Blythe." The two women broke into a shower of startled laughter. And then, oddly shy over this brief but telling exchange, they cantered down the echoing hall toward the gallery.

The morning ground on. Liza directed a harassed army of workmen, pleaded with laggard electricians, and cajoled some temperamental media types. Julian wandered in and out—whip thin and pale, pleasantly untidy in casual tweeds, his once blond hair curling over his collar. He gazed at Liza and Blythe over tortoiseshell half-frames and raised his elegant hands in benediction.

Liza regarded him with fond suspicion. "Julian. . . you won't forget?"

"Forget?"

"The *cross*, Julian."

She fanned the pages on her clipboard. "You're to carry it up from the vault, personally, precisely one-half hour before the ceremony—that was at your insistence, you'll remember. That would make it. . .?"

The curator clasped his hands behind his back. "Half-past three," he replied obediently. "And the security arrangements?"

"There'll be extra guards—armed." Liza wrinkled her nose in distaste. "They'll supplement our own security staff. Once it's in place," she added, glancing toward her secretary, "Blythe will switch on the new electronic surveillance system."

Julian smiled at her benignly. "Dear Liza, how you fret!" And he drifted off, cheerfully oblivious to the barely controlled chaos.

At noon, Liza stopped for coffee and a sandwich, managing one bite before being called off to settle another crisis. At one o'clock, the florist arrived. Liza had asked that the arrangements somehow evoke the Middle Eastern origins of the cross, and she was not disappointed. A snaking line of delivery-men bore flaming drifts of Turk's-Cap lilies, artfully interspersed with crinkly boughs of bittersweet, stark spikes of reeds, and plumes of dried grasses in containers of beaten copper. The effect was odd, lush and entirely wonderful.

At two, the caterer descended. Uniformed waiters and waitresses began to pace and fuss behind a long table stiff with white linen. Swiftly they set out neat rows of sherry glasses and platters of tiny finger sandwiches of cucumber and smoked salmon. Silver services were placed at either end of the table, one for coffee, one for tea.

At three, there was a hopeful calm. Liza, satisfied with the day's work, slipped home, showered, and changed into a suit. It was her best—a fine, Chanel-style fawn wool, set off by a simple white silk blouse with a jabot at the neck. For jewelry, she chose a long strand of pearls and matching earrings. Her hair she parted in the center, softly rolling the sides and securing the ends in a neat twist at the nape of her neck.

She scurried back to the museum and arrived, panic nipping at her heels again, just as the Livsay limousine was gliding to a halt beneath the large, arched entranceway. Julian was already descending the granite steps to a whir of news cameras, his hand outstretched in greeting.

THEY STOOD in a semicircle before their guests—the immediate Livsay family, Julian, and Victor Morneau—making a valiant effort not to wince before the assault of the television lights. Liza had positioned herself to one side, her eyes everywhere, her notes reduced to a single discreet file card, ready to prompt as needed. Directly in front of the little group, illuminated by a spotlight from the coffered ceiling, stood a small mahogany display case. Its glass top was covered by a swagged square of royal blue velvet.

Julian rubbed his hands together and tipped his head back. "Soon," he began, "we are going to see a piece of history before our eyes. A small object, but one which embodies an empire...fabulous wealth...epic battles. Indeed, I don't think I could be accused of being too dramatic if I said it symbolizes a change in the course of our own civilization." His smile was the charming one of a little boy caught in a fib, for Julian's tasteful flamboyance was legendary in museum circles.

"Its story began long, long ago, when the Emperor Constantine embraced Christianity. We can only imagine this man, walking one morning into the workrooms of his artisans in Constantinople, asking a favored one, perhaps, to fashion a cross for him. A few years passed and then, in A.D. 327, that cross, commissioned by the sole ruler of the Roman Empire and created by a nameless artist, was carried on a pilgrimage into the Holy Land by the emperor's mother, Helena."

Dear Julian! Liza thought. He was in his glory, his status as both scholar and curator fulfilled beyond his dreams.

"In the middle of the great wilderness described in the Old Testament," Julian went on, "and at the foot of Mount Sinai, Helena came upon a chapel built by Byzantine monks around a bramble bush they'd decided was the Burning Bush. So impressed was she by the monks' work and devotion that Helena left her son's cross there at the chapel, thus linking him to one of their new religion's most sacred sites.

"Two hundred years later, the Emperor Justinian enlarged the chapel, creating a fortresslike monastery. More centuries passed and the tiny walled commune in the desert was renamed St. Catherine's in memory of a young Alexandrian woman who, about A.D. 307, had been tortured to death for her Christian faith by a Roman emperor, and whose bones were discovered hidden on Mount Sinai.

"History made the Sinai a battlefield for the armies of Muslims and Crusaders, for leaders as various as Selim I, Napoleon, and Lawrence of Arabia. But the monastery, despite a never-ending siege by Bedouin tribesmen, clung doggedly to existence. At times its fortunes even flourished. During the Middle Ages, it became the object of a passionate, cultlike attachment. Churchmen, kings, and wealthy merchants in Europe sent priceless treasures to it in return for the tiniest relic of the virgin martyr, Catherine. The riches accumulated, largely uncounted and ignored by the simple, harassed band of monks. And amid that dusty tangle of gold and jewels lay the Cross of Constantine, its history only dimly recalled."

Julian's carefully modulated voice, so suited to the retelling of events gleaned from ancient manuscripts, was replaced now by that of another storyteller with a drama recent enough to exist in the minds of people still alive. Victor stepped forward and drew his audience along on the rising and falling warmth of his musical accent.

"The Russian czars, too," he began, "were among the powerful of Europe who sent money and treasure to the monastery—often their own exquisite icons—in exchange for other treasure, or perhaps a bit of oil said to have come from the bones of St. Catherine herself. One of those czars, Nicholas II, became intrigued by rumors that a cross that once belonged to another powerful ruler lay in the monastery's storeroom. He wanted Constantine's Cross for himself, and dispatched couriers to the Sinai, bearing payment of gold coins and icons.

"These couriers were successful in one part of their mission: they convinced the monks, who cared little for worldly wealth, to let them take the cross back to Russia. But the trip from the desert back to the grassy steppes of their homeland was long. They returned not to the Russia they knew, but to a country in the agonized throes of revolution. Nicholas was dead. His court and the rest of the aristocracy were either murdered or in desperate flight."

Victor was savoring his moment, and Liza reflected that if he had not been such a fabulous success as an art dealer, he could have made his living on the stage.

"The couriers," he continued, "discarded their rich clothes and carriages and became part of the hunted. We can only guess at what hardship and fear these men endured over the next months. What we do know, however, is that in the winter of 1917 a certain well-to-do Frenchman living in Paris was approached by two men with courtly manners and beggars' clothes. They offered him a quite magnificent cross for whatever he could give them. One aspect was not mentioned, of course, for those were dark times, but the Frenchman assumed the money would go to smuggling more Russians into the safety of Paris."

Here, Victor's tale became cryptic. He hinted—deliciously, Liza thought—at the identity of the people through whose hands the cross had passed. He declined to name them, though, in the interest of both professional ethics and security. As incredible as it seemed, there might still be some who wanted to settle scores almost seventy years old.

The cross, he told them, had remained in the same French family until recently, its existence known only to a few. But circumstances, as he so delicately phrased it, had forced the family to put it on the market. He had been approached to act as their agent in its discreet sale. With an attempt at modesty, Victor concluded that he was grateful to have been the overseer of the cross's final journey, after such a perilous history, to a safe haven.

"All this," he finished, "has been made possible by the generosity of one man."

Liza pressed her lips together and stared firmly at her clasped hands, for surely it would be unsuitable for the assistant curator to be seen looking at a member of the board with eyes so misted and cheeks so pink. She was both relieved and oddly proud that Penn's answering remarks were so brief and almost shy at his dismissal of all that he'd done.

"I am happy," he said, "that the Cross of Constantine will now be enjoyed by so many people. And it gives me particular pleasure to dedicate it, this afternoon, to the memory of my dear father William Livsay, here in one of the Cavendish galleries endowed by his father, Edmund." He stepped aside and, in a moment of hushed expectancy, pulled the fringed satin cord. The velvet cloth fell away.

Liza bit her lower lip softly but felt her eyes fill instantly anyway. The cross had lost none of its power to instill reverence and awe. Once the most indomitable man of his time had prayed with it at his breast. His aged mother had carried it on a heroic pilgrimage through the wilderness of the Sinai. Now, it lay before this gathering. The fussing news directors, the photographers fiddling with lenses, the elegant society women worrying about the drape of a hem or an errant strand of hair all forgot their preoccupations and fell silent.

The cross nestled on a raised bed of velvet. It was solid gold, six inches, no more, in length and richly encrusted with jewels. Each of the dozens of softly glowing pigeon's blood rubies was circled by a ring of minute gold beads. The center stone of the crosspiece was an emerald the size of a hazelnut. The workmanship was superb testimony to the vision and genius of the artist.

Liza didn't know what Penn had paid for it. She didn't think she even wanted to know, but knew it must have been a fabulous sum. That he had turned right around and given this rare article for public enjoyment filled her with wonder and no small amount of admiration. The applause began to rain down. *He deserves all of it,* she thought, and she too began to clap.

A short while later she tugged at his sleeve. "I promised that young man with the beard over there some photographs and an interview. You mustn't make a liar out of me, Penn." She already had Victor by the hand.

"You see how she drives me?" he said, smiling down on her. The circle gave him up reluctantly, for there was no man in the city that night whose company was so desired and who radiated so much glory in which others might bask.

Liza kept a firm hold on both men, shepherding

them across the gallery with quick, determined steps. "I though I'd *never* get the two of you together and this poor reporter's been—"

The smile suddenly vanished from Liza's face. She stopped so short that the two men were hard pressed not to spill their sherry. "Over there—look! Isn't that the man who was at the auction last week?"

Penn's eyes followed the direction of Liza's troubled gaze. "Christian Chase . . . ? So it is."

"What's *he* doing here?" Liza asked angrily, resenting even the smallest cloud's appearance on their horizon.

"I'd be surprised if he *didn't* show up," said Victor casually. "Everyone in the business is here to see the sale they missed. Why should he be any different?"

"Well, I think it's nervy . . . Penn, I think he's coming this way. He is—I don't believe it! The gall of the man. He must have the hide of an elephant!"

Penn laid a large, calming hand on her shoulder. "Relax, darling. I think we can afford to be gracious today." And indeed, Penn looked so thoroughly relaxed and in control that Liza felt at once reassured and a little bit ashamed.

Victor performed the introductions. Liza offered her hand reluctantly, hearing her own greeting sound stiffer than she'd intended.

"My congratulations to all three of you," said Christian Chase pleasantly. His smile was charmingly sincere.

Liza, if she hadn't already been told of his background, would have guessed it anyway. He possessed the smooth, cultured, and totally effortless British accent that immediately identified his elevated station in life. She wished, though, that he was just a shade less mannerly—it would be more in keeping with her image of him. What had she expected? Pushiness or smug superiority?

"Thank you," said Penn. "I think I can say that it's been gratifying all around."

Christian, one hand thrust casually into the trousers of a classic, gray flannel suit, looked over at the cross. "It's magnificent," he said, with frank and unforced enthusiasm.

"Indeed it is," agreed Penn, rocking slightly on his heels and looking, Liza thought, not unlike a new father at his child's bassinet.

"And that was a marvelous speech, Victor. I really enjoyed it. But what a job of research it must have been, working up the history of something like that. The provenance must weigh a ton."

Victor disclaimed the credit. "My staff—" he explained with a demure dip of his head and a small gesture with his glass "—they are excellent."

"That's good to hear, Victor. I take it, then, that you were well satisfied that there was nothing to the rumors about the cross," Christian commented in that agreeable voice.

His words were met with open-mouthed astonishment. "I wasn't aware," said Penn after a brief but nasty silence, "that there were any rumors."

"That's because there weren't any," Victor snapped dismissively.

Christian Chase smiled in his lopsided way and

shrugged carelessly. "You know how the art world is, Victor—loves a bit of gossip. I'm really very happy for all of you that there was no problem. Well, I should be going. It was a pleasure to meet you Mr. Livsay...Miss Downing."

He turned to go, but Penn, after a moment's visible struggle, lifted his hand and said, "Just a moment, Mr. Chase. I would like to know, please, what it was that you heard about the Constantine Cross."

Christian Chase stopped and turned back to them, his face open, the very picture of innocent concern. "Of course," he replied graciously. "Considering what you probably paid for it, I'd say you have a right to know everything about it—even the silliest rumors."

He paused, tipped his head back, and finished off the last of his sherry. Liza, for the second time in her life, felt she detested this charming stranger. "I had heard," he continued in his own time, "that there is another cross just like it in existence."

Victor laughed. "*Another* one?" he asked incredulously. "Meaning that this magnificent object in front of us is a fake? Really, Christian! And just where is this other cross supposed to be?"

"Back at the Monastery of St. Catherine," came the ready reply.

Liza saw Penn stiffen in indignation. "That really *is* an absurd bit of gossip, Mr. Chase. I can't imagine who would tell you such a thing. There's just no way that this cross could be the work of a forger."

"I didn't say that it was," Christian replied, unruffled. "Please don't misunderstand me." Genuine hurt seemed to shadow those startling blue eyes for the briefest moment.

Penn turned to Victor. "Surely there isn't any doubt about the authenticity of the cross!"

"Of course not," the Frenchman insisted. "I don't deal in slander or bad jokes." The pretense that this was an ordinary conversation evaporated.

"Then I don't think the public is well served by the repetition of such nonsense, Mr. Chase," said Penn with a cool calm that made Liza want to cheer.

But her elation quickly turned to anxiety, for she was not the only one who had heard this prickly exchange. Whit Manning, the *Times'* art critic, was standing just beyond Penn's elbow, and he was listening with undisguised fascination. There was the potential here for a very unpleasant scene indeed, Liza thought.

She rapidly collected her scattered wits. "Goodness, we've completely forgotten about that nice young reporter and the deadline he no doubt has to make." She wished Christian a crisp goodbye and, with a brittle smile, drew Penn and Victor away.

As she feared, Penn's temper was beginning to slip the leash. "What the hell was that guy trying to pull?" he whispered furiously to Victor.

"That's obvious, isn't it?" Victor said tightly. "It's one of the oldest, shabbiest tricks in the business!"

"What are you talking about, Victor?" Liza demanded.

"The game goes like this, Liza—if there was the slightest doubt about the authenticity of the cross, I would release Penn from our agreement instantly. Christian knows that. In fact, it's what he's banking on. The news that Penn had refused to buy would spread like wildfire. And where would I find another buyer then? Collectors and museums would avoid that lovely cross as if it were diseased. Its value would plunge. The only way I could recover any of my own investment would be to sell it for the value of the gold and jewels alone.''

Liza flinched at the thought of that awesome work of art reduced to a bundle of gold and gems. It was so much more than that! ''Is that possible, Victor?'' she asked, horrified.

''No! And he knows that too. I believe in the cross—I would stake my life on its authenticity. I would *never* see it degraded so!'' Victor was shaking, and Liza looked at him with real concern, wondering if such rage could make him ill.

Penn was nodding, his face dark with anger, but Liza was still confused. ''I don't understand, Victor. What would he stand to gain?''

''The cross, my dear Liza. Christian could approach me with an offer for something more than its worth in gold and jewels—but still only a fraction of its true value. He would have succeeded in driving the price down and putting me in an impossible position. After all, I am a dealer—I must buy and sell to make my living.''

''But why would Chase want to own something that he himself had devalued? Victor, it just doesn't make sense!''

''In the end, Liza, he will *not* have devalued it. He

will have increased its value." He saw her eyes widen.
"Yes, it's true. People will come to understand what
he did—they will realize there never was any doubt
about the cross's authenticity, that the rumors were
Chase's creation. But will they condemn him for it?
No, they will admire his audacity! He will have added
another colorful chapter to the history of the cross,
and its value will increase accordingly."

"But that's such an incredible gamble!" Liza said,
a note of desperation creeping into her voice. "And
even if he was successful, he'd still have to pay you a
great deal of money. I thought you said he lives hand
to mouth?"

"Oh, he does—he's no doubt doing the dirty work
for someone else, just like a hired thug."

"What's the answer, then?" asked Penn, his mind
leaping ahead.

They were silent a moment, three people considering a trap whose jaws were about to spring on them.
"Why not do nothing?" Liza suggested at last. "*We*
know what he's up to—let's just stand our ground!"

"But if what Victor says is true," said Penn, thinking aloud, "Chase won't stop with what he's done today. We have to seize the initiative from him in some
way."

"And there's another thing," Liza added glumly,
knowing now she had to tell them. "Whit Manning
from the *Times*...I'm almost sure he heard everything." She heard a sharp intake of breath from Victor, a short, unpleasant word from Penn.

"Then there is only one thing left to do," Victor
rapped out briskly, clapping his hands together. "We

will call his bluff. We will show everyone that we have absolute faith in the authenticity of the cross—and that, Liza, will be your job.''

"Mine?"

"Of course. I will submit the cross to you for verification before any money changes hands. Penn and I were going to attend to that tonight, over brandy, but it can wait. Subject it to every test you have, Liza. Check and recheck every item on its provenance. Only when you are completely satisfied that it is not a forgery will I—''

Penn flushed and shifted uncomfortably. "Look, Victor, you and I have done business for years. This really isn't necessary.''

"Not for us, Penn, no. But for the cross it is. I have no doubt that Liza will find it to be genuine, and in due time, we will share that brandy!'' He looked down at Liza and waited.

Liza searched Victor's face with all the detachment she could summon. There was not a flicker of unease in his eyes. No, Victor was not lying. She was sure of it. "Of course,'' she said, suddenly businesslike. "I'll speak to Julian and start in on it first thing in the morning. The sooner we put this tacky little incident behind us the better.''

She excused herself and set out to find Julian, hoping to tell him the news before anyone else could. There had never before been even a hint of impropriety connected to the Cavendish, and she knew Julian would be devastated when he heard.

But it was not her superior she came upon beneath the polished curve of the staircase in the pillared foyer. It was Christian Chase. She hesitated a second, unseen, watching him slip into a well-worn trench coat. Then, berating herself for cowardice on her very own territory, she squared her shoulders and entered the foyer, her heels making authoritative clicks on the floor. Halfway across, maddeningly conscious of his eyes on her back, she stopped and turned around. She favored him with a wintry smile.

It was definitely Liza's moment. She felt it acutely. The floor was circular, a starburst mosaic of rose Italian marble. She stood directly in its center, as if on a director's chalk lines on a stage. She was abnormally aware of the straightness of her back, the set to her chin, the glint of the gold buttons on her cuffs— the tiniest detail was crisply clear in her mind. She was sensitive to his expectant pause as their eyes held and he lifted a cashmere scarf slowly over his head. The moment was theatrical—not at all her style really—yet she savored it.

"It occurs to me that I have been rude, Mr. Chase. I should have thanked you."

"Oh, *Christian*, please—since we're colleagues, in a manner of speaking," he said. "And what have I done to merit your gratitude. . . Liza?"

She ignored the offensive familiarity. "We are always happy to have questions about our collection brought to our attention, because the integrity of this museum means everything to us."

One corner of his mouth lifted in what might have been a smile. "I take it, then, that you intend to consider your recent acquisition a little more closely."

"I do."

"And what form will this attention take?" he asked, methodically pulling on pigskin driving gloves.

"Tomorrow I'll begin a thorough evaluation of both the cross and its provenance."

"Commendable. But do you really think you are the person to do it?"

She blinked. How dare he question her competence? "I assure you, Mr. Chase, I am a very well-qualified curator," she retorted, wishing to heaven she didn't sound quite so prim.

"Yes, I'm sure you are," he said, looking for all the world as if he might pat her on the head. "And something else as well."

"I don't understand...." Her self-styled stage manner began to feel a good deal less comfortable.

"You are also the girl friend of the man who has a lot at stake in all of this, financially and otherwise."

Liza's eyes were the hot white violet of a flame now. Her voice began low and steadily rose, "If you are implying that I would deliberately alter my findings because of my relationship with Penn—that is the most despicable, insulting...!" Fury strangled the words in her throat.

But he was unmoved by her sputtering rage and merely smiled consolingly at her as he put a gloved hand on the handle of the Cavendish's huge front door. "I simply meant, Liza, that young women in love are frequently not in control of themselves. You *do* see my point?"

He left her there, with her scarlet-splotched face, and slipped out of the hushed old house into the

noisy Manhattan dusk. Curtain down, no applause—
her scene stolen by an arrogant interloper in her own
theater. Liza, known to her co-workers as the most
gentle of women, was overcome with fury. She aimed
an expensively shod foot at a fine brass umbrella
stand and gave it a swift kick. The only observer of
this tantrum was John the night watchman who concluded later, frowning over his mug of coffee, that
Miss Downing must have tripped and he did hope she
hadn't hurt herself.

"I TOLD THE CATERER to come back in the morning to
clean. We can live with the mess better than we can
live with your temper, Penn. And I've sent Peggy off
to the servants' quarters. Now, what's wrong?"

There had been twelve to dinner around the fine
old Georgian table, nibbling at quail, then pushing
hot lemon soufflé around the Flora Danica dessert
plates and otherwise driving the caterer wild with
frustration. They had, however, done justice to the
fine wines, if for all the wrong reasons.

Just the core of the group remained—Victoria Livsay, Penn and Liza, and Penn's sister, Alexa and
brother-in-law, Miles Kane. They were sitting in Victoria's large living room, a sumptuous place with
views west over Central Park and south down Fifth
Avenue.

Briefly, Penn told them. Liza listened, stirring her
black coffee needlessly, braced for a convulsion of
indignation.

"Oh, what impertinence—I can't bear it!" cried
Victoria, plucking at the square of lace-edged linen

on her lap. "No wonder you were so distracted all through dinner. And that explains Victor's and Julian's subdued moods too, no doubt."

Victoria was not at all like her son. She was as spare as he was sturdy, and where he showed the potential for becoming, in time, a large man, she remained reed-thin and uncompromising. She did share the thick, dark hair, but hers was disciplined and struck now by wings of silver at her temples. Her eyes were greener than his, her mouth straighter.

Liza had seen Penn's mother in moments when her restraint was softened by great charm. But now the habitually erect body in a simple dress made spectacular by perfect fit and the muted glow of cerise, was positively rigid. Victoria was seated by the fireplace in the chair she always took, a very straight, unpadded Queen Anne side chair—it was for others to fling themselves into the comforting depths of the down-filled sofas scattered about the room.

"And what are we to do now?" she asked, raising a finely-tweezed eyebrow.

Penn made a dismissive gesture. "It's being dealt with, mother."

"I should hope so," sniffed Alexa. "The man ought to be sued."

"For what?" said Penn, looking at his sister wearily.

Alexa shrugged a silk-draped shoulder. "Slander, or...I don't know, there must be something! Put one of our lawyers on it."

Miles Kane gazed balefully at his wife and set his gold-rimmed demitasse on the butler's table in front of him. "Don't be so quick to call out the legal types, Alexa," he scolded mildly. "It's getting to be your answer for everything."

Liza hid a smile behind her own coffee cup. She liked Penn's brother-in-law. A slight, sandy-haired man, he possessed a wry sense of humor and was a gentle counterpoint to his high-strung wife. He was also, she suspected, a silent sufferer.

Miles handled a lot of legal problems for his firm and would certainly know whether this troublesome problem had strayed into that realm. Liza was rather vague on the subject of the law. When her father died she had simply signed—perhaps too obediently—all the blue-bound papers slid across the attorney's polished desk with dizzying speed. The legal implications of the dilemma Christian had dumped in their laps had certainly not been her first thought.

Alexa smiled her assiduous smile. She had, Liza supposed, what was called "presence." It was the kind that allowed her to get away with the gown she was wearing tonight, a wealthy Gypsy's concoction of gold-shot rust silk with flowing sleeves and a skirt that drifted to varying lengths—the sort of thing Liza would have felt like a clown in.

It was certainly a very different "presence" though, from Victoria's. The mother's was silent, a force felt. The daughter's spoke more loudly, and Liza had never been entirely comfortable in her company.

"Well, what are you going to do about it?" Alexa demanded of her brother.

"Victor and I have agreed to submit the cross to Liza for an opinion. We will abide by her decision."

Alexa's extravagant gold and apricot mane jerked around. "Liza!" she breathed, and looked at her as if seeing her for the first time. At her feet, Alexa's beige-and-white Papillon fanned his feathered ears and gazed up at his mistress. Then, after a gentle flutter, he laid his head back down on the needlepoint pillow kept by the brass fire fender for his frequent visits. His mistress's outbursts were well-known to him and he was soon snoring delicately again.

Penn turned his brandy snifter in his hand and stared morosely into it. "Of *course*, Liza—who else?"

"But what does that mean?" persisted Alexa.

"If Liza says it's authentic, I buy. If she says it's a fake, I don't, and the cross is removed from the museum. It's that simple."

There was a moment of pandemonium—questions, objections, warnings—before Victoria stepped in to take control. "Stop it, all of you. And let poor Liza speak. You terrify her."

Liza, feeling the sudden silence keenly, decided she preferred the role of observer. She shifted slightly on the chintz-covered sofa and cleared her throat self-consciously. "Well, not *quite*, Mrs. Livsay," she began. "But I am sensitive to the concern of your family about unpleasant publicity. My guess, though, is that you have nothing to worry about." She turned quickly to Penn and they exchanged reassuring glances, the first time they had really connected since the day began its rapid disintegration.

"Liza, when you smile the sun comes out for my son." Victoria said it with neither approval nor disapproval, but simply as fact. Liza clutched hopefully at the comment anyway.

"Your *guess*?" Alexa repeated, ignoring her mother. "I think we need a good deal more than that, my dear."

"Oh, of course," Liza began earnestly, "I'll be performing a series of quite scientific...." But they weren't listening, and she knew it. It had been like that most of the evening, particularly when the aunts and uncles and cousins were there. She was, for the most part, excluded from the private jokes, the family gossip and knowing glances. Occasionally someone remembering his or her manners would toss her a bone of conversation. Liza had masked her irritation but wished all the same that Penn would notice and rescue her from her isolation. But that wasn't his place, she had admonished herself sternly. Either she was up to dealing with this family or she was not.

While the others now debated the merits of various methods of dealing with the troublesome Mr. Chase, Liza's gaze drifted about the living room. It was, she decided, a little lacking in domestic warmth, but not much else. Editors of decorating magazines had schemed and pleaded to photograph its stunning mix of various periods of furniture. Victoria, of course, was above such flattery and had resisted all efforts to invade the privacy of her home.

The decor was meticulous yet as feminine as its creator. The walls were a sunny apricot, the ceiling a pale sky blue. The ornate moldings were picked out in cream, and here and there were unexpected accents of coral. Aubusson carpets softened the polished parquet floors. On the walls, exuberant Picasso clowns hung companionably by tranquil Degas ballerinas. Only a woman as self-assured as Victoria Livsay could have held her own in such a room.

At Liza's side was a large circular lamp table skirted in eggshell silk moiré. A studied clutter of family photographs in sterling frames covered it. Liza smiled seeing Penn in his prep school uniform, Penn on his pony, Penn at the tiller of his first sailboat. And Alexa, of course—in her pram, playing field hockey at that girls' school in Connecticut, and looking surprisingly reticent in pristine white at her coming-out party. Liza's eyes stopped abruptly at a small photo of a woman she'd once caught looking at her, at a party, with stunning hostility. She was, it turned out, the woman Penn had been linked with the summer before Liza had begun dating him.

Her eyes hurried on to beautiful aunts and stern uncles, occasionally in the company of presidents. Liza had once overheard the Livsays sneered at as elitists. It was true they thought of themselves as special. It would be hard *not* to, she thought, given the number of judges, senators, doctors and the like who festooned the family tree. A certain standard of intellectual achievement and moral tone was expected—from the male side at least. The standards for the women were different, although no less exacting. Penn was continuing the tradition.

"Does it bother you, Liza?" She heard the soft rustle of silk and turned to find Alexa beside her.

"You've been entrusted with a job that's going to have quite an effect on this family, you know."

"I've been entrusted with finding out the truth, and no, that doesn't bother me." Liza's smile was faint.

"I'm curious—will you be able to do that? I really know so little about what it is you *do* over there in that glum old place."

"We have some very scientific tests these days. Our methods are not entirely subjective. But it's possible the question may never be resolved to everyone's satisfaction. We may have to live with some doubt."

"You might be able to, I suppose, but it would raise some problems for us. Look around you," Alexa said with a swoop of her scarlet-nailed hand. "You won't find anything fake here."

Liza pushed back a rising irritation. "No, I don't expect I would," she said quietly.

"And tell me, after all this publicity today—and heaven knows the papers will be full of it tomorrow, too—could you really recommend the Cavendish not accept the donation?"

"If I have to, I will, of course," Liza replied with growing wariness. What side of this was Alexa arguing for, she wondered.

Alexa frowned and plucked an invisible speck of lint from her skirt. "That would be hard, very hard, on all of us. But particularly Penn. I trust you understand that much about him."

"You surprise me, Alexa. Frankly, I think you're underestimating your brother's ability. Penn has done the right thing. And I don't think you should borrow trouble by speculating about possible public embarrassment." She saw Alexa's lips thin slightly at the bluntness of her words, and knew she had begun the first small tear in this tissue of civility between them.

"Well, whatever you decide, I hope you'll consider all the implications. I imagine the artistic side of you can be quite impulsive...possibly that's what's drawn Penn to you. We wondered about the attraction."

Liza was silent. How could she reply to that? Alexa stood suddenly. "I'll be watching how you handle this," she finished. "That will be more interesting, really, than your decision."

Liza sighed, finally feeling her exhaustion. The Livsays might forgive the near acquisition of an unsuitable work of art. But not an unsuitable daughter-in-law.

CHAPTER THREE

Angus had waited as long as his patience allowed. Surely by now, he thought, the plane carrying the overseas papers would have landed and the truck would have brought them in.

He left the cool, stone-walled house in the Old Town and set out on foot, heading for the hotel down by the water where the tankers plowed their determined path through the swarms of native dhows.

He had to make his way through the bazaar where the street was narrow and dark, shaded by the sagging awnings of the sidewalk vendors. Early as it was, it was noisy with the sounds of trading and the donkey bells. He threaded through the dark forms of women in their *jallabahs*, market baskets on their heads; careful as he always was to avoid the women's eyes.

At the end of the lane, past the wares of the copper merchants and the green mounds of fresh figs, he emerged into a blinding sun and a whole new world. Beyond the broad, paved boulevard, the smooth white concrete and glass of Aqaba's only luxury hotel lay shimmering in the mounting heat.

The clerk noted Angus's presence and automatically reached under the counter. "They just came in a few minutes ago, Mr. Cavanaugh."

"That's fine, Saad. Did you remember I wanted the New York papers as well as the London *Times* and *Le Monde*?"

"Yes, sir, they're all here." Angus added a tin of loose tobacco to the pile, handed over the necessary dinars, and walked back through the red-tiled lobby to the sidewalk café.

Over a glass of lime soda he began a rapid, deliberate search. On the front page of the second section of the *Times* he found what he had been looking for. Smiling, he folded the paper and leaned back to read the long article. With intense concentration and squinting against the sun, he pored over the printed page. When he was through, his eyes fell on the photograph that accompanied the story. It showed two men and a young woman standing near a display case, smiling.

He tossed the paper aside and leaned his elbows on the table. *Well, Christian, you failed,* Angus thought to himself. *I wonder what your next move will be, for if I know you, and I think I do, you're not finished yet.* But maybe, it occurred to him, Christian had never even made it to New York. Why else would these people look so happy?

He pulled the paper back to him and looked down at the picture again. Who was the woman? He knew who Morneau was, of course, and he'd heard about this fellow Livsay. The caption described her as the assistant curator. *Lovely little thing,* he thought. *She'd be the one Christian might go after.* He wondered if she would make his job more, or less, difficult.

"Poor girl," he said aloud. Almost a week had passed since this photograph had been taken and it would be night in New York now. "I wonder if you're still smiling?"

"EVERYONE OUT, JOHN?"

"Yes, that's the last of them, Miss Downing," said the uniformed night guard. "Will you be going home yourself soon? Seems as if you're practically living here these days."

"As a matter of fact, I'm staying tonight, John. That's what I wanted to talk to you about. I'm going to take the cross out of the vault. I'm moving it to the laboratory."

John nodded gravely. "I'll keep an extra sharp eye out."

"Thanks. And I'd also like not to be disturbed."

"Just leave it to me, Miss Downing. I'll even make sure the cleaning crew doesn't go down there tonight."

Liza laid a grateful hand on the man's arm and, as she turned to go, spied Julian. He was struggling with a briefcase, raincoat and umbrella, for the days had slid rapidly into the heart of autumn; ever since the unveiling they had endured a steady, icy rain.

"How goes it, Liza?"

It was all the invitation she needed. Julian was patient as Liza related the latest developments concerning the cross. "So you see," she concluded, "I'm struggling—I'd like you to come in on it now."

Julian frowned. Finally, he shook his head. "I'm afraid not, Liza. I won't do it."

Liza's voice was a small wail of dismay. "But Julian, why not?"

"Because it's your job, my dear," he said firmly, though not unkindly. "Oh, I'll go over your report with a fine-tooth comb all right. And it had better be a good one. But I won't involve myself in your decision-making."

"But Julian," she persisted, "the Cavendish has never had a gift this important."

"No, it hasn't. But you are important, too. There comes a time when you have to make decisions, stand by them, and take the flak. If you don't make the leap now, you never will."

Liza leaned back against a pillar and folded her arms across her chest. "There's something more, Julian. I feel I have to mention it...." And she told him of Christian's criticism, carefully avoiding the name of the critic.

"Good heavens, Liza! The thought never crossed my mind! I've noticed you and Livsay have been close. But you won't have any trouble keeping that separate from your work, will you?"

"Well, *I* didn't think so, but...."

Julian was suddenly serious. "You've got to have more faith in yourself, my dear. Otherwise you'll be looking over your shoulder all the time...and I won't always be there."

"So you're kicking me out of the nest, in other words?"

He touched the tip of her upthrust chin with one

finger. "Yes. And it's a long way down, Liza. Do us
both proud." He smiled, waved, and was gone.

LIZA PUSHED OPEN the heavy oak door marked No
Admittance that led to the cavernous basement and
descended the steep, worn steps gingerly. Under one
arm she held the pro on the Constantine Cross, prepared by Victor's staff. It was a weighty volume
printed on heavy paper, bound in red calfskin
and embellished by the gold crest of the Morneau
House.

Exemplary by any standard, the provenance provided detailed descriptions and colored photographs
of the cross taken from every conceivable angle. Its
exhaustive bibliography cited every known reference
to the cross, whether in ancient manuscripts, history
texts, diaries or letters.

Liza had cross-checked each and every one of
those references. She had zipped by taxi from one
library to another, from museums to university art
departments. She had interviewed history professors
and picked the brains of experts in Middle Eastern
languages. She knew more than most specialists
about Constantine's conversion to Christianity and
his decision to extend his influence into the Holy
Land. And now that history was coming alive. She'd
shivered when she came across, in a crumbling manuscript, the first reference to works of art commissioned by the emperor, among them a gold cross.

Yet it was a slow, grinding business sifting through
the embattled history of the Sinai, and there had been
nights with not more than a few hours sleep. But

stone by stone, Liza was building a strong case for the authenticity of the small, jewel-encrusted cross. That afternoon had seen the last of the pieces fall into place—confirmation from a professor of Russian history that the czars had been fascinated by the Monastery of St. Catherine, and that the monks' habit of bartering treasure was an indisputable fact.

The only thing lacking real documentation was this business of the French family, Liza thought as she headed down the arching, tunnellike hall. She wished Victor could have been more helpful there, for museums are traditionally cautious when an artifact surfaces after years of obscurity. Still, she argued silently, lots of agents found themselves bound by a promise of anonymity for their clients. Some wanted to avoid taxes on a sale, others were concerned about security because of the underworld of art thieves. Still others feared the humiliation—and this was apparently the case here—of their financial needs becoming public knowledge.

Victor had been firm about not divulging information, however, and Liza had to respect his decision. Everything else bore out the authenticity of his find, including its physical examination. She herself had photographed, x-rayed and measured the cross. She had evaluated each jewel and counted every tiny gold bead under a microscope. She had analyzed the method of construction and found it consistent with the period.

But Liza believed in instinct as much as in science, though she didn't care to admit it freely. She was not unlike a doctor who, with one hand full of laboratory reports, lays the other gently on his patient and ponders his diagnosis. She, too, wanted a time of stillness, a moment alone in which to feel the soft, rounded contours of the gold against her skin, to see into the rich depths of the jewels. She wanted it to speak to her. Silly, she thought. And it would never find its way into her report. Yet she would do it.

She withdrew a ring of keys from the pocket of her tweed skirt and let herself into the storage room. It was a small room, crammed with odds and ends of furniture, with only a tiny barred window high up on one wall. Quickly she switched on the single, unshaded light bulb suspended from the ceiling and thought with a sigh that despite the Cavendish's generous endowment, there would never be enough money to fix up this old dungeon of a basement. At the far side of the room was a large, gray floor safe. She knelt before it and carefully twirled the dial, using the combination known only to a few.

She inhaled, stilled her hands, and withdrew the cross from its shelf. She moved ever so slowly, holding it with care in both palms. Then, still not breathing, she stood up, turned around—and promptly dropped it.

Christian's reflexes were better than hers. With a quick swoop of one hand he caught the cross in midair. "You ought to be more careful, Liza. These things aren't cheap." He flashed the gold cross before her ashen face. "And close your mouth," he added softly. "It's hanging open, in case you didn't realize."

Liza did, but immediately made to protest his un-expected—and unwanted—presence. Once again his hand was faster. He clamped it firmly over her mouth. "Don't scream," he ordered. "I assume that's what you were winding up to do—it's really not necessary."

She jerked her head away angrily. "Give me that cross," she said with as much authority as she could muster, "or I really will scream. We have a security force here—"

"Yes, I know," he replied easily. "I passed the gentleman on the way down. He didn't see me, how-ever."

"Give it to me!" she repeated, her shock now replaced by real fear and mounting anger.

He complied, adding, "You might at least thank me. It wouldn't have looked very good on your job record, dropping the Constantine Cross and scatter-ing the rubies into a lot of cobwebby corners."

"I wouldn't have dropped it at *all* if it hadn't been for you," she snapped, clutching the cross to her breast and feeling the thud of her heart beneath the tissue of silk. "This is a restricted area, Mr. Chase. I don't know how you got in here, but the museum is closed. I will have to ask you to leave." She fingered the cross protectively and her eyes moved to the open safe door.

His glance followed hers and he smiled. "Surely you don't think I came here to rob you." His tone clearly indicated the idea was too absurd to give of-fence.

She wavered and felt color come to her cheeks.

"No...no, of course not...." Not even Christian Chase had *that* much audacity!

"I don't want much of your time, Liza," he went on smoothly. "You must grant other professionals access to the museum at odd hours. Surely there is no reason why you can't extend the same courtesy to me...is there?" His tone had become light and coaxing.

Liza could think of no reason to deny him. "What is it you want?"

"You must know—your decision about the cross. I feel responsible for what's happening. I noticed that it's been removed from display." Seeing her hesitate, he added, "Look, if it would make you feel better to go and notify the guard that I'm down here, I won't be offended."

Liza bit her lower lip softly, calculating. "No, that won't be necessary," she finally assured him. "I was just about to go into the lab. If you'd like to come...?"

He followed her into the lab, stooping automatically although the archway was high. It was a large room, more modern than the rest of the basement, but here, too, the windows were narrow and barred. One end was lined with deep storage shelves, filled with various pots, small bronzes, and other artifacts not currently on public display. Two high workbenches ran the length of the room, stools tucked under them. Pegboards held an array of picks, brushes, and the other specialized tools needed for the cleaning and restoration of objects in the collection.

Liza pulled out two stools, sat on one and laid the cross before her on a large square of fabric-covered foam. She pulled down a bench lamp and switched it on. Christian sat beside her, hooking one heel on the rung of the stool and draping an elbow over its low back. He was dressed more casually than she had yet seen him—light brown slacks, a Harris tweed sports jacket, an oxford-cloth shirt open at the neck. She smiled at him blankly, trying not to see him. She resisted any knowledge of the casual ease of his body or the oddly pleasing, expressive face. She did not want to be near the relaxed, elegant hands.

"Do you mind?" he asked, with a gesture toward the cross.

"No," she said, although she did.

Christian turned the cross over in his hands, his long fingers tracing its outline, running lightly around the emerald. Liza instinctively knew that it wasn't the first time he had handled something so valuable. His touch was too swift, sure, and professional. His eyes narrowed now in concentration and the lines at the corners deepened. He appeared, for a moment, to have forgotten that she existed. The silence unnerved her.

"You're familiar with Middle Eastern art, Mr. Chase?" she asked, her words a bit too rapid.

He put the cross back on the pad and turned to her. "I thought we were going to drop the formalities, Liza."

She flicked her wrist as if it didn't matter to her *what* he thought. "All right—*Christian*."

He looked pleased with the concession. "I've had some experience with it, yes."

"As an agent, I take it," she said, wanting to warn him that she wasn't entirely ignorant where his business reputation was concerned.

"I have one or two clients with a taste for it. I've been on a few buying trips for them. And although I deal mostly with European art now, I used to teach a course on Eastern art—but I confess to very dubious qualifications for it."

"Oh? And where were you on staff?"

"Oxford," he said casually. "But that was a long time ago and I've given up academic life entirely."

"Well, I'm sure your end of the business is a good deal more lucrative than lecturing," she noted.

"True," he acknowledged, "and much more interesting. There was something about trying to make a bunch of young girls really *look* at paintings, when they would much rather be doing something else, that wore thin after a while."

Liza could well imagine just what those girls were really interested in looking at. She had a sudden vision of Christian Chase in a lecturer's gown on a leafy English campus and found the image strangely appealing. "I understand you're also involved with security—as a consultant, or something," she prompted, suddenly curious. "That's specialized work, I imagine."

"Yes, there's quite a black market in art...but then I suppose you know all about that and how it can be messy at times. By the way, your security system here isn't up to much. It's really quite foolish of you to be down here alone with that cross. If I were another sort of person you'd be in a good deal of danger right now." His tone, as well as his words, held a distinct warning.

Liza was conscious of a sudden vulnerability. What if he did work both sides of the law and his earlier suggestion that she speak to the guard only a clever, comforting distraction?

"Why did you take the cross out of the vault tonight?" he asked.

It was none of his business, of course, yet Liza didn't want to seem either defensive or evasive. "I have all the facts I need," she calmly replied. "I think I simply wanted to be with it, alone, one more time."

She suspected that he would make some snide remark, but he surprised her. He appeared to accept what she'd said, apparently without the need for further explanation. He was silently staring at the cross.

"So you think it is genuine," he said a few moments later.

"Yes," she answered seriously, "I do. I intend to issue a press release to that effect very soon. Under normal conditions I wouldn't have to do that. But after the other evening...and what happened, we decided it was necessary."

"*We?*" he repeated, his clear blue eyes suddenly sharp. "You mean you and your friend Livsay?"

"Yes. And Victor."

"Naturally, Victor," he said. "He's an important part of this, isn't he? Tell me, do you accept the provenance as he's given it?"

"I suppose now you're going to point out that the French owner is unnamed. But," she said lightly, "as an art dealer you shouldn't need to be told about the ethics of protecting your client's anonymity. In fact," she added, unable to resist, "I understand you yourself deal with a good many anonymous clients." The blue eyes instantly narrowed and all at once she questioned the wisdom of provoking a man with Christian's reputation. She drew back a little.

"You know Victor well, don't you?" he asked.

"Yes," she replied, although that was not precisely the truth.

"Well enough to know that he's on the verge of bankruptcy?"

"What?" Liza was stunned by this unanticipated twist.

"Victor Morneau is broke," he replied flatly. He seemed to be assessing her blank-faced reaction.

"I don't believe it," she said at last.

He shrugged. "It doesn't matter whether you do or not. It's the truth."

Was it, she wondered. Victor's prosperity during the recent art boom was well-known. Even if he was broke, it did nothing to enhance Christian's credibility. More likely it was further proof of Victor's theory. And the idea of a scheme to stop Penn from buying, forcing Victor to sell for a lower price to Christian, was even more believable.

"I don't pretend to know all of Victor's personal affairs, Mr. Cha–Christian, but I'm sure Penn would be well aware of them. In any event," Liza added firmly, "Victor's finances have nothing to do with whether or not this is truly the Cross of Constantine."

"So," he said, "there's nothing I can do to change your mind."

Liza suddenly remembered Julian's warning. She had to stand by her own decisions. And she had made her decision in this case. Willing herself to look directly into those crystal blue eyes, she spoke crisply. "I believe it is Constantine's Cross. I don't know what your reasons were for what you did, but I hope you will accept that I can make a sound, competent judgment."

Unexpectedly, he tipped back his head and laughed. "Yes, I'd quite overlooked that! Perhaps it was watching you drop the cross that made me forget your professional qualifications."

Two dots of pink rose high on Liza's cheeks. She slid off her stool and clutched vainly at her dignity. "I have work to do, Christian. If you don't mind!"

He stood up with infuriating slowness. "That pale skin," he said. "It betrays you constantly, doesn't it? You had me fooled the first time I saw you—the stillness, the bearing, the utter simplicity. A pampered mistress, I thought. And then I saw the eyes, the fire there. Do you remember looking back at me?"

Liza brushed aside an ebony strand of hair that had fallen across her cheek. She did not want to hear this. "I've got to go," she said.

"It was the same at the unveiling—the cool, precise appearance, the control in front of the public.

But then there was that flare, that soft red mouth. Tell me,'' he inquired in his quiet, resonant voice, "which is the real Liza?"

"This," she said, "is ridiculous."

And then she laughed. Wasn't that how one defused these situations—with humor? As it was, she had precious few weapons against him. One glance was sufficient to tell her there wasn't a single aspect to this lean, self-possessed man that indicated any sort of weakness.

Her voice was exceedingly gay and a little bit mocking—he couldn't, wouldn't get to her with flirtatious sparring. "I'm sure I'm holding you up— I'll bet you're fantastically in demand in New York as the extra man. Don't you have some terribly fashionable place to go?" And a small, mischief-making voice whispered in her ear, "Particularly if they are old, rich, and female. . . ."

He smiled at her—slowly. "Not until tomorrow morning. . . ."

Was he extending a casual invitation to her? Did he think that she might be willing to spend the night with him? *Stay flippant and blasé,* she coached herself mentally. That would be how he expected a sophisticated New York woman to behave.

She gave him her second-best smile and said, "Do you think you could be a little less charming? I'm out of practice." Without thinking, she began to toy with the provenance, lining it up fussily with the edge of the table.

He watched her a moment, his manner indulgent. "I thought we could go—"

"Some other time perhaps," she said quickly. Too quickly. Her smile felt tight and unnatural.

"Tomorrow night then—"

"No!" It wasn't working. He was not a man to be dissuaded by light, casual words. She felt absurdly unhinged by him and that made her angry—at him, at herself, at this whole man-woman thing that was hopelessly awkward sometimes, yet undeniably delicious. There was something about their closeness in those musty, sensible surroundings that seemed so sweetly tempting.

With deliberate casualness she edged toward the door but failed to put the mile or so she needed between herself and Christian. He was with her, step for quiet step. Alarmed, she felt the pulse quicken in her slender wrists and in that vulnerable spot under the curve of her defiant chin. The indented corners of her wide mouth drooped slightly, making her look sulky. But her glance was purple heat.

He tilted his head and gazed at her thoughtfully. "If I'm wrong," he said, "I'm willing to be corrected. But I'll wager it must be tough on Livsay trying to live with such fire and ice."

"My relationship with Penn is out of bounds for conversation!" she snapped, trying to gain control of this runaway exchange.

Christian laughed. "You're loyal, and that's admirable. But he's a bit of a plodder, that friend of yours, I suspect. It takes a flexible, imaginative man to appreciate a volatile woman like you."

"Penn? A plodder? Don't you wish!" Now it was her turn to laugh. "Penn Livsay handles more money in a single phone conversation than you see in a year!"

"But I'm not talking business deals, my dear. I have something very different in mind—and you know that perfectly well."

One corner of Liza's mouth twitched dangerously upward. "God alone knows what a man like you has in mind. And the very thought of finding out is... is—"

"Is what?" he asked.

"Distasteful!" she snapped and thought, *oh, there are dark depths there, behind those cynical, cold, blue eyes!*

Christian had crossed his arms, his manner appraising. "A man can know everything, yet nothing, about a woman. Penn, for example—this is just speculation, understand, so there's no need for you to take offense—might know a thousand details about you from your politics to how you take your coffee, yet miss the essential woman. Another man, though, might know virtually nothing about you, yet feel he knows everything, everything that matters."

"You're playing games," she accused warily, lifting her lashes to him with difficulty.

"On the contrary, I'm speaking truths that for some reason make you very uneasy."

"I wish—" she began.

"I know, I know! You wish I would stop saying things that you don't want to hear," he said in that quiet, gently amused tone. "I'm sorry—it's not my purpose to upset you but it doesn't change the way you make me feel."

She thought later she should have seen it coming, for she had caught the way his eyes had lingered on her lips. Those lazy, complacent eyes of a predator, so sure of his prey. But the blunt intimacy of his observations had shaken her, and when he bent low and slowly kissed her startled lips, she did not at first resist.

For the next several moments, moments she could not count, the dim basement workshop, the Cavendish, the greater world ceased to exist. They alone, man and woman, possessed the whole of life. And when at last they drew apart, they stood quite still, their eyes fastened on each other.

Liza finally found her voice and whispered, "If this is supposed to be flattering, it's not!"

He ignored her meaning entirely. The fingers of one hand circled her wrist painfully, taking its measure. "There, you see? Nothing quite fits about you. You're so small, your bones so fragile, one would expect your voice to be high and hollow. But it's not that way—it's husky, warm...like wine." And his own voice touched her like the velvet paw of a panther, a caress before the kill.

Slowly, without taking his eyes off her, he reached behind him and shut the door.

She stared at him, and her ears filled with the sound of her racing, frightened heart. His eyes were so strangely bright she wondered if he would hurt her. But he didn't. When he kissed her again it was a soft kiss, a lover's kiss and she felt herself open to him unhesitatingly.

Instinctively, she met his tongue with hers, allowing him to probe and explore, to seek out all the hidden, sensitive places. She felt she would suffocate, yet she clung to the mouth that stole her breath and would destroy her reasoning altogether. Instinctively too, she crushed her breasts against his chest, responding without thought, knowing only a deep urge to submerge herself in him.

His lips, warm and delightful, slid along her cheek to her ear and she heard his soft, irregular breathing. "Please..." she whispered.

"Please what," he coaxed in a low voice. "Please love you more?"

He buried his face in the thickness of her hair while her entire being focused on the light, teasing fingertip that traced her jaw, ran down her throat and skimmed the slight swell of her breasts. "No," she whispered, trying to deny the wave of sensations his touch aroused.

Her head tipped back, partly in protest, partly in offering of her pale neck. His tongue grazed the hollow at the base of her throat and she heard a small moan escape her. She tried to hate him for making her expose such raw need, and found it impossible.

While one hand supported her the other began to trace the outer curve of her breast with an exquisite, mesmerizing stroke. She suddenly felt very naked. It was horrible, unthinkable, that this man, this stranger, could go so quickly to the core of her, could stir feelings that had remained hidden and dormant within her. Not even Penn had touched the woman inside her who was waiting, waiting. The man who could do that was dangerous, so very dangerous.

With that realization the world slid spinning away from her and her eyes flew open. She was shocked by what she saw, by his fierce concentration and obvious intent.

It was enough, at last, to make the fantasy turn to something more sinister. She pressed both palms against his chest and shoved, hard.

He stared down at her, his jaw tight and his breathing harsh. For one electric second the look that endured between them was achingly, searchingly deep. He shook his head and said on an odd, questioning note, "Don't, Liza. Don't try to tell me you find this distasteful."

"I do," she said unevenly. How could she have allowed this to happen? She prepared to shove again but he caught and kept those small angry hands.

"There's no need for that, Liza. You're quite safe. I wouldn't have done it if I didn't think you would be receptive." His voice was low, regretful.

She deeply resented what he had done to her. But mostly she resented that he was right. "Well, I'm not—not now!" she blazed.

Embarrassment and broken-off arousal were making her sharp and unforgiving. She was working herself up for a struggle, eyeing an escape. It was yet another blow, then, to see him wordlessly pick up his raincoat, turn, and without a glance in her direction, close the door behind him.

The pounding tension that had built and built, surrounding them like a visible, shimmering force-field, vanished, blown away in an instant by the draft of a closing door. Liza sank down on the stool, clutching the table for support. For a terrible moment she lost her sense of time and self. No man had ever made her feel that way. It terrified her. She hugged herself and tried to undo the hurt his arms had done. *It will stop,* she told herself.

But it didn't. The longing, an endless ache, had settled in her to stay.

CHAPTER FOUR

BAREFOOT AND IN HER SLIP, Liza wandered through the apartment. She had done all the small, boring chores, punishing herself. She had washed her brushes, taken out garbage, cleaned the film of talcum powder from her dresser and fixed herself an extraordinarily bad supper. One moment she wished she had someone to confide in, the next decided she wasn't the type anyway. She deserved this empty space.

In the living room she straightened a newspaper, plumped a cushion, discovered a coffee mug with a dry brown ring and took it back to the kitchen to wash. She was full of nervous energy, determined to hang on to her outrage.

Then she caught a glimpse of herself in the wood-framed mirror over the mantel. How awful she looked! She sank heavily to the edge of the pale apricot loveseat. Christian's lovemaking had been an ugly assault upon her body...no, he had been far too adept for that.

She rested her chin on her hands and stared disconsolately into the cold grate. A fire would be comforting, but she hadn't yet seen to getting wood in. She dropped to her knees and lifted the lid of the

brass log box—nothing there but last year's dust and
twigs. Her eyes traveled upward to the nearby
loveseat. There was a neatly folded afghan that she
had crocheted herself—none too well, but it was ser-
viceable. Suddenly spent, she dragged it down to the
floor and wrapped herself in it.

What did it say about her as a person, as the
woman who was about to become Penn's wife, that
another man, a man she didn't even like, had pro-
voked such a response in her? It had been purely
physical, she told herself, pulling up her knees and
hugging them. The feelings would pass, as surely as
they'd happened.

But her body stubbornly remembered what her
conscience wished to forget. Each time she thought
of his hands on her, she felt her limbs become warm
and pliant. In her mind's eye she saw the awesome
solemnity of the man, his eyes closed, bent over her.
To witness someone's need etched so nakedly on his
face—it was too much. She didn't want to know such
a thing about him.

And she couldn't bear to think that he'd also been
witness to her need, that he had actually heard her
whimper with desire. How was it that other people
could do these things so casually, touch another
human being's body so intimately yet without care or
affection?

She tipped her head back, resting it on the loveseat, and sighed. People thought she was so sensible.
And most of the time she was. She lived her life in a
steady, organized, predictable way. And then the
madness struck.

I've gone and done it again! she thought, pressing her forehead to her knees. She felt a kind of hopeless sorrow settle over her. She had planned it all so carefully—there was her job, and soon there was to be Penn. She had never thought any man, let alone Christian Chase, could do this to her. But he had. It was like waking to a bright, warm day and being struck by lightning.

With sudden firmness she stood and switched off the light. "I'll forget him," she told herself resolutely, walking into the bedroom.

It was cold in the high-ceilinged room and Liza shivered in the darkness as she stripped off the rest of her lingerie. She tossed it impatiently onto the chair by her bed, a thing she did not often do. She pulled open a drawer of the dresser and withdrew an old flannelette gown. She told herself, as she drew it over her head, that she wanted it because of the cold, but it really represented a stubborn rejection of both Christian and her body.

She lay down on the polished Victorian bed that had been her parents', pulled the blanket up to her chin, and waited for sleep. But the image of Christian's face hung over her.

Why him, she asked, and turned over onto her stomach. A need for fulfillment, a need that *he* had created, was the humiliating cause of her restlessness. She hugged the pillow to her, then suddenly she was upright, switching on the little night-light, wishing she smoked, wondering if she should go to get a glass of brandy. This bed in which she loved to read, dream and wonder, would not be a haven tonight.

Even sleep seemed threatening, perhaps bringing dreams she could not control.

If the memory of Christian was going to be an immovable presence, she thought, then at least she would make it work *for* her. After all, she told herself, if it weren't for him she wouldn't have all this damnable stuff to do! She punched the pillows against the headboard and grabbed the folder from the bedside table. She began to edit the press release with the energy of anger.

Yet at some point she must have slept, for she found herself crooked on the pillows, the pen in her hand but papers littering the floor. Something, a half-remembered dream, perhaps, was nagging at her. She snatched at it several times before finally catching the tail of it.

"Of course!" she said softly. She *had* heard something else about the cross. But it hadn't come from Victor and it certainly hadn't come from Christian. It was a long time ago and it was understandable that she hadn't made the connection. Or was it? Had she resisted it deliberately, for Penn's sake? That would be Christian's cynical explanation.

She rubbed her eyes and glanced at the clock. It was almost 5:00 A.M. *Well, why not,* she thought. She would probably need an early start on this day. She swung her bare legs over the side of the bed and groped for her slippers.

Half an hour later she stepped outside. There was a tinge of pink between the buildings and from down a side street came the thud and whir of a garbage truck beginning its rounds. At the museum Liza roused the puzzled night watchman, and skipped up the curving staircase to the private archives.

It was a tall room with four large, arched windows heavily curtained in wine velvet, its walls lined from ceiling to floor with bookshelves. Liza gripped both sides of the library ladder and pushed it along its ceiling track until she came to the section she wanted. She climbed three steps and ran her finger along the worn leather spines of the books. She knew exactly where she would find the one she was after, for she herself had cataloged it in her student days. At the time she hadn't paid much attention to it, but she had read it dutifully enough and typed a summary on a file card. Excited now, she extracted the slim, leather volume, took it back to one of the reading tables, and switched on the old-fashioned green glass light.

She was well-acquainted with the odd tradition of British explorers, gentlemen usually, who were fascinated by Africa and the great deserts of the world. These slightly balmy men would set out into the unknown with little more than a camel, a few porters, and their own cheerful innocence. Some were never heard from again, of course. Others surfaced years later, wearing the same khaki outfits and helmets, to give colorful lectures at some explorers' society. Calmly and ironically, they recounted the most hideous deprivation, torture, and racking tropical illnesses that would dog them to their graves. Then, their duty done, they would return to their country cottages and long-suffering wives to write their memoirs.

It was one of these obscure, quirky, private diaries

that was tickling Liza's memory. She found the chapter she wanted, leaned back in the oak captain's chair and crossed her slim legs. She read:

What an odd, ragtag assortment these monks are, and what a hard, lonely life they lead here in the center of this wasteland! Yet they go about their duties without complaint, a dreary round of long hours of prayer and meditation and the baking of coarse loaves of bread, which they give out to the starving nomads through a little window in the gate. They took me in, although I could have been nothing more than a burden to them. They gave me a room, as well as shelter for my porters and our camels. The monastery shows the wear and tear of the centuries of wind, neglect and the steady harassment by natives. And yet what treasure—a hodgepodge of gold and jewels jammed in every which way and forgotten, like the toy chest of some fabulous princeling—lies behind these aging, crumbling walls.

The monks are not an educated group and either do not know or do not care about what they possess. I counted over a hundred icons before giving up. There are ancient scrolls that must surely be tied to the beginnings of our Bible and would be a treasure beyond calculation to scholars. There were chalices and salvers and a little cross of gold, set about with precious jewels.

Liza's fingers tapped the arm of her chair. "And a little cross of gold...." She sat forward suddenly and began flipping through the book, searching for the date of the Honorable Mr. Nigel Bagley's expedition. She found it, and drew a sharp breath—1919—two years after the Cross of Constantine had been taken to Russia by the czar's emissaries.

But it meant nothing. The monastery held hundreds of treasures and there was surely more than one cross, although, naturally there could be only one that had belonged to Constantine. "And that one is *here*," she whispered. "I'm sure of it." The sun was well up before Liza left the library and went down to her office.

THE RESTAURANT PENN FAVORED for lunch was in midtown, near his bank. An artful mixture of mirrors, marble, and flattering shades of gray, it was stunningly elegant. The table decoration ran to simple crystal vases, each bearing one perfect, white calla lily. The service was quietly attentive and deferential. Penn rose as Liza slipped into the charcoal silk banquette, then brushed her cheek with his lips. "Cold," he pronounced, "and also very pretty." Her color was high from the sharp fall air.

Liza removed her kidskin gloves finger by finger and shrugged off her scarlet coat. "I walked," she explained.

"All the way?"

"These days are the best," she said. "You have to enjoy them while you can."

"You said something similar about spring, I recall. And summer. I can't quite remember about last winter. In those days I was still nattering on about budgets and attendance figures whenever I wanted to see you."

"I confess to rapture over the first snowfall—after that I prefer to enjoy winter's pleasures from the warm side of the windowpane."

"A drink, darling?"

"No, thanks. Wine would be pleasant, though—white, please."

They ordered omelets and salads, and alone again, Penn leaned forward. "Well?"

"I guess I don't have to ask what that means," Liza smiled.

"You have to admit I've been very good—for me—about keeping out of this. But I am curious. Have you finished your report?"

"I...I think so."

"Think?"

Liza leaned back against the banquette, her lips set in a slight pout. "Well, an anonymous owner always raises a little red flag for us."

"Victor's explained that, I believe."

"Yes, and it's neither unreasonable nor unheard of, although it's not ideal from my point of view."

"Is that all?"

"Well, I have dredged up a minor contradiction concerning one of the dates in the provenance. But this particular reference is very vague. And Nigel Bagley—he's the man who made it—was by no means a professional or a reliable source. He was eccentric to say the least...maybe even a little mad." Liza was conscious that she was running on in a rather skittish way, but couldn't seem to stop herself.

Penn's dark brows drew together in a frown.

"Have you spoken to this person—what's his name?"

"Bagley. No, he's dead."

"Liza!" Upset, he pushed his plate away.

She pressed her lips together, sighed, struggled for better words and couldn't find them. "Well, it irritates me," she said finally.

Penn's face was a study in reasonableness. "Look, if that's all you've been able to come up with I don't see why we can't contact the papers with a statement now. We could have a story running by tomorrow morning—possibly even tonight, if I make a few phone calls to the right people."

Liza twirled the stem of her wineglass. "Actually, I've been putting off calling Whit."

Penn looked baffled and for the first time there was brusque impatience in his voice. "I can't believe you would hold us up over something you yourself have to admit is a worthless scrap of information."

She dragged her eyes up to his. "I'm *not* trying to stall," she began.

"How else am I suppose to take it?" Penn demanded, bewildered.

"Penn, please try to understand. This is an enormous responsibility—I may see nothing like it for the rest of my career. Julian has left it entirely up to me and for that I'm grateful, if terrified. Call it overly cautious if you will, but I'm just not ready yet to take the last step."

The seafood sauce on the omelets congealed. Penn's eyes were dark and uneasy. "I'm sorry, Liza, but I can't help but think that the artistic side of you is dramatizing this.'' Those had been Alexa's words, and Liza knew she'd been discussed by the Livsays.

She tried to lay out her argument reasonably. ''You remember the scandal over the Greek bronzes that turned out to be fake? I don't want that for the Cavendish and neither can you.''

''But in that case, the evidence raised clear questions about their authenticity. Here, if I understand you, it's overwhelmingly in favor of the cross's being genuine.''

''True,'' she conceded with a defeated sigh.

''Then, do it, damn it—do it for *us*!''

A shadow passed over Liza's eyes. ''Penn, I was a curator before I was your friend. Please don't forget that.''

''I'm not likely to, if you choose to remind me. Frankly, I find it offensive that you do.''

''I'm sorry,'' she said stiffly. There was a brittle silence, then she drew herself up. ''It's just that there's a principle involved here,'' she explained. Her jaw began to tremble ever so slightly.

''Indeed there is,'' he said pointedly. ''It's called loyalty.''

Liza blinked. ''How did we get on to *this*? You have no cause to doubt my loyalty.''

''Look,'' he said, chopping the air with his hand, ''I'm not asking you to lie. I'm asking you to extend the same treatment to me that you would to a stranger. But look what's happened. You've gone so far in the other direction that you're applying standards of proof with me that you never would with anyone else. All, I suppose, so that you can pat yourself on the back and say that you were never guilty of favoritism!''

''Isn't that good?'' she asked, baffled. ''Even though *you* choose to put a very unattractive light on it.''

''And what about me and my family—have you honestly given a moment's thought to us and the impossible position you're putting us in? I've given a fortune to the museum, and you treat me like this—I don't deserve it.'' He turned his face from her, his jaw muscles working.

Liza sank back and fingered her napkin nervously. Her color was high now in a way that had nothing to do with health or brisk fall air. She and Penn were having what could be called their first fight. She knew who to blame. Christian's ghost, with his snide comments about her objectivity, sat at their table.

Penn, apparently, saw him too. ''All of this,'' he said, as he strangled a stick of French bread from the basket in front of him, ''is the result of one well-timed, loose remark from that Chase character.'' He started to put the piece of bread in his mouth and stopped. He looked up at her sharply. ''He's not *got* to you, has he?''

Her eyes were very bright. ''Of course not,'' she said angrily.

Liza was conscious of having made a choice, although she could not remember, later, precisely why or how she had made it. She did not tell Penn she had seen Christian again. It was a stupid and pointless deception, she told herself. But having done it, there seemed no way to go back—ever. And that

Christian had kissed her—and she him—she could certainly never tell Penn. He didn't deserve that pain. But this lie, or more precisely this choice not to tell the whole truth, seemed to have altered her relationship to Penn in a subtle but important way.

Anger, guilt and finally rebellion against the pressure *both* these men were putting on her caused the extraordinary words she heard spilling from her lips. "Penn, there is something I can do to settle this to everyone's satisfaction. And I'm going to do it," she announced.

"Oh? And what is that?" His face was disturbingly closed to her.

She felt her heartbeat accelerate. "I'm going to go to St. Catherine's Monastery and see for myself if there is indeed another cross."

She said it matter-of-factly, as if it was all well planned, when in truth she hadn't known what she was going to say until she said it. She hurried on in the face of his stunned silence, making it up as she went. "I can be there and back in a matter of a few days. It's the only way, Penn."

He crumpled his napkin and tossed it onto the table with a quick, hard snap. "Well, you can't go! That's all there is to it."

Liza's back stiffened. "That sounds very much like an order."

"It *is*. For one thing, it's not safe over there. I won't have you traipsing around the desert on your own—it's insane, Liza!"

Now it was Liza's turn to flare. "Won't *have* me—! I am not a child, and I am not yours to order about. I've traveled in the Middle East before and I can look after myself.''

"Pardon me, I forgot your nice little chaperoned vacations," he said, his voice dripping sarcasm. "And what does Julian think of this little jaunt?''

"He trusts my judgment," she said evasively and thought, *There! That's the second time I've lied to Penn in the past five minutes.* What was happening to them? To her? And after a few more heated minutes she was fleeing the restaurant under the amazed eyes of the maître d'.

She bent her head and pushed against the rising wind, darting recklessly through the midtown traffic snarl, beating out her anger in short, sharp steps. Whether her anger was greater with herself or with Penn she hardly knew and didn't care. Her erratic path led her along Forty-eighth Street and up Fifth Avenue but it was not until St. Patrick's Cathedral rose suddenly before her that she took any notice of her direction.

Breathless, she stopped and considered. The morning sun had vanished behind iron clouds and a damp chill was sinking through her light wool coat. She shifted miserably on her inadequate heels. Should she go back to work? No, she felt she'd had enough of the museum and the cross for quite some time. Home? But it was empty and conducive to brooding, second thoughts.

She decided that for the moment, anyway, she preferred her anger and the oddly stimulating freedom that sprang from a decision made—no matter how wildly impulsive—in the face of Penn's exaggerated disapproval.

Across the street a thin young man in washed-out jeans and Windbreaker lined up briefcases on the sidewalk and began to draw a few curious, potential buyers. The cases were line-for-line vinyl copies of the staggeringly expensive leather ones displayed for sale in the store window behind them.

Liza's eyes wandered to that window with its restrained yet sumptuous display and saw there, in Saks, the answer to her angry energy. She must need a thousand things, she thought. It had been ages since she'd traveled farther than Long Island. Clutching her purse to her, she skipped across the street and promptly lost herself in the seductive depths of Saks for the rest of the afternoon.

She emerged clutching a confusion of shiny boxes and pleasantly rustling bags. She'd bought a night-gown, two pairs of sandals from an end-of-season sale, a tube of lipstick, and a hand-knit Italian sweater—with a dizzying price tag—that she was sure she didn't need in the slightest. In a brief nod to practicality, she'd picked up on her way out a traveler's toiletry bag of sprigged cotton with lots of little compartments and tiny plastic bottles fitted neatly together.

The streetlights had just come on. A cold, gray rain was driving down and the streets were shiny and slick. There were cabs—long, yellow rows of them— but they were barely crawling and every one was occupied. Turning up her collar against the chill drizzle, she made a dash for Madison Avenue. The buses would be a nightmare, but her options at the moment seemed few.

They turned out to be even fewer than she'd guessed. She struggled through several shivering lines only to have the buses lumber by, too full to bother stopping. More than once she found herself elbowed out of the way or forced to duck dipping umbrellas. The odd bus stopped at what had been the rear of a line to admit a single lucky rider, thus setting off furious murmurs among those left behind.

Liza was jostled so much that she disregarded, at first, a small annoying tug at her elbow. But a larger, more persistent pull was too irritating to ignore. Exhaustion, aching arms, and trod-on toes produced a rare flash of snappishness in her.

"*Excuse* me!" she said sharply, jerking herself stiffly away from her jostling neighbor. "Pushing's not going to help."

"I thought limousines were more your style, Liza Downing," came the voice at her shoulder.

Her stomach did a curious little flip. He had on the same worn trench coat she'd seen him in at the Cavendish. It was splotched with rain now, the belt knotted crookedly and the collar turned up against the weather. His dark blond hair hung down across the high forehead and a fine beading of rain clung to the sharp cheekbones.

She managed a mechanical smile. "My style perhaps, but not my league, Christian...hi, how are you?"

He shoved his hands into his pockets. His eyes traveled from her damp lashes to her arms and back.

"Slightly better than you, I'd say—I managed a cab. But you look as if you've spent a pleasant enough afternoon in the usual frivolous, feminine pursuits."

"Feminine perhaps, but not frivolous," she returned. "I needed some things for a job I'm about to do. Where have you been this gorgeous New York day? Turning up more masters for your clients?"

"Just scouting. There's a new gallery uptown that was recommended to me."

There was an awkward, appraising pause. "Well, it's been nice seeing you again," Liza said with forced brightness. "Here comes another bus—if it's mine I'd better grab it while I can."

She made a few, futile leaps on her tiptoes to read the number on the bus, but he put a restraining hand on her shoulder. From his height he could see the hopelessness of it. "Forget it, Liza, this one's full and what's behind it isn't moving. I recommend you retreat, at least until the rush hour, or the rain, is over."

One by one he pulled the parcels from her and then, looping his arm through hers, he extricated her from the press of the crowd. She tried to decline the rescue, but the words died in her throat. His manner said the matter was not up for debate.

"I'm staying here at the Helmsley," he said with a nod to the hotel in front of them. "I was just on my way in when I saw you—you drew my eye like a flare with that red coat in the sea of beige and black. I was supposed to attend a lecture at the Met tonight but I'd much prefer to buy you a drink."

It was pleasant to have the troublesome packages

taken away, and pleasant to have that breadth of shoulder to deflect what was now sleet. They hurried under the wrought-iron arch and across the hotel's courtyard where the trees were decked out in fairy lights, multiplied a thousand times in the raindrops that hung from the branches.

There was a bar off the marbled lobby—very small, very dark, with lots of polished wood, beveled glass and fresh-cut flowers. Christian chose a dim, curved banquette and Liza slid in.

She asked for gin, Christian for Scotch. The flushed waitress virtually flew to bring the drinks and a silver bowl of almonds, along with, Liza was sure, more than their share of crab spread and tiny biscuits. The British gentleman had had his impact, apparently, on the girl from Manhattan, Liza noted wryly.

He raised his glass and held it out to her. "Here's to bad weather and Manhattan traffic," he said. "They brought you in out of the cold to me."

His eyes, so blue and laughing, and the odd, twisted smile that twitched up one corner of his mouth devilishly had their impact on Liza, too. She gave a small shiver and told herself it was the weather. "Well, to shelter anyway," she said, raising her glass and touching it to his. She took a small sip and set it down again.

Her hands strayed to her hair and tucked a straggling wisp behind her ear. She wondered how much damage the rain and wind had done to her. The smoky, flattering mirrors told her very little.

"You look fine," he said with disconcerting clairvoyance. "In fact, a little wildness becomes you."

He reached over and gently pulled at the tendril she'd hidden, drawing it down her cheek. Fascinated, he repeated the action at her temple and the side of her neck. Liza sat and suffered his attentions in silence, feeling his fingertips ruffle the almost invisible hairs on her skin, and experiencing a creeping disturbance in her blood.

"So," he said, "no work this afternoon?" It was a bland, polite inquiry so disturbingly at odds with the intimate gesture of his hand.

"No, not this afternoon," she told him. "And if you don't mind I'd rather not discuss my job. I've had a dose of it lately."

He gave her an appraising look, a look that by now she knew. "No, why should I mind? I'd be delighted to explore other topics with you. Incautious, intimate conversation in a good bar with a beautiful woman is one of life's great pleasures."

"Is it? I hadn't thought much about it."

"Then you ought to... because you look so extraordinarily relaxed and happy at the moment."

Her eyes flew up to his in shock. She *was* happy and relaxed, but not at all sure she ought to be. She gauged the strong lines and wise eyes that had incredibly, overnight, become fixtures in her life. His quiet strength unnerved her and gave rise to a nagging doubt about the prudence of choosing the path she'd just started down. She gave a small, careless shrug. "Well, you saved me from the appalling fate of the uptown bus at rush hour," she replied inadequately.

"Of course...but it's very easy, this being here with you. Don't you feel it?"

He had twisted the lean length of his body toward her. One elbow rested easily on the back of the banquette just above her shoulder. Then, with a smooth gesture, he undid the button of his gray flannel suit and the jacket fell open. Liza had an instant, indelible image of herself being pressed to that immaculate length of white shirt.

Quickly she averted her eyes and with a careless gesture of her hand said, "Well, of course, it's very pleasant here...."

"All right," he said quietly, the shrewd glance he gave her silently saying, "I won't press you if it bothers you." He could afford to retreat, Liza supposed.

She hated that about him. The knowingness. He had a way of focusing on her so intently that the rest of the world seemed to be blotted out. Even Penn didn't home in on her that way. It was flattering, yes, but most unsettling.

She stirred the ice cubes in her drink, then asked casually, "When do you go back to London?"

"I might go at any time...it depends on many things."

He spread some of the crab on two tiny rounds of toast and handed one to her. She took it for distraction, and instantly regretted it. Her neck muscles were tight and she swallowed self-consciously, feeling inexplicably shy.

"This is good, but hardly a meal," he said. "I'll take you out to dinner." It was a statement, not an invitation. "You must know New York well...."

"Yes, I do...I grew up here."

"Good. Then you shall tell me where to take you. You must know a thousand places."

At least, she thought. But these days had seen her eating mostly in Penn's favorite midtown restaurants. The food was either very plain—what is usually called "men's" food—or it was the very latest in French cuisine—very chic, a little odd and frightfully expensive. The last fashionable restaurant Penn had taken her to had served up minuscule pheasant breasts with raspberry sauce, arranged like a Japanese painting on an oversize white plate. She tried to visualize what would please a man like Christian Chase, gave it up as hopeless, and made a few tentative, safe suggestions.

He shook his head. "Expense account stuff—my clients are always dragging me to places like that. I was hoping you'd have an insider's edge on something off the beaten path."

His response stung ever so slightly and she replied a bit stiffly, "What interests you then—Chinese? Italian? Greek?"

He considered a moment, his eyes narrowing. "Japanese, I think. I fancy some raw tuna with that horseradish that makes your eyes stream. Please don't tell me you hate raw fish!"

"As a matter of fact, I love it," she replied grudgingly.

"It's supposed to be an aphrodisiac...did you know that?"

Color rose under her skin along her throat and swiftly faded again. "No, I didn't," she said bluntly, thinking something in that line was the last thing a remarkably vibrant man like Christian Chase needed. "I do know, though, what has to be the best Japanese restaurant in the city."

"I trust it's suitably tiny, hidden, and virtually unknown to all but a handful of insiders who jealously guard its whereabouts to keep it unspoiled."

She laughed, "You're not far wrong. It's a little hole in the wall up near Columbia University. When I was in school, we used to eat there all the time. Of course, we could never afford more than their iron pots of broth and noodles. Since those days I think— I hope—that some of us have gone back enough to atone for our penny-pinching student ways."

He sipped his Scotch and smiled at her slowly. "Good," he said, "I've made you unbend. You're laughing and you've quite forgotten yourself." The waitress was hovering, and with a swift gesture he indicated another round of drinks. "We've got a few hours to put in before dinner time," he reminded Liza.

Her mind ranged ahead with mingled feelings of dismay and eagerness to the evening that stretched before her. *You can still back out. It's not too late,* the cautious Liza said. *But you won't,* came another, softer whisper. Through lowered lashes she studied Christian and wondered what she was trying to prove. Accepting—or rejecting—this evening in his company seemed a futile exercise. It was all too effortless and pleasant.

He was speaking to her. She blinked. "What?" she asked, flushing.

"I was asking if you've done any bidding at the auctions for the Cavendish," he repeated.

"No, I haven't. So far that's been Julian's exclusive concern. I haven't had much experience, although I'm trying to remedy that. I've followed the sales and attend whenever I can. It's a dream of mine—foolish, perhaps, but persistent—to make some fantastically shrewd purchase for the Cavendish one day."

"Then I take it your friend Mr. Livsay was assisting in your education that night at the Fairchild Gallery?"

"That was to be strictly a private transaction although, of course, Penn has taught me a great deal."

"Including the perils of overconfidence and unsupported assumptions, I trust."

"If you're referring to the sale of the Renoir, then, no. I don't think that Penn could be blamed for that. After all, I gather you had unlimited funds to throw about and could have gone on bidding forever."

He leaned closer toward her. "I'll tell you a secret, Liza. That bid was my first and my last. If Penn had gone even five thousand over it, he could have had the Renoir."

She looked at him blankly for a moment and said in a still voice, "Then you took an enormous gamble."

"I did," he agreed flatly. "And if you want that treasure you dream about, Liza, you'll have to learn to do that, too. Tell me...would Mr. Livsay expect you to devote your considerable talents solely to the curatorship of his private collection if you were married?"

"Well, I could, of course," she replied carefully.

"But surely that would be a job more suited to a student," he pointed out.

"Oh, no, it's a major collection," she corrected.

"I don't doubt it. But if I gauge the man correctly, Mr. Livsay would reserve all the important decisions about acquisitions, trades and upgrading for himself. In any event, I think you'd grow restless in such a gilded cage. You love people. There's a strain of the public servant in you that always tries to relate art to society. I see it running through your writing and in the thrust of the changes you've campaigned for at the Cavendish."

"Now how would you arrive at a judgment like that?" she asked, laughing.

"You seem bent on making yourself a bit of a mystery...and a challenge, so I did something today. I went to the public library, said hello to the lions, and looked up the file on Liza Downing. For a very young woman you have quite a thick file, you know."

She choked on her drink, coughed and said, "Why on earth would you do something like that?"

"Let's say I had some time on my hands. I read the monograph you wrote on the vases and how you dated them through an analysis of costume details. It was lively and unusual...why do you blush?''

She bent her head and stared at her twined fingers. ''It was a very minor thing.''

''Don't put yourself down,'' he said seriously. ''It was an original bit of work and I read it with immense enjoyment.''

For some reason, she found a compliment from him impossible to accept gracefully. ''An elitist like you probably sneers secretly at my...philosophy. But I'm not apologizing. This may surprise you, but I wasn't on your side—*or* Penn's—at the auction the other night.''

He looked at her with exaggerated shock. ''What an extraordinary admission coming from you, Liza! Who is it Penn and I should feel murderously jealous of?''

''Marcus Johns,'' she said. ''Do you know him?''

''We've met...he never had much of a chance, you know.''

''No, which is a great shame. The Renoir really should have gone to a public gallery like the one in Washington. I only saw the painting from a distance. It was...thrilling. But will I ever see it again? Will anyone?''

''I suppose if it had gone to Penn, it might have belonged to you personally one day.''

''I never really thought of it that way,'' she said quickly, unsure if she should take offense at this odd twist of logic.

He looked at her as if he was...considering. ''I can make it happen....''

"What? I don't follow you."

"I can give you *La Baigneuse* for one perfect night."

She put her drink down and twisted in her seat. "You mean it's still here—in this country?"

"I mean it's still here—in the hotel vault. I can have it brought up to my suite so that you can see it for yourself. A private showing, if you like."

"A variation on the old let-me-show-you-my-etchings routine?" she bantered. But her heart raced and her eyes sparkled at him.

"Possibly. But a rare one," he smiled. "To be alone with that Renoir...to have it for...however long you choose—surely such a temptation is worth the risk of my company?"

It was just the sort of impulsive, romantic interlude that her secretary, for example, would applaud. It was also the kind Liza distrusted. Yet she'd cheerfully murder for the chance to examine *La Baigneuse* at her leisure. But Christian...such a lethal combination of tempting, disarming qualities. The wit and charm. The smooth-as-cream manners. And he was never, never boring. No, he couldn't be that. "It is tempting," she admitted. "I won't bother to deny it."

"Good. Then let's do it. What possible reason could you have to turn down an opportunity like this?" Her resolve was melting and he knew it.

She bit her lower lip softly. "None...none at all."

He carried their coats over one arm and with his free hand held her elbow and guided her across the lobby. Her heels clicked smartly on the marble and her stockings made a sensuous, swishing noise. She felt pleasantly female and alive in his male presence.

He motioned her to a chair in the seating area. "Wait here," he instructed, "while I make arrangements."

She watched as he spoke briefly to the desk clerk. The manager was summoned from his office and there was a hushed conference. A phone call was made, files checked, then Christian turned and crossed the lobby to her with his long, quiet stride.

"Done," he said, pulling her to her feet. "They'll send security to the vault and have it brought up to the suite shortly. It's crated, so they won't know precisely what they're carrying—only that it's valuable."

"I never thought about security, though heaven knows I should have. Look, I don't want you to put the painting at risk just for me," she said uncertainly.

He stood aside and directed her into the elevator. "That's hardly likely," he assured her, "but certain precautions will be taken."

His suite, large and airy, was attractively decorated in shades of soft yellow. There were pleasant groupings of traditional loveseats and chairs, even a small mahogany breakfast table in the window beneath the velvet draperies. Someone had sent fresh flowers—a Chinese bowl brimming with mauve asters sat on the console in the small, mirrored entry. A leather-topped desk held a controlled clutter of correspondence, glossy art magazines, and a stack of yellow legal pads, their pages covered in a firm neat hand.

The bed, Liza noted with relief, was out of sight beyond a connecting door.

He ordered white wine from room service and they sipped it, making light, distracted small talk until there was a knock on the door. Two dour men handed over a small, flat, wooden crate, nodded silently and drifted away.

Liza paced. She was suddenly, extraordinarily wrought up. It was here, this marvelous, glorious, achingly beautiful portrait. Something Renoir himself had created and it was going to be hers alone to thrill to—no cold, public gallery, no velvet ropes separating her from it, no buzzing crowds.

Christian propped the crate on the seat of a chair across from the sofa and paused, rubbing his chin thoughtfully. "I didn't think I'd be opening it, so it's rather well sealed," he said. "Just a minute...."

He vanished into the adjoining room and returned a moment later wielding a small, ivory-handled shoe horn. "My great-grandfather must be spinning in his grave," he said cheerfully. "This is part of a set he had made for him by one of London's best silversmiths way back when. But it will serve, I think." Carefully, methodically, he pried the front off the crate and set it aside. Shreds of packing material tumbled out. He scooped them up and set them on the floor.

Liza laughed nervously. "What a terrible mess I've helped create!"

"Never mind, never mind," he muttered, disposing of another handful. "It'll be worth it just to see your face. Ready?'' he asked, smiling at her over his shoulder.

She wrapped her fingers about her wineglass. ''Ready.''

There was a final layer of foam-backed plastic shrouding the painting. He grasped it and slowly peeled it off, then stepped back and watched not *La Baigneuse*, but Liza.

And suddenly the young Frenchwoman was with them, as alive as ever she was. The warm, lemon light spilled from the painting and fell on Liza's face. She caught and held her breath. That same heat, that same smell of opening flowers—only better, so much better for its being close.

Christian broke the silence gently. ''It makes you forget about the cold, gray day out there, doesn't it?''

''Yes. Oh, yes, it does. It's summer—high summer—again! Can you...can you tell me where it's going?''

He hesitated, pressing his lips together. ''No, I'm sorry. I wish I could—''

''No, don't apologize,'' she said quickly. ''I should never have asked.''

''It's all right,'' he said, taking her hand and leading her over to the sofa. They sat together as Liza absorbed the delicious pleasure of *La Baigneuse*. Without the public clamor, the hundreds of devouring eyes, the wonderfully painted beauty had regained her gentle composure. The grace of her private ritual among the flowers seemed to have been returned to her. Christian rested an ankle on his knee and was silent, his eyes moving from the French-woman at her toilette to the woman beside him.

Liza was pleasantly startled to feel his arm come around her shoulders. "I really shouldn't stay. We'll skip dinner," she told him.

"Why do you say things you don't mean?" he asked quietly.

"I don't think I do," she replied, running her fingertips slowly around the rim of her wineglass.

"You do it all the time," he gently corrected. "You say and do what you think people want you to do, even if it isn't what you want."

"And if that's true, what is it that I really want now?"

"You want to stay here, and drink this very good wine, and look at this very beautiful painting. And be the happiest you've been in a long time."

"So it's all right, then, for *you* to tell me what I want?"

"I'd like to think that I've simply given a very sensitive reading of your mood and needs."

"Am I really so obvious?" she asked, flattered by the analysis but piqued that he might find her transparent.

"On the contrary, you're something of a mystery to me. But somehow I've got it into my head that your moods have gone unappreciated...which is surely foolish. A woman like you can't lack attention."

She thought of all Penn's gifts and dinners, all the hours together that never made her feel like this and said, "Yes, it is foolish...you know, I've heard that you're a very dangerous man where women are concerned."

"Whatever I am, it doesn't change the fact that you like it very much, does it?" he asked.

"Doesn't it?...I'm not so sure that I like you at all." That was the truth, she thought, surprised at how easy it was to admit it aloud.

"Maybe that doesn't matter," he murmured. "Maybe liking has nothing to do with this...."

She felt his hand warmly and surely press her back into the curve of his arm. It was an easy gesture, with no hint of aggression. Her limbs felt only pleasantly languid. But she knew she shouldn't be here with this man at all. He knew too much about making a woman feel good.

Tomorrow...tomorrow she might regret her acquiescence. But now she could think of no place on earth she would rather be—certainly not her apartment. Christian had saved her from a great deal that night. Oh, not just the silly bus or the sleet or a solitary dinner of crackers and cheese. But a night alone with her outrage over Penn and the way he had treated her. The assumptions he had made. His anger that she had dared to think for herself—as if he owned her.

Maybe the phone was ringing that very minute in her empty apartment. Maybe it was Penn wanting to scold. Or placate her as if she were a child who'd thrown a tantrum and needed to be coaxed back into line.

But Christian, for all his subtle knowingness, treated her as if she was someone to be reckoned

with, both professionally and as a woman. He had
charm, and for reasons she didn't fully understand,
he had taken the trouble to read her work. That alone
disarmed her. Penn took an interest in her career, of
course. He was proud of it. But in a managerial
sense. He would never read—really read—her ideas.
Form, dazzling form, was his passion, not content.

It unbalanced her that a man who was reputed to
be an opportunistic fortune hunter on an international scale had sat in the dim, musty halls of the
public library and dug through her work. It seemed
oddly intimate, more than any other type of inspection could possibly be.

He confused her. Why couldn't he be as she expected him to be? Her mind was cluttered with a
dozen details about him, yet the man, the essence of
him, evaded her.

She thought she would never understand, never,
why she sat quiescent within the circle of that arm,
with his shapely hand lying along her upper arm. But
she felt so contented. She seemed to be able to summon nothing more than her voice, and that was faint
and full of secret, inner vibration.

But they talked—oh, how they talked! About
Renoir and van Gogh. The scent of heliotrope in a
French country garden, the smell of fresh-baked
bread in a Paris street. About the way one artist
caught sunlight, another shadow.

He said something, something outrageous and
funny and she laughed delightedly. Her head turned
on his shoulder and her eyes met his and something
arced between them. The smile died on her lips and

she lay against him, very still, listening with her heart.

A single finger turned her chin to him with a force she was helpless to resist. Everything about his power over her seemed out of proportion to the subtlety of his actions. She half heard a murmured denial from her lips and immediately felt the hungry, contradictory reply of her body. His light caress sent out sparks that ignited small fires of longing within her, quickening her pulse. Slowly he bent over her, almost tentatively, the touch of his lips exquisitely soft.

She watched, enthralled, as he removed the wineglass from her hand, then reached across her to set it on the table. The brush of his arm against her breasts was electrifying.

He kissed her again, taking his time, reacquainting himself with the warm, moist secrets of her mouth. With effort, Liza pulled away, drawing a ragged breath. Her eyes were bright and out of focus.

She wanted to damn him as a man who took and took from a woman. But how could she? How, when his mouth gave and his hands gave and his entire body seemed to exist for nothing more than raining pleasure on her? She stared up at the almost handsome, masculine face, the face of a man she'd been warned against. She didn't care what happened. Her eyelids fell shut, her lips half parted in a mute plea.

One arm cradled her while the other was devoted to the minute, sensuous exploration of her cheek, her ear, the flaring, elegant curve of her neck. Yet surely she pleased him too, she thought, unused to this kind of balance between a man and a woman. Hesitant at first, she insinuated a hand beneath his jacket and began a slow exploration of the muscles that flared out from his spine. His mouth sucked breath from hers in a short, harsh gasp. *So,* she thought, *you're not invincible, Christian Chase. I have my power, too....*

Yet her control was short-lived. He intended to let her play apparently only as much as he permitted. He kissed her again, but hard this time. Then suddenly he held her by the shoulders, away from him. His hands eased her around so that her back was to him. The Renoir sat in front of her.

She shook her head, stunned and confused. What was he doing? "Christian..." she began.

"Shh...!" he whispered, "*La Baigneuse*...look at her...she's beautiful, isn't she?"

"Yes...beautiful. But—"

"You are too, Liza. A beautiful, reverse-image of her. Her gold blond hair...your raven hair. Her pink skin...your ivory flesh. You delight my eye just as she does."

He painted them both with silken, erotic words, and Liza sat transfixed and trembling. He looked from *La Baigneuse* to Liza and she knew that he saw her like that. Without clothing. His hand rested knowingly on her back, and suddenly she wanted to feel like *La Baigneuse*, fully a woman, her skin bare and warm in the summer breeze. She wanted to feel his eyes touch her, like the glance of the sun.

It was as if he heard her heart's silent desire. With all the magical skills of a conjurer, he began to recreate that wondrous image of *La Baigneuse* in

Liza. She was wearing a simple dress of cream silk with a row of tiny pearl buttons down the back. Slowly, slowly, he undid those buttons, parted the dress and slid it off her shoulders. His unhurried fingers unhooked the thin lace band of her bra. It fell from her and was lost in the folds of silk that lapped at her hips just as the robe of *La Baigneuse* did.

Liza's hair was coiled softly on the back of her head. "Just like hers, at the point of falling into a man's hands," Christian whispered into her ear. She felt him pull the pins from her hair. It tumbled, heavy and lustrous about her slender shoulders.

Only her back was exposed to his hungry inspection. Liza had never known that the curve of a shoulder blade, the soft hollow along her spine, or the gentle swell at the back of her hips could be so full of sensitive nerve endings.

Her mind slid on the dreaming pleasure of the moment, playing, imagining. The vision of an artist was alive again in her. She knew instinctively that Christian shared that fantasy. *La Baigneuse* glanced over her shoulder, looking down on them benignly.

His fascination seemed endless as his fingertips explored, his touch almost reverent. Time passed, beyond her comprehension, till finally he brought his hands around her slender rib cage in a single, smooth movement, pressing her back to his hard chest. The sudden embrace staggered her, then a low moan escaped him as he took the weight of her breasts in his hands, his thumbs arcing back and forth across her nipples, turning her limbs liquid.

It might have gone on forever, but pleasure can be

so easily, so cruelly and totally shattered. He had begun to slide his hands under her knees when she heard the unmistakable intrusion of voices. People passing in the hall, she thought. But the low murmurs stayed close. There was a cough, and more words filtered faintly through the door. Whoever they were, they were not going away.

His sensitive antenna caught her tense distraction. He tried to kiss her back into his power but she resisted. In low coaxing words he assured her that no one could invade their privacy but Liza remained frozen in his arms.

He swore, raking his hair off his forehead and Liza shrank back. He stared at her in pained incomprehension. They were security guards, he explained impatiently, there to protect the Renoir. It didn't seem to bother him in the least that two men, strangers, were standing just outside the door as he did these intimate, soul-destroying things to her. The spoiled aristocrat in him, Liza thought, made him able to dismiss from his mind those in his employ. They simply did not exist for him.

But she was made of different stuff. The magic would not come back for her. Passion can't be ordered. It has its own immutable rules.

With shaking hands she dressed hastily in the bathroom and later, she rebuffed his insistence that he at least take her home. Alone, she fled to where she knew she should have been all along. . .anywhere but with Christian.

Oh, God, what had she done, she wondered despairingly. She had a right to be furious with Penn, but did she have a right to take comfort—or was it revenge—in another man's arms? She wanted desperately to see it as just an isolated but perfect moment of sensual pleasure that she as a woman had a right to know. Surely she didn't have to justify herself to anyone!

Yet the whole incident had curdled, leaving an unpleasant taste in her mouth. That she, Liza Downing, had been making love with a man she didn't trust and hardly knew while two detectives stood watch at the door—even the idea made her feel giddy.

And then she looked down at the parcels in her arms and remembered. She was going away, far away into the desert. Good, she thought. Good. She was leaving one man who wouldn't even try to understand her. And another who seemed only too eager to.

CHAPTER FIVE

BY THE TIME Liza had struggled home, night thoughts, raw nerves and a head pounding from too much wine on an empty stomach had eroded her confidence. She collapsed on the loveseat and wanted to die. In the briefcase tossed at her feet lay the useless press release she had labored over. Now it would have to wait until she returned from this absurd wild-goose chase in the Sinai.

But she didn't have to go, she told herself sternly. All she had to do was swallow her stupid pride and admit to Penn that she'd spoken in anger, and never had any intentions of going to the monastery—the idea had just popped into her mind and out of her mouth before she could think.

It was the sane, sensible thing to do. Penn didn't hold grudges. In an hour they could be together and everything would be as it was. She reached for the telephone, hesitated, and pulled back. She had a vision of Penn's telling Victoria and Alexa that she was finally behaving herself and canceling her trip. She could see the two women exchanging thin smiles and knowing glances, hear them saying, "Of course, we knew she would...."

She stood abruptly, walked to the window and

peered down into the shadowed garden. It was as clear to her as the rising moon that she'd reached a critical moment in her relationship to the Livsays. What she decided now, she realized, would affect the rest of her life. Suddenly she felt suffocated. Maybe she did need to get away and think—but to the Sinai?

Dear Lord, she thought, she didn't even know what it was she was supposed to do over there! All she had was one miserable scrap of information from the diary of a half-mad Englishman, and the innuendo of an unscrupulous fortune hunter. But she needed to be alone for a while, beyond the reach of any man. She laughed, but without humor, at the realization that the only place she could free herself from the force of two such dynamic men as Penn and Christian was the middle of a wasteland.

Perhaps I'm a little insane myself, she thought. All her careful work had been sabotaged again by that impetuousness so freshly stirred by Christian. Penn had been right. Christian *had* got to her, both in the way he meant...and in a way he could never have imagined.

She was in bed, though not asleep, when the phone rang. She set aside the light novel she'd been reading and went to answer it. It was Penn. He sounded wounded.

"It's not like you to be this way, Liza," he said.

"I know..." she agreed, and her heart constricted.

"You left so quickly...you were so angry. I've never seen you like that."

Her throat ached. "I'm not angry with you,

Penn," she said softly. "Only sorry for what happened today."

"I can't stand things this way, and I don't mean just today, Liza. It's everything. I'm here, you're there—it's not right, damn it! You should be here, beside me."

She pressed her eyes shut and murmured something soothing, apologetic.

"Forget what happened at lunch, Liza. Forget the cross—it doesn't matter. Let me come. Or let me send the car for you. Don't think, just do it—then marry me!"

She was almost, but not quite, crying. It would be so very easy. "I...I can't tell you what you want to hear right now. But when I get back, I promise...."

It would be hard, she knew, for a man like Penn to forgive her this.

IT'S STRANGE that once you've made up your mind, Liza reflected, events take on a life of their own and turning back becomes impossible. Julian hadn't been happy. It was the closest he had ever come to blowing up at her. It had even frightened her a little, for when a man of seemingly inexhaustible patience and sweetness suddenly flares, you take note. He had looked at her, hard, much longer than she'd liked.

"I seem to be caught by my own words, Liza. I only hope I haven't given you enough rope to hang yourself. But I said I wouldn't interfere and I won't. Still, I never expected this. I think you've been quite unfair."

Liza had hurried through the travel preparations,

afraid hesitation would be fatal. Her passport was valid, so there was no problem there, at least. She kept a savings account for emergencies, and although this didn't seem to fit the usual categories of illness, fire or flood, she withdrew it as soon as the bank doors opened the next morning. The museum could always reimburse her later.

It was not, she consoled herself, as if she'd be a complete innocent abroad—Penn's opinions notwithstanding. She'd dealt with the mysteries of the Eastern telephone system, the sanitation, or lack of it, the blissful disregard for the American obsession with schedules and reservations. She could haggle. She knew enough to set the fare with the taxi driver before getting in. And she knew when and how to dispense baksheesh for effect. The Sinai had, after all, changed a good deal since Nigel Bagley's day.

Clothes, she thought, standing before her open closet. She'd have to travel light, but she'd need a variety. Aqaba was in Jordan, where the rules about women's dress were strict. If she wanted to be treated properly, she'd have to be careful not to offend their customs.

She flicked the hangers, searching for something that would do for her brief stay in Aqaba. She pulled out a summer dress of muted brown-and-black check; it had a matching black linen jacket that would cover her arms suitably. She'd wrap her head in a square of brown silk tied neatly at the back of the neck. That was certainly subdued and modest enough, she decided, yet with the necessary authority and smartness it wouldn't hurt to have. Once she'd crossed over into the Sinai, life would be much more relaxed and permissive. But besides the cultural extremes, she would also have to cope with wild temperature fluctuations, so she folded into her suitcase cotton pants and tops plus a heavy sweater and jacket.

The last thing she did, before she boarded her midnight flight at Kennedy Airport, was drop an envelope into the mailbox. "Dearest Penn," she had written,

I know you are as eager as I am to have this matter settled, so I am leaving New York tonight. I was unable to get a seat on a flight to either Cairo or Tel Aviv on such short notice, but I had the good luck to get a cancellation on a charter flight to Amman. From there I'll get a connection to Aqaba where I'll arrange land transportation down to St. Catherine's.

This flight to Jordan is full of super-wealthy, super-courteous Arabs, plus a group of American engineers and their wives going over on some huge bridge-building contract—I've already had a nice chat with some of them here in the waiting room where I hurry to write this. So you see, I'm not going to lack for lots of good company!

It may be difficult for me to write once I'm in the Sinai, so please don't fret if we are out of contact for several days. I'll cable you with my return flight information the first chance I get. I hear them calling my flight now—I'm sorry if

I've hurt or confused you. I'm confused myself.
But we'll talk when I get back.

All my love, Liza

The first leg of her flight halfway around the world
was as relaxed and companionable as she had pre-
dicted. But when the Americans left at Amman, she
felt their absence acutely.

The trip on the small, furiously vibrating plane
down the coast to Aqaba was quite another matter.
Liza, the only woman aboard, shrank back into her
seat and prayed for the time to pass quickly.

LIZA WAS RATHER PLEASED with herself. It was the
best hotel—the only hotel, really—that it was conceivable for her to stay in. She had arrived, weary to
the marrow, to be told there were no rooms available. But she had refused to panic. Instead, she had
been quietly insistent, politely pigheaded and, when
the moment felt right, she tipped the clerk to check
the register one more time. Miraculously, a cancellation had appeared. She and the clerk exchanged
amazed and pleased murmurs. Liza went up to the
cool, shuttered room feeling she had passed her first
test very well indeed.

The room was large, spare and attractive, with
tiled floors, French doors and simple modern fur-
nishings. There was even a small but clean bathroom
off it. From the balcony she could catch the corner of
the Old Town and, stretching before her beyond a
band of white beach, the Gulf of Aqaba.

Quickly, she stripped, showered off a film of ocher

dust, and splashed herself head to toe with light co-
logne. Refreshed, she pulled on a gown made of
semitransparent white cotton gauze that felt cool
against her bare skin. It had wide sleeves and a flowing hem and the yoke was embroidered with threads
of hot pink and bright green. Both color and material
reminded her of the East and for a moment she experienced a thrill of pleasure. For the first time, she
had an acute sense of where she was.

She opened the double doors and walked out onto
the balcony with its attractive pots of brilliant,
unknown flowers. On the little white table, room service had left bottled European sparkling water, ice,
fruit and tiny almond cakes. She sank onto the
chaise. A sharp salt breeze coming off the Gulf lifted
the strange sounds of the street up to her.

There were crowds of men. A few were in traditional desert clothing, most in worn baggy suits, but
all wore the traditional headgear, a square of red and
white checked cloth folded in half and bound to their
heads by thick, black cords. The women were harder
to see. Quick-footed, hugging the sides of the
buildings, they were almost indistinguishable from
the shadows, in their long black robes and veils that
covered everything but their bright black eyes.

Letting the wind play with her hair, she lay there,
sipping the chilled water and allowing the tension to
flow out of her. Dusk began to fall, and the Gulf
became a dark opal, winking purple and magenta at
her. Lights from the bobbing fishing boats were its
fire.

She began to believe that everything would work

out, that a solution to her problems was possible. She did love Penn, she reflected, but was she in love with him? Did it matter? Suddenly she sat upright, staring at the horizon, a band of orange rapidly thinning and disappearing into the night sky, as if she herself were losing something. She felt an enormous need to see Penn. It was a heavy, pervasive longing and it shocked her, for she was not usually moved by him in quite this way.

She thought persistently of marriage to him, but just as persistently rejected the idea. She felt oddly dislocated. In coming here she seemed to have turned her back on her past, her present and her future. Although the days in Jordan are hot, the nights are just as suddenly cold. Liza began to shiver and went back into the room. Her eyes fell on the telephone. She had a clear vision of Penn back in his penthouse, sitting in his study as he did every night going over papers from the bank. All she had to do was pick up that phone and miraculously speak to him again.

He would share this with her. He would talk to her and fortify her. And if she weakened, she would only have to say, "Come get me," and he would. No questions. As easily as if she were still only those few blocks north of him. He would not embarrass her over this extravagant impulse. There would be no reproach, for it was his way to forget and forgive and get on with life. Oh, Alexa might gloat. But Victoria, whatever else she was, would be fair.

A small smile began to lift the corners of her mouth. He would, most likely, claim a holiday from this shambles. He would suggest, perhaps, that they stop off in Italy on the way back where he would lavish all sorts of attention and affection on her. If she was a fatalist—or a romantic—she would say that this whole escapade had been leading to just that: a grand adventure not in the Sinai but in the gilded splendor of some seventeenth-century villa overlooking a canal in Venice. It would be only natural, then, for her to share his bed and give them both the answer they needed so badly.

Moments later, Liza placed the call to Penn's residence.

"Liza? Oh, my God—I can tell from this horrendous connection you really *did* go!"

Was that laughter or just the sputter and crackle of the phone line? Liza stuck a finger in her unoccupied ear and shouted at Alexa.

"What? Penn? No, he's not here! I just stopped by to pick up some papers. He left them here for me with Peters."

"I thought—"

"You thought what?" Alexa's voice rose, faded, rose again. "But it's morning here, my dear!"

She'd forgotten the time difference. Wearily, Liza drew her hand down her face, erasing an image of Venice. The phone seemed to spit and snap in her ear like a malevolent beast. She asked about the letter.

"No, I don't know anything about any letter," Alexa told her. "And I don't suppose Penn does either. At least, he had precious little information to tell us about you before he left."

"Left for where—the office?"

"You don't remember? No, I guess not. You and

Penn were supposed to be spending the weekend out on the Island at the Ogilvies'. I don't know what day it is where you are, dear, but it's Saturday here."

"I. . . I'd forgotten about that, Alexa. But I've had more important things on my mind lately than sitting around drinking Bloody Marys on Ben Ogilvie's patio."

"Humph—it's debatable whether my brother agrees with you there."

Their conversation was full of little verbal hand grenades being bounced back and forth around the world. Liza spoke snappishly, not caring, knowing the connection was so bad that insults and whispered endearments would all sound the same on the other end—a hoarse garble.

"Message?" Liza repeated. "Arrived safely, everything wonderful, not to worry. And. . . give him my love." The connection began to fade. Alexa's reply was unintelligible.

IN THE MORNING, to give herself at least the illusion of control and purposeful activity, Liza showered, dressed, and walked briskly downstairs before most of the guests in the hotel were stirring. The lobby smelled of smoke, Arab coffee, and cloves from the bazaar across the street. Hungry, she went out to the terrace restaurant, ordered tea, and put together a meal from the buffet table that held a typical Jordanian breakfast of fish, cheese, juice, hard-boiled eggs and rolls.

The sun was a brilliant lemon yellow in the east. Despite a row of olive trees, arrayed like sentinels against the desert beyond, a hot wind was already spreading its yellow cloak of dust over the terrace, defeating the efforts of a young boy who labored resignedly with a reed broom. Liza could taste the dust, acrid in her throat, feel it seeping into her pores. She tugged at the high collar of her dress, plucked at her sticky hose, and bent over her notebook with renewed determination to get organized and out of Aqaba.

After breakfast she found what passed for a travel agency and made the necessary inquiries. He would be delighted, said the dark and engaging owner, to put her on one of their tour buses. He had one, by happy chance, going quite close to St. Catherine's.

Liza thanked him. "But I'm here on business," she explained patiently. "All I want to do is hire a car and driver."

The man's beautiful dark eyes became even larger. He was baffled. "But why would a young woman like yourself want to go alone into the Sinai when we can offer you companions, accommodation? And the meals are included."

Yes, she was sure that the tours were wonderful, she said. But she was not a tourist. The man studied her dolefully. He told her he would try. In the meantime, did the lady have the necessary passes?

Her visa and passport had got her into Jordan and would see her through the tiny southernmost tip of Israel that lay between her and the Sinai. But for the desert itself she would need a permit from the United Nations security group. This was a blow, and she set out with unease to find the small UN office.

Clutching a map penciled for her by the tour operator, she made her way through the noisy, squalid streets of the Old Town. Low, whitewashed houses crowded the narrow mud lanes. She passed by stalls crammed with bolts of dress material, fruit and olives, by carts offering freshly baked cinnamon cakes and lamb patties, by barber shops, book stalls, and copper merchants. Once, an aggressive and unsmiling soldier with a submachine gun slung over his shoulder stopped her and demanded to see her passport. Liza was outwardly calm but shaken by the incident.

She made a few more inquiries about guides and received either blank or uneasy stares. The heat became punishing and the lunch she bought from a street vendor was not agreeing with her. Her mind began to cruise in aimless circles. Defeat seemed imminent. She managed to get the UN pass with a good deal more explaining than she had been prepared to do, then doubled back to the travel agent only to be told, "Next week, perhaps."

Night was falling as she scuffed her way into the hotel, hot and unhappy, a headache pounding in her temples. She stopped at the desk, picked up her key and, on impulse, asked the clerk if he might help her. Like so many others that day, the young man seemed to view her request as bizarre, but he, too, promised to see what he could do.

More than anything now, she needed something cool to drink and a chance to gather her thoughts. She found the patio crowded almost entirely with men, their gazes openly curious, almost hostile. Or was she imagining it, she wondered. Her stomach did another little toss and she felt beads of perspiration form on her upper lip. She couldn't spot an empty table. She hesitated, feeling awkward and exposed.

"Excuse me, miss...if you're not joining anyone, perhaps you'd like to sit at my table?" He looked at her with meaning, as if to say he understood her dilemma.

Under ordinary circumstances Liza would have said no. But these were not ordinary circumstances. A seat beside a respectable-looking older gentleman suddenly seemed like a haven and she quickly accepted his offer.

"It can be hard on a woman alone in these Arab towns," the man said, drawing out a chair for her. "I noticed you earlier this morning in the lobby. I trust you don't think I'm too forward in asking you to join me?"

"No, not at all," she replied, sinking gratefully onto the chair. "And I hope you won't think I'm too bold in accepting...but I've never felt so self-conscious in my life!"

He smiled. "I'm Angus Cavanaugh, by the way," he said, half rising and extending a gnarled hand to her.

"And I'm Liza Downing," she replied, offering her own.

"You're American, aren't you?" he asked in the polite manner of all strangers who must make conversation. "I can always tell."

"Yes, I am, from New York. I'm here for a few days."

The man raised a walking stick to attract the waiter. Later, they exchanged more noncommittal pleasantries while waiting for their drinks.

He was elderly. British, she guessed, although his accent was unclear. He was short, rawboned, his arms and legs thin, although his stomach swelled beneath his beige shirt. He must have been away from home a long time, she thought. His thatch of thinning hair was pure white, his skin mahogany from more Arab sun than he would get from any business trip. And had his nose, perhaps, been broken once a long time ago?

His voice was gravelly. From alcohol and cigarettes, Liza suspected. And he confirmed at least part of that when, a moment later, he withdrew a tobacco pouch and some papers and began to roll his own cigarette. Liza found it harder to guess his age. The sun was cruel to skin in a country like this, and his was deeply lined and toughened. But his eyes were quick and intelligent and missed very little. He seemed delighted to have an English-speaking companion.

"You must be here on business, Miss Downing," he remarked. "We get very few single women tourists here. None, I would venture to say—"

"I'm an art curator back in New York," Liza quickly put in, "and I'm here on museum business."

"Is that right now! I'm surprised, though, that you'd be here on anything to do with art—Amman, or Beersheba, or Ismailia I could understand. But not Aqaba."

"Aqaba's just my jumping-off point," she explained. "Actually, I'm headed into the Sinai—with luck, that is."

The old man raised a tangled white eyebrow. "The Sinai—now that's a vast and godforsaken place for a young woman to be headed into. May I ask what your destination is there?"

"An old monastery called St. Catherine's."

"Ah, yes," he said slowly. "It's a name you often come across if you spend any time in the Middle East."

"You know, then, that it's reputed to have a fascinating collection of art...."

"I've heard stories to that effect, yes," he acknowledged, and once more smiled politely.

Their tall, iced drinks came. Liza sipped hers gratefully. She fanned herself with the menu card and watched the sun, a perfect red ball, balance itself on the dark blue waters of the Gulf. She had accepted Mr. Cavanaugh's invitation with mixed feelings, but now she was beginning to enjoy herself. Her stomach ceased its contortions. The breeze was kind on her brow. The thudding inside her head slowed.

Had she seen him, too, last night when she checked in? Perhaps. But he was the sort you always see hanging out in hotel lobbies from Singapore to Lima—lonely expatriates hiding from, or lost in, the past. At home only when farthest from it. Living on gin and meager pensions and haunting hotels for the arrival of newspapers from wherever it was they called home. Angus Cavanaugh was this type, she thought, glancing at a stack of much-read foreign papers that lay on the chair beside him. He had knowing, rather sad, eyes and an unmistakably educated voice that made her feel glad that fortune had put her here, if only to talk with him for a little while.

"I didn't know," he was saying, "that the monks are allowing foreigners in to look at the collection."

"Well, they're not, precisely. That is, I'm not expected," she clarified. "But I assume—"

He was shaking his head. "I hate to discourage you, Miss Downing, but you may not find yourself welcome when you get there. The monks have never liked to be disturbed. And since the tourists started pouring into the area, they've become particularly touchy about intruders." He pushed aside his glass and leaned forward. "Look, I don't mean to tell you your business, but a trip to St. Catherine's is not one I'd recommend under the *best* of circumstances to a young woman alone."

Liza smiled. "Thank you, Mr. Cavanaugh, I appreciate your concern. But I know when I explain to them the purpose of my visit they'll be more than happy to let me view the collection. And even if they don't want to take me into their hostel as an overnight guest, I'm not likely to find myself alone in the desert, am I, since you yourself say the area is full of tour groups?"

He looked at her sternly from beneath his weathered brow. "And with a tour group is the best place for you to be!"

"I can't be tied down like that," she explained. "My time is extremely limited...someone expects me home very soon."

"There are many miles of desert between Aqaba

and St. Catherine's. How do you intend to get there then?''

She spoke with more confidence than she felt. ''I've spent the whole day asking about experienced guides. Several people are looking into it for me.''

''Experienced!'' he repeated, stabbing the air with a crooked finger. ''That's the key word. You don't want just any fly-by-nighter. He'll have to speak English, Arabic, and Hebrew, too. And you'll need proper equipment—a vehicle with four-wheel drive, for example, and the right food and bottled water for traveling through the desert....

''El Tih,'' said Angus, balancing his chair on the back legs and staring out over the Gulf, ''the Wilderness of the Wanderer.... Just an empty gravel plain, but it's beautiful, beautiful in a way you've never seen. If you do go, Miss Downing, it'll touch you— change you in a way you never thought possible.''

Liza searched his profile for a moment, then lowered her eyes. She was silent, knowing somehow that no comment could, or should, be made.

Angus Cavanaugh pulled himself up in his chair and was suddenly brisk. ''Promise me this, will you?'' he said. ''Let me look into it for you, see if I can come up with someone really reliable to take you into the desert. I know a lot of fellows here in Aqaba who come from the desert Bedouin tribes—decent fellows who've come into town to earn extra money for their familes. Let me ask for you!''

''Really,'' Liza protested, ''I couldn't ask you to—''

''You're not. I'm offering.''

"Well, then," she replied, smiling at him with her eyes, "I would be very indebted to you, Mr. Cavanaugh."

They made arrangements to meet next morning in the hotel lobby. Angus Cavanaugh was sweet, Liza thought, as she climbed into bed a few hours later. But she knew he'd never show up.

OCCASIONALLY THE IMPOSSIBLE HAPPENS. For Liza it occurred in the form of a small, very dark young man with extraordinarily beautiful eyes. She looked up to find him suddenly there, silent and waiting, as she sipped the last of her breakfast tea. She dabbed her lips with her napkin and looked at him inquiringly.

His voice was soft and halting. "My name is Yaser Rahman."

"Yes...?" She smiled at him encouragingly.

"My cousin is Abdalmunem. He works here. At the desk."

Liza frowned. "Oh, Abdal—yes, of course!" She pushed aside the scattered remains of her breakfast and indicated that he should sit down, but he remained standing.

"My brother Hussein and I have been working in Aqaba. We are going to take our truck back to our family with some supplies. We come from a place— you call it an oasis, I think—near the Monastery of St. Catherine. We were not planning to leave for another few days, but if you are interested we thought we could work something out." He lowered his eyes. He seemed to find it excruciatingly painful to be speaking to a Western woman.

Liza had to restrain herself from jumping up and embracing him. They began to discuss details. "How soon could you go?" she asked. "Could you make it today—this morning?" He hesitated. She upped the already generous fee she had offered. He could, he said.

It was only after she had paid her bill and checked out of the hotel that Liza remembered Angus Cavanaugh. On impulse, she hurried back to the lobby. "There is a man, an elderly man, English, I think. He sometimes eats here. Have you seen him this morning?"

The clerk said he had not. She took a piece of hotel stationery. "Dear Mr. Cavanaugh," she wrote.

I have had great luck. Two very nice young men have offered to take me into the Sinai and, given the difficulty of finding guides, I have accepted. I do hope I have not inconvenienced you terribly.

She scribbled a few more polite lines about his kindness, about how interesting it had been to meet him, then stuffed the letter into an envelope. Sealing it, she gave it to the desk clerk. As she left the hotel she took one last look over her shoulder. Angus was already two hours overdue for their rendezvous. She had, she concluded, probably caught him yesterday in his only lucid moment of the day. Now, he was no doubt deep into a cache of illicit alcohol.

Poor man, she thought, and forgot him at once.

CHAPTER SIX

THE SINAI is an enormous wedge that cleaves Africa from Arabic Asia. It is that great and terrible wilderness of the Exodus. Across its broad, northern boundary lies the Mediterranean Sea. To the west is the Gulf of Suez and Egypt. To the east lies the Gulf of Aqaba.

The Monastery of St. Catherine, Liza's goal, lay in the very heart of the tip of the peninsula. From Aqaba, in Jordan, it was only a matter of an hour's drive west to Eilat, Israel's port town on the Gulf. From there, the road would turn sharply south, clinging to the coastline. Liza and her guide planned to follow that coastal highway as far south as the town of Nuweiba, once Neviot, where they would spend the night. From there, they would turn due west, into the desert, with the dark and distant pinnacle of Mount Sinai as their polestar.

Liza's courage had almost failed her when she first saw the truck that was to carry her so far from civilization. It bore no resemblance to that sturdy, four-wheel drive vehicle Angus had talked of. But then, that type of equipment was no doubt a Westerner's conceit. This vehicle had obviously done faithful duty to Yaser and Hussein for more than a few years,

Liza struggled to remind herself. It was an indeter-
minable make, pieced together from the remains of
others by means of bits of twine and wire. The body
was leprous with rust. The open back was heaped
with cartons and packages wrapped in brown paper.
Lashed across the top was an oily tarpaulin. Liza
averted her eyes as her best cream suitcase was
wedged in with the soiled cargo.

Hussein, if possible, was even more silent than his
brother Yaser. He was a large, splendid Bedouin with
swarthy skin and bright bits-of-coal eyes. Whether
the reserve of these two brothers sprang from shy-
ness, sullenness, a language barrier or even polite
custom, Liza could not decide. In any event, it was
her fate to spend the next hours locked in silence between the two men.

They set out into a land fashioned from dust and
set beneath a silver sky. The unaccustomed light
seared Liza's eyes, the sand roughened her throat.
She slid her large sunglasses over her nose and pulled
her scarf tighter about her head. The vehicle cork-
screwed wildly around bare hills baking in the sun,
passing lonely stone houses where scrawny goats
pawed patches of dried gorse and chickens pecked at
stones. Children with large kohl-rimmed eyes ran
after the truck, waving. Thin dogs scattered before
them.

But Eilat, when they arrived, was like a miracle. A
festive town, it was speckled with gay cabanas and
cooled by the sea breeze off the Gulf. The shore was
ringed by small excursion boats. Families picnicked
by the water's edge and children clamored for camel

rides. The trio of travelers stopped at a food stand on
the beach and bought a lunch of falafel, little fried
balls of chick-peas folded into rounds of pita bread.

At a gas station Liza ducked into the washroom
and quickly peeled off her now unspeakably wilted
dress. With a shudder of distaste she rolled it into a
ball and shoved it into the depths of her tote bag. The
cool cotton pants and T-shirt slid over her body like a
blessing. Bending over from her waist she brushed
the sand from her hair, then shook it free and shining
about her shoulders. Fortified and feeling fresh, she
skipped back to the truck.

They left Israel and veered sharply south. With
their home now somewhere out there in front of
them, Yaser and Hussein began to push, one taking
the wheel while the other dozed. Liza contrived to
get the window seat this time and watched in wonder
as the lush and beautiful border of the Sinai opened
up before her.

On her left, the Gulf, an unbroken band of cobalt,
unfurled to the horizon. Beyond it, just barely visible, lay a faint line of mauve that was the coast of
Saudi Arabia. Above her, a hazy orange sun hung in
a sky of unrelenting azure. To her right, a boundary
of jagged mountains sprang up, a stark and majestic
counterpoint.

They came upon long stretches of graceful doum
palms and thick clumps of prickly caper bushes.
Haphazard driftwood shacks of fishermen dotted the
beaches. Drying nets crisscrossed the sand. They
stopped only once, at an Arab seaside town. They
roused the owner of a coffee stand who had been

sleeping on a carpet spread beneath a palm to escape the sun and desert flies, and ordered mugs of steaming, aromatic mocha.

Toward the end of the afternoon, traffic on the highway increased. Clusters of low, whitewashed houses became more numerous. The pristine sands sprouted occasional bouquets of beach umbrellas. Inland, intensively farmed plots of land formed checkerboards of vegetables and flowers. Non-Arab hitchhikers, thumbing their way down to Sharm el Sheikh, dotted the shoulder of the road.

This part of the Sinai was the ancient home of the Tarabin and Muzeina Bedouins. But it had also become, oddly enough, a gathering place for rootless young people from all over the world. Perhaps it was the coral reefs, or the miraculous gold sand that spilled at the foot of the umber mountains. Or perhaps it was that India and Nepal had suddenly become old hat to this generation of youth—Liza couldn't quite fathom it—but this little town of Nuweiba had become a new magnet for a gaudy assortment of travelers with nothing more to their names than their scruffy backpacks.

Yaser and Hussein, Liza gathered, had relatives in town and would stay the night with them. The brothers departed in the truck, after arranging to meet her the next morning on the beach for an early start into the desert.

For Liza, finding accommodation was not so simple. There were no rooms to be had in the couple of attractive modern motels to which she wearily lugged her suitcase. The gravel under her sandals dissuaded her from trying the next one a mile or so down the beach and finally she settled for a bed in a small and plain hostel near the water. It was not the sort of place that invited lingering so, after stowing her gear in the locker provided and buttoning the key securely in a pocket, she set out for the beach.

After the long jolting ride it was a joy to let the salt breeze toss her hair and feel the muscles in her legs unkinking. She slipped off her sandals, rolled up her pants and strolled along the edge of the warm water, smiling at the antics of the swimmers in the surf. Her ear picked up Swedish here, German and Dutch there, and then something familiar, made odd by the incongruous setting—English, rising and falling in warm, honeyed swells.

Just ahead of her, beside a clump of palms, a group of men and women sat in a semicircle of bright canvas deck chairs. They were roughly middle-aged, she saw, although a few appeared quite elderly. Some had draped themselves with a patchwork of towels to hide from the still fierce sun but their bright red skin announced them as recent tourists.

Liza paused, watching them. They were unmistakably American and, more particularly, southern. Judging from the animated conversation, they were enjoying themselves immensely, sunburn notwithstanding. One woman in a gay cotton sundress, round-faced and plump, her hair a froth of silver curls, was standing as she snapped the sand out of an oversize beach towel. She glanced up and caught Liza's eye on her.

"Hello," she said, her voice a friendly drawl.

"Hello," Liza returned.

"American?" the woman asked, smiling broadly.

"Yes, I am—and I guess I don't need to ask if you are too," Liza said warmly.

The woman laughed. "No, I suppose not. I couldn't hide that even if I wanted to." She spread the towel back over the deck chair. "It's kind of nice to see a face from back home, isn't it?"

Liza agreed. "Especially for me. I'm traveling on my own."

"You're alone?" The woman glanced down the beach as if to confirm such an odd announcement. Her expression was a mixture of pity and horror.

"Oh, it's all right," Liza said brightly. "Lots of women are these days, you know."

The older woman looked doubtful. "I suppose... but a tour is so much more friendly, I always think."

"I suppose it is, but I'm just here on business."

The woman frowned as if trying to imagine what sort of business a young woman could possibly have out here.

"Anyway," added Liza, "you still can meet nice people when you're on your own—look at us."

The woman seemed pleased and said, "Well, there's a whole congenial bunch over here you can meet—"

"Oh, no...." Liza stepped back a bit.

The woman waved away her objection with one hand and with the other drew Liza toward the circle. "My name's Cora Parsons, by the way," she told her.

"How do you do," said Liza, then introduced herself.

"Look what I've picked up on the beach, every-one!" Cora chirped. The group chatter came to a halt and eyes turned eagerly to Liza. "This is Liza Downing from—"

"New York," prompted Liza.

"New York. And she's all alone here, if you can believe it!" she smiled. "I'll take you round, Liza. This is my husband, Lyn..." she began, indicating a similarly plump and friendly man nursing a can of soda on his stomach.

They were all equal to Cora's warmth and gathered Liza in like a lost child over her flustered protests. One man dragged a chair up to her, another scurried to provide a drink from a cooler.

"Have you traveled together as a group before?" Liza asked, accepting a drink.

"Camping trips, day trips—things like that," Cora explained. "This is the most ambitious jaunt we've ever taken, though. We planned it for over a year. We're all members of the same church, you see, and coming here was something we've always dreamed about. We've been to Jerusalem, Galilee, the Mount of Olives. This is the last leg of it, down to Mount Sinai. By next week we'll be home with enough special memories to last quite a while, I can tell you."

"Where *is* home, Cora?" asked Liza.

"Charlotte, North Carolina," she replied.

"It sounds like a marvelous tour. What did you enjoy the most?" Liza politely inquired.

"Oh, all of it! Every tiny step and that's the truth, isn't it, Lyn?" But Mr. Parsons, who was observing a spirited game of volleyball a little way down the beach, didn't hear. He probably, Liza suspected, would have named this idyllic haven as his favorite, for the moment, anyway.

A tiny, elderly lady in an enormous sun hat—Liza couldn't remember her name—was gazing toward the Gulf with some binoculars. Suddenly, she pointed and cried, "Here they are! Do you suppose they had any luck?"

Liza shaded her eyes with her hand and peered toward the shore. A motorboat was being pulled onto the beach by two Bedouins as a young couple was hopping out. The couple waded through the rolling surf, the woman lugging flapping scuba gear, the man hefting a basket onto his shoulder.

"Scott looks loaded down," remarked Lyn Parsons. "I guess that's a good sign."

"Are they with you?" asked Liza. The bronzed twosome appeared barely out of their teens and seemed unlikely members of the tour.

"In a manner of speaking," Lyn replied. "They run the tour—the practical end of it, that is. Reverend Clarkson, there, gives all the talks about the history of the places we visit." He nodded toward the thin, balding, pleasant man who'd been introduced as their minister.

"They look so young to be tour operators," Liza observed.

"Oh, they are. They're Americans, too. Cute as buttons. You'll love them!"

The two young people ground their way through the sand with their burdens, up the slight incline of the beach toward the clump of palms. The man was an unlikely looking guide, bearing more resemblance to the hippielike teenagers sprawled over the beach. His sandy hair exploded in a mop of bouncing curls from beneath a red bandanna knotted around his forehead. What looked like a seashell dangled from a cord around his neck. The old sweatshirt he wore over his bathing suit bore a faint trace of what might have been a college logo. Its sleeves had been cut off roughly at the elbows.

His partner looked as if she had been transplanted from a California beach. Her tall, lithe body was tanned a deep gold and a profusion of blond hair, bleached nearly white from the sun, floated about her shoulders. She wore a scrap of bright red bikini and gold chains, one about her neck and one about the preferred place of late, her nipped-in waist.

Cora, in her familiar manner, patted Liza's hand and said, as if reading her thoughts, "Don't let Scott's appearance fool you. He's got a good brain under all that hair."

"And he's good with his hands too," added Lyn approvingly. "Remember that engine trouble on the way down from Sodom through the Negev? We'd have been done as dinner without him!"

"Ladies and gentlemen, your supper," Scott announced, shifting the coarsely woven basket off his shoulders and onto the sand. Everyone strained forward, murmuring and curious. He knelt in front of the basket and pulled out an enormous, squirming lobster, to much laughter and applause.

"Real beauties!" exclaimed Lyn, peering into the confusion of feelers and seaweed. "They're not like the ones we see back home, are they?"

Scott shook his head. "It's a different variety over here—more like a rock lobster. You just eat the tails because they don't have claws like our own Maine lobsters. But they're fabulous eating anyway."

"I don't think there's one less than five pounds," said the tiny lady, shaking her head.

"Scott caught them with his hands—you can do that out there by the shoals where we were scuba diving." The girl had dropped to the sand not far from Liza, looking golden and lovely, with a healthy wash of color on her face from the diving. She noticed Liza suddenly. "Hi!" she said with an engaging openness.

"Hello," Liza returned. "That *is* an impressive catch. I had no idea you could get seafood like that around here. So far all I've had are variations on falafel and lamb."

"Then you shall eat with us," said the Reverend Clarkson. "We're going to set things up right here on the beach. And thanks to the skill and daring of Scott here, there's more than enough to go around." Then, noticing the question on the blond girl's face, he introduced Liza to her. Her name was Kimberley. Kimberley Wilde.

Liza began to decline sharing the meal, overwhelmed by the hospitality, but her protests were dismissed. Kim and Scott were enthusiastic too, perhaps welcoming company more of their own age. The girl drew up her knees and wrapped her arms around them. "Are you here on vacation?" she asked brightly.

"Actually, I came to look at some of the art here," Liza explained, "but thanks to all of you, it's beginning to turn into a bit of an adventure."

"Well, this is the place for adventure all right. Are you an artist or something?" Kim asked, looking at Liza with frank, cornflower-blue eyes.

"No, I'm hopelessly unartistic, to be truthful. I'm a curator," Liza replied a bit awkwardly, feeling the title sounded a strange note in these surroundings. She added quickly, "How odd to find a couple from an American city high in the mountains operating a business like this—wasn't it Boulder, Colorado, that Reverend Clarkson said you were from? It would seem more likely to find you in a ski lodge or something back home."

Kimberley laughed. "Operating a business is a grand description for what we do. That's our entire enterprise over there," she said, nodding toward the road behind them.

Liza turned and saw a battered vehicle, a queer cross between a school bus and a van. A small mountain of suitcases was roped to the roof rack and the whole thing seemed to be tilting precariously. "K & S Desert Tours" was painted on the side by an obviously amateur hand.

"It's not much, is it?" said Kim with a grimace. "But it was all we could afford, just getting started. And the roads through the desert are just murder on equipment."

"K & S" Liza read aloud.

"That's us, Kim and Scott. We run tours out of Eilat, mostly, into either the Negev or the Sinai. Sometimes I can't think why we bother, things get pretty wild around here. But we seem to be hooked on the place. . . for a while at least."

Kim retrieved a can of soda from the cooler and returned to sit, cross-legged and companionable, beside Liza. She seemed to be everything Liza was not—leggy, outgoing, perhaps a little brash. Even though she was at least six years younger than Liza, she seemed decades wiser. Liza concluded she was probably perfectly suited, in that way, to greeting and shepherding a constantly changing stream of strangers. Even though the unselfconscious exposure of an astonishing expanse of honeyed skin seemed at odds with the modest attire of this Bible-study group, they appeared to be not just accepting, but fond, of her.

She was the type of girl Liza didn't seem to meet much of in her circle. Sparkling chatter, with little held back, was more Kim's style than was cautious reserve.

"Scott and I came here as tourists ourselves—sort of," Kim rambled on. "We were doing the obligatory tour of Europe with our backpacks after college. . . you know, a little freedom between the books and the bills."

"I envy you," said Liza. "I would've liked to have done it myself, but finances wouldn't permit. After I graduated I went straight into the job I have now."

That was only partly true. Liza had been eager to get to work. Although her two summers in Egypt had whetted her appetite for travel, she hadn't thought herself sufficiently adventuresome to take off on foot wherever whim took her. And there was not enough money to travel any other way. But she held a secret admiration for those girls who, tanned and laughing, hitchhiked across Europe unencumbered by such boring details as train schedules and hotel reservations. She could well imagine Kim spending the night in some tiny square in a Swedish town with her pack for a pillow. Or lounging around the Trevi Fountain without a thought for tomorrow.

"We started in Scandinavia," continued Kim. "It was great, but we were camping out all the time, so toward the end of the summer we decided to drift south. We figured France, but then we were offered a lift by a fellow taking a truck straight through to Istanbul. He wanted company, and you know how hard it is to hitch a really long ride with someone and what a *hassle* it is to try to piece together a dozen rides to go a few miles in one day."

Liza nodded politely and murmured something she hoped was appropriate. In truth, she couldn't conceive of hitchhiking anywhere, let alone all the way to Istanbul with a strange trucker. "That's still a long way from the Sinai, though. . . ."

Kim rolled her eyes. "The Sinai wasn't in our plan at all! But Scott's a great one for going with luck so he said, 'Great! Maybe this was meant to be.' And off we went!"

Kim shrugged and tossed her blond mane off her shoulders while Liza marveled at the casualness of youth. "And was it meant to be?" Liza prompted.

Kim grimaced. "Well, Istanbul certainly didn't work out. Everyone seemed suspicious of us and looked at us—especially me—in a way that made me shiver. Right away Scott got us a couple of spaces on some ancient cargo ship going from Izmir to Haifa, and the less said about *that*, the better. Let's just say that we were absolutely thrilled to get on dry land in Israel.''

But berths on boats, even ratty old steamers, aren't free, thought Liza. There must be some money there—an indulgent parent perhaps. She wondered if Kim and Scott were married—it was so hard to tell nowadays. She glanced at the girl's left hand and saw a thick band of copper. She wouldn't ask what it meant. ''I imagine you found the atmosphere more relaxed there,'' she commented.

''Much more. There were lots of kids like us around and we felt right at home. We visited some kibbutzim, saw Tel Aviv, and decided we wanted to spend more time. Some friends we made told us about the beaches and resort towns that had opened on the Gulf. Just the word beach was irresistible, so we went down to Eilat and fell in love with it.''

Liza nodded. ''I can guess why—I just came through Eilat myself.'' She remembered the scores of bodies toasting on the sand, and knew Kim and Scott would have felt instantly in their element there.

''Well, the bottom line is that we ran out of money. But we didn't want to leave and our parents made it clear that there weren't going to be any more free rides. That's when Scott met a fellow who'd been running tourists down to Sharm el Sheikh.''

''An Israeli?''

''No, he was from Seattle—really, everybody passes through here eventually! Anyway, he decided it was about time he touched base again. He offered

Scott the bus for next to nothing, which is about all it is worth, and we took it. So, here we are!''

"Just like that?" laughed Liza.

"Just like that," Kim echoed. "We painted our initials over where his name had been. Scott takes care of the practical end of things—supplies, driving. I handle the bookings, food and motels. I also took a crash course in the history of the area so I could do some guiding."

"That must be difficult," Liza remarked.

Kim wrinkled her slightly upturned nose. "Not really. People on trips get bored easily, you know. And the heat gets to them. Pretty soon they'd rather you just shut up, or else they get down here to the beach and can't believe how gorgeous it is and just want to lie around all day."

"Now I heard that, dear," interjected Cora from the depths of her deck chair. "We *love* your little talks."

Kim laughed. "Oh, you're different, Mrs. Parsons! Not everyone has your determination, you know." And to Liza she added, "Bible-study groups like this really lap up the history part. Luckily for me, though, they usually bring along their own leaders like Reverend Clarkson. I'd be dead without him."

"Is it hard to get bookings?" Liza asked.

"Not really, I suppose. We slip a few dinars to the local tourist agencies. There's not much competition yet."

"I hear we're headed in the same direction—I'm going to the Monastery of St. Catherine. Will you be staying at the hostel there by any chance?"

"Don't I wish!" said Kim. "It's impossible to get into that place. I know—I've tried. Usually we camp out. There's a huge campground right there by the monastery on the Plain of Raha. But this group I've booked into a motel." Kim turned openly skeptical eyes on Liza. "If you got accepted into that monastery you have my admiration. You must have an official letter from the archbishop or something," she added enviously.

Liza was not inclined to expose the impulsive, ill-thought-out nature of her trip, so she smiled noncommittally, grateful for a boisterous knot of teenagers passing by who made conversation impossible. But she was reassured by the snippets of information she was gleaning from Kim. Even if the worst happened and the monks didn't invite her to spend the night after she'd talked to them, there was still this motel—or at least a campground with the basic necessities.

Scott ambled over, grinned at Liza and said to Kim, "How about organizing the swim now? We've got just enough light before we have to see about food for this gang."

Kim gulped the last of her drink and unfolded her golden body. "Come with us, Liza?" she asked, standing. "If you're a good swimmer we could use you to keep an eye peeled...I have my doubts about the stamina of some of our guests."

Scott pulled down the corner of his mouth. "Now, Kim, that's not her hassle...."

Liza was tempted. "I don't know...I'd like to, but I didn't even bring a suit."

"You don't mean you've come here and don't intend to swim the shoals?'' asked Scott, horrified. ''That's why everybody comes!''

''Not Liza—she's here for art,'' muttered Kim, stooping to gather towels.

Scott scratched his shaggy head. ''Still, now that you know—''

''Maybe she *doesn't* know,'' said Kim with what might have been impatience.

Scott looked as if this was highly unlikely. ''There are people on this beach who travel around the world just to swim or surf certain waters—Hawaii, California, Australia—and they say the diving here is as spectacular as you can find anywhere. I don't have that much to compare it with, but it certainly has everything—fish, coral, you name it.''

''Sharks,'' added Cora obligingly.

Scott laughed. ''Not where we're taking you, Mrs. Parsons, I promise. A baby gray did make a pass at me while I was catching lobsters, but it was pretty small and I was tucked back into the reef. There was never any danger.''

''I don't know,'' said Liza doubtfully. ''Any kind of shark, even a baby one, would tax my abilities and courage.''

''No, no, Scout's honor,'' said Scott. ''We'll stay right here in this bay where the offshore reefs keep out all the nasty stuff! The only thing you might run into is a lion fish, but I'm going to brief everyone on that,'' he added, dismissing what sounded at least as dangerous as the baby gray he'd encountered beyond the reef.

''Come on, dear!'' said Cora Parsons, heaving

herself from her chair. "Now, I'm not much of a swimmer," she added confidingly, "but I did plunk myself down in the Dead Sea. Floated like a cork—Lyn took all these crazy pictures. There's something about the water here that just bears you up, so I'm going to at least dog-paddle along the shore!"

Liza shielded her eyes and looked out over the Gulf of Aqaba. The horizon was dotted with the bright sails of surfboards skimming across the water on the offshore wind. The riders formed graceful arcs as they tugged at the handbars and leaned back over the water, guiding their tiny crafts. Closer in were swimmers, their snorkels moving along like miniature periscopes. And along the shore naked toddlers splashed in the breakers. Their free, water-slicked bodies reminded Liza of her own pale limbs and the decision was made.

Kim was eyeing Liza's body with frank appraisal. She bit her lower lip thoughtfully. "On second thought, maybe I don't have a suit that would fit you. You're very. . .petite. Do you know the motel down the road? Well, just off the lobby there's a little shop. You should be able to find something there."

So while Scott and Kim directed their group toward a row of striped cabanas, Liza plowed through the shifting gravel to the motel where only shortly before she'd tried to beg a room. The motel, newly built for the tourist trade, was long and low, hugging the palm-fringed beach. Its thick, stucco walls were bright white and formed bold geometric patterns with all the flavor of the East, as if they'd been cut out by a giant cookie cutter. The main entrance was set under a thick slab of concrete, cantilevered dramatically out over a sweeping driveway of crushed pink seashells.

To one side of the quarry-tiled lobby, Liza found the tiny shop that combined the sale of beachwear, candy, cigarettes and magazines. She squeezed in among the tourists from Tel Aviv, Oslo and Paris who were sorting eagerly through bathing suits that were not designed for the prudish. The bikinis were as flimsy as any you might see on the Riviera.

Liza tried on a one-piece in a pretty kelly green, turning this way and that before the mirror. She and her embarrassment held a heated debate. The suit contrived, by clever design, to reveal at least as much of her as a bikini would have. The legs were cut hipbone-high and the neckline, which stopped just short of her navel in front and the cleft of her bottom behind, exposed both sides of each breast.

The suit was really quite fun, Liza concluded. And it *was* the only one in her size. So what if it exposed more of her bottom than seemed decent? Considering what was lying out there on the beach, she wouldn't cause a ripple of interest. Satisfied, she pulled her slacks and top right over the suit and went to pay for it.

Back at the beach, she easily spotted her group of fellow travelers, standing in a little knot around Scott and listening intently while he gave his safety lecture. The lion fish was described, the spotted moray eel and stingray added to the list of creatures to avoid—although the latter two, he assured them, were unlikely to have penetrated the barrier reefs.

They divided themselves roughly into two groups, the nonswimmers and the timid who were content to dabble in the shallow water, and the others who wanted to try a little snorkeling. No one asked to go out past the reefs where Scott had earlier caught the lobsters and where, it was revealed, hammerhead sharks liked to congregate.

Liza stood still for the head count, noting that despite his whimsical appearance and laid-back manner Scott hadn't left much to chance. She wondered if, before drifting into his present mode, he had spent his vacations at some good, well-organized summer camp. His manner was remarkably like that of an experienced waterfront counselor accustomed to dealing with fractious children.

Kim, meanwhile, had waded into the water and, with the help of some Bedouins, was taking the boat back out to use as a base for the divers. Only old Mrs. Pepper was not going in. Not to be excluded, however, she had dragged her chair down to the water's edge, where, she informed them sternly, she was going to keep shark watch with her binoculars.

There were plenty of masks and snorkels to go around, and Liza took one. She stayed a little apart from the group, not wanting to add to Kim's and Scott's responsibilities. She waded ankle-deep into the surf and looked around her. The beach swept away on both sides, unsullied and peaceful, the water warm on her skin. She walked in a little farther and stopped to splash her arms and chest. Scott had pointed out an area where the diving was good but the water shallow enough to be safe. Kim was already there, bobbing in the graceful wooden boat. Liza stretched out in the water and, with long, easy strokes, headed in that direction. The Gulf water, she discovered, did have a marvelous warm, buoyant quality that made swimming virtually effortless. Liza was grateful that so little separated her body from the water's soft caress.

When she judged she was far enough from shore, she stopped and began to tread water as she took her bearings and adjusted her mask. The water was utterly clear. Below her she could see in perfect detail the beginnings of the coral reef. It was a fairy-tale sight, the coral resembling giant slabs of jade tossed into a bed of dazzling white sand. In the inky grottoes between the slabs, huge schools of fish glided like silver streamers rippling in the current.

Liza filled her lungs and dove, arcing neatly. Her pointed toes disappeared silently beneath the surface. She kicked straight down and found herself at once in a wondrous bubble of jade shot through with gold. Her hair drifted out into the sifted sunlight suffusing the water. She fluttered along the bottom, scattering schools of brilliant fish, then grabbed a piece of coral and pulled herself hand over hand along a ledge, marveling at the variety and beauty of the sea creatures. Reluctantly giving in to the need for air, she scissored to the surface and lingered briefly before diving again and again.

A few times she spotted other divers from the group and waved, but mostly she enjoyed a pleasant solitude, or company of a different sort. She joined a file of butterfly fish, yellow-and-black striped, felt the tickling fins of a brilliant parrot fish and steered carefully around tiny barracuda that were like slim, silver arrows. A pudgy grouper splotched with gold, black and scarlet presented its drooping, clownlike lips and made her grin.

Her discoveries were endless and glorious—flat, circular fish, entirely yellow, like a scattering of gold coins from a lost Arab dhow; a school of flame tetras, their long fins drifting backward, creating an underwater conflagration that could never be extinguished. Where a chunk of coral plunged into the white sand she caught a sudden movement and withdrew her hand just as a lion fish bristled, raising its shimmering, translucent fins in a ruff about its head. Liza recoiled. It was a singularly ugly creature, striped everywhere—fins, tail, mouth, even its eyes striped black and rust on white. The many fins along its back and beside its gills rippled like feathers. She took a last, fascinated look over her shoulder at the hornlike protrusions above its eyes, the droopy feelers at the corners of its mouth. Scott had been overly kind in his description of it, she thought.

At last exhaustion made her limbs feel heavy and she slowly surfaced. She spotted Kim in the boat and swam over.

"Want in?" called Kim, leaning over the edge.

"Thanks, I'll just hang here for a moment, I think," Liza said breathlessly as she grasped the side of the gently rocking boat. "I did so much diving before, it finally caught up with me!"

"The Gulf is warmer and saltier than ocean

water," said Kim. "It makes it easy to stay out a long time. Was it worth buying that outfit? It suits you, by the way."

"Thanks—for the compliment, *and* for insisting that I come. It's unreal down there!"

Scott suddenly broke through the surface, startling Liza and splashing Kim, who squealed and complained prettily. "Say, you're pretty good!" he said to Liza, shaking back a mop of dripping ringlets. "I passed you a couple of times down there, but you were involved in a lengthy dialogue. With a grouper, I believe."

"It's the water—it would make anyone look good," laughed Liza. "My diving skills are really pretty limited."

Several others were also in the boat, resting and drinking from the thermos Kim had provided. Reverend Clarkson had brought his camera, Liza noticed, and was busy snapping photographs of his obligingly giddy crew. The sun was sliding toward the far-off mountains of the Sinai.

"Time for a few more dives," said Scott, "then you can change and rest while Kim and I prepare a dinner for you to remember!" Kim smiled wanly and steadied the boat while people tossed off towels, roused themselves and began plopping overboard with varying degrees of grace.

On her last dive, Liza found a companion. A lacy angelfish, a giant cousin of the sort often found in children's aquariums, made a graceful pass along her side before bearing sharply off. Liza watched, delighted, as it made a sweeping turn and came back, brushing her legs and lingering, curious about this newcomer to the reefs. It had a pretty, pointed face and gay golden eyes, giving it an intelligent expression. The sharp upper and lower fins of its flat body swept back to form a flaring triangle. Other trailing, threadlike fins rippled behind it. Its sides were a shimmering, iridescent black, banded with gold and scarlet.

Liza followed it for a while, weaving in and out among the coral. She touched it, and watched it swim away shyly, only to return, seemingly as glad of fellowship as she was. Then it shot off, as suddenly as it had appeared, beyond an outcropping of rippling, scarlet brain coral. Liza felt an absurd sense of loss and swam quickly after it.

At the edge of the coral she stopped abruptly, for there the reef dropped off dramatically. Below her pumping legs was perhaps another sixty feet of water. Despite its depth, it was still as clear and sunshot as the water in the shallows. She was floating above a deep, pastel canyon of coral. It shimmered and glittered hypnotically, beckoning her, and she hovered there, struggling with a quite mad urge to follow the angelfish. She felt it drawing her, like a siren, into the deeper water. Yet she needed badly to surface and fill her lungs with sweeter air. The euphoria of being underwater so long was threatening her judgment. Frantic now to retreat from the abrupt drop-off, she twisted.

Then something seized her ankles. She felt herself tugged helplessly backward. This was no gentle brush of fins. She struck blindly, her arms flailing. As she thrashed, a hand shot out and gently gripped her jaw. Her mouth became a circle of astonishment. Her hair drifted in a veil before her face, each strand floating separately. She parted it with desperate fingers, unwilling to believe her eyes.

Her first panicked thought had been that she'd encountered an unpleasantly large fish. Yet she would rather it be a shark than Christian Chase. *I'm hallucinating,* she thought. But no, as she felt his fingers grasp her shoulders she knew he was quite real.

Suddenly her chest hurt. She signaled with one hand, her entire body straining upward. Then she felt his hands circle her waist, and with a strong, scissoring motion of his long legs, he sent them both to the surface in a shower of silver.

She was dizzy from lack of oxygen. Her heart hammered, both from the shock of Christian's greeting and from her own reckless flirtation with the angelfish. Speaking was painful but her anger was stronger.

"If you think this is funny—some sort of sick joke, or a threat. . .!" She coughed and had to stop.

He laughed. "Ever since I first laid eyes on you you've been flinging either dirty looks or wild accusations at me with absolutely no provocation. Are you always so bad tempered?"

"No—I mean, I'm not bad tempered. You frightened me!"

"And for that I apologize."

"You followed me," she said. Her eyes darkened and accused. *I'm so glad to see him,* she thought, *I can't be!* Yet there it was, a sudden lifting of her heart. It fluttered, a tiny fish trapped between them. Oh God—to have him suddenly back in her life again! It was the answer to a prayer she hadn't even known she'd offered up.

"I didn't follow you," he insisted.

"What then?"

"Later," he said. "On shore perhaps. We'll talk. But not now...."

There was a tight silence. She regarded his confident face warily. His strength seemed to radiate in circles across the surface of the water and to lap at her. Why had he come, she wondered, almost desperately.

She had been in the water a long time. Her breasts were rising and falling with her labored breathing. She tilted her small pointed chin to keep it above the waves.

"Here..." he said, simply and quietly. He made a slight gesture with his upturned hands.

Argument was beyond her. Unarmored, heart and body, she laid her cheek on his shoulder and they floated easily together, supported by the warm Gulf waters. She felt the stroke of his taut thighs on hers, felt the tiny underwater currents playing across her back from the lazy motion of his arms.

It was all so slow, so dizzyingly sensuous. Her limbs felt pleasantly heavy and languid. She was suffused by an unaccountable happiness. If only she didn't have to think! There were so many questions, questions that got in the way. She dragged her head from his shoulder with grim determination.

"You haven't just materialized, Christian—unless,

like one of the street merchants I ran into back in Aqaba, you claim that magic lamps exist. I hope you've got a more convincing sales pitch than he had.''

He tossed a dripping lock of hair off his brow and grinned. ''I concede that I deliberately followed you into the water, if that's what you mean. It wasn't my first choice as a spot to renew our friendship—although I must say it's turned out better than I thought it would.''

His eyes crinkled in that way they had and he smiled in the lopsided manner that she realized with a start she knew by heart. She pulled away from him as if his nearness burned her and she began to support herself in the water, making slow figure eights with her arms. ''*I* see. So now the truth comes out—but as always, so reluctantly, Christian,'' she said, desperately trying to hide her profound unease.

''Still so dreadfully volatile,'' he chided, his voice coolly amused, so detached and British. And to forestall another sputter of outrage he went on quickly, ''I would have spoken to you on the beach but before I could get to you, you were scooped up like some rare seashell by that gaggle of tourists.''

''They're very nice people,'' she shot out defensively, ''and they know I'm here, by the way, in case—''

''In case what, my dear?''

''Just in case, that's all.'' She twisted about suddenly, remembering the boat. It took longer than she'd hoped to find it. It had receded to a sliver on the horizon, apparent only because of the flash of Kim's crimson bikini.

"You've ventured rather far," he reproached, his eyes tracking her glance.

"No problem," she said flippantly.

"It might have been, if you'd been foolish enough to venture any farther over that reef. You're every bit as graceful underwater as the angelfish you were performing that sensual water ballet with, but I suspect you lack its natural ability. You need scuba gear to explore those cliffs—the undertow is treacherous, you know."

"I do know!" she snapped, but nonetheless increased her slow movement toward shore. "You were there—watching me—all that time?"

"Watching *over* you might be a more generous way of putting it," he retorted.

"And Scott said no sharks get into this bay," she muttered.

"Scott?"

"A friend," she replied, thinking it wouldn't hurt to remind this man there were people out there who'd notice her absence—perhaps Christian hadn't counted on that. But what had he counted on? It was almost as if he had known she would be there. Surely that was impossible!

She turned from her back onto her side, resolved to get to the beach as soon as possible. He'd promised her an explanation then, hadn't he? As she extended herself to kick away, the strap of her swimsuit slid over her shoulder and the plunging neckline fell open. She made a grab at the errant straps but succeeded only in getting a mouthful of water.

"Don't!" Christian said sharply. More quietly, he

added, "You're beautiful. In New York...that night...you were carved from ivory. Here, in this Arab light, you're molten amber...."

With one hand cupped under her chin, he supported her head. That gentle touch seemed command enough. For a brief moment, her cheeks took fire. Then, the desire to hide her nakedness deserted her utterly. Some barrier fell from between them and was swept away by the water. Water that freed her, bore her up, unleashed something deep inside her. Her arms inscribed a wide, graceful arc and she allowed him to look at her with unmasked appetite.

Hesitantly, she searched his face. His eyes were so blue. Bluer than the waters of Aqaba. She wanted to fall into them, to float forever in his mind's eye. It was a sweet pain, a pain that held him at its very center, yet it was outweighed by an inexpressible joy.

Before—with Penn—she'd existed in a state of self-conscious awareness of their growing intimacy. Even lost in his arms, she never quite gave up her mind's control over her body. She felt his need, and calculated her response. But this was different. With Christian there were no artifical stages, no weighing of right and wrong. Instinct alone ruled her mind, her body, and as his lips parted she felt her entire being rush toward him. She could not warn this away. She was a victim of his eyes, of the intense expression she saw there.

"Talk to me, Liza," he whispered. "Tell me what you're feeling. I want to know. Your words excite me...."

"I...I can't," she breathed. "Don't blame me if I can't be everything you want me to be."

"Liza, I don't blame you for anything. You excite me. Don't you know that?"

"Yes," she whispered against his ear. "But this... you...none of this relates to my life. It's a fairy tale. It's separate. How can I make any sense out of what you do to me?"

In answer he drew both hands down her neck and shoulders and slowly brought them under her breasts. Powerless to resist his knowing caress, she felt herself responding, the soft, smooth skin sensitive to his slowly circling palms. When his arms opened to gather her in, she pressed closer, willingly. Her nipples grazed the golden hair on his chest and went instantly, achingly erect. She shuddered and closed her eyes. Her hair floated on the water, cloaking their shoulders.

As his embrace tightened on her, they slipped beneath the water into a world of perfect silence and mystery. His hands slid down her back, and firmly, longingly, drew her to him. She felt his hard, male need of her in a way that stunned her. His lips found hers and she felt herself opening to him, as fluid as that gentle motion of the anemones swaying beneath their circling legs. He cradled the backs of her thighs with his strong hands, guiding them into place around his waist.

She locked herself there in an act of uninhibited need, her heart as tremulous as the sunlight that spangled the waves. They moved in a tender struggle, with all the grace granted by their weightlessness. Her fingers threaded desperately through his hair, tangling with the drifting strands as she pressed his head to her breast. His lips, moving over her nipples, set up answering spasms deep within her, till at last they broke the surface and drew long, shuddering breaths.

The waves rippling shoreward made their clinging bodies rise and fall, and they drifted on that hypnotic beat, reveling in their freedom, exulting in their ability to move against each other without restraint.

In that primitive, timeless medium, Liza felt more alive than she had dreamed possible. The sea had dissolved all the boundaries, and she scarcely knew which movement was hers and which his.

He cupped her chin in a tender grasp and said huskily, "Liza—you're so beautiful! We could finish what we began in New York. You want that...tell me you want that."

She averted her face, not wanting to admit it, though she knew he spoke the truth.

"Say it," he coaxed, "I want to hear you say it."

"You know I do, Christian...." The words of admission were out, for his hands were everywhere on her and his understanding of her too powerful.

Yet her woman's hands held power too, and that knowledge burned white hot within her. She stared at him, her own eyes as intense as the fiery blue ones that met her gaze. Slowly, with deliberation, she drew her hands down his lean torso and the flat of his stomach. Her thumbs made two slow arcs beneath the thin fabric of his swimsuit. The sharp sound of his breath being drawn through clenched teeth sent heat flowing through her limbs.

A sudden, strong swell pulled her from him. Christian clutched at her hand and said, his voice urgent and hoarse, "Wrap your legs about me again. Liza...please!"

The need in his voice, the unexpected tenderness and pleading destroyed her. With a moan she arched herself toward him and twined about him convulsively. His eyes glittered with a male triumph he didn't attempt to conceal and she felt his hands tighten on her hips as he guided her into position. "Oh, Liza... do you have any idea what you do to me? Hang on to me, hang on!"

She heard his short, low moans with delight, her own soft cries mingling with his. It took a long time, then, for a different sound to penetrate her consciousness. It was another voice—high, insistent, distant—calling her name. She resisted its intrusion but finally, reluctantly, drew her mouth away from Christian's and listened. She blinked and felt the cruel blow of the Arab sun shatter the spell she'd been under.

"Kim!" she cried with a small groan.

She heard Christian swear softly. "Who's that— one of those tourists?" he muttered.

"In the boat over there," she nodded. "Has she spotted us?"

He shook back his wet hair. A muscle was working angrily at the side of his jaw. "I can't tell." He passed his thumbs over Liza's cheeks, pushing aside the damp tendrils that clung there. "Liza...."

"We'll have to go back," she said unsteadily. "And...and maybe it's just as well."

He stared at her. Liza couldn't tell whether he was angry. . . puzzled—or calculating? But she did know that the magic moment had been destroyed. Brutally and totally. She was suddenly, sickeningly aware of people, voices, laughter, the raucous intrusion of a motorboat somewhere nearby.

Her passion had betrayed her again and the real reason Christian Chase was in the Sinai was still not clear to her. She yanked up the straps of her swimsuit. Her nakedness was no longer joyful but dangerous.

"You look tired, Liza," Christian said with sudden gravity. "Head back to shore now."

She would have preferred to kick away from him out into the Gulf, like a mermaid, free and graceful. But she knew he was right. She was suddenly deathly tired. She began a sensible steady crawl toward the beach, Christian hovering protectively at her shoulder.

The boat, too, was heading in for the day and as they passed close to it, Liza heard Kim's voice once again. "Do you want a lift?" she shouted. "Are you tired?"

The girl was kneeling on one of the rough wooden seats, her thighs braced against the pitching of the boat. Her silhouette against the darkening mountains was remarkable.

Liza, weighing her own strength against the already crowded boat, declined. "I can make it!" she called back. "Thanks—see you on shore!"

Kim hesitated a long time, her eyes not leaving Christian. "All right," she returned. "Be careful."

"You were right," said Christian from somewhere behind her.

"About what?" said Liza, stroking doggedly.

"The tourists you met. They're very nice—very thoughtful."

Liza, swimming now with real determination, thought: *You don't fool me, Christian Chase. It's Kim you think is very nice. And not because she's thoughtful.*

On shore, Liza scuffed through the sand, wringing out her hair, and sank to the sand in the shadow of a palm. Christian followed, unasked, and sprawled beside her, arms flung over his head, eyes closed. They were both tired. Neither of them spoke. Liza hugged her knees, protecting the breasts she had let him cup in his palms. She watched him, sideways, the first time she'd been free to study him without having to feign indifference or dodge those sardonic eyes.

His body was exceptionally trim, long through the thighs and torso, and his muscles well-defined. Was he a runner, perhaps? He had that sort of chest, broad beneath the thick tangle of fair hair.

Her eye was drawn to the pale line running along the top of his bathing suit, the single place that did not glow with a healthy burnish of tan. She looked down at her own arms, now brushed with bright pink, and felt the heat of an impending sunburn. Obviously Christian Chase did not spend all his time in the dark halls of museums, or even the candlelit salons of the wealthy.

She had a sudden, unbidden image of his lying like this beside some obliging woman, the type quite desperate for the companionship of a man so suitable in so many ways. Her gaze made a slow journey from the flat of his stomach to the point where his loins met the taut muscle of his thighs—as the gaze of how many women had? She jerked her head away and stared across the Gulf, and in her mind's eye past the pink hills of Arabia, around the world to Penn.

"You can't keep doing this, Christian," she said, quietly. "Following me, showing up wherever I am."

"Is that what I'm doing?" he asked, his eyes still closed. "I should have thought it was the other way around."

Her head whipped around. "Are you implying that *I* followed *you* here?"

"Didn't you?" His voice was mock-innocent. He turned on his side and looked at her, blue eyes flashing with irony.

"You know I didn't!" she snapped.

"I *beg* your pardon, I know no such thing."

How had he managed to twist everything so quickly? "I had no idea you were here," she huffed. "What a ridiculous idea—that I would travel halfway around the world and then skulk about some dusty, Middle Eastern town lying in wait for you!"

He shrugged, as if her motives were of no concern to him. "Isn't it equally preposterous to think I'd go to such lengths to follow you?"

She turned away, angry, for she had no answer. Or at least no quick, clever reply that would wipe the smugness from a mouth that said so much, even silent.

She started again. A rational, cool presentation of

the facts, she cautioned herself. "You confessed out there," she began, with a nod to the surf, "that you saw me on the beach and followed me into the water—"

"Confessed! You *are* conducting an inquisition, aren't you? Oh, well, if it pleases you—yes, that much is true. But I was hardly stalking you. As it turned out, it's probably lucky for you that I did find you, given your rash conduct on the reef. You might keep that in mind while you're being so critical of me."

She let that pass. "How long have you been following me?"

He sighed, picking out his words slowly. "I was having a drink on the terrace of one of the hotels. I saw you drive up with two young Arab men in a truck—who were they, by the way?"

"Guides," she informed him, "but that's not your concern."

He raised an eyebrow. "I see. And if you need guides, then the logical conclusion—in this part of the world, anyway—is that you're headed inland."

She regarded him gravely over the curve of her shoulder, reluctant to tell him anything. Yet what could be the harm? There appeared to be little she could keep from him, in any event. Perhaps being direct was the only way to deal with his smiling aggression. "That's right," she replied clearly. She lay back, her arms behind her head. "I'm going to St. Catherine's. But I suspect you already know that."

"Anyone could have guessed it, of course," he said, as if modestly rejecting a compliment.

"That's not an answer," she shot back.

His face was just above hers, and he was still faintly smiling. "Something's happened," he stated. "A little crack of doubt has appeared in that monumental certainty you had about the cross." There was triumph in his tone, as if a difficult pupil had finally got her lesson straight. Liza resented it bitterly.

Yes, she thought. *Oh, yes, something happened! On a perfectly marvelous fall day all bright and golden and full of promise I lied and fought with the man I love because of a shabby secret about you!*

"You're wrong," she told him in her best curator's voice. "If anything, I believe even more strongly it is Constantine's Cross. I'm just tying up loose ends— you know the museum's standards."

He looked at her for a long moment, long enough for her own gaze to waver. "And what about your friend's. . . are his as high as yours?"

"If you mean Mr. Livsay, you may assume his standards exceed any *you* may be accustomed to." She heard the defensive primness and regretted it— unless, of course, it helped deflate this man's insufferable ego. She turned onto her stomach and began to scoop and pour sand through her slender fingers.

"And what was his reaction to this little expedition of yours?"

"Oh, he raged and threw glasses and shattered mirrors at Antoine's, and we've vowed never to see each other again," she replied airily. For once, Christian looked unsure of what to believe.

She was quick to take advantage of this rare lapse.

She stopped playing with the sand and raked her still-damp hair off her forehead. "You know, you're very good at questions, Christian, but not nearly so good at answers—or perhaps you're *too* good."

"You've lost me, my dear," he replied evenly.

"I doubt it—I mean, you're a master of giving answers that reveal absolutely nothing. It's a kind of game with you, isn't it? And I, frankly, am sick of it."

"Well, by all means, Liza—let's stop playing games with each other." And he began to reach for her. Or at least she thought he did.

She sat up quickly, troubled violet eyes searching his. "Why *are* you here, Christian? What is it you want?"

He gestured carelessly toward the beach. "Perhaps I'm just like one of those young people—without a real purpose, here simply to enjoy the many pleasures of this splendid place...."

"Oh, spare me!" The taut line of her patience snapped. She began to scramble to her knees, but his hand caught her wrist, upsetting her balance and she was beside him again, her stomach pressed to his, their thighs touching. This time, though, what shot through her was not the pleasure his nearness had lately brought her, but anger, clear and bright.

She breathed hard and deeply, knowing it was purposeless to struggle. "I could scream—"

"You could, but you won't. It's not your style. That much I've learned about you."

"Have you also learned that I loathe deceit? You lie and you lie and you lie to me! I know it!"

"Then know this too—what you imagine I want from you is not the tenth of it. What I could have done to you out there—"

"Shut up!"

He fell silent, watching her. "All right...all right," he said finally. "But perhaps a woman of your type should be careful with the questions she asks. And of whom she asks them. It would avoid disillusionment." Casually he abandoned her and began to brush sand off his body. He had shifted the balance—as always, to his own advantage.

"That's it? That's all you have to say for yourself? But what about the cross?"

He seemed weary, or perhaps just bored. "Look, I'm sure it hasn't strained your intelligence to guess that I'm here for the same reason you are. Wasn't it your noble Penn who said so solemnly he wanted the cross to belong to the public? Well, I'm the public. I'm curious. That's all the justification I need or intend to give."

She had hoped to maneuver him into some damning admission. Now, his nerveless reply deflated her. She stared at him blankly. "Can you really have disclosed your purpose so calmly?"

"You're always thinking in terms of confession. It's one of the few objectionable turns of mind you have, Liza. You know, you and Penn may own the cross—or whatever cozy arrangement it is you've worked out between you—but you didn't purchase exclusive rights to an interest in it."

Liza flushed deeply, yet she couldn't allow him to overwhelm her so easily. "You wouldn't come here just to indulge your curiosity,'' she persisted. "That's a very costly whim!''

His nostrils flared with faint disdain. "You concern yourself too much with money.''

"Oh, no!'' she cried. "Money isn't *my* obsession.''

"Perhaps it just rubbed off on you, unbeknownst, from Penn.''

"And perhaps it just galls you to see another man with his money and family intact!''

"Don't push me, Liza,'' he warned, his voice low. And then, as if nothing at all had passed between them, he remarked, "Your arms are chilled. It gets very cold in the desert at night. Perhaps you didn't know that. Where are your clothes?''

"The group! I forgot all about them.'' She scrambled to her feet and peered down the beach. The light was fading, or shifting rather, washing everything with a bronzed pink. How long had they been lying there? And dear Mrs. Pepper on her shark watch— what had she seen through those binoculars? No impression except the wrong one could have been gained there.

CHAPTER SEVEN

THE BOAT had been pulled back onto the shore. Liza could see people, dressed now, reassembling under the palms. She had told them she was traveling alone. Somehow she'd have to let it drop—casually, of course—that she'd run across a friend. Friend! Wasn't *that* a joke. But she couldn't bear to think of their assuming she'd allowed a strange man to pick her up. They'd been so kind, so unquestioning in their acceptance of her. It was a small thing, perhaps, but it mattered to her.

She hurried away, half skipping, without a word of explanation or goodbye to Christian. He could do as he liked, she thought. She didn't much care.

"Here's our girl now!" boomed Lyn Parsons, shattering her hopes of slipping into their midst unobtrusively.

Kim glanced at her sideways. She was fussing with some food hampers. "Enjoy your swim?"

Liza managed a smile. "Yes, yes I did! I wonder... I was looking for my things...."

"There," said Kim. Her hand indicated a heap of clothes on one of the chairs, but her eyes were fixed on a point somewhere over Liza's shoulder. She began to smile then turned her large blue eyes expectantly to Liza.

Liza turned. Christian—of all of the nerve! The glance she shot him was venomous, the smile he returned pure sweetness. She grabbed her clothes and hugged them to her like a shield.

"Well!" she said with false cheer. "Apparently the Sinai is not to be outdone by Paris as a place to watch the whole world pass by. I've run into someone I know from New York, a...colleague."

There were various exclamations of pleasure and many references to the size of the world, after which Liza, with the thinnest of smiles, introduced Christian, stumbling over most of the names and receiving good-natured assistance. She saw the puzzled reserve that had greeted her melt into relieved geniality. So they *had* seen, she realized.

"Are you *both* curators, then?" asked Lyn. "It's funny to go all your life without meeting even one, only to meet two in a day. And here of all places."

"I'm sorry to disappoint you, Mr. Parsons," Christian replied, "but I lack a title as impressive as Liza's. I'm just a dealer. I work for myself." He made it sound like nothing.

"But you're not a New Yorker, surely. Not with that beautiful accent!" enthused Cora.

"No, I'm not," said Christian politely. "I'm a Londoner to the core, although I'm frequently in New York on business."

"You must cross paths with Liza a lot, then," Kim put in, looking up. She was about to spread a large checked tablecloth over the sand.

Christian seemed to hesitate before replying, and Liza wondered if he was taking time to admire the exceedingly attractive picture Kim made with her long, corn-silk hair lifting and falling softly about her shoulders in the wind. "Lately, it's been often enough," he said finally. "Our tastes are quite similar—we both have a passion for Renoir, for example." He smiled over at Liza with pure spite.

"Oh, I do think it's wonderful to have a love like that in common!" said Cora, and Liza smiled grimly at the woman's blackly humorous conclusion. Yet she began to relax, a small burden lifted. If nothing else, she had managed a convincing alibi for coming back from the sea with this man.

It was Reverend Clarkson, with his natural kindness, who said the obvious, that Christian should stay and round out the party. And having brought him into their midst, how could Liza now declare him unwelcome? Yet it was absurd to think of his joining the simple beach party of a group of unsophisticated tourists. Christian traveled, certainly. And presumably "summered" and "wintered" as well. But he was never anything as tacky as a tourist. His acceptance stunned her.

She strode away with as hurried a stride as her small legs could manage and jerked aside the canvas flap of the cabana. It was bad enough that he had intruded on her without invitation or apology. But to inflict himself on these unsuspecting people?

Oil and water, they'd be, she thought, stripping off her damp suit with a single, angry yank. Right now they no doubt found him charming. Well, they'd realize soon enough what a snobbish, materialistic.... She paused in toweling sand off her body. A twitch of a smile appeared at the corner of her mouth. *Let him stay!* she thought. Let him show himself for what he was. Let him find himself, just once, among people with whom his values held no sway. She pulled on her panties quickly. So long as he didn't hurt anyone with his airs—then, of course, bad tempered would be the worst thing he'd be able to call her.

She brushed her hair till it hung straight and shining, and tucked it behind her ears. She slipped into a cool white T-shirt and beige cotton pants, then knotted a sweater of oatmeal cashmere around her neck. In that odd light just before dusk her delicate skin lost the raw look and took on a pleasing sheen of deep apricot across her nose and cheekbones and along her arms. She finished with a flick of mascara, some lip gloss and gold hoop earrings. Feeling neat and fresh, she presently discovered herself almost eager to get back.

She found Christian deep in the preparation of lobster tails, a bottle of the local Stella beer in his hand. He, too, had managed to change, this time into tan pants and a crisp blue cotton shirt, open at the neck. Of course, she thought crossly, he would know all about fixing lobster, and was no doubt afraid poor Scott would ruin them.

But Scott seemed anything but offended. To the contrary, he, in his pale jeans and tattered sweatshirt, was hamming it up outrageously for everyone. He had added a second bandanna to his costume, this one bound about his calf—a bicycling custom, she guessed, that he had found too rakish to abandon. She noticed a hand-stitched appliqué, a bright rainbow, holding the seat of his pants together and wondered idly if Kim also counted needlework among her many talents.

It was a magnificent evening. In front of them, toward the unseen shores of Arabia, the sky had deepened, merging with the indigo of the Gulf waters. The lights of the Arab fishing boats had begun to wink and bob. Behind them, the sunset had stained the clouds bloodred and set jagged black mountains against an orange sky. The air was still soft and spice-laden. Scott had started a fire, one of several beginning to dot the beach as bathers drew close against the night.

"Let me help!" said Liza.

Kim had slid herself into a zipper-front jump suit, and very little else, in a rather shocking shade of apple green that made her tan even more remarkable. She was setting out the food and handed Liza, who felt like a wraith next to her, a tangle of napkins and cutlery to sort.

"Your Mr. Chase certainly seems quite a charmer," Kim commented.

"He is. I've often thought he could make a living simply by being captivating," Liza said breezily. And no doubt does, she added silently.

"You work together, is that right?"

"Oh, no. We have some professional matters in common, that's all."

"Too bad," consoled Kim.

"You think so?" She shrugged. "I suppose some people might say that, seeing him now." She glanced over at the fire where he was enchanting the ladies with a steady stream of flattering nonsense. She quickly drew Kim away from the lure, saying, "This looks marvelous. What have you got in all these bowls?"

Kim paused, set her hands on her trim hips and laughed. "Don't ask me the Arab names—really, I think it's all some variation on chick-peas and tahini—that ground-up sesame seed stuff. And this funny looking mush is eggplant mixed up with garlic and olive oil. It tastes a whole lot better than it looks."

"I suppose you scoop it up with this round bread," Liza said questioningly.

"Oh, yes—there's always pita for dipping with an Arab meal. I also got some lamb, in case anyone can't eat lobster. They do it up really well here. The marinade's got cinnamon or something in it, and they grill it over charcoal."

"I really admire you, Kim. This is an awful lot of work."

"Oh, it's not like this every night, believe me. Besides, I buy most of this from the motel restaurant. But we do try to make this part of the tour a little special. Nuweiba's such a gorgeous setting and this is the last time we'll really be able to provide them with a proper meal. Once we're in the Sinai we'll be roughing it and the food will be dreary. Tinned, dried—you know the kind."

Scott, with a spoon and tin can, chimed the group in to dinner. They drew their deck chairs into a rough circle and, with appetites built by salt air and exercise, set themselves to heaped plates. Christian, in charge of spearing the curled lobster tails from the pot, retrieved one and set it on a plate.

He handed it to Liza. "Say thank you," he admonished gently. "And do smile just a little. What will people think if you continue to scowl at me— even though, as the saying goes, you're just as pretty when angry."

"Thank you," she said icily.

"I hope you enjoy it."

"I'm sure I'll love it," she returned so fiercely that Scott, who had come up behind them, silent on the sand, almost dropped a very large bowl of salad.

Kim, licking her fingers with sensuous pleasure after picking apart her lobster, said cheerfully, "I get the impression you know the Middle East, Christian."

"Some of it," he acknowledged. "I've been on the odd buying trip over the years. A while back I got as far south as Sharm el Sheikh by way of Nuweiba. And before that, farther inland where I got to know a Bedouin clan—a small adventure of my youth."

"Youth!" cried Kim. You're not exactly ancient now," she teased.

Christian inclined his head. "Ah, but I feel it next to someone like you, Kimberley. Even so, I'm sure your knowledge of the East would put me to shame."

Kim giggled with a kind of liquid gaiety. She was just young enough to get away with it, Liza thought. With a start, she wondered just when had she experienced that heartbeat that moved her from girl to woman. It was long ago surely, for hadn't Penn been in her life, hadn't she been paying bills and signing leases and performing all those other tasks of card-carrying adulthood for ages and ages? Yet not until now, watching Christian with this lovely but younger child-woman curled at his knee, had she really felt old.

Christian must have been amusing, for she heard that rippling laughter again. With rancor, she surveyed his languid body, low in his chair. She slouched herself, crossing her slender ankles before her, and extended her lower lip in a soft pout. Why then did she feel instinctively that Kim was light-years older?

She watched the girl tug at a bottle of wine as Christian, grimacing, yanked at its recalcitrant cork. It gave suddenly, splashing them both, and Kim emitted a pretty shriek. In some way, Liza thought, Kim *was* older. She knew men. She knew them the way a sculptor knows the moist clay beneath her fingers. But there was still a void in Liza's life. How was it possible to feel both old and innocent?

The shadow of an arm suddenly fell across her lap. Christian was offering her a glass of wine. She said, under her breath, "You're shameless—"

"I'm happy," he corrected. "Of course, if you aren't enjoying the party, I suppose you could leave."

"*I* could leave?" she said in dignified fury.

"You don't think I should go just because you've been seized with the sulks, do you? I mean, you've only got a prior claim on their hospitality of what—an hour?"

She leaned forward and said sweetly, "Forget it. I'm staying. You couldn't run me out of an earthquake."

The wine was local and barely drinkable. But it seemed more appropriate there than any rare French vintage would have been. And it had, after the first, raw swallow, its intended effect. By degrees Liza felt fortified against the dropping temperature and began to relax.

Voices were raised and Liza cast an anxious glance to the men on the other side of the fire. Lyn Parsons was delivering an indignant recital of the woes of owning a business—everything from government paperwork to unreliable help. Christian was agreeing and Liza listened tensely for any hint of mockery or condescension.

It was a most unlikely group: an eccentric young man, a gentle clergyman, an unpolished workingman, a fallen aristocrat. Some spoke with a twang, taking liberties with the language, one with Oxford-educated correctness. Almost all were dressed modestly, one wore gently frayed but nonetheless "good" clothes. Yet the offense Liza feared Christian would give was noticeably absent. They had found their levelers, their common denominators.

Scott, cross-legged as he poked at the fire, talked of his plans to build up his business. "We'd like a whole fleet of buses," he was saying, "and specialized tours—desert, recreational, Bible, archaeological. We could even tie them in with lectures at one of the universities. Or lessons in scuba diving. There's really no limit, is there, Kim?"

Liza noted that Kim's agreement was reluctant. "This is hardly the most politically stable area in the world," she cautioned.

"But that's always true where the opportunities are wide open!" declared Scott. "How many places are left in the world where you can practically pioneer?"

"Brazil, parts of Africa, perhaps..." Reverend Clarkson offered, frowning thoughtfully. But Kim shuddered visibly, indicating that this represented the extent to which she was willing to rough it.

"What about home? Don't you feel the urge to go back?" asked Mrs. Pepper, looking puzzled and slightly worried.

At this both young people exchanged glances and Liza wondered what they had left behind when they fled to Europe after college. Perhaps there had been strained relationships with parents. "I guess," said Scott finally, "we've made a real commitment here. There just won't be the time or the money for trips home. Not for a while, anyway."

"And you, Mr. Chase," asked Cora, "do you keep a home somewhere or do you live out of a suitcase?"

"I do have a house, as a matter of fact, although I get to visit it a good deal less than I'd like. It's out in the country, a pretty place really. It's called Hawthorne Park, for the obvious reason."

Cora put down her plate and frowned. "Hawthorne Park...now why should that ring a bell with me?" She turned to her husband who merely shrugged. He had long since given up following his wife's mind along its many detours.

"Maybe you ran across it on a trip," Scott suggested.

"No, no, we've never been to England," Cora murmured now looking thoroughly exasperated. "Rhododendrons!" she cried abruptly with that expression of intense relief that comes when one is finally released from the torment of not remembering.

"Rhododendrons?" Lyn echoed. "What on earth have they to do with Mr. Chase's house?"

"They're my favorite flowers," she replied, to no one's enlightenment. "You know, they grow wild in the mountains around where we live. In the spring, the hills turn bright pink with them. Last year when I came across an article in a British magazine about a house that had a beautiful collection of rhododendrons, I clipped it out. I'm sure it was called Hawthorne Park!"

Christian nodded. "It's quite possible. There have been articles from time to time. Rhododendrons were something of a speciality of my great-grandfather's. Or was it my great-great-grandfather? Anyway, he established the beds. The gardens are now my sister-in-law Jane's special province. She has quite a marvelous hand with them."

"But—that place was like a palace!" cried Cora. She looked around at the others. "No kidding, it looked just like Buckingham Palace except smaller, which is still saying a lot."

Christian laughed gently. "Well, I don't know about that. It's really a great, drafty stone monster of a place, although not without charm, I suppose."

"How much land do you have?" asked Mrs. Pepper, explaining that she herself had farmed with her late husband for almost fifty years.

"I'm not sure...a few thousand acres perhaps. Some in forest, some in pasture or crops—not more than a dozen are gardened formally."

"Golly!" said Scott, expressing the general feeling.

Christian frowned. "I'm afraid it's an awful bother to maintain, but I'm rather stuck with it."

"How long have you had it?" Cora asked, still feeling the glow of having made this discovery.

"It's been in my family for about three hundred years," Christian told her. Suddenly he looked less sure of himself. Perhaps he wanted to change the subject but no one was inclined to let him, least of all Liza.

Her eyes were large and sweetly sympathetic. "How dreadful for you to have shoulder such a burden. Surely you have help, don't you?"

He looked over at her sharply. "Yes. My brother Alister lives there with his suitably large and active family. I'm afraid I'm reduced to an infrequent visitor."

"That must be sad for all of you," she said. She smiled with gentle malice.

"It is as a matter of fact."

"Still, I suppose having your brother there is convenient. It frees you for your many other activities...." He looked, she thought, as if he wanted to slap her. She decided she was enjoying herself after all.

"If I remember my British history," said Reverend Clarkson, bringing his fingertips together thoughtfully, "the reason you have these estates left in Britain is your strong tradition of primogeniture—"

"What's *that*?" demanded Kim in her blunt manner.

"It's a peculiarly British system whereby the oldest son of a noble family inherits everything, from the title to the last spoon. The rest of the children sink or swim according to the generosity of that first son. Am I right, Mr. Chase?"

Generosity, thought Liza. Could she tell them a thing or two! And while she reflected on those things, Kim pounced.

"Title! You mean you not only inherited an estate but a title as well?"

Christian gave a small twitch of a smile. "Yes, I'm afraid I've assumed that bother also."

Kim hugged her slender shoulders as if the very thought made her shiver. "So what is it—what sort of a title goes with Hawthorne Park?"

Christian shifted in his seat. "Viscount," he said.

Lyn Parsons knit his brow. "So that makes you what?"

"It makes me Lord Chase," he replied. He raised an admonishing hand. "But I shall be very angry if anyone calls me that. It would make me uncomfortable just when I'm having such a good time."

Liza stared at him, the interloper, the destroyer of her happiness, the marauder of her body. She stared at the charming stranger, the teller of amusing tales, the doer of flattering kindness to elderly ladies. She stared at this known liar and probable pirate. And at the man who was now, too, Lord Chase. The firelight softened the angularity of his cheekbones and he was tending more to handsome than homely. Her mind was a beautiful carousel with twinkling violet lights and raven-maned horses going around and around.

She shook back her dark hair, then stood shakily. "I'm afraid I have to go," she announced, just managing a smile. "I'm meeting my guides here so early in the morning. . . ."

"Liza—I'm afraid you're not," said Christian authoritatively.

"What are you talking about? Of course I am." She began to gather her things.

There was an attentive silence around the fire. "One question first," he said softly. "Your suitcase—where is it?"

"At the hostel. In the locker—Christian, why are you asking me this?"

"I put off telling you this because it's been such a pleasant evening, but now I suppose I must. I suppose, too, it's futile to ask you not to accuse me of treating you like some helpless woman, but earlier I made some inquiries. I'm very much afraid, Liza, that you've been deserted."

She looked at him blankly. "Deserted? What are you talking about?"

"Your guides—they've gone." He saw the blood drain from her face and said, "Apparently they weren't from a tribe around St. Catherine's. They come from a place down the coast, near Dahab. They never intended to bring you any farther than this. I take it," he added, "that you paid them in advance?"

"I did. I never thought that...." Her voice trailed off miserably.

"That was a mistake, of course. If you hadn't, perhaps they'd have taken you the rest of the way. Or at least just charged you for coming this far. But the temptation, apparently, was just too much. I won't embarrass you by asking what you agreed to pay. It was probably far above the going rate for this type of thing."

She didn't volunteer the information. She'd known from the beginning that it was. "I suppose I'm lucky I have my suitcase," she said bitterly.

"Yes," he said gravely, "I think you are."

"Are you sure? I mean, are you absolutely sure? They talked about going to visit some relatives tonight...."

"I'm sure," he said in a tone that left no room for doubt.

She sank heavily onto the chair. She was disgusted, more with herself than with the two young men. "I should have *known* it was too easy. One of them came to me when I was really discouraged and I thought then it was too good to be true. And, of course, it was. How could I have been so naive!"

"Don't be so hard on yourself, Liza," soothed Scott. "I'm sure their story seemed straight at the time."

"He told me he was a cousin of the desk clerk at the hotel. It seemed like a good enough reference. He probably lied about that, too." She pressed her fingertips wearily to her temples. "So I'm right back where I started."

Kim and Scott exchanged quick, questioning glances. "All our seats are taken," said Kim, "or you could go with us, of course."

"Look, please don't worry about this," Liza said quickly. "I've imposed on you enough already."

Kim turned to Scott. "Can you think of anyone?"

"Not off the top of my head. But don't get upset, Liza. We're certainly not about to desert you. I know a few people here—we'll come up with something."

"I think," Christian interjected calmly into the anxious murmurings, "we're overlooking the obvious solution. Liza can simply come with me."

Liza lifted her eyes slowly. A new light seemed to have fallen on the issue of the vanished guides.

"Well, then!" said Reverend Clarkson, greatly relieved. "There's the perfect answer. We'll all rest easier knowing you're in good hands, dear."

She excused herself a short while later and wandered off alone. Trapped, she thought, by her own hand, by her own eagerness to protect her reputation in front of these people. What reason could she possibly give that would sound halfway sane?

She had wandered toward the shore, weary of the effort of keeping up a false front. She stopped at the spot where a ribbon of silver trailed from the moon across the inky water to her feet.

Christian Chase was not the issue, she told herself

sternly. Her goal was very clear. Or should be—go to the monastery, find out what she could and go home. The fight with Penn, Christian's supposed "curiosity" about the cross—and certainly her unexpected and unwelcome physical attraction to him were all irrelevant. Should she not be glad he was here to help her?

When she felt the arms come around her she stiffened and lifted her chin but didn't turn. She knew who it was, though his fingers barely touched her. Gently he untied the sweater from around her neck and held it for her to put on.

"Where are you staying tonight?" His voice was low.

She suppressed a small shiver and slipped her arms into the sleeves. "At the youth hostel. . .down at the end of the road." He made some short, muffled sound and she said quickly, "It's fine—it has an adequate bed, towels, a view of the water, even."

"And gray sheets, sand on the floor, and things you'd rather not know about crawling around the corners," he added. "You'll take my room at the hotel."

She turned around and found him disturbingly close. "I can't—"

"It's not what you think—I'll find somewhere else."

"But there is nothing. I checked everywhere."

He shrugged. "I can stay on the beach if need be. I won't lack company."

She began to protest again but he cut her off. With strained patience he said, "Don't get me wrong—

arguing with you has become a delightful pastime, but it is getting late and I'm tired. Why don't I just admit right now that you're a very brave and resourceful young woman and you would never take advantage of me? That said, let's be sensible and agree that the best place for you tonight is in the hotel. You prove nothing by offering yourself up as a midnight snack to an army of bedbugs.'' As if the matter was settled, he told her how she could reach the hotel.

She averted her eyes, listening, her lashes lowered. "All right," she agreed.

He sighed, tipping his head back. "Something's still wrong. Why don't you just say it and be done with it? We have a long trip ahead of us tomorrow and I'd rather not spend it in frigid silence."

Her chin lifted defiantly. "I haven't said yet I'd go—you put forward the motion, Reverend Clarkson seconded it and a dozen people voted yes. But I wasn't one of them. No one seemed to notice that!"

He waited.

She crossed her arms before her, then hurled the accusation at him. "I think you had something to do with the guides' deserting me. I think you paid them to do it."

His lips went thin with anger and she drew back a little. "So," he said, "we're back to that, are we? More accusations and melodrama."

"It's the most convincing explanation I've had for anything that's happened in the past few weeks!" she bristled.

"Look," he rapped out, "I saw you drive up with

two strange men, which seemed like a damn stupid thing for you to do. I made inquiries out of concern for your safety. I have, if you recall, some experience in these matters—''

She was shaking her dark head. ''I don't think I'm that hopeless a judge of character. My instincts would have prevented me from going off with a couple of cutthroats. Yaser and Hussein were very proper in their treatment of me today—painfully correct, in fact. I don't think they'd have cheated me. I do think, though, that they might have been gullible enough to listen to some story concocted by a very convincing and manipulative man. And they might, I suppose, have accepted a generous tip to mute any lingering questions!''

''You're positively paranoid,'' he scoffed.

But she saw the whole scenario very clearly and it made her bold. ''Did you frighten them for good measure? Leave them in dread of some sort of scandal over a Western woman? Did you claim to be an irate husband, or better yet, my brother? Their culture would make them very vulnerable to that threat, wouldn't it?''

''We all imagine the worst when we're tired,'' he chided. ''You are tired, aren't you, Liza? A punishing trip, a vigorous swim, good food—''

''Don't patronize me!'' she said heatedly.

''And don't you be so snappish. It's unbecoming.'' He raked his fine, blond hair off his forehead. ''A young American woman in a Jordanian port town making arrangements to travel into the desert alone doesn't go unnoticed. Every crook and con man and worse was on your tail in less than an hour. You're lucky all you lost was your money." He paused, his jaw working. "Don't you *ever* think before you do anything?"

Perhaps it was the strain of travel, perhaps it was the wine she'd consumed, but suddenly stupid, uncontrollable tears were spilling down her cheeks. Seeing them, Christian seemed to relent, his small smile shatteringly sweet. Almost tenderly, he brushed her chin with a finger. "Forget I said that—I like you, Liza. In fact, I think you're terrific and I'm taking you with me."

She shrank under his touch. "I hate that," she said, her voice a bare whisper. It was becoming all too familiar. Each time he spoke, whether in anger or like this, his voice pierced her physically. Each time she flinched, expecting it to be hard and bruising, only to find his voice fell like a caress.

He gathered her hands into his and gave them a small shake. He ducked his head, trying to catch her eyes but she drew back farther and he relented— slightly.

"What has you so upset, Liza?" he asked. "What's my real crime? Tell me so that I may at least defend myself. Is it that I won the Renoir? Is it that?"

"No, of course not," she said unhappily.

"That I raised doubt about the cross? No, you thanked me for that, I remember. Is it that I'm bailing you out of a fix and it offends your sense of independence?"

She shook her head, her hair sliding across one side of her face.

"No, I thought not. Shall I tell you, then?"

"Can I stop you?"

"No, you can't. What is bothering you, Liza Downing, is that you and I went straight to the chemistry with each other. That's not unusual, you know...."

Liza inhaled sharply. "It is for me," she said in a very small voice. It sounded like a confession and she hated that.

"You're usually such a tightly controlled woman. You're threatened by anything that overwhelms you or can't be analyzed. You're not in the habit of clutching at men in darkened basements or—"

"Stop it!"

His voice was velvet, coaxing. "Shh...if it bothers you so much we'll deal with it—somehow. For now, try to think about what's important."

Her head was bent, her lips not more than an inch from the strong hands that still pinned hers to his chest. She was nursing a murderous resentment and a thunderous headache.

Suddenly he slid his hands over her shoulders and began to massage with skill. Her mind shrank from him but her body was hungry for his touch. Under his fingers her taut muscles became pliant. She was weary now and the anger began to flow out as easily as it had come.

The anger was better, she thought. It made her mind clear, her resolve strong. She lifted long lashes and gazed on his strong, aristocratic features in wonder. Her face lighted up with a dreamy smile. "There are moments...moments when I think I catch a glimpse of another Christian Chase...a man who's prepared to be tender. A man who isn't perpetually aggressive or working some angle."

"Of course—there are many sides to me," he replied, smiling down on her benignly, "and I hope you'll come to know all of them. Intimately."

"What a daunting thought!" she said archly.

"I find it infinitely exciting to think about getting to know all the Lizas." Slowly he caressed her cheek with the back of his hand, his touch warm and gentle.

"I'd love to hold you to the light like a jewel and turn you so that all the facets glint and glitter.... I care for you, Liza," he said suddenly.

That was what she dreaded most. That he might really care about her. That this man might possess the capacity for tenderness as well as passion. It would be hard to go home and get on with the business of forgetting him, although forget him she would have to.

She said, "I think you're a skilled illusionist. You can create any effect you decide will give you the desired result. You no doubt have many reasons for what you do, but caring for me isn't one of them. You'll never convince me you understand the meaning of caring for another."

"I think I already have," he said smoothly. "That's why even though your words are often hard, your eyes are soft. There's fear...but there's wanting, too."

She exhaled slowly. She felt as if he was tearing her in two. "Passion...yes, there's been that. But I could never feel for you . . . what I feel for Penn, for example.''

He flinched slightly, then quickly recovered. "I can accept that," he said. "What you feel for Penn Livsay wouldn't interest me much. It's pretty thin fare, I suspect. But what you feel for me—I'm satisfied with that. Your eyes go a wonderful, smoky violet and you tremble. It excites me tremendously. Give it a chance, Liza.''

"Give what a chance?" she flung at him. "Lust?"

He looked at her sadly, as if he believed she was determined not to understand. "An ugly word," he said softly.

"Yes," she snapped. "An ugly word, but it happens to fit!"

He shook his head slowly. "It doesn't. When there's feeling, when there's love—"

She wouldn't let him finish. "But we don't have that, do we!" she snapped, turning the knife in her heart. "But Penn and I do, and that's the point. We've got the other half of the equation.''

"Love . . . but no passion?" His tone was curious, teasing.

"Don't! Don't deliberately turn everything I say upside down, Christian! And don't insult the sort of life I've chosen to live . . . my values.''

He looked both amused and exasperated now. "I'm *not* insulting you. How can you say that? I'm trying to know you.''

"Well, you can't. Our lives are like night and day. Anyway, I don't owe you a thing, least of all my most intimate feelings.''

"Stop wishing me away, Liza," he whispered, stooping slightly to peer into her eyes. "I won't go. You can't hide from me...and you can't hide from your own feelings."

She laughed without amusement. "I'm not. Believe me, I'm not." She hesitated, weighing the risks, then admitted, "It's true...I am attracted to you. And that's fine—for you. But have you for one second wondered what happens to me when Penn finds out?"

"There's no reason why he should," he observed quietly.

There was a small rebellion brewing in her eyes. "There's *every* reason. There's honesty, for one. Without that there's nothing."

He looked distracted and drew his fingertips across the soft underside of her jaw as if deciding what to do with her. She felt twin flares of desire and anger, a soul-destroying combination for her. She was thinking of the future, of what it would be like to see another man's face whenever she looked at Penn. She could never do that.

"Don't start," she breathed. "You've got to leave me alone—you must!"

"Is that what you really want?" he demanded. "Think, Liza...think before you answer me."

She *had* thought. She'd done nothing but! Her mind had turned ceaselessly ever since she'd first laid eyes on him. She felt harassed and unhappy, and her shoulders sagged. "Christian," she pleaded, "don't do this to me! I've worked so hard—you can't know—and I've built something worthwhile and precious. But you can damage it with incredible ease. You might even destroy it. I think you've already started. If that happens, I'll never be able to fit the pieces together again. It will never be right again. Do you understand what I'm telling you?''

There was not a hint of comfort in his eyes. "No, I don't think I do. Why do you invest me with all this sinister power over your life? It takes two, you'll recall—that's what this is all about. You'll have to take the responsibility for your own life, I'm afraid, my dear.''

Her eyes flickered over his somber face, his bleak and beautiful bones. "I think I hate you," she told him. "I know I do.''

He laughed suddenly, disarming her utterly. "Marvelous! Every great love affair needs a little hatred. You know, don't you, that this is what we have here?''

"A love affair—or hatred?" she inquired acidly. She thought it a fair question.

His voice was low and set off a chain of small explosions throughout her. "Oh, Liza...my sweet, fiery Liza! You will have such fun finding out—I promise you...."

He released her then and she struggled for a foothold in the shifting sand. His tone had turned hard and offhand when he next spoke. "If you are as intelligent as you are lovely, you will be in the hotel parking lot in the morning. I'll wait until eight o'clock. No longer.''

She raised her eyes in a passionate protest. "But I haven't said yet that I'll—''

He ignored her. He drew a key from his pocket, pressed it into her palm and closed her fingers around it. "The room number's on it," he said coldly. He stared at her for a moment, a silent command, then was gone.

Liza wandered off alone, picking a path through the dark forms of sleeping bags strewed about the beach and among the circled campfires, where young people still sang and strummed guitars. Beneath a clump of palms she saw a small, tethered donkey and stopped to pat its dusty coat.

The animal shuddered, provoking an angry buzz from the sandflies dislodged from his back. Liza tugged a handful of hay from the nearby bale and fed it to him.

Deep in her own thoughts, she perched on the edge of the bale of hay and watched the donkey chew contentedly. She had two clear choices. She could go back to New York now, a failure. Or she could accept Christian's offer. The latter could work, of course, if she could shift the tone of their relationship. Why couldn't they be neither adversaries nor lovers, but simply friends?

If she did go with him, she would have to be careful, hard as that was when the threat couldn't even be defined. Christian was a man who liked to control. He was a man, therefore, to be resisted. He could ruin everything, and she would have only herself to blame. Men who invaded and awakened desire were to be distrusted.

She knew her mistake. She had let a stranger understand her better than her most intimate friend.

There were a thousand, thousand things he did not know about her, yet somehow he had uncovered the most important thing.

"Christian," she murmured, and grieved to say it, "I allowed you to know how you make me feel."

CHAPTER EIGHT

THERE WAS A SMART BREEZE from the Gulf. It lifted his fine hair easily from his high forehead. He wore light beige bush pants and a matching shirt with the sleeves rolled back to his elbows. The laces on his tall, worn hiking boots were wrapped several times around his ankles. A poplin sun hat that had seen much use sat carelessly on the back of his head. He had put the jeep in the far corner of the sandy parking lot.

Liza inhaled deeply, squared her shoulders, and found her voice. "Good morning...."

Christian looked up but didn't stop working. "Morning! Knew you'd come. That goes in the back," he said, indicating the suitcase in her hand. "You did the right thing, by the way."

"Still so sure of yourself, aren't you?" she said, dragging her luggage to the rear of the jeep.

"No arguments now," he warned. "You came— I'm happy. Let's leave it at that."

She couldn't, not quite. "I'm not here," she reminded him, "because of you." His grin was so disarming her voice lacked the necessary snap.

He raised his palms. "Whatever you say—I'm determined not to ruin this."

She gave a short laugh. "What's to ruin?"

"A lot."

She put the suitcase down. Hands on her hips, she tilted her head. "I think," she challenged, "I regret coming already."

"No, you don't—chuck that in with the rest of the things. Time's wasting."

She complied and began to poke about in the array of boxes. "I should be contributing," she told him, waving a hand at the supplies.

He finished shoving the last carton into place and gave the securing rope a final tug before glancing at her sideways. "Somehow I don't foresee your consuming vast quantities of food," he said.

"That's not the point," she returned. "I must pay my way fair and square."

He shrugged. "There's always the gas," he said, unconcerned. "If you want, you can pay next time we fill up."

She nodded seriously. "I will. . . what's in all these things anyway?"

He slapped various boxes and bottles in turn. "Canned food, biscuits, bottled water—some for us, some for the radiator. And gasoline, extra tires and some treats, candy and such, for the Bedouin children we'll see along the way. It's not a long drive but it's rugged. You have to be prepared in case something goes wrong—engine trouble and that sort of thing."

Liza tried to look appropriately attentive and sensible. She peered into the toolbox and inspected all four tires solemnly.

"Do you drive?" he asked unexpectedly. "Really drive, I mean—shift gears and all that."

Liza hesitated. As a New Yorker she didn't keep a car but she'd once taken lessons and was in possession of a legal, if unused, license. "Sure," she replied.

"Good," he said. "If you can relieve me just a bit we can make it in a day and a half. I don't want to wear you out though." He was looking at her sharply, as if gauging her endurance level.

"I'm not fragile," she informed him crisply.

"No, I've noticed that you're healthy," he observed.

The sly, erotic word play—she couldn't have it.

"Look, if you and I are going to survive this trip together, Christian, we'd better establish some ground rules—"

He gave a final, jarring slam to the hood. "Say no more. That was my mistake. Let's just relax and think of this as a vacation. You like to camp out, don't you? All American girls do, I hear."

Liza smiled, thinking of the dusty summer day camps she'd gone to all her growing years, camps that smelled of hot tar and exhaust fumes rather than pine and toasted marshmallows. She thought, too, of the summer past and Victoria Livsay's "cabin" in Maine with its stout log walls and gold-plated taps in the bathrooms.

"I beg your pardon?"

"I said *Atwa*. That means peace, in Arabic," he explained.

She looked down at his outstretched hand, hesitated, then slipped her own into it.

"Atwa," she said.

They could have continued on a branch of the new highway that had brought Liza down from Aqaba, but Christian chose to cut west immediately into the desert. "We'll bypass the chaos of the tourist route and all that goes with it," he said, as they bounced onto the narrow, unpaved road. "This way you'll get a real feel for the Sinai. And why should we stay in some dreary motel when we can spend the night in the camp of a real desert sheikh?"

Liza, clutching at the dashboard for dear life, glanced wistfully over her shoulder at the smooth blacktop they were leaving behind. "You're joking— a real sheikh?"

"In the flesh. Don't worry though, I won't let him carry you off into his tent. I'll tell him you're mine."

"What makes you think," she said with cheerful malice, "that I'd want to be rescued?"

They had reached a broad plain studded with palms and tamarisks and thorny acacias. The Gulf had receded into a thin blue thread behind them. Christian raised his arm. "See that? That's our goal."

Far ahead, the plateau erupted into jagged red and mauve granite mountains. The tallest, a bare stark shaft of rock, was Mount Sinai.

Liza felt her heart thud. "It looks so close. . . ."

"Distances are deceiving in the desert. We won't reach its foothills until tomorrow afternoon at the earliest."

There was no sign of life or water. She turned and searched his face. "Are you *sure* you know your way?"

His crooked grin was slightly wicked. "If you doubt my sense of direction, here—" he pulled out a dog-eared map and tossed it into her lap "—you be our navigator."

She undid its many folds and spread it out. "Well, for starters, there's just a big blank space where we're heading—not a road, not a town!"

"You were the one who wanted to come here. If you think now you should have stayed home—"

"Oh, shut up," she said, "and keep your eyes on the road!"

The jeep was the single moving object on a huge gravel plain that stretched to the horizon. If Liza had expected a classic desert out of a storybook, with rippling silken sand dunes, she was disappointed. Those, Christian explained, were much farther north near the ancient caravan routes that joined Arabia with the Nile valley.

Here was only a sharp escarpment of limestone, chalk and pebbles. There was no soil to support the smallest wisp of green and only an occasional stunted acacia twisted from between boulders. Colors were muted—dusty mauves, ochers, umbers and grays. Even the sky had been bleached to a pale yellow by a white-hot sun. It was a land so harsh only the barest existence could be scraped from it. Yet every pebble and grain of sand was sacred to some culture or people. Only the foolish or insensitive could look down on it and see just a bare waste, Liza thought. It possessed a grave beauty that quickened the pulse, a stillness so great it sang.

Christian put his hand on her arm. "What are you thinking, Liza Downing?"

"I'm thinking that no matter what misunderstandings brought me here, I'm grateful to have seen this. Thank you, Christian, for this moment."

His voice was without sardonic undertones. "You are very welcome, Liza."

The driving demanded almost fierce concentration, yet they exclaimed, here and there, over a cluster of *bustans*, the mohair tents of the Bedouins. And once they laughed in delight at the dipping silhouettes of some camels, moving across the horizon as if on springs. At noon they stopped in the shade of a granite outcropping for a lunch of rolls and cheese. Later, as they roller-coastered down a steep granite hill, Christian said, "You're smiling—I like that."

"Even if I'm smiling at you?"

He downshifted and they began to climb up out of the depression. "That depends, I guess."

She peered at him over the top of her large sunglasses. "I was thinking you look like Lawrence of Arabia on a slightly updated steed—this is where he led his Arab armies, isn't it?"

"Hereabouts, I think."

"He was blond too...or was that just in the movie version?"

"If my history serves me, he was—what the hell!" Liza had let out a small shriek. Christian hit the brakes, hard. His hand shot out across her instinctively, keeping her from sliding into the windshield. "What on earth is wrong with you—"

She was jabbing at the map. "We're here—that's it!"

"*What's* it?"

"The Wadi Watir you said would lead us to the sheikh's camp—it is, isn't it?"

He unclenched his jaw and said it was. "But *please*...don't ever do that again. I thought you'd seen a body or something."

She flicked her hand at him. "Your nose is out of joint because my skills as navigator have turned out to be considerable. I'll bet you gave me the job the way you'd ask a child to count out-of-state license plates to keep him quiet."

"I acknowledge your expertise," he grumbled. "Now grab hold. This will be rough."

The Wadi Watir was one of many riverbeds that scored the desert and served, during the dry season, as roads. Twisting, erosion-chiseled notches, they sliced deeply into the rock. The jeep hung for a moment at the lip of the wadi then, tail up, began a sliding descent.

"Frightened?" asked Christian.

"No," she said, although she was. Very.

"Good. There's no need to be frightened ever with me, Liza."

She shot him a quick, sideways glance, but all she could see behind his dark aviator glasses was the network of lines etched at the corner of his eye. No need, she thought, despairing. She was headed into the vast desert wilderness with a man who barely deigned to explain himself, and she was not to be frightened—ever!

The deeper they went, the colder it got. The sheer granite walls blocked off almost all sunlight. When they reached the floor of the canyon, they pulled on jackets and tucked sunglasses away. The river had dried up almost completely, breaking out of the ground only in isolated pockets. At times the canyon widened dramatically into a valley hundreds of yards wide. At other times it narrowed, leaving barely enough room to pass.

The jeep jounced and swayed over the boulder-strewed bed. Christian had to swerve constantly to avoid the debris of rock slides. But he seemed more challenged than wearied by the demands of the drive and there were moments when Liza wondered whether the drama of a lurching turn that sent her slamming into him had quite been necessary.

Toward late afternoon, the wadi began to even out. They passed a squat pyramid of stone. "A tribal border marker," Christian said. "That black slash on it is a curse, in case anyone coming into the tribe's territory is an enemy."

"The handiwork of your friend, the sheikh?"

"Relax," he smiled, his grin exhibiting fine white teeth against his deep tan. "Ibn-Bader is a most hospitable man."

They began to pick up speed as they climbed out of the wadi toward another brown plain. The wind sang past Liza, whipping her hair about reddened cheeks. It carried his voice on it.

"You're lovely, you know. Have I told you that yet?"

"Can't remember...." Her voice was light. She affected disinterest.

"I shall, then. A dozen times before nightfall...."

"I suspect you tell a dozen women that quite regularly."

"And if I do?"

"Then I'll value it accordingly."

"I'll tell you anyway. A hundred times. I think you need it."

She slid down in her seat and burrowed deeper into her jacket.

"You're lovely—there, that's twice."

She tucked one leg under her and regarded him reflectively across her shoulder. "I think you're making fun of me. I should be angry with you."

He squeezed her knee. "You don't look angry. You look excited. Why don't you admit you're glad to be with me?"

She brushed off the offending hand. "Never, not even under some exotic Eastern torture, which is a fair description of this drive, by the way. Look—I think we've got company at last."

Where there had been only a bare, flinty waste, now a shimmering, palm-fringed pool, the oasis of Furtaga, floated before them. Barefoot children who had been tending sheep abandoned their charges and ran beside the jeep, laughing and waving their long switches. In the distance, what looked like a row of coal-black birds turned out, as they neared, to be women steadying pails of water on their heads. They were returning to the circle of *bustans*, their gowns billowing wide and winglike.

Christian brought the jeep to a smooth halt before the largest tent. He was immediately recognized and engulfed by a group of boisterous greeters. It was very much a man's show, and Liza was momentarily ignored. She waited, unsure of protocol. Even the women of the tribe held back, although their large, kohl-rimmed eyes were intelligent and watchful above their veils.

The flap of a tent was thrown back, a man emerged, and a path opened at once through the crowd. This, then, was Ibn-Bader, Liza thought, watching him stride toward Christian with raised arms. He was an old man, less vigorous than his splendid, black-eyed sons, but an imposing figure still. His skin was as dark and lined as old leather, his jaw firm, his gait proud. While many of the young men wore pants and shirts, he kept to desert dress— tall riding boots and a sweeping *arabaya* with a wide belt studded by a curving dagger.

Liza looked about her at the evidence of a hard, frugal life. The *bustans* were low and dark with sides made of woven goats' hair lashed together with thongs of camel hide. She caught glimpses of dim interiors with canopied beds made from the stout ribs of palm fronds. Fat, freshly filled waterskins hung from poles beside the doors. Lying about helter-skelter were sacks of lentils, milk-filled gourds, old tin tubs and supple camel whips. Scruffy dogs nosed through piles of refuse and, behind the tents, hopeful goats stretched their thin necks to nibble the desiccated twigs of acacias.

Christian strode back to the jeep and began to pull out the gifts of tobacco he'd packed. "The sheikh would like me to present you to him," he told Liza. "After that, I'm afraid I'll have to leave you to your own devices for a while while we discuss old times. It would help if you didn't take offense. There's a pretty strict separation of the sexes in a Bedouin camp."

Liza hopped out and stretched her protesting muscles gingerly. "I'll manage. Should I try to make friends with the women, do you think?" she asked, following Christian to the sheikh's tent.

"There's no harm, but you'll find them shy and I doubt that any of them speak English. Perhaps you'll have more luck with the children and the candy—that's a universal combination."

Ibn-Bader greeted her with elaborate courtesy, bowing deeply in the traditional *salamat*. The younger men remained silent and staring, not precisely hostile, but very curious. Liza was scrupulously polite, said little, and soon drifted away unremarked.

Attracted by a bizarre cacophony of growls, wheezes, snuffles and roars, Liza sought out the camel enclosure. The sheikh had a large, prosperous herd. She found them milling about on their powerful legs, their strong, graceful necks dipping and swaying. They looked down their disdainful, slit noses at her, their beautiful, long-lashed lids opening and closing lazily. Their mobile mouths twisted contemptuously.

Liza leaned on the rough wood barrier, smiling at the willowy females suckling their ungainly, velvet-eyed foals. Cautiously, for they pulled back their lips to show mean, yellow teeth, she amused herself by feeding them handfuls of sorghum straw from their troughs until Christian came to collect her.

An extra rug had been laid by Ibn-Bader's own fire for the visiting couple. With the light failing, candles had been arranged, too, in their honor. The desert sky was now varying shades of purple, only the faintest trace of orange outlining the mountains.

"The saying is that every good Bedouin has a very black teapot," said Christian, indicating that she should sit beside him, cross-legged, on the rug. "Ibn-Bader's, you'll notice, is very charred indeed. It means he's offered his hospitality to strangers many times."

"But seldom to a Western woman, I suspect. Am I to be the only female here?"

"Yes. The women will serve first, then eat by themselves when the men are through."

The crowd around the campfire grew as the younger men returned from settling the herds for the night. The sheikh's wife, Nura, appeared bearing a huge copper pot. She was shrouded head to toe in black, a dancing shadow, silent except for the tinkling of gold coins around her ankles. A heavy and beautiful turquoise necklace swung from her neck.

Ibn-Bader began the steady rhythm of eating—dipping into the stew pot a charred round of pita that Nura had cooked over the hot coals. Liza glanced discreetly at Christian and, seeing his slight nod, scooped out some meat for herself. It was a coarse, sweetish meat that she couldn't identify. Goat, perhaps, she wondered. She saw Christian rub his stomach and nod in vigorous praise of the food. With a nervous smile she followed suit. From the expression on her host's face, she knew she'd pleased him.

Conversation around the fire was spirited and emotional, full of the high, rapid tongue-clicks of the desert language. The Bedouins, Liza reflected, were a strange mixture—wild, some would say, yet courtly and obsessed with hospitality. They seemed to value freedom above all else, and Arab literature was full of praise for their courage and independence. But next to their freedom, she knew, they loved poetry, and nearly all Bedouin men prayed that a poet would be born into their family.

When the pots were cleared away and bitter coffee poured into tiny cups, the men lay back and smoked as one of Ibn-Bader's sons recited. It was, Christian whispered, a story of loneliness and courage and long-suffering. But it hardly needed translation, Liza thought. It was joy enough just to listen to the music of the boy's voice, the crickets singing with him, and to watch the fire send thin, golden spirals of sparks into the night.

Later Christian asked her, "Regrets?"

"None...well, a passing one, perhaps. When Nura gave the stew pot to the dogs to clean."

He laughed. "You were very brave."

They were walking slowly away from the oasis into the desert. Ibn-Bader had begun the reading from the Koran, the saying of prayer beads, and his guests had politely absented themselves. There was an eerie, extraterrestrial quality to the night desert. The vast arch of the sky, strangely soft over the stony land, glowed with brilliant stars and meteors that plunged flaming to the earth. Sound floated easily in the emptiness. Liza heard a flapping of wings, the hoot of an owl and, far off now, the muffled stomping of the camels.

"Just the word oasis conjures up such lushness. Yet it's still harsh here—how do they manage!" she wondered aloud.

"As they always have," Christian answered. "A little farming, a little herding. More and more of the young men are lured to the cities, though. The sheikh distrusts education and resists any modernization. He thinks it will kill the old ways, and perhaps he's right."

"It must be worst for the women...."

"The women are highly prized, of course, but in much the same way any chattel is among people who own so little. I suppose you found the sheikh's attitude toward the women offensive."

"Their culture, their circumstances are so different from ours—I think it would be very presumptuous of me to pass judgment on Ibn-Bader."

He had taken her hand to help her over a pocket of shifting gravel. When, after they were on firmer ground, he hadn't released it, she did not try to withdraw it. "Perhaps their ways aren't so very different from ours," he mused. "We like to think ourselves civilized where women are concerned, but maybe we just dress up the same attitudes in different clothes. Take your Mr. Livsay...I imagine he's very traditional—"

"I know what you're going to say," she cut in. "And you're wrong. Penn's very modern."

"Oh, I have no doubt he's liberated enough to approve of, or at least not to be threatened by, your rather dazzling success. All the same, I'll wager he would rival Ibn-Bader in possessiveness where his woman's concerned. It would take a strong-willed woman to remain a true equal in marriage to him." Abruptly he asked, "Are you going to marry this man? I noticed a ring in New York. Nothing now."

Liza felt her bare finger. "I thought it wiser not to bring jewelry."

"That's not an answer—"

"You pry—"

"And you evade constantly. Coyness doesn't become you, Liza. I've seen you and Penn together, remember."

"All right, the answer to your question is that Penn and I aren't officially engaged but—"

"Yes?"

"But I've been thinking that a Christmas wedding would be nice." This surprised her, for she had been thinking no such thing. "You assume too much, you know," she added crossly, "with all these personal questions."

She felt a sudden desperation. So, he was going to make a battle out of this trip after all! She hated these games men and women seemed to torment each other with. They nearly always ended so badly. And there'd be no winning, ever, against a man as experienced in frivolous love play as Christian Chase undoubtedly was.

"Liza, you're brooding." His voice was low, serious, familiar. "You're filled with an odd guilt over what you feel—or don't feel."

"You don't know what I feel!"

He raised an eyebrow, but was silent.

Above them, one star shone brighter than the rest,

and in its extraordinary light she noted for the first time a small dimple near the corner of his mouth. It deepened briefly as he looked down on her upturned face.

"I should feel sorry for you," he said, bemused, "a young woman alone, as I hear, against all that wealth and power of the Livsays. But I don't. Oddly enough, I persist in feeling sorry for Penn."

Liza tossed her head, a spirited gesture, and laughed. "If there's one person on the face of this earth who deserves less pity—"

"I'll tell you something else you don't know. You're not in love with him."

She should turn right around and leave, Liza thought. Yet she waited, for what she hardly knew. He let go of her hand and lighted a cigarette, one of those small twisted ones the sheikh had rolled. It was the first time she'd ever seen Christian smoke.

"I don't know how experienced you are with men, of course, and it's your business how much you intend to tell me—"

"Not a word!" she shot back.

"But my guess is—and this is no reflection, let me stress, on your ability to please a man—that you have decided not to have much to do with this business of love. Hence the lack of haste on your part to formalize your relationship. But Penn doesn't share your reticence, does he?"

She bit her lower lip softly. "He has... until lately."

"First the Renoir, then the cross... it would only be natural for him to want to firm up his claim on you."

"How cold you make it sound—as if I'm an invest-ment, too!"

"Not necessarily. Livsay's subject to the same in-securities as the rest of us, surely. Or is he that plastic?"

She tossed him a quick, angry glance, then spoke slowly, choosing each word. "I am cautious," she conceded. "It's the result, I suppose, of being alone for so long. Penn is, too, although his reserve is more deliberate. A necessity, really, of his onerous busi-ness responsibilities."

He drew on the cigarette, inhaling the smoke deep into his lungs. "But marriage, or a love affair, if that's all it's to be between the two of you, isn't a business proposition. Where's the romance, the glit-ter? And I don't mean the family money and what it buys—parties, presents, limousines—"

"I know what you mean. And I happen to think that Penn and I have something that goes beyond all that, something of substance...."

She delivered herself of a small lecture on values, all the while thinking Christian's version of love was unrealistic. Did he think it was all wonder and showers of stardust? And sex the first shining thread drawn through the loom? But love, she maintained, didn't happen with that blinding radiance. Not a love that would last.

"There's a poem," he said, "that I'm reminded of...

Where both deliberate, the love is slight:
Who ever loved, that loved not at first sight?"

She quickened her step, moving ahead of him. "Nonsense," she said, "silly, sentimental—"

"Charming and wise," he countered calmly, butting the cigarette out, "and as true as when Marlowe wrote it a few centuries ago."

She tore impatiently at the elastic band that held her hair back in an untidy braid. She shook her head, loosening the dark mane.

"Good...I like it best like that." His fingers combed through her hair, taking out the last of the braiding. "It suits the Liza I know."

She suppressed the small shudder his fingers moving lightly near the nape of her neck caused. "I've told you—there's only one of me." Briskly she continued to walk, Christian matching her pace.

"You bear scant resemblance right now to a pampered society girl. Or a curator in that pretty but too-perfect suit you wore to the unveiling."

She was indignant. "I happen to like that suit!"

"I'm sure. But it's a contrived look, isn't it? A woman's uniform used to be a housedress. Now you've traded it in for a new uniform—perfectly tailored and in the best of taste and worn with a frilly blouse or something so the men won't be too alarmed by your competence."

"Spare me, please, your half-baked theories on working women. And stop that!" She brushed away the hand that had not ceased its play with her hair, and wished it back at once.

"You think you've changed the subject. I won't allow that. We were discussing the facets of your personality."

She glared at him. "Why should I be the one who's always cross-examined? I know virtually nothing about you. Nothing that matters, anyway."

"You mean Victor didn't rush to tell you all about my fall from grace and subsequent need to work like everyone else?" With detached pleasure he observed the telling shift of her gaze.

They came to a tall shaft of granite. He turned and set his back against it. "Come here," he said, lifting his arms.

Her breathing was uneven. "I won't," she said mutinously.

But she did. He kissed her and she laughed, giddy and reckless. This Liza was a stranger to both of them. He lifted her and she was as light as her sudden hope. When he set her down a voice warned against this lethal pleasure, but in her heart she was delighted.

"I won't make it easy for you by being less gentle," he told her, suddenly serious. "I won't give you even the illusion of being forced. There'll be no excuses later when you have to face your doubts about your devotion to Livsay—"

"But I have no doubts," she said unsteadily.

"Nor devotion."

It was a cruel assault she would not have thought even him capable of. "Don't be unfair, Christian. Don't spoil it—please!"

"Spoil what? Your affair with him? With me? Your innocence?"

She couldn't answer. She didn't know. So much had been thrown into chaos by one tender command.

Slowly she raised her eyes and found his. Such a pale, beautiful blue in the starlight.... She looked into them, entranced. Had she always known, she wondered, or just now understood? It was *this* man who stirred her. This man who made her laugh, wonder, fear—but *feel*. It was he who gave her this awesome sense of *being*.

He kissed both her cheeks, quickly and lightly, then whispered, "Are you still frightened, darling?"

"No...a little." She was thinking that she'd never stopped wanting him, not from the first moment she'd seen him. Now she didn't want to stop and he knew it.

"Don't be...don't be." He kissed her eyes. "I won't do anything you don't want. Do you understand it now, darling? This is how love's meant to be, Liza. Just this unplanned coming together. The moment, nothing else."

She couldn't speak. She was well beyond words and that was answer enough. He guided her arms around his neck. "Try passion just this once. Trust me, it will be our secret. I don't kiss a woman like you and tell...." His fingers traced her profile, the soft line of her jaw, the vulnerable curve of her neck.

"Such a vivid beauty," he whispered, drawing a veil of ebony hair across her sun-touched cheek. "There's no more perfect setting for you than this." He bent and skimmed the edges of her parted lips with his own, murmuring, "I love your mouth, I love what you do with it—if only you knew!"

He kissed her then with such a savage sweetness that all the stars in the heavens seemed to fill her

breast. The invader was welcome now and she could
only give what he had come to claim.

He kissed her temples, her hair, he filled her ears
with his own choked cries and she strained against
him, desperate and a little mad, wanting only to
drown in him.

Suddenly he was holding her at arm's length, his
muscles rigid. His fingers gripped her shoulders and
she struggled, uncomprehending, in a fury to return
to his embrace. She saw his head turned aside, his
cheek pressed hard to the granite. Sweat formed a
sheen on his brow. His parted lips suggested agony.

She wanted to hold him in her arms, comfort him.
Passion was pushed aside, replaced by an anxious
caring. "Christian...Christian?"

His smile shattered her with its sad tenderness. He
seemed to have found whatever discipline he had
reached for within himself. He smoothed her hair.
"We have to go back now," he said simply.

"But—"

He laid his finger lightly on her lips, silencing her.
"I would like nothing more, my dearest Liza, than to
lay you down and make love to you as you deserve to
be loved. But I've risked our welcome here long
enough, and if I don't stop now, I won't...."

She felt she was dying a small death. He held her
again, and they stood together, swaying gently, listening to each other's heart beating; waiting for the storm
to subside. Finally they walked back to the camp,
carefully apart.

It was a timeless scene. The encampment of the
Crusaders' armies, Liza thought, probably hadn't

looked any different—just the great black arc of the sky with its bright stars and beneath them, the answering flicker of the fires. The camp had settled in for the night. A few dogs were still about, worrying bones left over from dinner. Some women were spreading out the rough sacking on which the unmarried men would sleep, outside the tents.

The day had been hot, the declining sun warm gold, but now it was colder than Liza had considered possible, even in the desert night. She hopped from foot to foot, muttering over the inadequate contents of her suitcase. Christian ambled up to the jeep, hands shoved casually in his pockets.

"Nura's laid a fire for us—and none too soon, apparently. Your teeth are chattering."

Liza tossed a scrap of peach silk back into the depths of her bag. "I'll have to sleep in my clothes. Somewhere between here and Manhattan my nightgown changed from lovely to ludicrous."

He hiked himself up on the running board, retrieved a fat bundle and tossed it at her. "Sleeping bag," he said. They were back in Ibn-Bader's realm now, and they were distant, proper friends again. But the transition had been hard won.

"What time will we leave in the morning?" she asked.

"Early—as soon as the camels bellow."

"I hope those animals are well tied up. Do you know how big they are? Their feet are like platters."

"I shouldn't worry. They're far too valuable to the tribe to be allowed to roam. And too unpredictable as well. Although they're usually docile they can turn quite nasty."

"Now you tell me! I wish I'd known that while I was so blithely feeding them this afternoon."

"That would have spoiled your fun. Anyway, I was watching."

Her stomach did a quick flip. It was very seductive, this business of being under Christian's eye, being protected. It would be easy to be passive, to forget that she had a mission here. Something more to guard against, she told herself, more in duty than enthusiasm.

She lapsed into a brooding silence as they plowed doggedly through the sand, back to the circle of *bustans*. Their fire had been set to one side, in the shelter of some palms where the wind off the plain was less fierce. It welcomed them with a cheerful sputter and pop. Christian set to work at once, scraping the sand level and rolling out the sleeping bags. He placed them on opposite sides of the fire. He was pointedly ignoring her.

Liza burrowed into the soft down depths of her sleeping bag. She rested her chin on her hand and watched him. He tossed a few more sticks of acacia into the fire, releasing the column of orange and silver sparks. Later, in his sleeping bag, he lay with his face turned to the fire, one hand thrown back over his head, and seemed to sleep.

Liza stared at the strong column of his neck, at his long, fine hands, at his rawboned wrists with their thatch of golden hair. Firelight on Christian's cheeks...firelight on Christian's hair and on his eyelids. She would remember that amber wash on warm skin as long as she lived.

But how to return to Penn after this dangerous

detour, she wondered miserably. She had thought her feelings for Penn unshakable. Now they seemed a weight, a burden to be borne.

This business with Christian—perhaps her only defense was to label it clearly for what it was, a temporary madness, a sexual obsession, and not confuse it with anything deeper. She was a mature woman with a woman's needs. Surely she ought not to feel guilty about that.

She turned her face to the desert. She listened to the sound of the fire speaking softly, the keening of some unseen bird. Would she ever find her way back to Penn? For the idea of love, once thought, could not be erased. She couldn't pretend that out there it hadn't burst on her like star fire.

No, she decided, you can't fall in love with someone you don't trust. It was futile and reckless, an act of self-destruction to love Christian Chase.

His voice came to her softly. "Liza? Good night, sleep well...."

If at all, she thought.

CHAPTER NINE

MORNING DIDN'T COME RELUCTANTLY to the desert. The black velvet retreated before a searing heat and a burnt-orange sun. Liza stirred on a bed canopied by palm fronds spangled with pink gold. A soft scrunch of gravel near her ear and a muted giggle nudged her awake.

She opened an eye in time to catch a swoosh of black and two bare feet, ankles encircled in turquoise. She opened the other and saw Christian on one knee before the fire. He had bathed, shaved and shaken a semblance of neatness into his clothes. He was waging a small war with a lopsided cooking pot.

She smiled sleepily, stretched, and struggled up onto an elbow. "Morning...."

He looked back over his shoulder. "Good morning. Stay where you are and I'll bring you breakfast—such as it is—in bed."

She hid a yawn behind her hand. "Was there some gauzy creature here? Or did I dream it?"

"She was no dream, although she might certainly be described as dreamy—that was Shukria, Ibn-Bader's youngest daughter. She brought us a gift of fresh pita dough. She offered to make it up, too, but

I thought it might be rather fun to do." He looked at her sternly. "Why are you laughing?"

She was remembering Nura the night before, her lightning-fast patting and flipping of the dough that formed the thin, crisp bread, the mesmerizing grace no doubt born of years of practice. "It's just nice to be waited on," she said, and thought, *this will be a show*.

The water had come to a boil and Christian busied himself with tins of tea and sugar and powdered milk. Liza grabbed her tote bag and took herself off to the spring to wash up. Anxious not to blunder into an offense, she gave wide berth to the rounded backs of the men, prostrate at their morning prayers. She inhaled deeply, breathing in a pleasant mix of charcoal and mocha. As she plunged deeper into a tangle of brush she startled some bulbuls, little sand-colored thrushes that exploded skyward, making her jump, then laugh aloud. She had forgotten her night thoughts. She was happy.

She returned to find Christian poking morosely at the coals. "Smells wonderful," she said, sinking to her knees beside him.

His smile was crooked and guilty. "I'll give you one I *didn't* drop in the sand."

"Harder than it looks, is it?" she asked cheerfully. She looked askance at the charred lumps steaming in the coals.

He speared one with a sharpened stick. It fell, rather hard, on the metal plate. "Should I be nervous about feeding you? I don't know how good a cook you are. We'll remedy that some day."

She labored through a mouthful. "A valiant first attempt," she commented. It was rock hard and burned on the outside, raw and doughy on the inside. Christian stared at her and she at him. They dissolved into adolescent laughter and fed the rest to the dogs.

LIZA SETTLED BACK in the jeep and adjusted her sunglasses. They had had a protracted, warm and noisy send-off from the camp. "What a great long conference you had with Ibn-Bàder and the men— what was all that waving of arms about?" she asked.

"We were discussing the best route," Christian explained. "The riverbed splits down here a bit. The branch I'd intended to take, the Wadi Ghazala, is the shortest, but the sheikh thinks we're too close to the rainy season to use it. He suggests the longer but less risky branch."

"Rainy season? Here?"

"It starts up in the mountains, where we're headed. There's not enough vegetation to hold water, so it all comes rushing down the wadis." He lifted his arm and pointed to a red splotch high up on the steep canyon wall. "That's a flood marker there."

Liza craned her neck. "Not that high, surely!" she exclaimed. "We've only come through the barest trickle of water so far."

"I've never seen it myself, but this hardly seems the time to find out. We'll keep on this road heading southwest. We should pick up the main highway through the Wadi Saal sometime this afternoon. It will mean enduring an extra couple of hours of desert, but that's all."

When they came to the divide in the riverbed Liza tossed him a glance and asked, "Are you sure you know which is which?"

He reached over and squeezed her hand, his eyes still on the road. "Where's that sense of adventure we talked about?"

There was a superior twist to one corner of her mouth. "Still here, Lord Chase," she replied, "or I wouldn't be sitting beside you."

He conceded the point. "You were very game about everything last night, from the mysterious stew pot to the various beasts that weren't in it."

She grimaced. "What *was* in that pot? No, don't tell me! I wouldn't have passed up the experience for all the air-conditioned comfort in the world. For one night, anyway."

"We'll see if you're as cheerful tonight. I warn you we've left anything resembling civilization behind. We're headed into the most desolate hundred miles on the face of the globe."

He was depressingly accurate, Liza discovered. If yesterday's trip had been uncomfortable, today's was torture. They became lunar travelers, bouncing under a baking sun toward distant dunes that seemed to run from them. The mountains remained a stubbornly unattainable ripple of red on the horizon.

They developed wordless rituals, their throats too raw for unnecessary speech. If Christian stopped suddenly, Liza hopped out to scrape the thick film of dust off the windshield. To her also fell the unceasing watch for the giant, ugly acacia thorns that could destroy the tires and leave them helpless. She signaled him by placing her hand over his on the vibrating stick shift and pointing out an approaching tree. Christian's attention was consumed by the constant shifting of gears as they ground their way up sliding hills of gravel, fell into gullies, or braked for the unexpected hazard of a rockfall.

She would have liked to close the window against the wind that blew a thousand pieces of grit down her shirt and under her cuffs, but it would have turned the jeep into an oven. Painful chafed bands appeared around her wrists and neck and under her bra.

Though she scanned the horizon, they never once passed a sign of human life. Once she spotted a long curl of brown dust she thought might have come from another car or at least a camel. But it was a khamsin, Christian said, a sandstorm, luckily traveling away from them.

They stopped for a brief lunch of bread and cheese and canned soft drinks. Liza noticed with alarm the raw red rings around Christian's eyes. She remembered her offer to help with the driving. She repeated it and felt both relieved and guilty when he declined in a distracted way saying, "When we get to the highway, perhaps." They poured water from the plastic jugs over their faces and renewed their skidding, crablike progress across the moonscape of boulders and wind-whipped sand.

Yet regret would not have been the proper word for what Liza felt as they moved across that fractured landscape. She was oddly elated and grittily determined to live out the experience. Only once did courage desert her, when the dark, lazy shadows moving over the hazy white sun turned out to be huge Egyptian vultures attracted to their movement in the empty desert.

How odd, then, to strain, wheels spinning, over a low swell of dark green flintstone and come at once upon life and color and honking horns. The broad cleft of the Wadi Saal opened out before them, a modern highway striping its back. Cars, transports, military vehicles, tour buses whizzed by. Bouncing and grinning and hanging onto their hats, Liza and Christian lumbered down the face of the flintstone to join the convoy streaming toward the Plain of Raha.

They quickly found themselves passing tent villages as they approached the base of Mount Sinai. Modern day-glo tents were staked close by the hide tents of the Bedouins. Liza shaded her brow and strained to see the people already working around fires, preparing the evening meal.

"They look different from Ibn-Bader's tribe," she remarked. "Their dress is more modern. And I think they're taller and perhaps fairer as well."

Christian nodded. He was relaxed now, driving slightly slumped in his seat, one wrist tipped casually over the bottom of the steering wheel. "They're Jebelya," he answered, "descended from the original one hundred Wallachian slaves Justinian sent to serve the monks of St. Catherine's. They've remained aloof from the other Bedouins over the centuries. When they did intermarry it was with Egyptian women. They've maintained their physical differences and still aren't completely accepted, I understand."

"You're very knowledgeable on such an obscure topic," Liza observed.

"I did some reading before I came," he said, dismissively.

"So did I," Liza told him. "But I certainly can't toss off facts like that."

"Nor should you have to. Your job was to concentrate on the cross and that you did. I'm a bit more of a generalist than you are, my dear. Anyway," he added, "I can't take all the credit—Kimberley and I were talking the other night. She's a very bright girl."

Jealousy speared her, silly and inappropriate and utterly beyond her control. It was a deep, green pool in the pit of her stomach. "She is," she said tightly, willing herself to forget it.

They stopped at the flaring foot of Mount Sinai. Around them, others were spilling out of cars and tour vans. Most, despite an obvious eagerness, were strangely silent as they looked up at the peak where Moses was said to have received the Ten Commandments. The dark, jagged silhouette was awesome against the setting sun. The high, sweet pealing of evening prayer bells climbed its face and fell back on them.

The monastery was set tight against the base, isolated in a limitless tumble of boulders. It was virtually unchanged since Justinian had sent his architect and builders in the sixth century to fortify the little Chapel of the Burning Bush. The same five-foot-square blocks of granite etched with Maltese crosses endured as walls and ramparts. It had turned out, though, to be an unlucky location for a fortress. The beleaguered compound had been helpless against the Bedouins who embarked on centuries of harassment by rolling boulders down on the hapless monks. Justinian's architect had paid the price for his error with execution.

Yet the monastery, a self-contained village, survived. The tops of the inner buildings were just visible over the thick outer wall. Liza could see the cross of the chapel, the campanile and the unexpected dome of a mosque for the servants.

To one side was a blessing of green in that wild and austere setting. A garden had been laid out, lush with cypresses and palms, orchards and grape arbors, and the beautifully tended rows of a kitchen garden. An ancient aqueduct poured cool water into this oasis, and peacocks, kingly and complacent, strutted the paths.

Liza's heart rose into her throat. It was exotic and wonderful, and suddenly she couldn't wait. She began to gather her things together. What would she see behind those walls? What answer was waiting for her? Go easy, she cautioned herself. She couldn't just rush into the monastery. The monks were hardly likely to take seriously some bedraggled "tourist," with a grime-streaked face, beating on their door.

Quickly she took out comb, compact and tissues, set them on the hood of the jeep, and began to repair the ravages of the drive. Her hands were shaking a little. As she fussed, she remembered Scott's rueful admission—and his warning.

"The truth is," he had said, "we've never been inside even once. Every trip we ask the monks and every trip they refuse. If a thousand years in this desert and Kim's nagging hasn't worn them down, I don't know if you will. I think they feel the tourists have just taken the place of the natives in badgering them."

"But I'm not a tourist," she'd argued. "Once they understand that—"

"Liza, if you have some picture in your mind of jolly little men with bald heads, flowing robes and saintlike smiles on apple-cheeked faces, making cheese and fruit liqueurs for the New York gourmet trade—well, you're in for a shock. They're simple, religious men who work hard at dreary jobs and just want to be left alone."

Liza finished pinning a neat coil of hair at the nape of her neck. She glanced back at the charming garden. She had a city girl's faith in the goodness of all who work the earth and tend growing things. *It's going to be fine,* she told herself.

She heard a discreet clearing of a throat. "Oh. . ." she said softly. She'd been dreading this moment.

"If you're through primping," Christian said, "shall we go?"

She put her lipstick back in her cosmetic bag and closed it with a firm click. "I'm going, yes. But not with you. I appreciate your bringing me here and I'm grateful for meeting the sheikh, but from now on I have to manage on my own."

His eyes were hard. "Somehow I thought you and I had teamed up—pooled our resources. Now where do you suppose I got that impression?"

"There's no need for sarcasm, Christian. I just can't afford to be indebted to you for anything else, that's all."

"Because of the cross? Or because of what happened—or nearly happened—between us?"

"The camping, the fun and games—it's over, Christian."

He crossed his arms against his chest. "I see—it's business as usual, then."

Her eyes searched his for a moment, hurt and confused. "It's the way it *must* be. Don't you see? If there were even a hint of collusion between us—"

"Collusion! I seriously doubt anyone would suspect the moral Miss Downing of such a nasty crime!"

"It doesn't matter. If people knew we were together there'd be enough questions. I didn't ask for this problem—I didn't ask to have you here. And I'm certainly not going to help you get into the monastery. You'll have to make up your own story."

He swung his bush jacket over one shoulder. He started walking. "Suits me fine," he called, "and it works both ways, I take it."

"Of course," she said, grabbing her purse and scrambling to keep up with him. "I'm not worried— my interest is official. Yours is idle at best."

"Well then, let's see, shall we?"

A chain stretched across the road and on the other side a Bedouin, a guard, Liza guessed, squatted on the ground. He wore a shapeless suit jacket over a long robe, and the traditional cloth headdress. She was a long time getting his attention, but eventually he heaved himself up and sauntered over to the chain.

"I wish to see the archbishop," she said slowly, distinctly. She pointed at the monastery for good measure.

The Arab's hand jerked in a blunt, dismissive gesture. "No tourists," he said gruffly, and turned his back on her.

"No, no, not tourists!" Liza cried. "This is business. Very important business!"

The man half turned, a bit sullen. "Monks praying now," he informed her.

"When will they be through?" she asked quickly. She didn't want to give him the chance to go away again.

The guard relented more because he was anxious to get back to his cigarettes and tea, she suspected, than because of her powers of persuasion. But finallly he did unhook the chain to let them both pass, and that was all that mattered.

"Now what, do you suppose?" Liza asked. They were climbing the steep incline to the double wooden doors. There was not a soul about.

"The obvious, I'd say." Christian reached up and took hold of the monstrous iron ring suspended from the tall door. He struck hard, three times.

A small hatch high up on the main door swung open and another native guard leaned out. His welcome was no warmer than the other's had been. Liza racked her brains but this time she got nowhere. The guard steadfastly refused to allow these visitors entry.

"You have business, too?" the man suddenly asked. He was looking now at Christian, who had remained a silent observer of Liza's frustrated pleas.

"No," he said, "I'd like only the kindness of a bed for the night."

The guard narrowed his eyes. "Nothing more?"

"No, just a bed...oh, and I have this." He pulled a piece of folded paper from his shirt pocket and stretched, passing it up to the hatch.

Liza's mouth dropped open. She eyed Christian with distinct suspicion, then the Arab. He read the paper and his expression seemed to change in some subtle way. He glanced quickly back at Christian then vanished, slamming the hatch behind him. A moment later they heard the dull scrape of the great doors being pulled back on their ancient iron hinges.

The guard waved Christian in.

"Wait," Liza cried, panic rising. "Where am I supposed to spend the night? Christian, ask him if I can at least have a room, too!"

The Arab stopped abruptly. He raised a warning hand. "No women!" he said brusquely.

"I don't believe this—you're in and I'm out? Are you going to allow that?" she demanded furiously.

He picked up his duffel bag and smiled. "What choice do I have? Anything else would be...collusion, I believe you called it."

Liza glared at his retreating back. "You tell him I'll be here in the morning," she shouted. The door closed with a resounding thud.

"IT'S CALLED BASIC SHELTER—no comforts, but a roof and some privacy." Scott held Liza's suitcase in one hand and with the other yanked at the bus doors.

"I'm a nuisance," Liza said apologetically. She had run across Scott and Kim in the campground and poured her frustration out to them.

"Don't be silly," Scott chided. "Anyway, I'll bet you'll be at least as comfortable as Christian up in that buggy old place."

"I'm not surprised Christian succeeded," Kim remarked. "He'd be a hard man to say no to."

Liza's jaw worked in irritation. Certainly she'd had little success in denying him anything. And the implications were frightening. If he found something in there, if he succeeded where she failed, the newspapers and gossip columns would have a field day with it. It would be an intolerable humiliation. No one would forgive her—not Penn and Victor, not Julian, not herself.

Scott said goodbye, then left; he was to meet with Reverend Clarkson to discuss the next day's trip up the mountain. Kim stayed, helping Liza brush sand from the aisle of the bus, spread the sleeping bag, and wrestle with a balky window.

"You and Christian, you're really more than casual acquaintances, aren't you?" Kim asked without preamble. She was sprawled on a seat, all legs and golden skin. "He seems to. . . get under your skin easily."

Liza looked up quickly. How very frank green eyes can be, she thought. "We. . . he has that ability. But

I'm sure the experience is not unique to me." She was annoyed to feel herself flush.

"I'm not very subtle, am I," said Kim, sounding not at all apologetic. "Scott's always telling me to bite my tongue."

"I think you're outgoing and refreshing," Liza replied diplomatically. "You must find that an asset with your job."

"The problem is, people come and go before I get a chance to know them. I guess I've developed the bad habit of making up for it by going straight to the point—or the jugular, as Scott says. I hope I didn't offend you," she added, frowning as if recalling others whose feathers she'd ruffled.

"No, don't be silly, of course you didn't," Liza said quickly, for that was the truth. She really was enjoying Kim's company. Her personality was so different from her own that Liza was always being surprised.

Kim tipped her head back against the window. "He's got such yummy manners. And that accent—I could listen to it all day," she said, returning, inevitably, to the topic of Christian.

"Yes, he does have an interesting accent—but the manners are changeable, according to the circumstances and company," Liza said, an ambivalent moth about Christian's flame.

"But he's not at all stuffy. Not the way you'd expect a lord to be. He's...." Kim pondered.

"Approachable?" Liza offered.

"Yes, that's it exactly. There wasn't anyone in the group who didn't feel comfortable talking to him, even after they found out who he is."

Liza did battle with her demons. She wished to be fair. "He was a pleasure that night in Nuweiba. And there have been other times as well. . . ." She pulled her knees up and hugged them. "But there were also moments when he was arrogant, pushy, and generally unbearable."

Kim smiled, as if she found these not at all undesirable qualities in a man. Liza's answering smile was cockeyed and sympathetic. "He's the *last* person I'd have chosen for a travel companion. In fact, for reasons I can't go into, I was a little afraid of him."

Kim sat forward eagerly. "Really? Are you still?"

Liza blinked. "I'm not sure!" She was surprised at her own answer. "Once the matter of being with him was rather abruptly taken out of my hands, I admit I enjoyed his company. There's an undeniably generous and charming side to him." Deliberately, she hadn't alluded to his prowess at lovemaking. There had to be some limit to these confidences, no matter how pleasant.

Kim's lips curled slyly. "There's a light in your eye when you talk about him—right now, for example— did you know that?"

"No," Liza replied, "I didn't. I'll have to watch it."

"Why on earth bother? If a man like that is interested in you, you might as well enjoy it!"

The corner of Liza's mouth twitched downward. "Oh, he's interested in me all right. But only as a means to something else. You see things very differently in the clear light of day, I'm learning."

"A means to what?" Kim demanded.

"I don't know," Liza said, knowing Kim would find that a hopelessly inadequate reply. She did herself.

"Well, I think he's sexy," Kim bubbled.

"He's disturbing," Liza said seriously. "That doesn't always translate to lovable or desirable. Except," she conceded reluctantly, "in a base sort of physical way, I suppose."

Kim's small white teeth seized her lower lip, biting back a smile. But her eyes danced, telling Liza she was quite hopelessly transparent. Soon they both surrendered to helpless laughter.

Liza hugged her stomach and felt the stiff soreness there. Her muscles ached from the jolting ride and her eyes still stung from the clouds of dust that had floated about her since leaving Furtaga.

As soon as she got back to Eighty-third Street, she planned to stand in the shower for hours and hours, and even then she despaired of ever getting the grit out of her hair. Or of removing all traces of him. What a tangle it was—hopes lifted only to plunge. Anger burning bright and pleasure at his nearness just as incandescent. And now the afternoon's collision with reality.

"The proverbial penny for your thoughts," said Kim. "Are you brooding, meditating, or dreaming?"

Liza pondered and finally said, "All of them. I'm confused. I'm frustrated and a little scared. And... and as alive as I've ever been in my entire life!" She turned astonished eyes on the younger woman. How did it happen? How, when she was fussing over the mundane matter of cramped muscles, had this soaring joy burst through?

She rested her pink cheek on her knees and asked of no one, "Can you be exhausted and full of life? Can you dislike a man and miss him the moment his back is turned on you?"

This illogical mix did not baffle Kim. "It's natural," she pronounced, nodding with an air of wisdom. "Men like Christian Chase inspire the most amazing behavior in otherwise levelheaded women. *Especially* in levelheaded women—you're one of those, I suspect."

"To the marrow," Liza replied honestly, although she supposed coming from Kim the assessment was not a compliment. "I've been known to deviate wildly from time to time, however," she added in disgust.

Kim flicked her wrist in a gesture of exasperation. "So? You're five thousand miles away from home in a very strange land. You're supposed to spread your wings. Women pray that someone like Christian will suddenly loom on a foreign horizon. I can tell you you're the envy of every woman on our tour—not sexually, of course," she added in her blunt way. "Athough...do you remember Mrs. Johnson? Short woman, nice clothes?"

"The one with the rather startling red hair?"

Kim nodded. "She's divorced. And lonely. She practically trembled every time he made the most casual remark in those rippling tones to her. And when he offered to show her how to eat lobster—I thought she'd dissolve right into the sand."

Liza smiled thinly. "I'd gladly deliver him into her hands...no, forget that. The poor woman would have no idea what she was taking on! I didn't. But there are still times when just the thought of going back to New York makes me feel like a kid resisting the end of summer vacation."

"And you feel guilty about that," Kim hooted. "Why do you think Scott and I never went back to the States? We're playing permanent hooky."

"But you work hard here," Liza protested. "I've seen you—there's hardly a moment you can call your own."

Kim shook her golden mane. "Hard physical work isn't necessarily real work. What we do here has an air of play and unreality about it. We both know that even though we don't talk about it."

Liza searched Kim's face. "That surprises me. I thought you were committed to the life you're building here. In fact, Scott said—"

"Just talk," Kim said with an aggressiveness that made Liza glance at her in surprise. "We aren't married, you know," she said suddenly.

Liza hesitated, unsure of the proper response. "No, I didn't know," she said simply.

"We feel married," Kim asserted. "But I think one of the reasons we didn't go home was that if we did, we'd have to face up to a decision. I suppose you don't approve of our relationship...." There was a small note of challenge in her voice.

Liza spoke cautiously. "I don't disapprove. But I wouldn't choose it for myself. It just seems...confusing. As if the opportunities for misunderstanding and pain are greater, not less. I need firmer ground...."

"That's why Christian's thrown you into such a dither, isn't it? He doesn't play by your rules. Tell me, has he ever mentioned his feelings for you?"

"No," Liza replied emphatically.

Kim regarded her pityingly. "Why don't you ask him?" she asked.

Liza's violet eyes held something akin to panic. "Is that what you'd do?"

"Sure. It beats not knowing."

"Somehow I doubt that. I've caught him more often than I like looking at me with an infuriating smile on his face."

"Maybe," said Kim, "looking at you makes him feel good!"

"More likely," Liza retorted, "he finds me slightly absurd. He teased me, to put it mildly, about my work when we were back in New York. That made me mad—darn mad—but I could take it because I'm sure of my ground professionally. But if I thought he found me ridiculous as a woman—"

"You're convinced, then, that there's nothing more going on here than the little thrill of having something on the side while you're away from home?"

Liza winced. "I'd hate to put it in those terms," she said, her memory jerked painfully back to Penn.

Kim saw it all as such a great and glorious game, she thought. The advances and retreats of sexual flirtation—she dared them with laughter and youthful gaiety. The way the green eyes looked lazily from beneath long lashes. The way she moved in those jeans whenever she was around Christian, unconsciously yet with meaning. Liza had noticed it. She was aware of an irrational jealousy and it depressed her.

And she was impatient with moodiness, even though far from free of it. She thought herself thin-skinned and far too sensitive—this charming child was her emotional elder. Christian, she realized, was drawing her into the maelstrom she had always avoided. She craved calmness, yet he persisted in wrenching her eyes open to undreamed of and unsettling sights.

She didn't want to fall in love with a one-dimensional man, an exotic stranger encountered far from home, the fantasy figure who loomed so large in Kim's imagination. She wanted to be able to say with peace and sureness, "This is the man I love." Wasn't that why she had waited so patiently for the revelation of Penn the man? Not Penn Livsay the wealthy, international investor. Not Penn Livsay the social giant. Maybe there hadn't been the sharp excitement she felt when she'd had a kiss torn from her in the dark basement of the Cavendish. But neither was there this tormenting doubt.

Yet that was exactly what she'd done, she thought, anger rising in her. She'd allowed her blood to be stirred by the desert wind lifting a man's hair. By a bronzed arm clutching a steering wheel. She'd given away a patiently-won love for a few days—no, not even that—a few minutes of passion in a desert oasis.

And what would become of her when she got back
to New York? Christian would be gone, of course—
perhaps with the cross. She'd be left with two
choices. She could be silent and enter into a dishonest
relationship with Penn. Or she could confess and lose
him. She thought he would forgive her much, but instinct told her he would not forgive her dalliance with
Christian Chase. She remembered one night last summer, sitting on the patio of the Livsays' weekend
house overlooking Long Island Sound, when Penn
had offered, unasked, a detailed but not surprising
confession of his liaisons with other women. She'd
had little to offer herself—her chaste infatuation
with a professor of archaeology who chaperoned the
dig in Egypt, a brief romantic interlude with the
pleasant, helpful young lawyer who had settled her
father's estate for her. They counted even less, now
that she'd experienced this earthquake of emotion
for Christian.

Kim's voice pushed into Liza's musings. She was
saying, "So far you've assumed the worst. But what
if he said he really cared about you? What if he
wanted to keep on seeing you once you get back to
New York? What would you do then?"

What indeed, thought Liza.

Much later, she lay alone in her sleeping bag and
listened to the final prayer bells from the campanile
rise and fade in the darkness. She wondered if Christian was thinking of her. Was he wrestling with the
same questions?

No, she thought fiercely, she wouldn't speculate.
She wouldn't torture herself. She had to concentrate

on her job and on her responsibilities. And right
now, it looked very much as if she would need Christian's help to do it. She couldn't afford to alienate
him and that was the simple truth. It was her last
thought before the profound sleep of utter exhaustion.

SHE WOKE with a fierce headache and a dry mouth.
The sun had already turned the bus into an oven. She
opened bleary eyes to see Christian striding across the
rocky ground toward her. He looked fresh and bright
and impossibly smug.

She drew her fingers through tousled hair, recognized the futility, and gave up. No doubt the only
women he saw in the morning had dewy skins, were
attired in lace bedjackets, and had every hair miraculously in place. She dragged herself up into a sitting position against one of the seats.

He rapped a noisy tattoo on the side of the bus and
stuck his head through the doorway. "I've seen you
look better, Liza," he said cheerfully.

"*I* didn't spend the night in a proper bed," she
snapped. Her voice was fuzzy with sleep.

"I don't know how proper it was, but I slept, and
the shower was refreshing. Breakfast was simple but
nourishing."

Liza set her jaw and reined in her temper. "It's not
so bad here," she muttered.

"It's awful here," he corrected. "You'd have done
better spending the night out on the sand. How fast
can you get yourself freshened up?" he asked briskly.

"Why?" she inquired testily.

"Because," he said, "I have made the acquaintance of a very nice priest, a Brother Damion from Athens. We had a productive chat over tea this morning, and he's agreed to give us *both* a tour of the monastery—if you hurry up."

"Five minutes!" she promised. Without embarrassment or a thought to the skimpiness of her attire, she lightly kissed his cheek. He accepted the kiss with bemused grace.

"Turn around," she instructed, noting the slow journey of his eyes, but there was no edge to her voice. He did so, with a small sigh, and she drew on the slacks that had been hanging over the seat back.

Moments later, fresh and neatly if hurriedly dressed, Liza left with Christian for the monastery.

CHAPTER TEN

BROTHER DAMION was young and olive-skinned, with thick black hair tied back with a cord. He wore the loose, dark robe, broad waist sash, and fezlike hat of the Order of St. Catherine. The robe was rusty and threadbare with age, the hem gray with dust. Scott was right, Liza thought. These *were* poor, hardworking religious men, with an exotic, faintly Oriental appearance to them.

Brother Damion had met them at the doors and now led them down the dark, arched tunnel of stone Liza had watched Christian disappear into the night before. The monk's voice was halting, accented and soft. He had a shy way of hanging his head and clasping his hands behind his back as he walked, but his bright eyes and smile betrayed pleasure. They emerged into a large courtyard and the sudden assault of the sun. Liza had expected it to be silent and deserted except for a few monks lost in contemplation. Instead, she found it filled with Bedouins squatting around the Well of Moses, talking animatedly, smoking and holding various bits of work in their laps.

The outer battlements were crowded with white-washed stone buildings. Exterior staircases climbed steeply up their walls. "Why, it looks just like a Mediterranean fishing village!" Liza exclaimed in a low murmur to Christian. "Brother Damion and the rest of the Greek monks must feel right at home."

They examined a domed mosque adorned by a minaret, and a tiny Byzantine church with a wooden roof. Everything was so archaic and charming, and Liza was wide-eyed with wonder. They walked, their footsteps echoing, through the empty dining hall, past long refectory tables, and exclaimed over the peeling religious murals that covered the walls. They climbed a narrow, open staircase that hung on the outer wall and strolled the parapets, stopping to peer out the holes where once pilgrims had been hoisted up on slings, so that the monks wouldn't have to open the gates and risk attack.

"And this?" Liza asked, pointing to a small window in one of the walls.

"For the bread," Brother Damion told her. "We give it to the hungry." Liza ticked off one more thing Nigel Bagley had described accurately. She began to wonder if she dared press this monk about seeing the treasure. But Christian was still showing only the casual interest of any other tourist, and she kept silent.

Back in the courtyard, they passed a low white building with its own small terrace and plants thriving in clay pots outside. "The archbishop's rooms," said Brother Damion. "I know, Mr. Chase," he added quickly, "you would like me to ask permission to see the treasures. . . ."

"If you could," Christian said. "We've come a

long way and Miss Downing and I would be most grateful.''

The young man hesitated a moment, a struggle written clearly on his face. He nodded. "But I cannot promise," he warned.

"What do you think, Christian?" Liza asked, poking distractedly among the plants after Brother Damion had been admitted.

"I think we're lucky we got this far. Brother Damion's fairly new here. I suspect he's a bit lonely still and that's why he latched on to me. The others I met were older and a bit on the gruff side. I think he'll give it his best shot, but whether he has any influence over the archbishop I couldn't begin to guess."

It was half an hour later when the monk emerged. "It is good," he said, beaming. "The archbishop has given me work to do in the library. You may come with me and stay for as long as it takes me to do it."

Liza shoved her hands in her pockets to keep from clapping. "Thank you, Brother Damion," she said. "We'll try not to get in your way."

They followed his flapping sandals up the stone steps and stopped before double, carved doors of Lebanon cedar. The monk withdrew an enormous iron key from his pocket and unlocked the padlock that secured a heavy, drooping chain. The doors swung open and Liza and Christian fell silent, stunned by the splendor that lay before them. Monolithic granite columns supported a vaulted nave that glowed with gold leaf. Chandeliers of gold and silver glittered above intricate, jewellike mosaic floors. There were wall panels carved with the crests of the

Crusaders and erected by the knights. Others glowed with murals depicting Biblical scenes of angels or Moses, or portraits of Justinian and Theodora.

Beyond the exquisite little side chapels and the rows of plain wooden benches for the monks was the most sacred area of the monastery, the original Chapel of the Burning Bush. Following Brother Damion's example, Christian and Liza slipped out of their shoes and stood barefoot on the rich, Oriental carpets, before an altar bearing heavy silver candlesticks. Silently, the monk motioned them over to a small, intricately grilled window. Outside was a low, beautifully kept shrub. It was descended, he whispered to them, his face glowing, from the bramble bush of the Bible.

From the chapel, they were led into a narrow alley. They rounded a sharp corner and came all of a sudden on the hunched back of a monk, who was seated by the dark doorway of a squat, whitewashed building. Liza brushed the worn, purple robe and turned to apologize, a smile on her face.

With a choked cry, she stumbled backward into Christian's arms. From beneath the cowl of the monk's robe, sightless eyes were turned up to her. A bony hand stretched toward her. For a moment she reeled.

"Brother Stephanos," their guide said, with a gesture that made Liza feel as if he was introducing her to the skeleton and expected her to say, how do you do. "He was truly a saint," Brother Damion offered by way of explanation, "so the archbishop gave him this place of honor guarding our ossuary."

"Ossuary—a charnel house? Where bones are kept?" asked Liza, edging away from the macabre sight of a gowned skeleton complete with staff in its upraised hand.

Brother Damion nodded. "Here, we dig up our dead after five years and place their bones in this building. Would you like to see?" he asked hopefully.

Liza felt Christian's hand tighten painfully around her elbow. "Yes, Miss Downing and I would like that very much," he said. He smiled down on her with meaning.

"Of course!" she agreed briskly, understanding, with the help of Christian's spur, that they must endure anything in order not to offend.

The dank building was every bit as unpleasant as Liza had feared, but between the two of them, she and Christian managed to work up enough enthusiasm to please Brother Damion. They exclaimed, with what they hoped was appropriate interest, over ghastly niches filled with skulls—and worse, the bins of unsorted bones. The strong, musty odor made Liza grateful she'd had no time for breakfast. Outside again, she inhaled the dry, hot desert air with profound relief.

Across the alley, under a stone arch, lay yet another elaborately carved door. *The library,* Liza thought. She bit her lip softly and glanced at Christian with bright eyes, rivalry forgotten in her anticipation. Inside, Damion paused by an old trestle table and opened an enormous, leather-bound book. He took up a straight pen and dipped it in a crusted pot of ink.

He handed the pen to Liza, saying, "If you would both sign the registry, please. It is required of everyone who comes."

Liza bent, signed her name, and filled in the other spaces for date, address and affiliation. Quickly and, she hoped, unobtrusively, she scanned the entries above her own. She drew a deep breath, thinking once again how close she'd come to having the entire trip turn into a fiasco. The previous guest, one Antonio Mordini from a museum in Rome, had come five months before. A Martin McCready from the University of Edinburgh was the only other visitor for the entire year. Had she known the odds against her, she'd have thought long and hard that afternoon at lunch with Penn when she'd blurted out her intention to come here. She stepped back and watched Christian sign the registry in a strong hand. Odd, she thought, how this man who'd created the problem, was the one providing her only chance to solve it.

Accustomed as they both were to working daily with masterpieces, neither was prepared for what they found in that library. Liza heard the British explorer's description echoing in her ears, "... the toy chest of some fabulous princeling." Little seemed to have changed in the decades since Bagley wrote that, she thought. Row upon row of shelves were jammed with artifacts in no discernible order—icons, triptychs, gold chalices, jeweled candlesticks. There could be no value assigned to them and Liza abandoned any attempt to fully comprehend what she was seeing.

There was a second, even larger room off to one

side, sealed by a heavy wire screen. It held, Brother
Damion told them, several thousand ancient manuscripts. These, unlike the artifacts, were neatly
shelved and labeled. The church had sent specialists
to catalog the precious texts in Greek, Arabic, Persian, Coptic and a dozen other languages. "You
mentioned Constantine, I think," the young monk
said. "In there we have the Old and New Testaments
commissioned by him and sent to us by Justinian."
He volunteered the information simply, without any
hint of boastfulness.

Liza felt a little thrill of shock run through her. If
Constantine's Bible had come here, might not his
cross as well? What had all seemed academic back in
New York seemed electrifyingly alive here.

"I will not be able to let you into the manuscript
room," Brother Damion added apologetically. "It is
the special domain of Brother Spiros, who is in
Athens for medical treatment right now."

Christian assured him that was no problem. "Although we'd love to see the manuscripts, of course,
they're not what we came for."

The monk lifted his palms in a gesture of helplessness. "I'm afraid there is no list of our possessions.
You said a cross?"

"Yes," Liza said eagerly, "in gold and jewels—
very beautiful."

Brother Damion rubbed his thin beard thoughtfully. "There are many crosses...but perhaps I know."
He walked along one row of shelves, frowning, then
stopped. "Here," he said, obviously pleased. "Yes,
this one is very fine."

"Oh, Brother Damion," Liza breathed, "it's exquisite!" She reached out and traced the lines of the cross the monk held reverently in his hands. It was silver, the crosspiece bound by gold and set with a large ruby encircled with pearls. It stood about fourteen inches high on a base of solid gleaming gold. "I'm afraid this is larger—it was made for an altar, perhaps," Liza said respectfully. "The one we're interested in was made for one man, a very wealthy man."

Brother Damion shook his head. "As you can see, it is impossible for one man to know everything that is here. Some day, there will be a record of everything. We began with the manuscripts because they are so fragile. Soon someone will come to do the icons. But it will take many scholars and much more money than we have right now to do it all." He looked over his shoulder at a library table, stacked with ledgers, at the far end of the room. "I am afraid I must begin my work now and leave you to do the best you can." With that he excused himself, removed one of the ledgers from the pile, and bent over it dutifully.

"Can you believe he apologized?" said Liza. "As if it's a burden to sort through all this! I could float away I'm so happy!"

Christian looked less pleased. "Before you do, may I remind you that there are thousands of things here and we can stay only as long as the good brother can be spared to keep tabs on us. When he's through, we're through."

Liza dumped her handbag on a table. "You're

right—I couldn't bear it if we were kicked out now, after seeing all this.''

''I suggest we divide the area up. You take this side and I'll take the other. Be careful when you use that stepladder—it looks as if it's been here since day one. And no getting carried away dreaming about what even a single shelf of this would add to the glory of the Cavendish.''

''Nor you, calculating what the commission on it would mean to your bank account,'' she retorted. He hadn't liked the dig—she could see that from the faint narrowing of his eyes. Instantly she regretted it, feeling she'd taken a very cheap shot at him. They separated stiffly and started to work.

The curator in Liza was alternately exhilarated and horrified. Such exquisite things, dull with dust and in total disarray! She would have loved to get down to the basics of her profession—the sorting, identifying and describing. It crossed her mind more than once that she should march right up to the archbishop's little house and volunteer—enlist, really, for it would mean at least a few years' work.

The morning wore on and Brother Damion stayed at his books, his pen making a steady scratching noise. Liza sneezed with the dust, blew wisps of hair from her brow, and made a snail's progress down the shelves. She did not give in to the urge to exclaim loudly over every discovery. She felt that Brother Damion would believe his trust in them more justified if they appeared scholarly and serious. But soon she and Christian were sharing a quiet communication. There was a special joy in a glance exchanged, an excitement signaled, a nod and a smile, or simply a moment of silence over something particularly beautiful.

Yet as the shafts of sunlight piercing the tall windows shifted and lengthened, Liza despaired of finding what she'd traveled halfway around the world for. They had inched their way along two sides of the room and were within a few feet of each other when Liza said with irritation, "Christian, I believe you've brought me here for nothing."

He didn't look up. "I didn't bring you anywhere. All I ever did was make a simple comment over a glass of sherry. How was I to know that under that conservative suit beat the heart of an adventuress?"

She slumped in a chair and rubbed her temples. Christian sat on his heels beside her, rummaging through a bottom shelf of not very interesting brass bowls. She watched him idly. She was tired, but restless and dissatisfied. It was as if she'd rushed through a rich meal greedily. She was over full yet couldn't remember any of the exquisite dishes she'd consumed.

The light spilling through the elaborate grillwork fractured into a thousand smaller beams. Her eyes followed the specks of dust swirling in large lemon clouds about her. It was so distracting that she might have nodded off for a second had not a beam, in one of its infinitesimal steps across the heavens, suddenly hit something, setting off a tiny, golden explosion.

She cocked her head and looked again. The fire was out now, but an afterglow remained. Sticking out from the edge of an upper shelf was a small semicircle of gold. It was just a tiny piece, perhaps an inch wide and half again as deep. Liza blinked, then abruptly straightened. She grabbed Christian's shoulder and shook it.

He shot her a distracted, almost annoyed glance. "What?" he muttered.

She stood up. "Look," she said. "Look!"

His eyes followed hers, then moved back. "I'm not a mind reader, Liza. What is it?"

"Second shelf from the top, six inches in from the right," she rapped out impatiently. She extended her arm and made a few futile leaps for it.

"I see it now," he said. He slipped his large hands around her waist and drew her back. "Here, let me." He took a small library stool and stepped up to pull the gold shaft down, along with a choking rain of dust.

Slowly, carefully, his long fingers brushed away the gray film. Liza felt her heart hammer. As the color of each stone was exposed, each swirl of detail uncovered, she nodded. But the revelations only confirmed what she had known at first glance, so totally had she memorized each line of Constantine's Cross.

Her eyes lifted and met his. So, he had been right after all. This was his victory. Yet what did it say about what lay in the vault in New York? And what conceivable profit, she wondered, was there for him in all of this?

She found no answers in his face, only a schoolboylike elation. "If it were not," he said in her ear, "that we might distract dear Brother Damion from his duties, I would pick you up and kiss your very pretty mouth."

He turned to the long library table, pulled a linen handkerchief out of his pocket, and laid the cross on top of it. He pulled up two wooden chairs, indicating the cross was hers to inspect.

Liza pressed her hands together to still their trembling and bent over it. Christian was silent, letting her concentrate. She worked quickly and surely. At one point she reached into her purse and retrieved a small notebook and pencil. She jotted down various figures in neat columns. She ran the pencil point back and forth between entries made before she'd left New York and those just made. Finally, she brushed aside strands of dark hair that had fallen across her flushed cheeks and sat back.

"Well," Christian demanded, "what have we got?"

"We've got," she replied, sounding weary, "a cross that is identical in virtually every detail to the one in the Cavendish."

He looked at her sharply. "You're sure?"

She made a small gesture toward it. "It's the same size—and by that I mean I don't think it varies by as much as a millimeter. The rubies number the same— twenty-eight. The weight of the emerald in the center is harder to calculate, but it's approximately the same. The gold detailing follows it swirl for swirl... see here?" She showed him her photographs and the rough sketch she'd drawn in the notebook.

He glanced at it and said, "It seems that way to me, too. But you're the only one who'd know, of course."

She hugged herself as if she hurt. *Two* identical masterpieces.... It was possible, but not reasonable. This one had lain here, untouched, for years—perhaps since Nigel Bagley had held it. Yet someone knew it was here, someone had spoken to Christian about it.

"Christian," she said in a small voice, "the dust on this cross was horrendous. You saw it—breathed it—yourself. It simply has *not* been disturbed for a very long time. I don't know what that means, but it's a piece of the puzzle. If...if you could tell me where you first heard about it...."

He shrugged. "I go to so many places, Liza—it could have been a cocktail party, a gallery. I'm sorry I can't help you—believe me."

A shadow passed across her eyes. Perhaps no one had told him. Perhaps he knew it himself and had led her here. Perhaps this was some elaborately orchestrated plot, from the casually dropped hint at the unveiling to his sudden appearance at Nuweiba and the vanished guides. Even here he might have told her which side of the room to search, setting her in the path of the cross, and bided his time until she stumbled across it. Her mind teetered between doubt and belief.

Absurd, she thought. How could that profit him? Victor's theory hinged on the cross in New York being judged, ultimately, as authentic and Christian's comments a ruse. Yet here was a second cross, just as he'd said.

"This isn't...what I'd imagined at all," she began. "I owe you an apology...." She couldn't find the words. She was ashamed.

"You thought I lied." He said it gently. There was no condemnation in his voice or in his eyes.

"Yes," she said.

"Right until now?"

"Yes." She averted her eyes.

"It's all right, Liza." His hand covered hers.

"No," she replied clearly, "it's not. Something will have to be done. I'm not sure what yet. But I think—oh, Christian, I'm so terribly afraid—that Victor and Penn have been sold a fake! And there's so much money involved. And there'll be such a scandal and public embarassment—" She stopped. The Livsays' reaction, the newspapers, the loss and the snickering—she hardly dared think about it.

She looked up at Christian. His eyes were on something far away that only he could see. She couldn't read his feelings from his profile. But when, at last, he turned to her, he was smiling. And that was not, somehow, what she'd expected.

"No BREAKFAST, no lunch—I could eat a camel!" Liza muttered. She was speaking to herself. She had, luckily, the camp locker room to herself, for an observer might have concluded the desert sun had severely affected her.

She was also smiling. Her bare feet were light on the cool, concrete floor. She hadn't known it was possible to be this happy. She and Christian, after thanking Brother Damion warmly, had walked the garden paths for ages. They'd shared their excitement over everything they'd seen. They'd discussed this land and its people, held hands and sat silently

under the cypresses, laughing at the haughty peacocks. She had even told him about the Bagley
diary—silly thing to have held back, she admonished
herself.

But tonight, she thought, they'd talk only about
themselves. She wanted to know everything, everything about him. They were done with wary games,
with loaded, entrapping questions. And if he spoke
of love...she wouldn't be afraid. The love she'd felt
swelling in her breast like some rare, night-blooming
flower back at Ibn-Bader's camp was blossoming
now in the clear light of day. It was real. The acceptance of it both calmed and excited her. She wanted
only to be with him. Hurry, Liza, her heart sang.

She had showered and shampooed her hair. It had
dried almost instantly and now she began to tie it
back. She stopped and shook it free, remembering
the way he had run his fingers through it approvingly
in Furtaga. She passed over makeup, thinking it unnecessary on sun-kissed skin. But she did lavish
mascara on her long lashes and clear gloss on her
lips. She removed the plain little studs from her ear-
lobes and replaced them with gold hoops.

She had one clean outfit left and now she dug it out
of her suitcase. It wasn't special—just another pair
of tan pants and a T-shirt. But the pants were fresh
and the top a bright cherry red with a flattering
scooped neck, a perfect complement to her skin and
hair. She tugged it on over her head and wondered
what on earth they would eat. There was precious little food left in the jeep and what there was certainly
wouldn't do justice to the evening.

He'd probably suggest they drive down the highway to one of those restaurants where they could get something fresh. Funny, she thought, to feel so excited about going out on a date in a jeep to some dilapidated roadside stand made out of rusty scrap metal, where the food might be questionable. Yet she was more thrilled than she'd ever felt dressed in silk and pearls, slipping through Manhattan in the isolated luxury of Penn's limousine, to dine on oysters and champagne.

She pressed her eyes shut and set her jaw against the sudden pain. Penn—there was so much to tell him. All of it unpleasant. Where would she find the strength? She shook her head as if to toss off this burden of disloyalty. Soon enough she'd have to face him. Tonight she'd find her happiness and in it, her courage. She turned to leave, her step as light as her heart.

At the edge of the road she had to pause. She was trembling inwardly, her blood rushing to her ears. Nerves, she thought. She was like a schoolgirl, her self-consciousness excruciating. She hated it and she loved it. Across a barren stretch of ground she saw him. He was so tall it was easy to pick him out. She was stunned that she could miss him so acutely after a couple hours' separation. He looked up, saw her and waved. She heard her sharp intake of breath and hurried to him.

He had been doing something with the motor. Now, he slammed the hood, tossed a wrench into the back, and wiped his hand on a greasy rag. He hadn't changed. "Hi," he said.

She perched herself on the fender. She felt absurdly shy. "Problems?" she asked.

"Some. I think I've got it fixed now, though."

She nodded. "Good...." And, when nothing more was forthcoming from him, she asked, "Are you hungry, Christian? I am."

"I suppose so." He was tossing the keys distractedly in his hand. His manner wasn't cool, precisely, but it lacked the easy intimacy of the afternoon. The extra effort she'd taken with her appearance seemed lost on him.

"If you'd like, I could fix us something from our supplies. It will be boring, but...."

"I was going to suggest you eat with Scott and Kim tonight if you can find them," he said.

She was confused. She had no desire to share the evening with anyone but him and was hurt that he felt the need for more company. "I could ask them, I suppose...but you'll eat with us too, won't you?"

"I'm eating with Brother Damion tonight," he said bluntly.

"Brother Damion?"

"Yes—he asked, and after all he did for us I didn't feel I should refuse. You can see that, can't you?"

She closed her ears to the impatience in his voice. "Yes, I can see that," she replied. Her smile was mechanical. Her eyes filled with ridiculous tears of disappointment but she didn't cry. "I don't suppose I could come?" she asked, deserted by her pride.

"Afraid not—no women and all that."

"Well," she said, hopping down and hiding her hurt behind brisk movements, "perhaps we could meet later? At the very least we have to make our plans for returning to Aqaba.'' She had assumed they would go back together. Now, having said it, she felt the chill threat of another rejection.

He gave her a perfunctory pat on the shoulder. ''Could we leave that till the morning? It's been a busy day. I thought I'd go straight back to the dormitory after dinner to catch some sleep.''

Something inside Liza crumbled. Had she misjudged his mood and misread his signals *that* badly? She searched the mask that was his face. It was so hard to understand what intimacy meant to men. This whipsawing was playing havoc with her ego.

Then suddenly he was kissing her cheek and saying goodbye, then crossing the ground with his long, loping stride. She slammed her hand down on the hood in a fit of pique. ''Damn!'' she said. Yet he was only doing what she herself would have done had the monks allowed her to dine with them. If he weren't so scrupulously correct he wouldn't be the man she had fallen, with alarming speed, so deeply in love with. She rubbed her arms and sighed. Well, she certainly wasn't going to eat alone.

She found a bored Kimberley at the strangely empty bus. ''Where's the gang?'' Liza asked.

Kim sighed. ''Reverend Clarkson's got them all at a little chapel partway up the mountain. They're doing their Bible study tonight. I sent some food with them. And Scott's over gabbing with some of the other tour guides—I won't see him for the rest of the night. What's got you down? Things not go well at the monastery?''

Liza shook her head. "Things went great. Better than I hoped."

"So?"

"Well, it's just that I wanted to talk to Christian tonight about...everything. And he's gone off to spend the evening with the monks."

"Looks like we've both been deserted. It's hardly flattering, is it? Why don't we fight back by having our own party!"

Liza gave a short, rueful laugh. "I can contribute precisely one box of crackers, a can of sardines, and half a bag of dried apricots."

Kim jumped up and brushed sand from her cotton slacks. "Forget that!" she said gaily. "We'll drive down the highway to a tourist stop I know. It's run by a young Egyptian couple. The food's good and the crowd's even better. Game?"

Kim drove with more enthusiasm than skill in the failing light, but they arrived safely enough and squeezed in among the usual assortment of battered and rusting vehicles. There was Western music blaring from somewhere; and the air smelled deliciously of charcoal and cinnamon.

This was just what she needed, Liza thought. Noise and people and Kim's offbeat, irreverent conversation and peculiar brand of common sense. She had fallen out of love with one man and in love with another in the space of a heartbeat. That might terrify her, or sound like the plot of a second-rate film, but Kim, she guessed, would find it predictable and wonderful.

It was a perfect night. The stars were silver, the

hills blue, the sands deep yellow. They bought lamb and pita and a spicy tomato and onion salad and took it to eat at an outdoor table. Liza discovered she had at least two versions of everything Kim wanted to know about Christian. Kim was decidedly partial to the more roguish account. She had decided not to tell the younger woman about Penn, but confidences are easily given far from home.

Kim brought her hands together in a single clap of delight. "I begin to see your problem.... Problem— what am I saying?" She widened her large green eyes for effect.

Liza was uneasy. She was a reluctant and bewildered stranger to the world of multiple male friends. "I didn't plan this. I didn't want it. It just...happened," she said miserably.

Kim pushed a can of soda aside and rested her elbows on the table. "You're what? Late twenties?" she asked. "C'mon, you're susceptible. This Penn of yours had you to himself for a long time and never asked—or gave—a firm commitment. If another man comes along and makes himself attractive— well, that's not your fault."

Liza's lower lip pouted thoughtfully. "Really?"

"Really!" said Kim with authority.

"All right, then," Liza said, laughing. "I'm tired of feeling guilty for falling in love. I'm not even going to feel guilty for having a good time tonight while Christian's stuck eating bread and watery soup under the stern eye of the archbishop."

"Now you've got it," said Kim. "C'mon, let's go

in. I'll introduce you around and we can get some coffee.''

The air had become suddenly cold just as the last thin slice of bloodred sun fell behind the mountains. The two women grabbed their purses, deposited their paper plates in an old oil drum, and ducked into the plain, cinder-block building.

The dining room was small, crowded and very noisy. There was an open kitchen at one end in which charcoal fires burned, sending clouds of greasy soot to mingle with the thick cigarette smoke. The crowd was noticeably young, European, and high-spirited. Kim and Liza paused, blinking as their eyes adjusted to the dim light. Kim stood on tiptoe, straining to find a couple of vacant spaces for them. Suddenly her jaw dropped. She shot a nervous glance at Liza.

"What is it?" asked Liza.

Kim hesitated, a struggle on her face. "Maybe this wasn't such a good idea. It's awfully busy tonight."

"But you love people—and I don't mind, honestly!" She, too, craned her neck for an empty table. And she, too, saw the cause of the peculiar expression on Kim's face.

She felt the blood drain from her cheeks instantly. It was a double blow. To see Christian sitting there, hunched over a table, stirring a cup of Turkish coffee, was bad enough. But *him*, as well? Shock had driven his name from her mind, but there was no mistaking the snowy hair, the mahogany skin, the grizzled hand resting on the knob of the walking stick.

Liza closed her eyes and rubbed the bridge of her nose, willing herself to think clearly. Why would the old man from Aqaba be here? She looked back at them. It was clear from the way their heads were bent close, from the intensity of their gestures and speech, that this was no casual encounter.

Why had Christian lied to her? A dozen explanations assaulted her, all appalling. She felt Kim's fingers on her wrist. "Perhaps he has an explanation...."

"I'm sure he has," Liza replied tightly, "but none I want to hear. You see—oh, it's too complicated and I can't go into all of it. But that man with him—I met him in Aqaba. It can't be a coincidence that he's here."

"You think it has something to do with you?"

"I *know* it does. A lot of things I didn't understand are beginning to make sense. I don't know why or how, but I've been tricked. It's beginning to fit in with a theory about Christian that someone else told me."

Kim tugged at her. "You're scaring me, Liza. Let's get out of here. I gave you very bad advice about that man. He's no good, and I'm taking you back with me."

Liza lifted her chin. "I'll go back. But not before I have the pleasure of watching him try to explain this away in that oh-so-smooth manner of his."

She plunged into the crowd with Kimberley at her heels. As she fought her way to his table she was amazed to find herself in possession of a cool calmness. Anger had made her mind very clear.

It was the old man who saw her first. He wiped his stubby chin with the back of his hand and half rose while flashing a warning at Christian with his eyes. But Christian was staring into his coffee and it was Liza who intercepted the alarm.

"Please don't bother to stand," she said, waving a hand carelessly and sitting without invitation. Christian's head jerked up and she noted with grim pleasure that it was his mouth that hung open this time.

"Liza—" he began, his nostrils flaring slightly. Christian Chase wasn't used to being caught off guard. But she gave him credit—his manners always saw him through anxious moments "—I believe you know Angus Cavanaugh," he said in his most civilized tone.

"I do indeed," she said with frigid courtesy. "Good evening, Mr. Cavanaugh."

Angus had recovered from his initial shock. "Good evening, Miss Downing," he said. "It's good to see you looking so well. And in such good hands. I must say I was worried about you when I got back to the hotel and found you gone."

"You did get my note, didn't you? I left it with the desk clerk." She raised a sardonic eyebrow.

"Oh, yes indeed. I'm sorry I didn't get back to you in time with more satisfactory guides than the ones you apparently ended up with. I missed you by less than an hour."

He was smiling, courteous—and patronizing. She hated it. "That's all right, Mr. Cavanaugh. It takes time to place overseas calls. That is what you were doing, isn't it, Mr. Cavanaugh? Telling Christian where to find me?"

Angus's eyes swung to Christian for guidance. The act spoke eloquently of secrets from which she was excluded. She said, bristling, "I'm sure the two of you would prefer that I leave for a moment so you can get your stories straight. But I have no intention of accommodating you."

Christian passed his hand over his face as if exasperated. "Liza, you have to believe I would have taken you into my confidence before this, but—"

"No!" she flared. "I don't have to believe anything you say, ever again. You were caught—isn't that about the sum of it? If Kim hadn't brought me here, you'd have let me go on thinking you were back at St. Catherine's. So don't pile one insult on another, please."

A muscle in his jaw worked furiously. "I'm sorry," he said.

She was stiff with indignation. "Sorry you were found out—not sorry you lied."

His voice was low and lethal. "I never lied to you in any way that counts. You made assumptions...."

More than you know, she thought, hot with humiliation. She shook her head slowly, disbelief widening her eyes. "Is that how you define truth—by degrees?"

"Liza, calm down. Please...there's no need for accusations and hysteria."

And suddenly she hated him, hated the voice, the discipline, the icy, cultured calm. What she had once seen as devastating charm now seemed chilling superiority. She wanted to slap him, to shatter the control. Instead she asked furiously, "Can you look me in the eye and tell me now that you haven't been working all along for someone?''

"I can't deny that," he replied quietly.

She turned her head away, her lips thin and pale. Her voice was hoarse when she spoke. "Victor warned me about you. So did Penn. You're probably every despicable thing they said you were. But at least I know now where we stand."

He leaned forward, blond hair falling across his brow. "No," he insisted, "you don't know. But I'll tell you—"

He was stroking her hand. When had he started that? "Don't!" she cried, withdrawing her fist. "It won't work this time, not the handholding nor the—"

She saw embarrassment on Angus's face and broke off. Did he know about that, too? Was that the plan— make love to her to render her blind and obedient? Oh, how she had rewarded him!

She hugged her purse to her. "Kim?"

"Right here, Liza."

She felt the firm young hand on her back. "Let's go."

She thought the night air would help. And then she felt the blow, a terrifying wave of nausea. She fought for balance. Cold sweat beaded her face. She ran to the edge of the desert and was ill until all that was left was fear.

The exhaustion was complete. It numbed her mind, seeped into her flesh and bones. She had only the dimmest recollection of Kim bedding her down like a baby in the sleeping bag an hour later.

CHAPTER ELEVEN

SHE HEARD FOOTSTEPS on the gravel and at first paid little attention. She was still floating at a deeper level. But low voices raised pinpricks of fear on her arms. She started to pull herself up but a hand bore her down. Another pressed her mouth.

Her eyes sprang open and she saw his face looming close, close enough to count every tiny line at the corners of his eyes, to feel his breath on her. His gaze held hers, heavy with meaning, and slowly he released her. He sat back on his heels on the floor of the bus.

"Sorry about the hand. I hated doing that. But if you'd made a scene, brought people running—"

"You needn't have bothered. It's not my style—remember?"

"Kim said you'd been sick—I'm sorry."

It was then that she saw Angus behind him at the bus door. "It hits everyone sooner or later," the old man said, "the water, the food. We've brought you some sweet tea."

Liza felt the stirring of a small rebellion in her stomach. She closed her eyes briefly. "I couldn't..." she began.

"Just sip it. It'll help. Believe me, I know."

"I don't want your tea and sympathy, Mr. Cavanaugh," she said. "A straight answer would do more for me right now."

He looked almost meek, she thought. "That's what I've come for, Liza," he said. "I don't want you thinking badly of Christian on my account. It upset you last night when he said he was working for someone. . . ."

Liza envisioned the sort of person who would employ Christian's less savory talents and felt a shudder of distaste. "It did—it does," she replied.

"You must know, then. He's been working for two people, really, although they're as unlikely a pair as you'll ever find hiring a high-class agent like Christian."

She wondered if she even wanted to know any more, if she was strong enough to take another blow. She took a deep, unsteady breath. "And who are these two people, Mr. Cavanaugh?" she asked.

"Christian's been working for me. And a dead monk named Brother John."

Christian took control then, as he was accustomed to. He eased Liza up and into the front seat, opened windows, poured tea from the thermos. Then he sat across from her, legs braced in the aisle. Angus lowered himself to the top step. They gave her time. She stared out at the pink haze of morning, focusing, sipping tea. Presently her stomach settled.

"Did you know," she asked Angus, "who I was when we first met in Aqaba?"

"No, but I did very soon after. My only thought when I saw you standing on the terrace was that a young woman was looking lost. I wondered if I might help. But as soon as you told me a bit about yourself the pieces came together. The face had already been nagging me—I'd see your picture in the paper. You're an unusual and attractive woman, Liza. You'd draw attention to yourself in the States or Jordan.''

But Liza wasn't interested in flattering digressions. "The *Times*?" she asked. "The story on the unveiling?"

He nodded. "You gave me quite a start. Things were happening much faster than I thought they would...although with Christian on the job perhaps no development, even your popping up in Aqaba, should have shocked me."

Her eyes went to Christian and back to Angus again. He was badly dressed, rumpled, eccentric. He had none of the polish and urbanity of the others who glided through Christian's world. And certainly a simple monk, now dead, never had.

"Perhaps," said Christian, "we should go back to the beginning, Angus. Liza's a very thorough woman and I doubt we'll get away with less."

"London, you mean. And Bernard—all of that?"

"Only if you want to, Angus," said Christian with what Liza took to be extreme gentleness.

Angus shrugged his bony shoulders. "I don't mind. Not anymore...." He was silent for a moment, as if gathering memories. "It started in the war years, Liza," he began, "long before you were even born. I was a reporter, then, for a London newspaper. The owner of the paper was Bernard Chase."

Liza glanced at Christian and he nodded. "My father," he confirmed.

"Bernard asked me to cover the fighting in North Africa—Alamein and Tobruk. I'd seen duty myself as a young man and thought I was toughened. But it didn't work out that way. Oh, I did my job and filed my stories on time—usually. But inside me something was happening. I was a man writing about boys dying and I hated it. When the war was over I found I couldn't go back. I'd lost my taste for the old life. They say it's an occupational hazard of being a war correspondent," he said with a hoarse, humorless laugh.

"I don't know... but there are more than a few of us hanging around the corners of this world. Bernard couldn't keep me on as a regular, of course," Angus continued. "I kept moving—Cairo, Jerusalem, Khartoum. But there's always a story in those places, and Christian's father was good enough to buy pieces from time to time to keep me going."

"It wasn't a matter of being good, or charitable, Angus," Christian interjected. "You were one of the best. You still are. You see a side to life others can't or don't want to see. Father loved your work. He looked forward to everything you sent."

"Your father was a fine man, Christian. Never a word of reproach from him. Or dumb questions, either." And to Liza he added, "There's no point trying to hide it. You've guessed anyway, I'm sure. I started drinking pretty heavily... some times worse than others. During one of the bad times I ended up here. I'd finished an article up in Suez and I'd heard a lot of talk about some monastery stuck away in the desert. I had a little money in my pocket and nothing better to do, so one day I found myself on the brothers' doorstep, banging away with the same great knocker I expect you and Christian used.''

Liza thought about the reluctant welcome the tourists were receiving now and wondered what the monks had made of a solitary, probably drunken stranger. She accepted more tea from Christian, tucked her bare free up under her, and turned back to Angus.

"They were used to odd bits of debris washing up from that sea of sand around them. . .did you know that in the Middle Ages prisoners were sent on pilgrimages there? They were made to cross the godforsaken waste on their hands and knees, bound in iron shackles around their necks and ankles. But that's another story. Anyway, they picked me up—literally—hauled me in, nursed me, fed me.

"The archbishop put one particular monk in charge of me. He spoke a little English. He was old and had been relieved of most of his other duties. I think they were glad to pair us up. He could attend to my soul, and I could keep an eye on him, too. It was my good luck that he turned out to be a patient man, because I was a trying sort of swine when I was cut off from my primary source of contentment.''

"This monk," said Liza, "is he the Brother John you mentioned?" When Angus nodded, she asked, "And is all this going to work its way through time and two continents to *my* doorstep?" She looked between the two men, utterly bewildered.

"Oddly enough, yes," said Christian. "You've turned out to be the key. . . go on, Angus."

"This isn't a happy fable about the reformed drunkard, Liza. I couldn't exist in John's world any more than he could in mine. But those were good days for me. If I wasn't at peace exactly, at least I wasn't so full of the self-destructive rages. John and I became friends during all those days that I worked in the garden and he sat reading. I paid several visits to the monastery over the next few years. John and I exchanged letters, too.

"His last letter was rambling and shaky—he was almost ninety when he wrote it—but I'm convinced his mind was as fine as it ever was."

"When was this, Angus?" She'd slipped into a less defensive way of addressing him without realizing it.

"It was 1955, in the spring. He was troubled. Something from the past was preying on his mind. He tried to tell the young monks who were nursing him, but he knew they thought he was senile. They were humoring him, not really listening."

"But he thought you'd listen. . . ."

Angus's eyes danced. "Sure—one crazy man's courtesy to another. Besides, I'd listened to the story once before. When he first came to the monastery, one of his duties was to clean the library. He liked the job because it was peaceful and allowed him to escape the watchful eyes of his superiors for a while. About that time—the early 1920s—a young man came to visit the monastery. He was a scholar. John said he had a letter from a high church official giving him permission to study the manuscripts with an eye to cataloging them.

"John remembered him as a very intense person. His specialty was Coptic dialects. He showed him his notes, not that John could make any sense out of them, of course. But he was impressed by the man's quick mind, and he found him pleasant company, too. The scholar would often sit chatting, watching John at his cleaning. One day, John was polishing a cross—yes, Liza," he said, noting the little jerk of Liza's head. "The man admired the cross and questioned John about its origins."

"What did John tell him?"

"Nothing that he wanted to know—like most of the monks in those years, John had very little education. All that was important to him was that he liked the cross. He liked to care for it—he said it had a special feel in his hands and that sometimes, when he was alone, he held it while he was meditating.

"About then, the visitor left. Said he was going back to Istanbul to a library there—something about dating a manuscript. He returned a month or so later, stayed a while, then left again. There was one final visit about a year later. So far as John knew, he never came back to St. Catherine's again."

Angus paused then, and Liza leaned forward, resting her elbows on the metal bar that separated the front seat from the steps. "That's it? I thought you were leading up to the cross's being stolen—"

"Nothing so straightforward, I'm afraid. The next time John went to see the cross it was right there where he'd left it. But he said it was the oddest thing. The cross felt... wrong. Now I'll have to admit this about Brother John—for a religious man he had a

strong streak of superstition running through him.
The more he brooded about it, the more he came to
believe that the young visitor from Istanbul had
'spoiled' the aura of the cross when he'd handled it.''

"Did he tell his superiors?''

"He mentioned it. But what did he have to tell
them—that he no longer felt peaceful when he held
the cross? Who would pay any attention to that?''

"You, apparently. . . .''

"Who am I to make another man feel foolish,
Liza? In his last letter he wrote,

Angus, I have spent almost all my life in this
little community. But you—you go everywhere.
You see things, hear things. Some day, you will
hear a story about the cross. Some day, you will
find out what I couldn't.''

Angus paused, his eyes strangely misty.

"So I wrote him,'' he went on quietly. "I promised
him. He died soon after that. Years and years passed
and I ended up in Aqaba—I was doing a series for a
British magazine on the resurgence of a fundamen-
talist branch of Islam. Anyway, one morning I happened to pick up a newspaper at the hotel. There was
a story in the art section about the surfacing of a very
valuable cross. A big New York wheeler-dealer was
buying it to donate to a museum—some kind of a tax
scam, no doubt.'' Liza shifted uncomfortably at the
gruff and cynical dismissal of Penn.

"Well, John, I thought, this one's for you. It's not
much to go on, but maybe it's as good as we'll ever

get. That may sound crazy to you, Liza, but... well, I loved the man. That's the long and the short of it.''

"No, Angus, it doesn't sound crazy to me," Liza said. She knew all about doing lunatic things for love.

Angus rubbed his hands and became suddenly brisk. "I thought of Christian—I knew he'd become some sort of expert in art security. It was asking a lot, I know. Maybe he should tell you this part himself.''

Christian brushed his fine hair back off his forehead. "There's not much more to say, really. Angus cabled my London office. I was in Rome at the time buying some oils from an old family friend. My secretary managed to track me down and set up a phone conference between Angus and me. Actually, I'd already been considering going to New York for the auction at Fairchild's. I had a client who'd been after me to get that Renoir for her. She wanted it back in France. I wasn't really sure I wanted the job, but Angus's call settled the matter.''

"Not that I could afford his usual fee for this sort of sleuthing," Angus put in. "I'd have to write for a year just to make his hourly rate.''

The two men laughed, but Liza wished Angus had left that unsaid. Christian had invested a great deal of time and money in this business. Would he have done that if he hadn't expected some sort of return? "I wish you had trusted me," she said quietly. "I wish you hadn't felt the deceit necessary, Christian... at least, not after we came to know each other better.''

He leaned forward, his expression utterly serious.

"I wanted to tell you everything. But you weren't exactly cordial to me when we first met, remember. You made it very clear that you were aligning yourself with Penn and Victor. Can you really imagine Penn allowing anything to disrupt his grand and highly publicized gesture? Especially something as vague as the fretting of a monk who died twenty years ago?"

Liza raised a warning finger. "You can stop right there—I don't want to listen to you malign Penn and Victor. Your own methods are hardly above reproach. All you did was stir things up, sit back, and wait for me to hand you the answers, all neatly gift wrapped."

"Something like that," he conceded casually, "although I didn't anticipate your impulsive trek to the Sinai. I was stunned when Julian told me. You don't know what a chase you led me, Liza."

"And I only hitched a ride down here yesterday, Liza," Angus told her. "I guess the reporter in me is still kicking. I know it looked bad when you walked into the restaurant and saw us—but there's been no conspiracy to deceive you."

She looked at Christian, reaching for the trust she'd had in him. But it stayed stubbornly just beyond her grasp, although not beyond her sight. She said to Angus, "He's told you about the cross we found?"

"Yes, and an odd feeling it gave me. As if John was speaking to me. Liza, I made a promise. But there's only so much I can do, or even Christian. You're the one with the skills and knowledge to sort this out. Will you do it? I'd be forever grateful. . . . ''

Liza leaned back and stared out the window. "I have an awful feeling that there's some sort of fraud in all this. We may be forever in *your* debt for alerting us to it. . .although it may already be too late for Victor."

"What do you mean?" Christian asked quickly.

"Penn hasn't paid for the cross yet—I suppose it doesn't matter if I tell you that. And if I advise him not to buy it when I get back to New York, then Victor will have to absorb the loss, which will be substantial, I'm sure. If, as you've said, he's already in financial trouble, he may never recover, although I suppose he could always. . . ."

"Always what?" Christian prompted.

She was going to say that he could recover its value in gold and jewels. But she felt as if she was speaking from a script that Christian had written, and she rebelled. "Nothing," she said crisply. "We're not at that point yet." She looked at him with eyes that were veiled with sorrow and reproach. How could you have used me so calculatingly, they asked.

Angus felt the lull acutely. He cut into it, saying, "I knew there was a lot of money riding on this deal, Liza, but I had no idea until last night that some of it was your fiancé's. It puts you in a hell of a spot, and I'm sorry about that."

"Thank you, Angus," she said, with an emphasis that made it clear she felt Christian had shown no such consideration for her.

But it was more than Christian's attitude irritating her. It was the fear that she had come within a hair of making the most costly, humiliating blunder of her life. She had been so sure of her research that she'd been ready to put out an international press release based on it. A tiny shiver of horror shook her.

"We'll have to go back and look at the cross in the library," she said. "There must be something I've missed." She frowned, chewing distractedly at the corner of her mouth. Suddenly she slid to the edge of the seat. "Angus—before they let us into the library, they made us sign a registry. When you came here after the war, did you have to sign one, too?"

"I . . . yes, yes, I did. Why?"

"Because if nothing has changed here in hundreds and hundreds of years, isn't it possible that the young manuscript expert from Istanbul had to sign one, too? And since nothing seems to get thrown out, isn't it also possible that the registry is still in there somewhere?"

Angus and Christian exchanged glances. "I suppose so," said Christian, "but I don't know where it would lead us. . . ."

She was already standing and clambering over his long legs. "Anywhere. I don't care. As long as we get going."

They began to grind their way up the hill to the gates. Liza felt Christian's fingers circling her wrist, holding her back a little. His voice was low. "You're still angry," he said. "I can see it in those small, quick steps."

"I'm not," she said with conviction.

"But you *are* finding it hard to get back to where we were with each other."

"I'm trying, Christian...but I need more time. For now, let's back away from the 'we.' I can't handle that yet."

"You know, contrary to what Victor probably told you, I don't do everything for profit. Some things... but not everything."

She withdrew slightly from him. She had to. "We've got work to do," she insisted.

"I thought you were beginning to relax, to trust your instincts."

And to imagine our future, she added silently, *all the time you were winning my trust and picking my brains.* She wanted him, yes, wanted the warmth, wanted all of it. Yet how could she trust herself to be rational? She'd have to make the best of a bad job and get back home where she belonged. Somehow she had to regain control of her life.

He studied the set of her small jaw. "This resentment is so unnecessary."

"But I *do* resent the way you've disrupted my life. I resent the fact that I'm five thousand miles away from home and the people I care about—because of you."

"I thought you came here because you wanted to uncover the truth?"

"That truth may hurt people who've been good to me. And how have I repaid them? By practically bedding down with you behind their backs."

He began to laugh. "Sex again....''

Her hands went to her hips. "You really can't stand the idea that there are men in this world who are kind and generous, can you? Even now, when you're obviously a success in whatever it is you do for a living, you still allow your own brother to scrape by, supporting what is really your responsibility!'' She saw the anger in his eyes but didn't care.

"And who was your source for that bit of gossip— no, don't tell me! The malice is familiar.''

There was a loud crash and they jumped. Angus had his hand on the knocker. He looked from one to the other of them and sighed. "Okay, kids, no fighting in church.''

Brother Damion escorted them to the library where Christian began scanning the rows of registers. He took hold of one of the giant, cloth-bound volumes and yanked, powdering them with dust. He opened it at random and the brown page crumbled at the edges and broke loose from its hand-sewn binding. He replaced it carefully. "That one was from 1942," he said. "You're right, Angus, we'll be at this for a while. We have no name, no date. If we're lucky we'll spot an educated hand at intervals of a few weeks. Perhaps some reference to the church's permission to see the manuscripts. Then, if we're very lucky, we'll see it again after the space of a year.''

Liza wrinkled her nose at the smell of must rising from the stacks of registries. "I'll leave you to your business, gentlemen,'' she said, and walked to the other end of the library where the cross lay waiting on the table.

She rummaged through her bag and retrieved a leather case about the size of a large cigarette package. It had a tiny brass lock and brass hinges, and the leather was soft and shaded by years of gentle use. Liza felt a smile lift the corners of her mouth, as she did nearly every time she held it. Nestled inside its fitted compartments was a miniature set of tools commonly used by archaelogists.

It had been a gift from her father. She had just finished reading the story of Schliemann and the gold of Troy and announced with all the gravity of a sixteen-year-old that she, too, was going to be an archaeologist. Some parents might have ignored such a fancy, or given a lecture on more practical professions for a young woman. But Charles Downing had responded by engaging his daughter in a lively discussion of tombs and treasures, and leaving at her dinner plate the next night "a little something" he'd seen in an antique store near the university during his lunch-hour stroll.

Liza surveyed the fan of brushes of different shapes and sizes. She ran a fingertip over the fine picks, each with a special point and angle. Finally she chose a fat sable brush with a mellow, ivory handle and set to work. When the worst of the dust was gone, she took a smaller brush, about the size of a lipstick brush, and moved it down the cross in quick short strokes. Using the tiniest surgical tweezers, she removed specks of grit that had lodged in the jewel settings. Next she used a specially treated cloth that she removed from a sealed plastic bag. At last, when the cross was cleaned to her satisfaction, she bent over it with a magnifying glass.

From the other end of the library came periodic coughs and sneezes and irritated muttering that made her smile. But for the most part she was lost in her soothing, rhythmic task. She didn't know how much time had passed before she looked up and found Christian and Angus standing over her. Her heart was pounding in her ears and her breathing was quick. There was an odd light in her eyes.

"You've found something," Christian said, lowering his angular body onto the chair beside her.

"Yes," she murmured, happy. The defensiveness was gone from her voice and she laid her hand over Christian's. "Look at this," she said. Their heads came together over the cross, his fair, fine hair mingling with her darker strands. "At first I thought it was just the dirt," she said excitedly. "But I've cleaned it, and it's even more pronounced. You must know something about jewels. . . ."

"Something," he admitted.

"Then look at the rubies. Hold them up to the light."

He raised the cross to the window, squinting. "There's a slight cast to them. They're pinkish."

"That's right," she said, her voice betraying her agitation. "The rubies in the New York cross are deep red, pigeon's blood—the very finest. Now, look at the emerald in the center. Use the magnifying glass this time."

He bent low over it. "There's a slight flaw in the upper right-hand corner, a milkiness underlying the green. It's not the finest stone either."

"Exactly. And the gold beading around the stones. . . ."

Christian shook his head. "They look perfectly fine to me—beautiful, in fact."

"The process for making this beading has been lost to us," she told him. "We just don't know how they produced those perfect, minute chains of beads. But these, while painstakingly made and still very lovely, seem almost clumsy compared to the ones in New York. Also, this cross feels fractionally lighter. I can't give you the difference in grams without my scale, but I'd say it's gold over another metal. Or it may even be hollow."

Angus seemed deep in thought. "It still looks pretty dazzling to me," he announced. "You two aren't splitting hairs, are you?"

"Oh, no," said Liza quickly, "when you've seen the real thing, you know it."

"Liza—do you know what you said? Did you hear yourself?" Christian was staring at her.

The terrible weight was gone, she realized. The corners of her generous mouth curled gently. "The cross in New York is the true Cross of Constantine," she affirmed, "just as I said it was. This one is an exquisite fake."

Christian regarded her now with an intensity verging on fierceness. "Why fake—why not a copy by a lesser craftsman...a student of the original craftsman, for example? A duplicate might have been made. And the way the treasure of the Constantine empire was plundered, a thousand people, bandits even, could have sent this cross here in return for a blessing."

She raised her palms in cheerful concession. She was so relieved that she was prepared to be endlessly agreeable. "Sure—anything's possible. But the artisans of one of the most powerful rulers in history simply did not stamp these things out like prizes in a Cracker Jack box, Christian. And don't forget that whoever made this lacked the knowledge available at that time about the gold beading. No, call it a hunch, call it instinct, but I'm sure this is more recently manufactured.''

Angus's sigh was long and weary. Christian drew up a long leg, resting his ankle on his knee, and drummed his fingers on the table. Impulsively, Liza reached out and laid her hands on both men's. "Oh, come on, you two!'' she cajoled. ''This means Penn and Victor are safe! And if you can't be happy for them, at least be happy that Julian won't have to sack me for gross incompetence!''

Christian looked at Angus from beneath his brow, then turned those cool blue eyes on her. ''There's something you'd better see. . . .''

She searched his face but it was closed to her. Silently, she rose and followed him to the other end of the library.

His long finger slipped over the fragile paper of an open registry and stopped halfway down. ''Here,'' he pointed.

She bent low. The ink had faded from black to a pale, transparent purple. The old-fashioned handwriting was slanted and European. She rested her buffed nail under the line and read aloud, ''September 22, 1921. . . André—''

She went white and groped for a chair behind her. Her eyes when she looked up at the two men were large and stricken. Almost against her will she dragged her gaze back down to the book. She swallowed hard and summoned her voice. "September 22, 1921, André Morneau, Marseilles, France, at the request of His Holiness, Father Basil Andropoulos."

She sat back, silent. Christian reached across her and turned a few brittle pages, supporting them with both hands. "And again. . ." he said.

She looked obediently. The date was October. The final entry, this one in another volume, was dated May 14, 1922. "It's a common name," she blurted out a little wildly.

"Yes," said Christian, as calm as she was desperate, "but this is not a common situation." He took her hand and drew her up. "A little fresh air is in order, I think."

They walked the worn path of the herb garden. Liza bent and picked up a sprig of thyme, drawing it through her fingers and inhaling the familiar, calming fragrance. They found a low stone bench and sat.

Angus lit another of his misshapen cigarettes and said, "Tell us what you know about Victor's grandfather, André, Christian."

"The official version or the unretouched one?"

"There are two?"

"Oh, yes, as there are with most of us," he said pointedly. "But the one André put out for public consumption was more distorted than most."

"Did you know him?" Liza asked.

"No, he died long before I became involved in my father's art dealings. Even Victor's father, Henri, was in semiretirement then. The Morneaus liked to be thought of as an old, elite family. Not aristocratic, to be sure, but part of the wealthy merchant class. They gave the impression that the money, and the paintings, came rolling down from generation to generation and that the sons acquired their eye for art along with mother's milk.''

''Yes, that's the impression I've always had,'' said Liza.

''It was true for Victor, perhaps Henri, but certainly not for André. The truth is, André rose from one of the worst slums in Europe. His mother was a prostitute, his father unknown. Violence and crime were part of everyday life for him as a child.''

''But he overcame all that,'' said Liza. ''He was an educated man, if we can judge from John's story.''

''Self-educated. But he was no Coptic scholar, my dear. The fact is that the founder of one of the greatest art houses in the world started out as a small-time crook and a smuggler. He began, according to the stories my father heard, as a deckhand on boats running between Marseilles and the Middle East. He saw the smuggling going on, the profit to be made. Even as a boy he knew that he was quicker, smarter than the men he worked for. Perhaps André just had a natural eye for it, but he could see that a lot of junk was being passed off as the real thing by the shrewder dealers in the East. He knew that if he was going to keep from being stung, he had to learn everything he could.''

''His diligence must have paid off handsomely,'' Angus remarked.

''Indeed it did. Over the years, with his financial wizardry and shrewd eye, he built one of the greatest art houses in the world. It was a feat of enormous boldness and vision. He was buying up certain kinds of art years before anyone else was paying attention to it. Now those canvases are fetching upwards of half a million dollars.

"Henri built on the base his father provided. He made solid, if unexciting, decisions, consolidating the wealth. And he lived the life André dreamed of for him. He married well and moved into Parisian society. André, you see, knew that his money had brought him a great deal of acceptance. With his quickness and photographic memory, he'd acquired the speech and mannerisms of the upper class, too. But he still suffered subtle, social slights that left him bitter all his life."

"I've never seen any evidence of Victor's being snubbed," said Liza.

"No, Victor was his grandfather's fulfillment. By the time he was born, people had forgotten the ambiguous origins of the Morneaus. They were a fixture in society; their business was powerful and prestigious. The economy was on Victor's side, as well. The great families flocked to him to buy or, if their fortunes were in decline, to sell discreetly through him. Have you ever seen Victor's home in Paris, Liza?"

"No, but Penn and I are planning to go there next...." *How long ago all that seemed,* she thought. She looked quickly at Christian. Something passed between them and was gone before she could identify it.

"Yes...well, it's exquisite. Victor's wife, Sylvie,

has a marvelous hand. They also have a delightful
château in Limoges and a boat moored in Cannes.''

"Hardly the life-style of a man you claim is teeter-
ing on the edge of bankruptcy," Liza observed.
"Anyway, how does all this tie in with what we
found in the monastery?"

"Oh, I don't think we need a script to imagine
what happened," said Angus, exhaling a long stream
of smoke. "Can't you just see a young André
Morneau, ambitious and restless? He hears talk
about treasure hidden away in St. Catherine's, and of
course he wants to see it."

"But the letters of introduction—" Liza protested.

"I'm sure André was clever enough to talk himself
into the confidence of some minor church official,"
offered Christian. "How many could call his bluff
on Coptic languages—look at Brother John."

"Just think how the man must have felt when he
saw inside that library!" said Angus, slapping his
thighs. "He must have been half-mad with frustration."

"Especially," added Christian, "the day that
Brother John showed him the one thing he loved
above all others. By asking him the right questions,
André must have realized that the monks didn't
know what they possessed. But I think André must
have guessed—something so rare, so fine, that all the
other treasures paled before it. So he conceived a
plan that, like all of his schemes, was so bold it risked
everything he was working for."

"But if it worked!" cried Angus.

"Yes...the deckhand from Marseilles who was

born in a brothel would possess an emperor's cross. But first he had to make sure it was worth such an investment."

"And that's where the trip to Istanbul came in?" asked Angus.

"Yes, although why there I don't know."

"He went to a library there," said Liza, her voice emotionless. "There's a book in it that contains the first known, detailed reference to the cross. I know because I used a copy of it myself to confirm the provenance." It was a bitter thing to admit. She and Victor's grandfather must have shared the same quickening of the pulse when they read it.

Christian frowned down at her dark head, worry in his eyes. "After that he must have gone straight back to St. Catherine's to make a careful study of the cross—measuring, counting, sketching—all the things you did, Liza. During his longer absence he had a copy made."

"We can assume that by this point in his life, André was on intimate terms with the best forgers in the business," said Angus. "It must have cost him everything he had."

"Yes, but it was vital that the forgery be the best so that no one would uncover his plan for years and years—he hoped never. And it worked. After his last trip to the monastery, when he switched the crosses, no one suspected what he'd done. Only Brother John sensed something was wrong, but the forgery was so good that no one would listen to him."

"But then what, Christian?" asked Angus. "Did he just hold on to it?"

"I doubt André ever saw it in terms of a quick profit. He probably guessed that some day his investment of thousands of dollars would be worth millions. But knowing what we do of his pride and ambition, I think he dreamed of the day when the cross would be a great coup for the House of Morneau. He wanted to found a dynasty, not just make money."

"So maybe he put it away like a trust, a guarantee for all the grandchildren he might never live to see," mused Angus.

"And it might have remained a family secret even longer had not Victor proved to be the weak link," said Christian.

As each detail unfolded, Liza felt herself shuddering under the blows. Now she sat huddled, looking like a lost child. "I made it all terribly attractive, didn't I?" she said. "The publicity I arranged, the champagne...."

Angus glanced at her with alarm and asked quickly, "Why would he have made his move now, Christian?"

"Victor had invested heavily in a group of artists who never received critical acclaim. He lacked his grandfather's eye. That alone wouldn't have undermined him, though. Unfortunately, Victor loves the good life a bit too dearly. And he also has a fondness for gambling at Monte Carlo. As so often happens, a fortune made by the genius of one generation was stabilized by the next and destroyed by the greed of the one after that."

"Aren't you a fine one to be criticizing another

man for abusing family trust!" Liza flared so unexpectedly that both men flinched. "Your hypocrisy disgusts me sometimes!"

"Don't talk about things you don't understand, Liza. Just because you're feeling guilty and a little foolish—"

"My, oh, my," said Angus, shaking his head. "Have you two been like this from the beginning? I think I started much more than I bargained for."

But Liza wasn't listening. "Why should I feel guilty? I'm the one who's been used—by you, by Victor, and maybe even by Penn! But you—you were the worst. You used me, not just to solve this little mystery, but to amuse yourself along the way!"

She stood up. When had Angus left, she wondered, looking around. She hugged herself. What had happened to her that she'd fought with Christian in front of that poor man? She'd never done anything so rude before. But she had done a lot of things she'd never done before since meeting Christian Chase.

"Do you really think Penn was in on this, too?" he asked.

"I don't know...he was very angry with me when I told him I was coming here."

He reached out and ran a tentative finger down her arm. "You're hurting pretty badly. But please don't add me to the list of those causing your pain. I had no hidden motives for what I did. It was all for Angus."

She removed herself a step from his touch. "Are you going to bring on the violins next? Do you really expect me to believe that you went to all this trouble for the sake of one of your father's old employees, a pathetic old man honoring a promise made years ago to a dying monk?''

He took her shoulders and gave them a single, hard shake. ''Don't you—can't you—trust anyone? I thought when you left that suffocating prig you were going to marry, when we were together in Furtaga and working together in the library, laughing and loving, that it was all so clear to you. You were going to make a dreadful mistake, you know.''

''Maybe I was. But walking right into another one isn't the brightest solution, is it?''

''Is that what a relationship with me would be?''

Relationship, she thought bitterly, and said, ''I'm not interested in being your current plaything.''

''Well, in that case, you'd better get yourself back to New York in a hurry so you can make up with Mr. Livsay. You needn't bother to invite me to the wedding—I can see it all now. In fact, I can see your whole life in numbing detail.''

Furious, she grabbed her handbag and turned from him but he caught her. *''Liza!''*

His hand was heavy with anger. It was a terrible thing, for she'd once known it light with tenderness. But she would not feel that again. No, never again! She spun away and ran down the path. The dream had been broken forever.

The steps the monks had cut into the mountain were steep and worn but they led away from him and that was all that mattered. She bent her head and labored up them, stamping out her anger. Victor must have thought her such a fool. He just hadn't counted on her coming here. And except for that, he'd have won. Yet she couldn't claim a victory, for her reasons had been personal, not professional. She'd only been grandstanding against Penn's effort to control her.

Her breath began to come in quick, unsatisfying gasps. She'd climbed high and the air had thinned and grown cool. Before her was a ledge of granite thrusting over the rock-strewn valley. She lowered herself onto it, her energy spent, and offered her face to the strong, reviving wind.

Long, layered bands of color swept away from her on both sides. They were gentle gradations of gray and beige, blue and mauve and more blue—the desert, the Gulf, the coast of Arabia and the sky. The single break on the smooth canvas was the toylike monastery on the valley floor, the only movement the black-and-white *shaharira* birds that circled and floated on the air currents.

This was where the mystics came and sat for days in contemplation, Liza recalled. Slowly she felt that timeless vista work its magic on her, too. In the stillness she listened for her heart. She crumbled a twig and watched the pieces take flight over the valley.

If the emptiness she felt was any indication, she had little left to lose. Yet if she followed where her heart still wanted to take her, she had so very much to gain. For could it have hurt this much, she thought, if she didn't love him with every fiber of her being? Christian had seen her pain, offered her comfort, and she had run from him like a child.

And suddenly she was standing, tossing her pride to those eternal winds, skipping down those steps and flying to that final chance. How long had it taken her to climb that high? To surmount her doubt? Where would she find Christian, she wondered. In the garden still? At the jeep? Or would he have gone back to the monastery already? He and Angus were to have lunch there and visit the archbishop. The monks had remembered and welcomed Angus. It was a letter from him, in fact, that had gained Christian entry that first afternoon.

The foot of the mountain was riddled with fissures. A sudden movement drew Liza's eye to the arch framing one of the grottoes. She stopped, startled by the unexpected sight of lovers on the harsh mountainside. But lovers they surely were—that was no gentle embrace, but one in which two bodies formed a single, molten column.

She stared with a detached scrutiny born of shock. She thought with perverse admiration how beautifully suited they were. . . Kimberley so tall and lithe, the perfect female counterpart of Christian's lean maleness. Their limbs were the same rich gold, their mingling hair a sun-touched silver. . . .

Christian stood with his legs slightly apart, his back braced against the wall. His hands were resting on Kim's hips as if supporting her. Kim's slender arms were thrown about Christian's neck. She was offering hungry, parted lips to him. In response, he covered her mouth with his, drinking in the young woman's need of him.

Liza began to tremble. She was filled with a jealousy so intense she felt ill. Never had she known an emotion to own her so wholly, to fill with such agonizing rage.

How could he do this? Kim is a child, she thought furiously. She pressed her fingertips to her temples and fought back a rising tide of nausea. No...no, that kiss was not being forced from her. She remembered Kim's probing questions, her fascination with Christian.

She lowered her dark head and stared at the two of them through stormy, narrowed eyes. She hated it, the watching, but she couldn't seem to stop herself. She saw Christian take Kim's upturned face in his hands and put a wrenching end to their kiss. And she saw from the look Kim gave him that the parting was painful. Liza shrank back against the mountain, praying to remain invisible.

They were speaking but she couldn't make out their words. Christian was holding Kim at arm's length, pinning her shoulders against the rocks. There was something close to desperation branded on Kim's young face.

Hugging herself, fighting back a flood of tears, she watched their secret, intense exchange. Hating him, loving him, she watched Christian lay his palm on Kim's forehead as if trying to calm a fever. Suddenly he bent and bestowed a kiss on the girl's flushed cheek.

Liza knew that kiss, the softest kiss imaginable. She dug her nails into her palms as she felt her heart pound and the hot blood rush to her ears.

She would have fled then, but Christian took

Kim's hand and drew her out of the grotto. Liza caught and held her breath. It would be the ultimate humiliation to have these two people—the man she loved to the point of madness, the woman she'd confided in like a sister—see her now.

But she was to be spared that blow, although dealt another. Kim and Christian were lost in their own world. They wouldn't have recognized her, Liza thought bitterly, if they had tripped over her. Christian drew a hot-cheeked and obviously overwrought Kim along the narrow gravel path among the boulders. It led to one of the rock ledges hanging out over the valley, where the hermits came to meditate. Liza froze as they passed within a few feet of her.

She was staggered by this blatant revelation of Christian's character. Kim was married...well, as good as married, she thought. And so young. He really was just a professional seducer after all. Watching Kim melt and mold herself to him, Liza had seen how she herself must have looked—helpless and hungry under those skilled fingers.

What could poor Kim possibly have to offer him that could make him unleash his arsenal of weapons—besides her young body. She had no keys to some fabulous treasure. No man whom he could hurt through her. You couldn't count Scott—who would want to hurt that boy? Yet he *would* be hurt. Devastated—and that was what was so despicable.

She was assailed by anger and shame that she had brought this creature into the midst of good people. By fury at the brutally casual way in which he could destroy another couple's relationship for the sake of his trivial needs—like a giant crushing an entire universe and never feeling its death beneath his heel. An enormous, poisonous resentment began to bubble inside her.

Moral indignation was all well and good. But the most painful hurt was the childish one, the one of the schoolroom—that old, familiar enemy, jealousy. It curled and twisted in her stomach. She could almost taste it.

She moved slowly at first, painstakingly picking her way past the ledge. But then, when she was sure they couldn't hear her, she ran finally, stumbling over the rocks, not caring about the scrapes and bruises, wanting only to distance herself from Christian.

One by one, her refuges had fallen away. She was left with herself—and that was the answer, of course, she raged. She would leave this place and depend on no one, ever again. Instinct had warned her the night she turned in her chair at Fairchild's and saw him for the first time—he was a predator. He would devour her. She should have listened to that whispered warning.

Her heart remained the only rebel against her sure knowledge of his treachery. It remained shamelessly, stubbornly hungry, craving what he was at that very moment giving another woman.

It was then that she knew with sickening certainty that tomorrow would not be soon enough to leave him.

CHAPTER TWELVE

SHE THREW HER THINGS into the suitcase, scrunching, slamming and muttering. Scott regarded her with amazement.

"But how will he get back?"

"Feet, camel, hot air balloon—I don't care! He'll charm a lift out of someone, I'm sure. Probably female. He has a way with women...." She pressed her lips into a thin line. She mustn't make Scott share her pain.

One corner of Scott's mouth was caught up in a wry twist. "I suppose so," he said doubtfully.

Liza looked up from her packing, suddenly worried. "You will do this for me, won't you? I don't have anyone else I can ask."

"You know I don't mind helping, Liza, but—"

He was wavering and she cut in firmly. "All you need to do is tell him—if he should ask—that I'll leave the jeep in the parking lot at Nuweiba. He'll remember. I'll get other transportation up to Aqaba."

Scott shook his curls and frowned. "I'll do it, Liza, but I wouldn't be a friend if I said I liked it."

She reached out and touched his hand. "I know. But I have my reasons, Scott. And I have no guilt about relieving him of his jeep. Believe me, he owes me.... Now, if I keep on the highway and drive straight through, I should be able to make Nuweiba by evening. Is that right?''

"Yes," he said reluctantly. "It's a straightforward drive, not like the route you took down. You'll only come to one split in the road. Part goes north to Nuweiba, part south to Dahab. But it's well marked, and if you have any sense of direction you can't get lost.''

Liza nodded confidently. "Good," she said, and began to check her assembled belongings, unaware of the growing and uneasy silence.

Scott's voice was very soft. "It's Kim, isn't it?" he said. "What happened—did Christian express an interest and discover that she was not, to put it mildly, offended?''

Liza stopped abruptly and sank to a seat. She wanted to deny it but knew her face had already spoken. "I'm sorry, Scott—I've been so stupid, thinking only of myself.''

Scott was slouched in the driver's seat, his back to the steering wheel. His smile was lopsided. "It's not your fault. Sometimes I see more than I let on....''

"It is my fault," Liza said earnestly. "People in pain can be awfully self-centered. There's no excuse for running roughshod over everybody else's feelings.''

"I'm not surprised, you know. I've seen it coming. She's been restless as a cat ever since that picnic. But I don't blame Christian. In fact, I kind of like the guy.''

"*I* blame him, Scott," she said, presenting a

defense for Kim. "He's a much older man—he should never have taken advantage of her."

"I know Kim pretty well. . . I'd say it's a question of who took advantage of whom. Don't get me wrong, though. I'd still marry Kim in a minute. My generation's supposed to be pretty free about this kind of thing. But in spite of the way I look, I'm probably more conservative than most people. I work hard, I want my own business. What could be more middle-class American than that?"

"No one's fooled by anything as unimportant as clothes, Scott. There isn't a person on your tour, for example, who doesn't see a lot in you to admire!"

He gave a short, humorless laugh. "I guess Kim saw something, too. A life sentence to drudgery and never enough money."

"But Kim isn't materialistic," Liza protested, trying to undo some of the damage she'd done. "She's just as determined as you are not to take money from your parents."

"Yes, but not for the same reasons. I can see that now. I wanted this business to be all mine. I wanted to grow up and be independent."

"And Kim?"

"I think it's mostly rebellion. She wants to reject her parents' values just for the sake of saying no. It's funny, isn't it, how rebelling against family can be both good and bad."

"Does she have a difficult relationship with her parents?"

"Not really. Her folks dote on her. They're well-off—her dad's a pediatrician. She says she hates the way she grew up, but I think it was easy for her to go off on her own, knowing she had all that to fall back on. That's the appeal of Christian.''

"I don't follow, Scott...."

"He's the perfect mix. He offers money and class and luxury beyond anything she's ever known. But he's just exotic enough that she can still feel as if she's doing her own thing and being a little bit wicked.''

Liza recalled the shock of Christian's embrace in the very proper confines of the Cavendish and thought, *yes...a little touch of wickedness does sharpen the senses.* She glanced at Scott's touchingly open face. She began by feeling sorry for him but concluded it was misplaced sympathy. He was wise for his years and would probably survive this much better than she.

"What will you do now, Scott?" she asked.

"Just keep on going, I guess," he replied with a faint smile. "Let Kim do what she wants to. There won't be any hard feelings. Well...almost none.'' Suddenly there was a look of real pain on his brow. "Do you think there's any chance of the two of them really getting together?''

"No," Liza said with certainty. "Lord Chase is not the type to be tied down, although he's not above taking his amusements where he finds them.''

Scott stowed her gear, checked the oil and tires and otherwise acted like a mother hen. "You've got the keys?" he asked.

"Yes. Christian gave me the spare set when we left Nuweiba, something he'll regret dearly,'' she said with some satisfaction.

"How long do you think it will be before he notices the jeep's missing?"

"With luck, several hours. Perhaps if I'm *very* lucky, not until tomorrow morning when he gets ready to leave." She climbed behind the wheel.

Scott pawed the sand morosely with his sneaker, his hands stuffed into his pockets. "I can't talk you out of this?"

She turned the key in the ignition. "He's the kind of man who has to control. If I stay, that's exactly what he'll continue to do."

Scott sighed, acknowledging defeat. "At least take some advice from an old hand at crossing the desert. Link up with a tour bus or some sort of official vehicle. You'll have company, you can stop when they do to get gas, eat. There's safety in numbers if you have a breakdown."

"Will do," said Liza brightly.

They looked at each other, briefly self-conscious, then smiled. They leaned forward and kissed quickly. "Goodbye, Scott—and thank you."

"Goodbye, Liza—and good luck." He stood there for a long time, watching the brown plume of dust from behind the disappearing jeep, before turning and heading quickly back to the camp.

Liza eased the jeep across the rutted plain and onto the highway. It would be a tedious drive, but the road was smooth and at the end her first real bed in days awaited. With a determined tilt to her chin she pushed and pulled her way through the unfamiliar gears. Gradually she built a rhythm to set her thoughts to. She was finished, he was finished, they were finished. She added a litany of his faults. Greed, arrogance, duplicity.

With several miles behind her and the jeep behaving well, she entered a phase of confidence. It's right to be active, to take control, she told herself. No good ever came of giving up as much command over life as she'd been willing to cede to Christian. She stopped once for lunch, once more for a catnap. It wasn't until midafternoon that she felt the first twinge of doubt.

She wondered if she had misjudged the problems of the drive. The monotony of the straight, flat road began to induce a kind of hypnosis. Her eyes stung and there was the threat of an ache behind her temples. She blinked, twisted her head from side to side, and stretched protesting muscles.

Another worry came to haunt her. The more she thought about it, the surer she was that Scott hadn't lasted an hour before breaking down and telling Christian what she'd done. Typical of herself, she thought in disgust, that even in anger she'd fussed over details, with no stomach for real thievery.

What then, she wondered. He'd be furious, of course. And he'd come after her. He'd need time to locate another vehicle, but her head start wouldn't mean a great deal. He was a much faster driver than she was.

She gripped the steering wheel tighter and flexed her fingers. She craned her neck and peered into the rearview mirror. Exhaustion was fertile ground for fear. Paranoid, Christian had once called her.

"Not this time," she muttered.

Ahead was a cluster of road signs, a shed and some gas pumps, some rusting cars and a few tethered donkeys. She eased the jeep off the highway and cut the engine. The silence flowed over her like a blessing. She climbed out, still feeling the vibrating in her bones. While the Bedouin owner filled the tank, she bought a can of soda and walked over to the road signs. Dahab, Sharm el Sheikh, Nuweiba, she read. And Ghazala. Where had she heard that?

From Ibn-Bader, of course, she thought. It was the wadi Christian had wanted to take on the way down. She snapped her fingers. This was the edge she needed, the advantage she'd given away by telling Scott her plans. According to the map Christian had given her to study, she could cut at least an hour, possibly two, off the rest of the trip by taking this diagonal route.

She strode to the edge of the wadi and peered over—bone dry, not even a small eruption of water. And even if the heavens were to open right now, not enough rain could fall to cause trouble in the time it would take her to travel it. If he was somewhere behind her now, gaining on her, he'd never, with his silly male assumptions, think her resourceful or strong enough to choose this route. The very thought of outsmarting him sent fresh energy rushing through her. Even the knowledge that it would be a more demanding drive seemed welcome. It would keep her alert and be safer, ultimately, than that flat, unending highway.

The road took her across a stretch of pebble desert, then began to descend slowly into the wadi. The walls were not particularly high and she had lots of light. Learning to control the jeep became a bit of a game to her and she caught herself smiling. She flirted with the idea of buying a small car when she got home. She'd take trips, she decided, drive to Vermont, take up skiing.

She'd have to. There'd be hours to fill. If Penn had known anything about the false provenance, she could never forgive him. If he hadn't, she could never forgive herself for her betrayal. Either way, it was over.

A few miles into the canyon she came across spots where the river gurgled from the ground. The tires spun on the wet pebbles. Twice she fishtailed on large, flat rocks. One stretch of shallow water lasted almost a quarter of a mile before giving way to dry ground.

It was because she was searching the sky for storm clouds that she failed to notice the small things—in this case acacia thorns, a wind-borne drift of the two-inch spurs. One flat tire she could have coped with, but the two gashed tires she discovered after a jarring stop were beyond her strength and supplies.

She kicked at a perfectly good tire in ill-tempered frustration and perched on a boulder to ponder her fate. Not a hint of life, human or otherwise—no, that wasn't entirely accurate, she thought, noting the vultures cruising overhead. The sight of those broad, blunt wings settled one option. She would *not* stay in the wadi. Travelers were so few and far between that she could walk out before anyone else came along to give her a lift.

Yes, she thought. That was reasonable, practical, sane. By her estimate she wasn't more than half an hour from the broad escarpment overlooking the coast. Once there she could flag down help. *Now don't be dumb, Liza, think,* she commanded. *Your hat. And your purse and that bag of nuts and a jacket.*

Around a twist in the wadi the stream rushed out of the ground and pushed her to the walls of the canyon. The walking was more difficult there and she was forced to scramble over boulders. At one point a rock slide cut diagonally across her path, forcing her back into the water. It was flowing faster, now, the current quilting the surface. She inhaled sharply and spread her arms to keep her balance.

As the stream rose, rocks vanished. She tripped and scraped herself more frequently. She stopped to scan the granite walls for a place to climb out. It didn't look promising. *Damn!* she thought. No path up, and the river, which had bubbled intermittently, now did so constantly. She had kept her jacket knotted about her waist. Now she put it on and slipped her sunglasses into the breast pocket.

A wave washed against her. The frigid shock of it set her in motion again. The water had become a thick soup of brown and rust, picking up silt as it went. The sky had been pinched into a narrow blue streamer above her. Soon, she thought, she'd round a bend and there would be the coastal highway. And cars and people and help.

But when she came to the bend she'd been slogging toward, the color drained from her face. There was no outlet to the Gulf, only another narrow plunge deeper into the ground. A low roar rose as the water was forced faster over the rocks. Rapids were forming, yellow froth riding on them.

With both hands she smoothed back the lank hair that had fallen across her face. She willed herself to be calm, but the rising river wasn't allowing her the luxury of time. Already it was foaming at the small of her back. It was a time for firm measures, she decided. She must make the current work for her, not against her. A dash for the end of the wadi, straight down the middle, was the only way.

She took her wallet and passport out of the tote bag and buttoned them firmly into a pocket of her jacket. She discarded her sunglasses and a couple of pens that might be dangerous if she fell. Suddenly she laughed. The whole wretched affair loomed more comic than tragic. What a ludicrous end it would be if she died here, she thought.

She wondered if they'd find her body. And how long Penn would mourn her. She even wondered whether Blythe, her secretary, would remember to water the plants in her office. "And can't you just see them adding this to the cross's history?" she muttered a little wildly. "Young woman curator," she went on, "dies in the Sinai Desert while researching origins of priceless cross." It would make a marvelous headline and add a few dollars to someone's pocket. Maybe Christian's. It was then that she realized she was not far from hysteria.

But the hysterics were doused by the next wave that loosened her grip on a boulder and knocked her hard into the water. She felt the sharp edges of the stones and knew her palms had been cut even though there was no pain. Her mouth filled with thick brown water. She felt the sand in her throat and gagged. She blinked, frantically clearing her eyes.

She was committed now, ready or not. She groped forward, half walking, half crawling. Then, without warning, the riverbed fell away and she was floating freely. She tread water for a moment, groping for a footing. There was none. "This is it, Liza," she told herself. She stretched out and began to stroke.

There was a painful thud between her shoulder blades. Something tugged at her jacket and snarled her hair. Shuddering in revulsion, she fought free. With relief she saw that it was only the stump of a dead acacia, torn from the wall of the wadi. But the thorns that had already cost her so dearly had now left ugly red, stinging streaks down her neck and wrists. She watched the twisted brown roots swirl away and wondered what else might be floating down the river toward her.

She was not without hope. The rising water was bringing the plateau closer and closer. She searched for some promising spot where she could grasp a rock and pull herself out. It would take strength, of course. And the river would try to suck her back. It might even be an unnecessary risk if the wadi outlet was around the next bend. But submerged boulders and undertows and trees being tossed about like twigs might also be there.

She saw a zigzagging break in the smooth rock wall. She grabbed for it, her fingernails becoming ragged as she clawed for something to grasp. She worked her toes into a narrow crevice. Her legs seemed to have turned to jelly but with a last, enormous effort she broke the hold of the water and heaved herself up. With surprising agility, given her battering, she scrambled backward into a niche just big enough to hold her.

She scrunched up into a tiny ball, her knees to her chest, and rested her face against the cold rock. She stayed there, fighting for breath and watching dispassionately the livid swelling of her hands. She had lost the ability to feel pain.

It was a brief respite. The dirty water was again lapping at her toes. She inched her way out of the niche and craned her neck upward. The plateau and the end of this ordeal were just a few feet away. But to get around the overhanging rock she was going to have to lean out over the river at a risky angle. Courage didn't enter into it. It was simple necessity.

Tears of exhaustion sprang to her eyes. "Christian, I blame you for this!" she muttered. He had been the cause of every insane thing she'd done. He had made her run away from Penn to Aqaba. And he'd started this fool's flight as well. He had made her hate him, love him, then hate again. And now it was all going to be for nothing. It was going to end here in this godforsaken gully!

Exhausted, she wanted to stop struggling, to let go and flow with the water. It would be easier and there was no sense trying to go on. She simply didn't have enough strength left.

"Liza!"

"Leave me alone, Christian."

"Liza, look up here!"

"Christian, I'm tired . . . let me be."

"Liza, open your eyes and look at me—that's right!"

She struggled to obey but it was so hard. Her eyes were raw and swollen from the sand. He was leaning out from the lip of the wadi. He put his hands to his mouth and shouted, "Stay where you are—I'm coming down!"

She nodded her understanding and watched as he eased himself over the edge and dropped gracefully to the shelf just above her. Quickly he grabbed her wrists and drew her up to him. She wanted to hold him and never let go but he took her shoulders and turned her to the wall.

"You're almost to the top, Liza, just a little bit more. . . ."

"I tried so hard, Christian—"

"I know, I know. Here, one more push, Liza." His hands spanned her hips and suddenly she was on the plateau. He was with her, holding her, shaking her, beside himself with joy and anger. "God, you're so cold," he said, running his hands over her. He shrugged his jacket off. "Put this on," he ordered.

She let him do it, unable even to summon the strength to raise her arms. The last time she'd seen him he'd been polished and handsome. Now, his clothes were rumpled and his hair uncombed. He looked exasperated. "Please don't lecture me, Christian, I couldn't bear it," she said, her voice small and her eyes closed.

He drew her in and pressed her head to his chest. "Stay close," he commanded. She didn't reply, except by burrowing deeper into him like a small animal.

"You came—"

"Your luck, you foolish, impulsive woman." He kissed the top of her head.

"Scott told you?"

"Yes, being wise. It was a marvelous scene—like one of those medieval assaults, with Scott pounding the door down with that great knocker and the guards shouting and the monks running around wondering if history was repeating itself. You'd have loved it."

"I doubt it. . .you must have thought I was a child, running off like that."

He looked down at her thoughtfully. "No. I didn't. You'd had a bad shock. The bottom had dropped out for you when you learned about Victor. It's only the dishonest people who are armored with cynicism against those disappointments."

So, she thought, he puts it all down to that. Scott hadn't mentioned Kim. And neither would she.

He scooped her up. "It's almost dark and you're soaked through. The jeep I commandeered is a few hundred yards back. Let's get to it while we can still see."

He set her down and was soon pulling supplies from the back of the jeep. He unzipped a sleeping bag and spread it out flat in the shelter of the wheels. Gently he helped her lower herself onto it. One of her ankles had begun to swell. Bruises she couldn't re-

member receiving began to assert themselves. The
cuts smarted.

"I've got aspirin," he said, kneeling beside her. He
shook a few into her palm and offered her a can of
fruit juice.

"I don't know that I can drink anything more,"
she told him, "not after what I swallowed in the
wadi."

"You had your shots before you came, I hope?"
he said anxiously. "If not, we'll fix you up in a clinic
the first chance we get."

"How did you find me—here, off the main road?"
she asked.

"Luck, mainly. But I was also beginning to learn
my lesson about you. You're nothing if not gutsy
underneath that demure exterior. You had a very
small head start on me. I'd broken all the speed limits
down that highway, and I still hadn't overtaken you.
I couldn't understand it. Then it hit me like a
thunderbolt—the Ghazala route. Given your state of
mind and temperament, plus the fact that you were
probably quite sick of driving, I figured you must
have taken it. The thought made my blood run
cold—I knew the rain had started in the mountains."

"But you weren't behind me, you were somewhere
above me."

"I couldn't risk the road. And I was almost into
Nuweiba by the time I figured out what you'd done.
So I drove like a fool right across the top of the
escarpment, strewing the desert with bits and pieces
of the jeep as I went. I kept stopping, looking down
in the wadi for you. When I spotted the empty jeep

awash in the water I hardly knew what to do. Finally I found you, but only because the red of your T-shirt caught my eye.

She began to shake. The numbness had worn off and there was not an inch of her that did not ache. She was deathly cold.

Christian was suddenly brisk. "That's enough talk. You have to get out of those clothes and get some sleep. I'll find you one of my shirts...."

"We're not going into Nuweiba?"

"It's night now, if you haven't noticed. There's no road up here, not even a camel track. A wrong turn could drop us right into the wadi."

"Are we far from the coast?"

"No, we're very close—you almost made it, you know." He ran his finger down her nose.

She tried to smile but even that hurt. She felt funny and light-headed and really didn't care where she spent the night, as long as sleep released her from this torment. She began to pull at her shoelaces but the knots were hard and sodden, and her fingers clumsy with cold.

He watched her and said finally, "I'll do it." He worked swiftly and gently and with a skill that made her wonder. He spoke to her as he eased off her things, quiet, soothing words she later couldn't remember. With his broad back he shielded her naked body from the cruel edge of the wind.

He was beginning to slip her hand into a sleeve of his shirt when suddenly she lifted her slender arms to him. "Christian, it hurts. Make it stop."

He hesitated only a moment, then lay beside her,

pulling an opened sleeping bag over them. He engulfed her totally, holding her tenderly, pressing her two small hands to his chest. He gave her his warmth, moving his hands repeatedly over the chilled flesh of her back. He rocked her gently, stilling her trembling.

On the mountain, in her jealousy, she'd wondered what had happened to her love for him. Now she knew. She had not wept it away. She had not reasoned it out of her system nor outrun it. No one else would ever have this power to move her, this capacity to lift the stars out of the heavens and set them in her breast.

He began to speak but she laid her fingertips on his lips. "No more words," she whispered. "They frighten me—more than floods and rocks and the night."

"You mustn't be frightened," he said, holding her as if she was made of glass and might shatter beneath the slightest touch, as if his deepest, most passionate prayer was to grant her his protection.

She felt an intoxicating mix of power and joy, as if she'd unfurled a mystical scroll and seen the meaning of her life. And her life, she knew now, was centered on her love for this man. He was the missing half that would join with her to make up the perfect totality of her existence. She yearned for that completion with the sweetest pain.

Her palm lay like a blessing on his rough cheek. "Christian...." She counted her heartbeats, waiting for comprehension to break over the sharp planes of his face. His eyes, like two bright dots of moonsilver, flickered as he searched hers. "Please..." she whispered.

She had glanced at oblivion back there in the raging wadi, and a chill hand had closed about her heart. She had caught sight of an eternity deprived of his love, his touch, the exquisite sensations she experienced when he was near. Even now, safe and sheltered by him, she had to face the reality that in the morning he might well be gone. A bleak lifetime without him stretched ahead of her—but tonight, tonight she could own it all.

"Liza, what are you saying to me?" he murmured. "Is your body really all you trust me with?"

Her heart shook within her. "I need you, Christian. I want to make love with you...."

"Are you sure, Liza?" he asked, looking perplexed and oddly reluctant.

"You will make me sure, Christian...."

A low cry was torn from somewhere deep inside him as he drew her closer. He smoothed the hair from her brow and laid a dozen small kisses there. He kissed her lips, urging her head back against the pillowed sand. She shivered slightly and he paused to gaze into her eyes, his expression concerned.

She felt a dull tightening about her temples, then a sharp, shooting pain. She rubbed her forehead with the back of her hand, angry at this intrusion into her world of perfect pleasure. She tried to burrow into him away from the little knives that attacked her brain, but the pain pursued her, moving down her neck and into her shoulders. Another pain arced through her, making her cry out. She squeezed her eyes shut, willing the pain away.

His lips brushed her forehead from temple to temple with exquisite tenderness. "Liza? Darling, your forehead is damp. Are you feeling ill?"

He was hovering just out of reach of her splayed fingers when all she wanted to do was drown in him. She struggled to reclaim the joy. "Please—it doesn't matter! Nothing matters but us. Not Kim or why you came here or any of the other women you know. I need you...I love you. Don't you know that? I love you so much!"

"You've been through so much," he whispered. He was hushing her like a fretful child. "I should have thought—"

"Christian, I'm cold," she cut in desperately.

"You're not," he said sharply. "You're bloody burning up!"

She felt a flash of incomprehensible annoyance. She said peevishly, "I am not hot—I'm cold! Don't pull away from me like that!"

Suddenly she was churning with contradictions. She was terrified that he would stop making love to her and angry, too, that he couldn't seem to understand that she was offering him all her desperate, unconditional love.

What was he talking about, she wondered. *Why* was he talking, now of all times! Oh, it hurt so much. The least noise echoed and pounded. She clenched her chattering jaw and said, "Christian, what's the matter?"

"Hush darling, hush," he crooned. "I'm here and you're safe...." He folded her to his chest and started to rock her with the gentlest care.

She didn't want to be safe. She wanted to be loved, to be a woman. Why couldn't she make him under-

stand that! It was as if he existed on the other side of
an invisible but soundproof wall.

She opened her eyes and that hurt, too. His own
eyes were hooded, the moon-silver eclipsed by a dark,
indecipherable look.

"Try to lie still, Liza," he said. "There's almost
nothing I can do for you tonight. But you mustn't
thrash about."

She felt defeated. Her head ached and her thoughts
tangled and collided. Her mind stubbornly refused to
focus. One thing she knew, though: he had rejected
her. Yet surely he'd wanted her at least as much as
he'd wanted Kim. And he'd come all that way to save
her...no. No, he'd come in anger. He'd come because he was a man who had to have his own way.
He'd come to punish her, and oh, God—this was punishment enough!

He was whispering something in her ear, words she
couldn't catch, words that were fuzzy and far away.
Suddenly she thrust her arms around his neck. "Oh,
Christian, I *did* want you to care...I *did*! It doesn't
matter now. You know I love you! If only you'd cared
just a little...."

"Darling, I do care, very much. But you mustn't try
to talk now...."

His voice was receding, then was lost to her. She experienced a brief, giddy rush, a sensation of floating.
And then, nothing. Not ecstasy or loss. Not even that
terrible confusion.

SHE DIDN'T SEE the pink desert light that broke over
the Gulf of Aqaba the next morning. Or the toylike
caravan of vehicles that threaded along the coastal

road just below the plateau where she lay. Nor did she see Christian's anxious face peering into hers, pale beneath his tan, drawn from a night of listening for each of her shallow, rapid breaths. There were small rays of light in the dark cloth of her eyelids, but she resisted sight, wanting only to withdraw deeper into blessed unconsciousness.

She did feel his hands dressing her, because every nerve ending in her body cried out. And she felt him lifting her into the jeep, swaddling her in blankets and anything else he could get his hands on to insulate her against the bone-jarring trip down the escarpment to the highway.

At some point there were other voices and she struggled to answer them. Yes, yes, I'm fine, she tried to say, although she wasn't. There was a new face, too. It was a woman's face and she was smiling. Liza smiled back. Somehow she trusted this woman. She had hands that were swift and sure and gentle.

But Christian—where had he gone, she wondered. Once she thought she heard him talking to the woman who was with her all the time now. But she couldn't be sure.

She floated in that twilight world of fever, alternating between moments of half-conscious confusion and longer periods of deep, drugged sleep. It seemed like an eternity, although later she was told it was no more than a few days.

Christian saw to flying her out. Liza closed her mind to the details of the trip. She endured it stoically through firmly gritted teeth, praying silently for release from the ache in her bones and the persistent throb behind her temples. She longed for the sweet, familiar depths of her own bed like a pilgrim in sight of his shrine.

Although her perception of her inglorious return from the Middle East was fuzzy, one detail stood out clearly. Christian had changed—they both had—and the change chilled her heart. She had the painful impression that he was doing his duty by her—seeing her to safety and comfort because he was, after all, a thoroughly proper British lord. He was stiff, correct, distracted. And the woman in her cringed and shriveled before his ruthless scrutiny.

It was all such a shambling end to what had begun as a great adventure. She had wanted him to love her. Instead, he'd nursed her. From an attractive, vital woman, she'd collapsed into an ashen, stringy-haired burden. A thin girl with smudged eyes he'd had to hold as she gagged up muddy floodwater. There had never been a word of reproach from him over the thousand details he'd been saddled with—he wasn't that type.

So much for romance, Liza thought, as the Manhattan skyline slid over the horizon and touched the wing of her plane.

CHAPTER THIRTEEN

WINTER ANNOUNCED ITSELF with a snap, turning breath white, cheeks scarlet and skies lead gray. Skaters cut figures at Rockefeller Center, chestnut vendors added the rich aroma of their offerings to the air and farther up Fifth Avenue, Connie McKay studied the white wicker lunch tray before her.

The soup bowl was empty—almost—and that was good. But she frowned over the untouched roll and the custard, only a single spoonful dipped out of it. When she heard the shower running she went into the bedroom, put fresh sheets on the bed and straightened the pile of magazines, which, she suspected, were largely unread. She dusted the night table, checked the ice water in the thermos and poured a fresh glass, setting it on the tray beside the little bottle of bright red capsules the doctor had left.

"Your afternoon pill," she said, when Liza came out of the bathroom wrapped in a plain terry-cloth robe.

"Thanks, Connie, I won't forget." Liza shook the towel off her head and her damp hair fell in loose curls about her shoulders.

She sat in front of her dressing table and began to rub her hair dry. Her eyes fell on the jars of makeup.

She considered using some but discarded the idea. She was still listless, even though the doctor had said she could go back to work, half days at least, on Monday. She ran the brush through her hair, letting it fall naturally about her shoulders, patted some moisturizer into her skin and let it go at that.

Connie stole a sideways glance at her, her lips thin with disapproval. She knew how much even that effort cost her young charge. Her square, capable hands plumped the pillows and pulled back the comforter. "Back into bed with you now," she ordered.

Liza stood and untied her robe. "I'll need a fresh gown," she said. "Something covered."

"I thought this would be right—my, you've got such pretty things!" Connie's broad, ruddy face creased with pleasure as she held up a nightie of pale mauve silk strewed with tiny violets of a deeper purple. It had thin straps and a deep neckline trimmed with ecru lace. The matching bedjacket had neat little shoulders, a high neck, and long sleeves that ended with a flounce of the same lace. It was French and Liza's best. She slipped it on obediently, making sure the tie at the neck of the jacket was secure. She'd have preferred something less pretty for the afternoon's ordeal, but Connie loved to fuss. It made her a very good practical nurse.

After she had tucked Liza into bed Connie asked, "What refreshments will I make—tea? Or will men prefer sherry?"

Liza shook her head firmly. "No refreshments at all, thanks. This is strictly business. When they're gone, though, I'll probably need some brandy.'' She smiled at the older woman bleakly.

Connie put a hand on her generous hip. "Are you sure you're up to this, dear? I could phone them all right now...."

"No, I'm not sure," Liza answered honestly, "but I've put this off as long as I can. I heard the phone ring earlier, Connie. Was there a message?"

"It was that nice Mr. Sloane checking up on you. He didn't want me to wake you, but he said to tell you everyone at the museum is dying to have you back next week."

Dying of curiosity, Liza thought, dying to know whether the jewel of their entire collection was going to be snatched from them. It hadn't gone unnoticed that the cross had been removed from viewing immediately following the unveiling. No one had bought the lame story about a loose stone being spotted. Reporters had been hounding poor Julian, according to Blythe, and although he'd been calm he'd been unable to stop the gossip.

"Oh, and Mr. Livsay phoned, too. He wanted to confirm that he and Mr.—"

"Morneau?"

"Yes—they'll both be here on time."

Liza sighed and leaned her head back on the pillows. Part of her wanted to get on with her task, part of her shrank from it. Only the fever and the doctor's stern orders had postponed the showdown this long.

Connie was resistant when Liza gave her the rest of the day off. "As soon as you've shown them in,"

Liza told her, "you can go treat yourself to a movie and a dinner out—you've earned it."

Protectiveness and curiosity made Connie want to stay on, but Liza was oddly adamant for a woman who'd been so tired and disinterested. Connie was discreet about her elite clientele, but that didn't mean she didn't like to have her own inquisitiveness satisfied. When, at five o'clock, she had shown three, not two, attractive men into the bedroom, she closed the door on the apartment with the greatest reluctance.

Liza accepted Penn's kiss to her cheek and Victor's to her hand politely but indifferently. Christian made no move toward her. He stood apart from them, his arms folded across his chest, looking idly at the top of her antique dresser. Liza felt herself flush as his eyes moved over her silver-backed brush set, her favorite French perfume, the card that sat propped against the dozen red roses—the card that bore Penn's name and an affectionate message.

She hadn't seen Christian since their first day back in New York. He hadn't even said goodbye; there'd only been an offhand note left with Connie saying he was going to London. No explanation, no mention of what had passed between them, not even a reference to the cross and what was to be done about it.

He was looking very much the English gentleman today, in gray flannels, a navy jacket with some sort of ornate silver and gold crest on the pocket, and what looked like a school tie. His skin still bore the mark of the desert sun; that warm bronze was enhanced by his crisp white shirt.

There was a brief outbreak of nervous small talk.

Victor was elaborately solicitous, inquiring after Liza's comfort. He sat down, stood, sat again and straightened the crease of his expensive, pin-striped suit. Penn's greeting of Christian was correct, right down to the firm handshake. Everyone was being so terribly civil that Liza could have screamed.

Penn took the chair beside Liza in a proprietary manner. Despite all the right words, he had a belligerent set to his heavy jaw she thought did not bode well for the meeting. The conversation moved awkwardly toward the inevitable. Liza began to regret turning down Connie's suggestion of tea. At least she could have hidden behind the ritual duties of pouring and passing and the small silences could have been filled by the nibbling of cookies.

Victor adjusted his immaculate cuffs, crossed his legs and smiled. "So, my dear, did the doctor finally decide what it was that affected you so unfortunately?"

"No, not really. It could have been strange food and water, a virus, infection from the acacia scratches—more likely, a combination of them all."

"When Penn told me you'd come home with such a high fever I thought at once of all the really dreadful things you could have picked up in the Middle East. I suppose we must thank Christian for acting so quickly to get you home safely to us." He flashed a brilliant smile at Christian who was leaning against the wall with loose-limbed ease.

Christian's face remained a mask and Liza said nervously, "I don't remember much at all—perhaps that's fortunate. Christian arranged everything, a nurse, a whole block of seats on the plane. I don't know how I'd have made it otherwise. I'm making plans, by the way," she added to Christian, "to pay you back for all that expense. I'll have a check for you next week."

Penn's voice was brittle. "I had no idea. You should have told me, Liza." And to Christian he said, "I can write you a check now." He began to reach into his breast pocket.

Christian smiled thinly and turned his eyes to the bed. "Well, Liza—is Penn paying?"

She flushed in anger and embarrassment. "No— Penn, this is my responsibility. I won't take a penny from either of you." Quickly she multiplied the cost of the air fare times six—the museum would never authorize payment for an entire block of seats— added the fee for a full-time private nurse, and then suppressed a small shudder. She added seeing the bank manager to her list of Monday chores.

Now it was Victor's turn to protest. "But I asked you to investigate the cross. It is certainly my responsibility and I will pay Christian."

"Liza's health is a personal affair," said Penn, "so the matter is settled." He reached again for his checkbook.

Liza closed her eyes briefly. She should have anticipated this squabble. Penn had made no secret of the fact that he bitterly resented Christian's going to the Sinai. He'd wanted an explanation, but Liza had been too ill and Christian, up until this morning, had been in London. Now, she wondered at the wisdom of inviting the three of them together. She looked at each man in turn. There was anger on Penn's face, anxiety on Victor's, watchfulness on Christian's.

She folded her hands before her, inhaled, and said, "Penn, the cross that Victor gave you is undoubtedly the original Cross of Constantine."

The tension drained visibly from both men. They laughed. Penn said, "Wonderful news, Victor! Your decision to entrust this business to Liza was a wise one."

Liza turned somber eyes on Victor. "I don't know if you'll agree with Penn when I tell you what else I know." She decided to state it as fact, not theory. She didn't want to debate endlessly with them. She said, "The cross was stolen from the Monastery of St. Catherine in 1922 by Victor's grandfather, who left a forgery in its place to cover his tracks."

She leaned back against the pillows, waiting for the inevitable explosion. There was a moment of absolute silence. Penn gawked at her, seemingly unable to grasp what she'd said. For a moment she thought she caught revulsion in his eyes. He pulled back ever so slightly, as if she was still the feverish carrier of some Eastern illness.

"I'll tell you what we know, Penn," she said at last. "I think some of this will interest you, too, Victor." As she told the story, the Frenchman walked to the window and looked down into the garden, his hands clasped behind him. She was unable to see his face or gauge his reaction. Penn was easier to read. He was quite red with anger.

"What we don't know," she concluded, "is how much you knew about all of this, Victor. I'm hoping you'll tell us." And this was the hardest for her. "I'm also hoping you'll tell us what your part in all of this was, Penn."

Penn stood so abruptly he almost tipped the little lyre-back chair from the dressing table. "I can't believe that I'm hearing this, Liza. That you would implicate *me*.... I can only conclude that you're still sick—or this man Chase has had yet *more* influence on you! But because you're not yourself yet, and because I will not discuss private matters in front of a stranger, we'll drop it for now."

"It's not that easy anymore, Penn," said Liza sadly. "Too many people are involved in this now. We've lost the luxury of privacy."

He looked at her as if realizing for the first time that this was not the same woman he'd parted from only a couple of weeks before. When he spoke again, something of the public Penn Livsay had replaced her almost-fiancé.

"I knew nothing," he informed her. "Victor, you and I have done business together for years—what on earth were you thinking of?"

When Victor turned around there was no shame on his face. There was a proud defiance. "I did not deceive you, my friend! I put into your hands one of the greatest treasures in existence. I charged you not a penny more than it was worth. I gave you exactly what I promised!"

"But it was stolen—"

"It came down rightfully to me from my father and grandfather!"

"But you knew its history," Liza protested.

"Better than you, my dear. Did you also find out, while you were busily uncovering all these terrible things about my grandfather, that when he arrived in the monastery he saw ignorant servants lighting fires with the pages of irreplaceable manuscripts? That he saw jewels being dug from priceless treasures to sell for a few dollars? Icons being tossed into dustbins? Can you imagine how he felt, a young man who loved art, who was fired by a genius for it? When he saw that cross, when he knew for sure what it was, he did conceive the plan you described. But I do not sit in judgment of him."

There was a heavy silence in the room. Liza hadn't expected this passionate defense from Victor. He was not bowed by the revelation of the story she herself had shed real blood to learn. She glanced down at the pale pink scratches on her wrists, which were just now beginning to really heal.

Victor drew himself up and fixed them all with his piercing black eyes. "Are you going to tell me I have any less right to my inheritance than you do to yours? You Penn—was it not your own grandfather who built the Livsay fortune on factories that worked children and maimed their fathers? The very money that you so grandly give to this or that charity was won in death and disease," he said roundly.

"And you, Lord Chase—your family, being so old and noble, has even more to account for. Your pastoral home was built on shipping profits, was it not? The China Trade, the East Indies, Africa? And have I not heard that there were slaves stowed below the decks with the cinnamon and silk?"

Neither Penn nor Christian had answered Victor. Small furrows of pain formed on Liza's brow and she shifted uncomfortably. "Really, Victor, I see what you're getting at, but we are dealing here with something quite specific. The Cavendish can't—"

"Yes, Liza—what about you and this lovely museum over which you preside so delightfully? Are your hands so clean? Are you now going to look into the history of all your pieces to see at what point in history they were stolen or smuggled or changed hands wrongfully? No, of course not. You can't and you won't."

Liza looked reluctantly at Christian. "Well? Don't you have anything to say?"

He shrugged carelessly. "He makes a point—life is never as neat as we want it, nor history so convenient."

She whipped her head around. "And you, Penn?" she asked, baffled by the turn in what she thought would be a nasty but cut-and-dried confrontation.

Penn raked his short, dark hair with his fingers. "It's a rather humbling argument Victor makes. None of us, apparently, can afford to be self-righteous about this business. Perhaps if we handle it delicately, some good can be salvaged. I wonder, first, what the legal problems are."

Victor spoke confidently. "There are none, Penn. Too many years have passed for the monastery to make any claims on the cross. No court would hear the case. And the things we have talked about today, while we may believe them, are still speculation. There is no real proof."

Penn stood and began to pace the small area by Liza's bed. "I'll have my lawyers look into it at once, of course. But my guess is like yours—the cross is legally yours to sell."

"Do call your lawyers!" said Victor with a dramatic sweep of his hand. "You will find that I am correct."

"Is that all this comes down to?" Liza cried. "Legalities?"

"What would you have us do," asked Victor, "take it away from the public and put it back on a shelf in the monastery?"

"Victor's right," said Penn. "We should put it back on display because it's exactly what we said it was. Victor, I'll pay you and—"

Liza was incredulous. "But what about the monks?"

"I told you," he snapped, "I'll have the lawyers look into it. Maybe there can be some sort of donation—anonymous, of course. Look, I just don't *know* yet. In the meantime, Liza, you're to speak to no one, and certainly not to the press." He stopped, suddenly realizing they were not the only ones in the room. He lifted his chin and narrowed his eyes. "And now, Mr. Chase, what is it you want out of all this?"

Christian smiled slowly. He looked very much the way he had that night at Fairchild's—determined and devastatingly confident. "I have what I want, Mr. Livsay," he said, glancing at Liza.

Liza flushed scarlet, remembering their lovemaking.

Was it punishment or kindness that so much of it had been blotted from her memory? It must be kindness, she thought, if he could be so cynically amused by his conquest of her.

Penn looked slowly from one to the other. He began to say something, thought better of it and asked, "You have no plans to take this any further?"

"Where would I take it? To a court? I'm not the injured party. To the press? All three of you would hit me with libel suits—no, Liza, don't look at me like that. Julian has the reputation of the museum to think of and I have no doubt he'd sue me in a minute."

Liza looked down at her hands clasped tightly in her lap. "I don't know what to think. An hour ago I'd have said there was not a shred of defense for what you did, Victor. Now I think I understand your actions. But I can't condone them. And I have to wonder about my own contribution to all this. . . ."

"I want to speak to Liza alone, now."

She looked up at Penn. "Yes," she said. "I think we do need time alone."

There was a long silence after Christian and Victor had closed the door behind them. Both she and Penn knew that something vital had shifted in their relationship.

Self-consciously, Penn sat on the edge of her bed and took her hand in his. "I'm relieved to have Chase out of here," he said. "It's been difficult for me to accept his involvement in all this."

"Knowing you as I do," she said gently, "I can understand that."

"I'm going to make sure you're protected in all of this, Liza. By the lawyers, of course. We'll bring in the firm's public relations people to deal with the press, too, if it gets that far." He gave her hand a small shake. "Look, I'm terribly worried about *you*. You must give me credit for that much at least."

"I *do*," she said earnestly. "But I'm more concerned about what's right and proper than about myself."

"You're a first-rate curator, Liza, but you don't know a thing about money. At least not on the scale I deal with every day. This isn't like returning a purchase at Saks, my dear. My family's tax lawyers have been planning this for over a year."

Her chin was trembling and she turned her face abruptly away from him. "I thought art was our bond, Penn. . . I guess I was wrong."

"No, not wrong. But naive, perhaps. I know there's a lot about my life you don't understand, Liza. But I thought you were at least sympathetic and would make the effort to learn."

"I did try," she said, very close to tears.

"Well, it's not showing."

They both glanced miserably at the closed door and made a visible effort to control their emotions. Neither one was attracted to the idea of having a common lovers' quarrel within earshot of Victor and Christian.

Penn drew his hand across his face in a weary gesture. His voice was hoarse. "Something happened to you while you were gone. It was Chase, wasn't it?"

Liza's breath caught. There was a part of her that

hurt for both of them. "Yes," she said quietly.

He looked at her, his face surprisingly vulnerable. "Liza, if you...did something, we can get past that. I'm not completely antiquated, you know. I understand that women these days have sexual interludes, too. I've not been without my own diversions since I met you...but I suppose you know that."

"I guessed," she said. She stared at a spot on the comforter in front of her, feeling unbearably small and sad. How could she explain to Penn that she'd hoped for love, settled for sex and in the end been cheated of both?

"It's painful for me to think of you with another man. I hurt for *you*, thinking of your first experience in some wretched little motel in the Middle East. But it's not the end of the world and it doesn't have to be the end of us."

She ignored his hopelessly warped image of her relationship with Christian. "Doesn't it, Penn? Somehow I can't see your forgiving me that."

"Don't be silly. I don't think of you as tainted or some such thing just because you've been with another man!" He made an effort at casual laughter that was telling in its failure.

"No, Christian's not the issue between us, Penn. I *have* been naive, have misjudged your world and my place in it. Your mother and sister saw how ill suited I am to it. The things that are important to you will just never be at the top of my list. Look at me, Penn, and tell me that you don't believe deep inside you that our relationship is a mistake. Tell me you wouldn't be relieved if it were to end for us right now."

But he couldn't look at her and that was answer enough. She couldn't deny that it hurt. Inside she cried a little, for she had once cared very much for Penn Livsay. Or at least for what she thought he stood for—integrity and competence, stability and the family life she'd never known. All those things were still there, she supposed, but the man had been diminished in her eyes.

He leaned over her and she inhaled his familiar scent. He kissed her gently, a lingering kiss, a kiss of goodbye.

OUTSIDE THE BEDROOM WINDOW the last leaf detached itself from the poplar tree and joined the golden pool that lapped at the garden wall. The autumn conflagration was over and a true winter night was drawing in on them, darkening the room.

"They say there'll be snow tonight."

"Not so soon, surely," said Liza.

"A freak storm. My taxi driver told me on the way up from the hotel. He seemed quite indignant."

He was standing by the window, one hand on his hip, drawing back his jacket, the other resting on the sash. There had been little talk since Penn and Victor left. Liza was sad and distracted, Christian sensitive to her struggle, allowing her to live it out. He was a man who seemed comfortable with silence and she was grateful for his presence.

She sat amid a profusion of pillows, her knees pulled up, nursing a glass of sherry he'd brought her, saying, "You're pale, even for you. This may help." She had watched with amazement this man moving easily about her apartment, heard him opening her kitchen cabinets, listened to his footfall on her floor. It made her feel shy yet tremulous and excited at the same time.

She rubbed her arms. "The temperature is plunging. I don't think our ancient heating system is prepared any more than we are for this."

He reached out a hand.

"What?" she asked.

"Up. Into the living room. You can lie on that charming loveseat of yours. I saw an afghan there for your legs."

"But it's colder in there than it is right here."

"I'm going to build you a fire," he replied. "It's one of my talents I've yet to demonstrate to you." He drew her legs over the side and steadied her as she wriggled her toes into soft, warm mules.

"Somehow I've never imagined your attending to the simpler domestic duties," she said. She smoothed the little jacket, tugged at the lace hem, and wished devoutly it covered more. The thin, sprigged silk of the gown clung uncompromisingly to the curves of her figure and outlined each thigh separately.

"That shows your appalling ignorance of my life," he said cheerfully. He took her hand and led her into the living room. "There's an entire wing of Hawthorne Park that still doesn't have central heating. I woke up to cold stone floors every day while I was growing up there. Even now, in the wing where Alister and Jane and the children live, you need a fire in every room in the winter."

"Sounds exhausting," she said, looking about her own tiny dwelling.

"It is," he said. "I think if it had been up to me I

might have sold the house for a school or a hotel. Not that I don't love it, but I really lack the necessary time and abilities to run it. My brother was more than willing to tackle it, though.''

"But does he enjoy it? I had the impression that it was...a burden to him.'' She thought he might be angry but he only smiled.

"No one forced it on him, Liza. Least of all me. It's a struggle, admittedly, but one of his own choice. He's always loved the fishing, the farming. If you went there you'd probably mistake him, in his Wellingtons and torn sweaters, for one of the dairy hands. He was devastated when we were sent away to school. He wasn't much for books.''

"And you?''

"I loved school. Later, I loved my work. After my father died and the problems really came at us, it was the most natural thing in the world that Alister go back to run the estate while I provided the funds to keep it going.''

"Is that when you sold your London home?''

"Yes," he said, with a brief look of pain. "We needed the money to refinance, make major improvements—there'd been virtually no modernization, and what was done was mostly for the benefit of the cattle, unfortunately. Jane still labors in an antique kitchen and where she gets her cheerful disposition from, I'll never understand.''

"It must have been heartbreaking for you to see so many family treasures go. Particularly the paintings.''

He gave her a wry smile. "Some good came of it. I

traveled, made contacts, and discovered that I had a calling of sorts. I had assumed that I'd go back to teaching when I was through with the disposal, but I was enjoying myself. That was lucky, because I couldn't afford to go back to the university. The kind of money I was beginning to make was too desperately needed, not just for the estate, but also by the dozens of employees who depend on it for a living. I saw, too, that I wasn't alone in my predicament. There was a major breakdown of many of the great fortunes of Europe. I'm well aware of some of the gossip that attends my coming and going from the homes of ladies of a certain age. But discretion often means that no defense is possible."

"Christian, I'm as guilty as the gossips—I listened."

"I know," he said, and kissed the top of her head.

She didn't want to be forgiven. "But I was beastly to you—how can you be so casual about it?"

"It gave us some marvelous fights. I loved them." Without ceremony he picked her up and laid her on the loveseat. He placed the afghan over her. "What's for dinner?" he asked.

She sighed and shook her head a little. He was a difficult man to track. "There's steak, I think. And the makings of a salad. Does that sound too American? I still can't eat much, but Connie insists on getting things she thinks will make me strong."

"Connie's wise. You listen to her. The agency recommended her highly to me. I'm glad it's worked out."

He prepared a creditable meal. "Better than the pita," she informed him brightly. She ate dutifully from a tray on her lap, he from the floor beside her. Later, in his shirt-sleeves, he gathered up the plates and washed them in the sink. Liza lay back with her coffee, smiling at this British lord puttering about her minuscule kitchen.

When he came back into the living room he opened the brass fire screen and threw another log onto the fire. He was right. It was burning well. The fire and a tiny desk lamp in the corner provided the only light. Outside, a fine snow was powdering the rooftops and slurring softly against the dark windowpanes.

He folded up his long legs and sat on the rug, his back to the loveseat. She couldn't see his face. "When you come to England I'll show you the gate house that I keep for myself. It's tiny—not meant at all for my height. And there's no great art or Georgian antiques. Just a jumble of mismatched chintz sofas and chairs and a very friendly Welsh dresser with some old crockery on the shelves."

She bent her head. Her lashes swept her cheeks. "Christian...."

"If you want to see the gold service plates and marble busts you'll have to pay your two pounds and take the tour of the main house with the rest of the tourists," he warned with smiling eyes.

She reached out to touch that fine, blond hair, stopped, and pulled her hand back. "Christian, no...."

"All right, tightwad, I'll sneak you in the back way."

She inhaled and tried again. "I would love to see your home but—"

"Then when—when will you come?" He turned suddenly and faced her squarely, an intensity in his eyes that made her breath catch in her throat.

"I can't come. Not ever."

"You can—and you will," he stated.

"*No*, Christian," she said firmly. "It was grand and wonderful in a terrifying sort of way. I won't deny that I was caught up in a crazy, romantic passion for you—you know that only too well. But I'm not made for affairs. It just isn't me. I would be hurt, eventually, just as I was hurt once by. . . ."

It still hurt. Even now. Just the *thought* of his touching another woman with desire tore at her heart with an astonishing pain and made sane thought almost impossible.

"Ah, those stormy eyes. . . I've come to know them so well. Too well, perhaps," he said quietly. "There's still something standing between us, isn't there, Liza?"

She shrugged. "There are a number of things between us, I suppose," she said, attempting indifference.

The angle of his brow was skeptical. "Like our competitiveness over the Renoir? Our battle over the cross? Our sexual sparring? They made your mouth deliciously sulky and your eyes flash. I loved it—it excited me. But this—whatever it is," he said with quiet intensity, "it's hurting you, isn't it? I can't stand to think of you in pain."

There was an edge to her voice. "I'm *sorry* if you

find it disconcerting,'' she said, plucking absently at
the scalloped edge of the afghan in her lap. ''In an
odd way, I came to accept our battling. I even came
to love the pain of loving you. But that was my
risk...and my punishment. What I can't come to
terms with is the fact that my recklessness spilled over
onto other people.''

''What are you talking about—Victor brought this
down on his own head. And Penn? He can look out
for himself, my dear—better than you know.''

For a moment her mind skittered dangerously and
courage threatened to desert her. *No!* she thought
vehemently. Better to have it out. Better to know.
She shook her dark head and said, ''No, it's not
Penn, or Victor. We were all players who knew the
rules. We weighed the risks against the possible gains
and made our decisions. But the night I begged
shelter from Scott and Kim—the night you got into
the monastery and I didn't—I brought two very innocent people into our problems.''

He looked askance at her. ''Oh, come now! I hardly think those two were irreparably damaged by their
brief exposure to *us*,'' he retorted.

''No? Then let me enlighten you. Look, I know
that you and I were never bound to each other. I
know that you're an intense, passionate man and
women find you very desirable—''

''I wish you would dispense with the defensive preamble, Liza. Just say what you have to say.''

''All right,'' she said, stung to sudden fervor. ''I
wish you hadn't seen fit to use Kim to satisfy your
needs! Even if she wasn't entirely unwilling, she was

still in way over her head with someone like you."

"What do you mean I *used* Kim?"

His expression was so incredulous that she almost faltered. "I had been walking on the mountain the day I left St. Catherine's and I...I saw enough." Her mind drifted, remembering, and then her eyes shot up to his, challenging. "And wasn't it typical of Scott and his kindness that he didn't confront you with it that day he went to warn you I'd left with the jeep?"

Christian drew one hand slowly down his face. He sighed and asked, "He knew, too?"

"Yes...I blurted it out," she answered, deeply ashamed. "I was so concerned about my own wounded pride! And what did I have to lose? You and I had no relationship to betray—there was no 'us.' But Scott and Kim had invested a lot in each other, and with a few careless words I shattered it."

He shook his head ruefully. "Let me ease your conscience, Liza. You shattered nothing—I had already done it."

"Oh, I could see *that* quite well...although how you can speak of it so easily I can't understand."

"No, no, I don't mean the kiss. That was nothing. You see, I told Kim that I thought she should leave Scott."

Liza's eyes were enormous. "My God, you did that? What did you promise her? Castles? Titles? Royal receptions? I guess when you saw that it wasn't going to work out with me, you went running straight to her. And you certainly didn't waste any time, did you?"

"It wasn't that way at all, Liza!"

"But you *did* kiss her," she insisted, probing the wound brutally.

"Yes, I did," he snapped.

"Oh...." She sank back against the pillows and hugged the hurt. She'd asked for it, but oh, God, the wound went deep.

He made a visible effort at controlling his temper. "Liza, I'm not going to abet you in this self-indulgent, masochistic imagining. I'm a man, and when a beautiful young girl kissed me, I kissed her back—"

"Don't," she began, "I don't want to hear it—"

"Well, you're going to! Ordinarily I don't talk about the women I know behind their backs. But you brought the issue up and you at least owe me a fair hearing. Will you give me that much?"

Her reply was a sulky silence, but he went on anyway. "After you left the monastery, I became worried about you. I thought you might do something impulsive—silly thought, wasn't it—Kim told me she'd seen you take the path up the mountain. We climbed together for a while but there was no sign of you. I started to go back, but Kim wanted to talk. The gist of her story was that she was miserable. She was utterly fed up with the life she was leading—the so-called romance of the desert wears thin after a while, you know."

"Well, I knew—or suspected—that she was...I don't know—restless, I guess. Distracted. I put it down to youthful energy," said Liza.

"I don't think that would account for such misery

and desperation. She was in tears and she begged me to take her away. She promised me...well, rather a lot.''

"But who made you the great arbiter of other people's lives?" Liza demanded.

"I didn't choose the job, remember—it was thrust on me quite unceremoniously," he replied. "I hate wasted time—you above anyone else should know that. Kim was going to leave Scott anyway and I thought for his sake as much as for her own that she should get it over with."

"But she and Scott had such plans! Dreams!"

"She hated that life, you know. She had an entire catalog of complaints—the sand in her shoes, bad food, demanding guests. The desert was either too hot or too cold. She despised it! You're a woman, and from what I can see around me, you're at pains to make your own surroundings comfortable and pleasant. Surely you can sympathize with a girl who wants to have things ordered and beautiful for once.''

Liza's indignation had deserted her. She was dismayed by her misreading of the situation, and saddened by Kim's and Scott's blighted relationship. "Whatever happened to working things out with the man you love," she murmured, more to herself than to Christian.

"I don't know, Liza," he said quietly. "It's still there, I suppose. But the man has to be right, the woman, too, and the dream has to be the same. It just wasn't for those two. And from the way she behaved toward me, I could see that she was going to bring a lot of bitter disillusionment to Scott. The next man she threw arms around,'' he added brutally, ''probably wouldn't have said no.''

Liza remembered Kim's clinging arms and her tear-streaked face. She remembered, too, Christian's sheltering, supporting arms and the way he'd kissed her with such tender concern. How different it all looked now in the light of this new knowledge!

''I was so jealous,'' she admitted, shaking her head. ''I was just spitting mad at an unhappy young woman who was begging to escape.... I suppose she thought you could give her some kind of instantly perfect life.''

''Well, all I can say is that she had some very odd notions about what my life's like. On the surface it looks glamorous, I suppose, but she'd have been disappointed in very short order, I assure you. For a tough, unsentimental kid, she harbored some remarkably romantic notions.''

''Oh, there I can sympathize with her,'' Liza told him. ''A woman resolves to be sensible. She vows to be totally practical about men. She tears off the rose-colored glasses with a vengeance—no rash decisions for *this* generation! Love will be the product of a series of considered judgments. There'll be no rude surprises in *her* marriage.''

He watched her with intrigued, smiling eyes. ''It all sounds quite dreadful—and very threatening to us poor males.''

''You don't know the half of it,'' she returned with grim cheer. ''Learning all the terrible details about your beloved becomes a kind of holy quest. You know he snores. You know he leaves soap scum in the bathroom sink. You know he sometimes eats right from the saucepan when he thinks no one's around. You *especially* know his bank account, his earning potential, his thoughts on mortgages and childrearing. You enter marriage armed with these details, each one a link in the chain mail about your heart. You'll be immune to shock. And of course the joke is it *never* turns out that way. Never.''

"All these depressing, common-as-dirt details about man's frailties—did you uncover them dutifully about Penn?" he asked.

She dimpled briefly. "Oh, no. I spoke in general. Penn's never been unfastidious in his entire life. I suppose he may well leave soap around the bath, but I never knew it because someone else was always there to whisk it away. I did once see him throw a terrible temper tantrum over a tennis game and smash a perfectly good racket—that kind of thing, the insistence on having his own way, I knew about. But there were so many other things I missed. Things that masked entirely different and less noble motives.''

And she thought of the factory with poorly paid workers whose labor eventually provided the funds for *La Baigneuse*. And the staggeringly generous donation of the Cross of Constantine, which was, at the same time, a mammoth tax manipulation. She felt a shudder of revulsion travel the length of her spine. Not at Penn—he had a right to do as he wished. No, what she shrank from was her own naiveté. She felt she'd aged a lifetime since that night at Fairchild's.

"So all your careful planning did you no good. In the end, you were disillusioned anyway," he said gently. His eyes were very soft and sad for her.

She smiled with equal sadness. "In the end, it didn't matter. Love, it seems, refuses taming. It had one great surprise left for me."

Several emotions overwhelmed her—dismay, chagrin, apprehension. Yet when it's needed most, courage often floods in like a warm blessing. Now, when she lifted her face to him, her gaze was clear and unwavering.

"I fell in love with you like a sky diver leaping into the void," she told him. "I had no idea of the end, yet there was no turning back. I made as ungraceful a leap into love as there ever was, I suppose, yet it was thrilling. I thought I knew enough about you to warn me off such madness. But you made me feel what it is to be a woman, and in the end that's all that matters. When you pulled me out of the wadi, I knew nothing except that I loved you... and wanted you. You were my whole world."

Color flooded her cheeks and her eyes were bright, but the honesty was cleansing and she didn't for a moment regret it. Then suddenly he was bending over her, frowning and smiling, tucking a loose strand of hair behind her ear and kissing her cheeks.

"And I wanted you, too, my darling—so very much! It was an agony of self-denial, for which I'd like due credit, not to have made love to you right then and there."

"You're teasing me," she said. One small tear spilled over and slipped down her cheek.

He brushed it away with his thumb. "Teasing. . . a lot you know, Miss Downing! Do you really think women are the only ones who feel the world go spinning out from beneath their feet? I had been obsessed with you ever since I first saw you at the auction. I couldn't eat, I couldn't sleep. I saw you everywhere. When I found out you'd slipped away from me in New York and flown to the Sinai, I almost went mad with frustration. But when I pulled you out of the wadi I knew that my arms possessed all the joy that life can possibly give. It was right there—in you! And I prayed and gave real thanks for the first time in my adult life."

She saw something, then, etched on the craggy planes of that dear, dear face, something she'd never dreamed she would see. She saw helplessness, and the capacity for pain. This time it was he who waited. His eyes willed her to understand, to let go, finally, of the pain and misunderstanding that had separated them.

"I didn't know," she cried. "Oh, God, I thought all you could possibly want from me was the comfort of my body—a few hours of human warmth against the night. . . ."

"There were so many things I wanted to tell you, Liza. But you wouldn't have heard me—you were so sick! All I could do was hold you to me and try to bring you safely through. I do love you. Believe it, darling. . . ."

She drew her fingertips tenderly down his cheek, following the groove that ran beside his mouth. "Oh, Christian, how? When?" she breathed.

"I don't know—the very first night perhaps."

"If only you had told me. I was in such agony. I thought—oh, you can't imagine all the things I thought!"

"How could I, in the beginning, Liza? There were too many issues, too many doubts," he said. "I'd already lied to you about why I was in New York. I didn't want to be rejected the way you were rejecting this or that theory about the cross. You were in a mood to disbelieve, darling, not to hear that I loved you. Later, on the way back to New York, you were so ill. It didn't seem like the time for a man to tell a woman that she had become the center of his universe."

Silently then, and with ritual care, he pulled the afghan from her lap and spread it on the floor before the fire. He took her hands and drew her down to it. They faced each other on their knees. The room became their entire world, dark and silent, haunted by beauty.

He whispered, "Once, you told me love doesn't happen this way...."

"And now I know it can. It has...."

He pulled the tie that closed her jacket and it fell open. Slowly he slipped the jacket off her shoulders. It drifted softly down, creating a shallow pool of silk and lace about her knees. She didn't dare move, didn't dare breathe. So much to share, so much unsaid, yet they were silent. Her heart hammered in her breast.

His eyes slid over her, lingering on the telling rise and fall of her bosom. He smiled at her, the barest lifting of his lips to give her loving encouragement.

Oh, God, he was not to be torn from her life! The full understanding of what was happening washed over her. She could only wonder at the blessing of it, and cling to him, light-headed from shock and incoherent joy.

For a moment her cheek lay against his, and she was suffused by a feeling for him that was so achingly tender, so unbearably beautiful, so perfectly peaceful.

And then he pulled away from her and searched her face. His own became transformed, the lips grave, the eyes full of solemn wonder as he embarked upon a course from which he could not turn back.

Under his fingers the slim straps of her gown fell and she knelt naked before him in a silken drift of violets. Beside her the coals broke and murmured in the grate. The snow spoke softly at the window, but her heart's calendar had stopped at spring.

Gold-flecked amber firelight stroked her thigh, her shoulder, the outer curve of her round, pale breasts. He stared at her, mesmerized, yet controlling her with the velvet touch of his glance alone. And then passion flared in his eyes and the storm took him.

With a moan torn from deep inside him he seized her and bore her back against the afghan. He kissed her eyelids, her parted lips, the hair that cloaked her slender shoulders, her breasts. His heart listened for her response and his body replied, urging her higher and higher with his perfect knowledge of her need. He did not shield her from his weight, knowing instinctively that she hungered for it. She lay beneath him, feeling as fluid as the firelight flowing over his back.

When at last he reluctantly pulled away from her to undress, she was in an agony of wanting. She strained toward him mindlessly, pleading. She was frantic for the return of his melting touch. But his lovemaking continued as he stripped off his shirt. He loved her with his voice. The aristocratic smoothness was gone now, his voice rough and broken with passion as he uttered words of love and need that made her blood surge white-hot throughout her.

Naked and beautiful in the firelight, he knelt beside her, stroking her from her knees upward, reveling in the caresses they tenderly exchanged, till the last of her defenses fell. "Love me," she moaned, "oh, Christian, love me!" She splayed her fingers against his bare chest, tangling them with his hair. She was filled with such an enormous need she thought her heart would burst.

His hoarse, whispered promise that the pain would soon be pleasure was fulfilled. This was love made perfect, male and female need realized by the gift each had to give. A balance was struck so fine that every part of her being vibrated in perfect concord. There was fire in her limbs, love in her heart and peace in her soul.

Oh, how he knew her! Instinctively, totally, his whispered endearments drawing her into the spiral of his building passion.

"Let it happen, my love," he whispered against her ear. "Just let go and it will happen. Trust me, my darling...I have you...I have you...."

Trusting him, letting go as he commanded, she began the fall through a pounding surf of molten gold. The final joy was almost unsupportable, a joy they shared as she heard him call her name over and over again.

She lay quite still. *Strange, how good the weight feels,* she thought. The fullness. . . the completion. He was sleeping so soundly, like a child. The fierce concentration of his lovemaking had been replaced by the soft pout of exhaustion.

She watched the firelight flicker and leap on the ceiling. How long had she lain like this? How long ago had he held and supported her through her dreaming rush to knowledge? She didn't know. Time had lost its meaning for her. Now she held him protectively in the circle of her arms and cherished his defenselessness.

She smiled, and a pure, sweet happiness flowed into her heart. And then she, too, slept.

Epilogue

SIMPLE PLEASURES. They're the same all over, Angus thought. He settled down with a contented sigh to his coffee, his almond cake and his papers. They were a week old, of course, but that was one of the good things about life here. Time just wasn't the master it was in other places.

Still, even if he might not have wanted to admit it, today Angus Cavanaugh had been impatient. A clock-watcher, in fact. Today he knew exactly what the papers would hold for him. He chose the London edition first.

They had been married on Christmas Eve. It was a small affair, but the society editor's account was lengthy and glowing. The ceremony was, she wrote, dazzling in its perfection. The assembled guests were varied, encompassing lords and ladies, secretaries and artists, curators and professors. But they were united in their devotion to the two people whose union they'd come to bear witness to.

The bride was given away by her employer and attended by a Miss Blythe Conroy. The best man was the groom's brother. A plump-cheeked four-year-old named Emma had been flower girl and her brother, a bashful Master Nicholas Chase, in short velvet pants, had borne the simple gold band.

The chapel was a vision. The pointed windows were swagged with evergreen. The pews were capped with holly and trailing ivy. There were white candles everywhere, long tapers at the altar, tiny ones scattered along the sides—"No other light, Christian," Liza had said as they sat before the fire planning the wedding. "The candles will be for the stars of the Sinai where I fell in love with you."

She was a serene winter bride in a slender, floor-length sheath of the finest silk jersey, the neck high, the long, tight sleeves fastened by rows of minute pearl buttons. The tucks across the shoulders were as delicate as those on a baby's christening gown.

Angus laughed. Serene—she hadn't been that when she'd seen him with Christian. No, not by a long shot! Spitting mad and ready to take them both on, she was. With cheeks on fire and eyes that could wither a man.

Her bouquet, tiny and delicate, befitting such a petite bride, was a circle of deep green boxwood dotted by mistletoe berries. "I'm going to cut it myself from the courtyard at the Cavendish," Liza had told Christian. "I love the museum and I'm leaving it and that's my one and only regret. After the wedding I'll dry some of the bouquet. And when I miss the Cavendish I can smell that wonderful scent—and cry a little—but the memories will be wonderful. . . ."

She wore her hair in a crown of French braids through which more tiny sprigs of boxwood and baby's breath were twined. Angus's shaggy brows came together. He wasn't much good at translating this business of fashions and hairstyles, he decided. Were French braids different from plain old pigtails?

Whatever, he thought. She'd been beautiful with sand and twigs in her hair, too.

"After a honeymoon in Switzerland," he read, "Lord and Lady Chase will divide their time between Hawthorne Park, their home in England, and an apartment in New York. They will pursue joint careers in art and will be traveling extensively." So grand, it sounded, thought Angus. But he knew better. He remembered Liza's letter enclosed in the wedding invitation he'd received.

We'll be living in the apartment over the gate house, planning, poring over the catalogs from the auction houses—a working honeymoon, the beast!

I'll never be out of old pants and rubber boots. He says I'm to learn about some cows called Brown Swiss. And about fly casting for salmon. Do you think that's possible for someone who was raised in Manhattan? Christian says if I can swim through a flooding wadi I can wade through the Tyne to catch our supper!

But mostly we'll be getting to know each other. Do you realize how little I know about Christian, or he about me? What an awesome thing marriage is! Where do we find the courage?

In the same place Christian found it, Angus thought, *when he heard you were gone and he took off after you into the Sinai. With his blazing anger and his fear for you. And a great, consuming love from somewhere deep inside that* knows.

Liza had concluded,

Dear Angus, you'll think of a hundred excuses not to come to our wedding—no time, no clothes, or a story to pursue. We know and we understand. But *you* must know that it is you above all others whom we would have beside us on that day. For without you, there would be no wedding. Without you and your caring about a promise made long ago to Brother John, I would not have my own heart's desire—this man I love beyond all else, and this new promise of a life full of blessing. . . .

Angus sat for a very long time, watching the great scarlet ball of sun extinguish itself in the indigo waters of the Gulf of Aqaba and thinking how sometimes in this difficult life, a knot is at last unraveled and a peace descends in the most unexpected way.

The bestselling epic saga of the Irish. An intriguing and passionate story that spans 400 years.

FIRST...
The Defiant

Lady Elizabeth Hatton, highborn Englishwoman, was not above using her position to get what she wanted ...and more than anything in the world she wanted Rory O'Donnell, the fiery Irish rebel. But it was an alliance that promised only ruin....

THEN...
The Survivors

Against a turbulent background of political intrigue and royal corruption, the determined, passionate Shanna O'Hara searched for peace in her beloved but troubled Ireland. Meanwhile in England, hot-tempered Brenna Coke fought against a loveless marriage....

ANTIGUA KISS
ANNE WEALE

The exciting new bestseller by one of the world's top romance authors!

Christie's marriage to Caribbean playboy
Ash Lombard was to be for convenience only.
He promised never to touch her. That was fine
by Christie, a young widow whose unhappy first
marriage had destroyed the passionate side of
her nature—but it wasn't long before she
learned Ash had no intention of
keeping his word. . . .